Rachael English is a presenter on Ireland's most popular radio show, *Morning Ireland*. During more than twenty years as a journalist, she has worked on most of RTE Radio's leading current affairs programmes, covering a huge range of national and international stories. *Going Back* is her first novel.

Going Back

Rachael English

First published in Great Britain in 2013 by Orion Books,
an imprint of The Orion Publishing Group Ltd
Orion House, 5 Upper Saint Martin's Lane
London WC2H 9EA

An Hachette UK Company

1 3 5 7 9 10 8 6 4 2

ISBN (Hardback) 978 1 4091 2983 7
ISBN (Export Trade Paperback) 978 1 4091 4525 7
ISBN (Ebook) 978 1 4091 4521 9

Typeset by Input Data Services Ltd, Bridgwater, Somerset

Printed and bound by CPI Group (UK) Ltd, Croydon, CRO 4YY

The Orion Publishing Group's policy is to use papers
that are natural, renewable and recyclable products and made
from wood grown in sustainable forests. The logging and
manufacturing processes are expected to conform to the
environmental regulations of the country of origin.

For Eamon

Prologue

Janey O'Hara threaded her way along Washington Street, past Macy's, around the fast food carts and through the clusters of tourists at the Famine Memorial. She was behind time, but no matter. She would get there in the end. What was it her dad always said? There was no point in rushing to be late.

Janey had never intended to spend the summer in Boston. New York had been her choice, only her friends had made different plans. But with just four of them, they hadn't been able to rent so much as a cupboard. That was how they'd ended up in a minuscule apartment with three other Irish people. Two bedrooms, seven sleeping bags and not a moment's peace. She had called her mother in Dublin for a good moan and was sorry she'd bothered. When her mum heard they were living in Brighton, she'd started to laugh. Back in the dark ages when she had gone to America on a student visa, she'd lived only a few streets away from where Janey was staying now. She said that sleeping on the floor was good for the soul. Oh, and she warned her to watch out for the rat. Sometimes Janey worried about her mum.

It was funny to think that twenty-three years before, Elizabeth Kelly, as she was then, had lived in the same neighbourhood. She rarely spoke about Boston. If anyone asked, she gave a well-worn line: it was very pretty, almost everyone had an Irish relation, and people talked about money all the time. This made Janey smile. 'Sure, that description fits half the cities in the world,' she joked.

Following the rat phone call, however, her mum did e-mail a list of places she remembered. *If you're bored one day*, she wrote, *you*

I

can see where the old folks hung out. Mostly, the list was made up of bars with names like The Purple Shamrock and The Kinvara. The shop where she had worked was there too. Janey had only been in Boston for a few days when she went to look for Anderson's Electrical. Up and down the street she'd traipsed for the best part of twenty minutes, before coming to the conclusion that her mother's one-time workplace was now a discount clothes store. She had whipped out her phone and taken some photos all the same, to prove she had gone to the trouble. Her mum put great store by 'going to the trouble'. It was up there with politeness and perseverance and all the other stuff she banged on about when she was in bad form.

Janey was on her way to the bar where her boyfriend worked, The Old Shillelagh Tavern. Aidan said she shouldn't be taken in by the name; he reckoned the owner wouldn't be able to find Ireland on a map. The mid-June sun was obscured by pale cloud, but there was a simmering warmth to the day that she had never experienced at home.

That night they were going to a motel to celebrate her birthday. Aidan, who had chosen the place, said it was fairly basic. She didn't care how grotty it was, or what they had to pay, so long as there was no danger of an uninvited Irish head peering around the door. Plus, it sounded like such a grown-up, American thing to do.

She had been going out with Aidan McNamara for nearly a year, and she was mad about him. Stone mad, as he would say. He had lots of funny sayings. If she was being picky, he wasn't the best-looking man on the planet. But he was so amiable. He was also incredibly clever, even if sometimes he hid it well. Aidan's main talent was for living. When Janey was feeling stressed or down, ten minutes in his company and life felt like an adventure again. He was from Clare, and her friends called him Hawaii because of the way he greeted people. 'How are ye going on,' he'd say, his accent making the first three words sound like the fiftieth state.

When she reached the bar, he was sitting outside, his head stuck in a newspaper. The sports pages, no doubt. Starved of his usual ration of Irish sports, he was attempting to teach himself baseball.

He looked up and gave her his loopy grin. 'At last,' he said. 'I was beginning to think you'd run away. I'll have to go back inside in five minutes.'

'It's a good job you love me so much, then,' said Janey as she leaned in and kissed him full on the lips. She had no time for any cheek-pecking nonsense. Then she sat down and manoeuvred her metal chair in beside his so they could have a really enthusiastic kiss. Daft as it might seem, there was more privacy out there on a city street than in their apartment. 'How are the Red Sox doing?' she asked.

'OK … I think. I don't know as I'll ever get a handle on that game.' Aidan turned over the paper. 'Actually, for once I was reading the serious pages: a piece about two builders. Brothers.'

'What sort of skulduggery have they been up to?'

'Nah, it's not one of those stories. The two of them bought a load of derelict ground close to where they grew up, and now they're putting up a swanky development. They want to attract new people to the area. Rejuvenate it. Despite the economy and that.'

'Pffft,' she scoffed, 'you can bet there's plenty of cash in it for them. I'm sure they're no better than the crowd at home.'

He squeezed her knee. 'You're a shocking cynic.'

Janey took a look at the article. Or rather, she looked at the accompanying picture. There was something familiar about one of the brothers. She could swear she'd come across him before. She was about to say as much to Aidan, but stopped herself in time. She would only sound like a fool.

'So,' she said, 'I was talking to my mum.' Her voice must have revealed her concerns because her boyfriend said nothing about the madness of ringing home when she'd only been talking to her mother a couple of days before, on her actual birthday. They were supposed to be saving money.

'How was she?'

'Doing her best to sound perky but making a poor job of it. I hope she's OK.' Janey ran a hand through her tangle of hair. 'She's going out tonight with her old college friends. The crowd she came here with.'

'That's good.' He paused. 'Isn't it?'

'Once she doesn't get all maudlin about her lost youth.'

A couple of months back, Janey had gone hunting for photographs from the summer of 1988. There was a colossal box of photos in the spare room. Seriously, there was a time when she couldn't get a new pair of socks without someone feeling the need to record the occasion. She had rummaged and sorted for most of the day without finding even one picture of America. She'd said as much the next time Michelle was there. Michelle Rooney was her mum's best friend, and she had been in Boston too. They'd both muttered and clucked and said there weren't any photos because back then no one had the money for a camera.

Janey had thought no more of it, until a week or so later she'd come home from college to find the pair of them in the kitchen poring over a wallet of photographs. Michelle had blushed before blurting out something about having forgotten they existed. The colour was off-kilter, and some of the shots were so blurred it was hard to be sure what was going on, but it looked like they were taken at a party. The rest of the Boston gang – Orla, Peter and Donal – were there, looking young and thin and drunk. The shame was that her mum was in just two of them. In one she was posing with Michelle. In the other she was with an unfamiliar dark-haired man. He had the air of an American; his shoulders were broad, his face tanned and his smile stretched from ear to ear, like a cartoon character. Janey had raised an eyebrow. 'Where'd you find the handsome guy?' she'd asked. 'Him?' Michelle had replied, Oh, he was just a lad who worked with Peter.'

It was almost too easy to say her mum looked beautiful. That's what people always came out with when they looked at old photos. The thing was, it was true. Even the ridiculous mane of hair and the outsize plastic earrings weren't enough to distract you from her face, and the way it glowed. Her expression was open and trusting, like nothing bad could happen. Janey hadn't known what to say, so she'd smiled and made a comment about the big hair. How, she wondered, did her mother feel when she looked at the pictures? Was she a different person in those days? More optimistic? Less uptight? And if it had been such a happy time for her, why didn't she like talking about it?

Then she chided herself for being unfair because there were times when her mum was brilliant – really entertaining and young. This was how it should be because she *was* younger than most of her friends' parents. When life was good, she looked young too. And not in a phoney way like half of the women on their street. When she smiled, her face did move; her little nose scrunched up and her blue eyes spoke of devilment.

More often, though, she was all closed in and distracted. She looked as if crossness had been etched onto her face. Janey's dad claimed she had little enough to be cross about. Maybe this wasn't so true any more. After all, their marriage was hanging together by the flimsiest of threads. But the dark mood pre-dated her mother's current woes. On top of this, there was her 'too much perfection' routine: going out of her way to take the burned dinner or the small dessert, and getting up excessively early to do mundane tasks that didn't need doing at all. As much as Janey loved her mum, there were days when the martyr act was a bit of a pain.

'Overcompensating,' Janey liked to say, although her mother had such a straight and narrow life, it was impossible to imagine what she was overcompensating for. Aidan, as was his way, had concocted a silly story about her having a secret past. 'Elizabeth – the wild years,' he joked. Janey told him to get away with his old nonsense; she knew her mum and she knew this couldn't be true.

On the other side of the Atlantic, Elizabeth was giving herself a thorough talking to. She didn't want to go out. She would prefer to stay at home and read, or have a long sleep between cold sheets. She stood beside the shower, rocking on her heels, telling herself she had no choice. An age had passed since her college crowd had last met up. Who could say when the five of them would be together again?

There was big news. Happy news. Her old friend, Donal, had called to say he was getting married. Elizabeth had told Janey but her daughter, seeing love and sex as the domain of the young, had made a noise that sounded something like *eeew*. It was the noise she usually reserved for when the cat left a dead mouse on the doorstep. Even though they lived in Oregon, Donal's fiancée was from Boston, and that's where the wedding was due to take place. 'Promise me you'll come,' he'd said. 'Just imagine the nostalgia of it all.'

Elizabeth knew it was wrong to envy her daughter, yet she felt a tight sensation in her chest when she thought about Janey in America. At that age, you always looked forward to a night out. It didn't matter how insecure you were, and as a student she'd been burdened with a thousand pointless insecurities, there was always possibility in the air. There was time to grow into what you wanted to be. At least Janey knew her own mind. Elizabeth had pretended to be an adult when in reality she had bent to the will of others like a wisp of grass on a windy day.

Janey had sent her some photos of Winter Street, where Elizabeth had worked during her own student summer. From what she could tell, all of her landmarks were gone. She supposed this was to be expected. Look at what had happened to Ireland. Sometimes, she would be telling Janey a story about the 1980s, then realise she might as well be talking about the 1880s. It would make as much sense to her daughter.

When old footage came on the television, even she was taken

aback by how foreign the recent past appeared. Back in the last recession, Dublin had looked faded, its streets filled with angular cars and thin people. Reluctant as she was to over-romanticise the past, Elizabeth did carry happy memories of those years. When she had first arrived in Dublin from Thurles, a shy and dutiful eighteen-year-old, the city had seemed crammed with excitement and promise.

To be honest, she found it hard to navigate her way around the incessant change of the past twenty-five years. The Ireland of her childhood had been a make-do-and-mend sort of place. Then, in the blink of an eye, the country was all boom and profligacy. Now the nation was so broke that her husband – an engineer, for God's sake – was working in the Middle East.

Elizabeth looked at her watch. Seven o'clock already – she needed to pull herself together and get dressed. First she reached into the bathroom cabinet and plucked out her tablets. When she was calmed, most of her petty concerns abated. She no longer worried about whether she still had the knees for a short skirt or could remember the name of Donal's bride. Her hair was in a bob now, so it wouldn't take much drying.

Before he went away, Liam had told her that she was no longer twenty-five or even thirty-five, and it was time she lost the long hair. It made her look haggard, her husband had said. That one sentence had lingered at the back of her head ever since. On her bad days, up it would pop, and she would have to close her eyes to try and banish the memory. The strange thing was, she didn't believe that Liam had meant to hurt her. Casual cruelties had become an ingrained part of their marriage.

Perhaps she was the one woman on the planet with no desire to go blond, but Elizabeth had never dyed her hair. It was the same pale brown as when she was twenty-one. These days there were a depressing number of greys, most of which she removed with a pair of tweezers. When she'd gone to have her hair lopped off, the stylist had oohed and aahed about how soft it was. 'Virgin hair,' she'd said, which had provided them both with a good giggle.

As she gave her knees one last check, Elizabeth thought about how she would explain the Liam situation to the others. An entire chemist's shop of pills wouldn't prevent her from fretting about that. Only Michelle knew the full story: that there'd been more to his departure than a shortage of work. Her husband had been having an affair. He claimed it was over, but spending some time apart felt like the easiest way of handling things.

It was a night, she reckoned, for keeping the focus on the rest of them. For remaining vague. When she was a girl you were taught not to whine and wail. It was drummed into you, like the county towns of Ireland or who was patron saint of what. Nowadays people saw things differently. Failure to go around sharing all the intimate details of your life meant you were repressed. Such an ugly word. Elizabeth gave a little shiver. She didn't care what her friends said; she planned on sticking to what she knew. Besides, if she started talking, where would she stop?

One

June 1988
Boston

Chapter 1

Elizabeth rested her head against the side of the phone booth and exhaled. Her left eyelid twitched. It always did when she got flustered. She tried not to look at her flatmates, although they were pretty hard to miss. There the two of them were, a short distance down the street, pacing back and forth like even a moment's rest would bring bad luck. Under the mid-afternoon sun, Peter O'Regan's Ireland soccer jersey took on a synthetic gleam, and Donal Mulvihill's spindly legs looked so pale they were practically blue. Behind them a row of brown and red apartment buildings shimmered in the heat.

She told herself that this was simple. All she had to do was keep the phone pressed to her ear and carry on talking. 'I miss you so much,' she said. 'But I'll be home in no time at all.' She threw a quick glance in the lads' direction. When they looked at her, they'd assume she was still chatting to her boyfriend. In actual fact, the line had been dead for five minutes or more. The problem was, the instant she ended her charade the two would come bounding over, desperate for information. Then they would see her damp eyes.

It was Peter and Donal who had decided she should ring Liam to get the result of the Ireland–England match. Donal said there was no point in him calling home because all the family would be in the pub watching the football on the big screen. Peter said he would do it, except his mother would want to know if he'd been to mass. But, they pointed out, if she made the call not only would they get the score, she could engage in some long-distance cooing.

'Go on, Elizabeth, you know you want to,' said Peter, his heavy-lidded brown eyes giving her an imploring look.

'Oh, and we'll need a match report,' chimed in Donal. 'We'll want plenty of detail if the result is good. Not too much if it's bad.'

'Which it will be,' added Peter.

She had teased them for a few minutes, reeling off lists of all the other things she had to do. They both knew she was only play-acting. Three years of friendship meant they were well aware of each other's quirks and games.

The moment the quarters clunked down the chute, Elizabeth realised she had made a mistake. Somehow, Liam made 'Ireland one, England nil' sound like abject defeat, and 'I miss you' sound like an accusation. It was well for her, he said, and not in the jokey way he normally used the phrase. To be fair, his bad humour wasn't directed solely at her. Three of his friends were actually in West Germany for Euro '88. Thumbing lifts and sleeping rough and ringing at all hours from autobahn service stations to let him know what a wild time was being had. Poor Liam was at home in Tipperary, working through a rain-sodden summer. So she tip-toed around his ill-temper, assuring him it was work all the way in Boston with no time for going on the lash. But his words, and his tetchiness, stung. Before she knew it, there was a volley of pips, and he was gone.

Elizabeth was sure that if you asked anyone who knew her, they'd say it was a wonder she was in Boston at all. She wasn't cut out to be an emigrant; she was too much of a home bird. She'd heard these lines a hundred times, especially from her mam and dad. She had assured them she'd be back in October. After all, this was 1988, not 1958. Going away for the summer was what students did. Her explanations fell on stony ground. In her parents' world, when people went to America, they stayed in America.

Liam too had been perplexed. He could understand, he said, her university friends wanting to go. Now they were about to graduate, what had they to keep them in Ireland? There was little prospect of any of them getting a job. And it wouldn't do them any harm to expand their horizons. 'But you're different,' he said. 'Surely you understand that?' As he often pointed out, he had a steady job so she didn't need to find work just yet. She could stay at college and become a teacher, like she'd always wanted. Did she not realise that everything was falling into place for her? That was something else everyone said about Elizabeth: she was lucky.

It had taken months of coaxing and cajoling – and just the teensiest bit of sulking – to get Liam onside, but now that she was in Boston he was getting awkward again.

She had hardly placed the phone back on the hook when Donal and Peter came darting towards her like greyhounds out of the traps. A well-upholstered couple with a little boy of two or three were forced to leap out of the way. The child began to wail. 'Goddamn idiots,' yelled the father. Elizabeth's eyelid gave a robust twitch.

'The face on you,' said Donal. 'I take it the news from Stuttgart isn't good?'

'How bad was it?' added Peter.

She smiled at her friends' downcast faces and put an arm around each of them. 'Boys,' she said, 'I have a surprise.'

There were only five of them in the grimy, unfurnished apartment on Lantern Street. When Americans asked, Elizabeth liked to stress the 'only'. She knew that sleeping ten to a room didn't bother some people, but she couldn't have handled living in one of those apartments where everybody tumbled out the door in the morning like towels spilling from an overstuffed cupboard. She had heard of one set-up where twenty-four Irish lads shared a house. You would swear there was a competition for the dirtiest, sweatiest living experience.

Their street was a stone's throw from Boston University, and for the bulk of the year it was colonised by American students. During the summer months, the young Irish took over. For Elizabeth's generation, spending a summer in the United States was as much a student rite of passage as getting drunk on cheap cider or having your electricity cut off. No doubt most of those who took the trip told their parents they were there to earn money. They probably told each other they were there for the adventure. But, if many were honest, what they were really doing was getting a sense of America, seeing if it was somewhere they could call home. In the trademark dark humour of the Irish, they were known as 'trainee emigrants'.

In the late afternoon, the flat roof of the apartment block was cooled by a light breeze. Music from a transistor radio, its sound tinny and indistinct, drifted over from the next building. Elizabeth and Michelle had spread out their sleeping bags on the pitted concrete and were basking in the sun, the unfamiliar warmth tickling their skin. From where they were sitting, Elizabeth could follow the curve of Lantern Street as it meandered towards Commonwealth Avenue. Directly across from them was a three-storey, red-brick apartment building, the mirror image of their own. On the corner was a small grocery store, its windows festooned with scraps of paper advertising flat-shares, removal vans and second-hand textbooks.

Michelle and Elizabeth had become friends on their first day at university in Dublin. Elizabeth remembered sitting in the cavernous lecture theatre, part thrilled by the newness of it all, part terrified that she didn't know a single person there. Imagine her joy, then, when the girl beside her – a vision of cool in a black mohair jumper and battered Doc Martens – had revealed that she felt exactly the same. The two had escaped to the canteen where they'd bonded over the shared experience of being the first in their family to go to college. Shortly afterwards, they had met Peter and Donal, and the four had decided to rent a house together.

'And get this,' Michelle was saying now, her dark curls appearing to bob in time with her voice, 'the cereal was full of marsh-mallows – and some of them were in the shape of leprechauns.'

'You're making it up,' replied Elizabeth as she fanned herself with the *National Enquirer*. Michelle worked in a supermarket

14

and appeared to have brought home the entire news-stand.

'I swear. I asked the woman if it was breakfast or dessert. She smiled at me, but no doubt she was thinking, "Where do they find these people?" Of course, I can't say anything to the folks at work. I can't say, "Listen, we have food at home, only it's less imaginative," because then they drone on about Ireland being the Third World.' She looked at a grinning Elizabeth. 'Don't laugh, some of them genuinely believe that.'

'Don't I know. I must bring a box of that cereal home with me. I can see my dad's face. He's suspicious of anything more new-fangled than porridge.'

Elizabeth's father was a one-man campaign against fripperies and self-indulgence. Syl Kelly had left school at fifteen to work in the sugar factory in Thurles, and he'd been there ever since. In his view, most modern youngsters were educated beyond their intelligence. He had been especially baffled to hear of one local lad who was going away to 'find himself'. 'Finding a job would be more in his line,' he'd said. At college, when trapped by the ramblings of one of her more pretentious classmates, Elizabeth had fantasised about bringing her dad up to Dublin and setting him loose. He would have been in his element, threatening them with snagging turnips and the like. Needless to say, she had never snagged a turnip, although she agreed with Syl's old-style common sense more often than she would care to admit.

'The two boys are going for a few drinks later,' she said. 'To celebrate the result. I don't know as I've ever seen them so excited about a soccer match. Do you fancy going along?'

'I was planning on writing a letter home.' Michelle frowned. 'They'll get anxious if they don't hear from me soon.'

'Peter's meeting some of the lads from work. You never know, you might be missing out on the love of your life.' Peter was a labourer on a large construction site. Every evening, he came home moaning about the heat and the dust, but the pay was good and the social life was even better. He had already accumulated a considerable group of friends, most of them Irish.

'Tuh,' said Michelle. 'If they're friendly with Petie, you can guess what they're like. It'll be a bonus if they can lift their knuckles off the ground.'

Elizabeth lay back on her sleeping bag and laughed. 'You're a cruel woman. Will Orla be about? I've a feeling her standards aren't quite so high.'

'I heard that,' said a flat Dublin voice.

Damn, thought Elizabeth, as she sat up again.

An instant later a blond head peeped over the parapet. 'Actually, I have plans,' Orla said. 'One of the girls in the café has set me up with her brother.'

Elizabeth did her best to warm to the fifth flatmate, but some days this was hard. Orla Finnegan had endless self-belief and a scarily sharp tongue. Men flocked to her like birds after a plough.

Orla plonked herself beside them and stripped down to her pink underwear. Her green eyes fixed Elizabeth with a condescending stare. 'Calm down, pet. We're on our own up here. No men to distract or old women to offend.'

Elizabeth didn't think that she'd done anything to prompt this jibe; it was just part of the game that Orla played. Everybody had to be pigeonholed, and Elizabeth's place was as the prim, prudish flatmate. 'You ought to be careful,' she said, picking up her sun cream and offering the bottle. 'You know how quickly we burn.'

Orla shook her head. 'Answer me this, Elizabeth. Were you ever young?'

'I don't follow you,' she replied, hating the nervous squeak that had replaced her normal voice.

'You see, I have this feeling that you've always been a grown-up. I can picture you at primary school with your solemn little face. Telling the rowdy boys they'd be sorry if they didn't complete their jigsaws to the best of their ability.'

'I went to an all-girls school,' she said, immediately cringing at the silliness of her response. It was always the same. Give her a couple of minutes, and she'd think of something witty. In that instant, though, her brain was frozen. Strictly speaking Orla was Michelle's friend. 'There's no real harm in the girl,' she'd insist. Right then, as she braced herself for another onslaught, Elizabeth wasn't so sure.

Orla was fixing her hair into a high ponytail. 'You know what I was thinking? Before you go home and get shackled for good, you should have an adventure. With a big Boston man. Someone who'll give you a bit of a rattle. And a few stories for the grandkids.'

'Now, now,' said Michelle, who usually intervened if the tormenting went too far. 'Orla, why don't you tell us about this fella you're meeting tonight?'

Elizabeth stayed quiet. Best, she thought, to draw a veil over her boyfriend's sulk. Further evidence of Liam's unhappiness would only bolster her flatmates' belief that some day soon she would pack up her belongings and head on home. They had cause to be sceptical. At college, she had spent most weekends back in Thurles, often disappearing on Thursday and not returning until Monday. During their previous two student summers, when her classmates had flitted off to England or Germany, she had stayed in Ireland. Throughout those autumns she had listened with envy to their tales from InterRailing trips through France and Italy and Yugoslavia: tales that grew taller with every telling.

This time, Elizabeth was determined to prove her friends wrong. She wanted to experience America. Not that she harboured any fanciful notions about seeing the Grand Canyon or Las Vegas or New Orleans. What she enjoyed were the small differences: groceries in brown paper bags and big traffic lights, steam rising up through pavement gratings and women wearing runners with business suits.

Plus, despite what Orla might think, Elizabeth craved another few months of being a make-believe adult, sitting up half the night talking about matters of no consequence and listening to Donal and Peter turn insulting each other into an art form. That seemed in every way preferable to real adulthood.

*

It had never occurred to Danny Esposito that he would miss his big brother. How could you miss someone whose life was dedicated to nagging and interfering? But now that Vincent had left, the grey and white clapboard house had all the atmosphere of a funeral home, and Danny felt too big and clumsy and loud. At that moment, he was doing his best to stay quiet. He padded across the porch, trying to avoid the creakier boards, hoping his mother wouldn't wake.

The silence was punctured by the rasp of a familiar voice. 'Is that you, Danny, love? I need a word.' He winced before turning around; there would be no escape this evening.

'Hey there, Mrs O'Connor, how are you doing?' Bridie O'Connor and her husband, Mossy, lived next door. Despite the temperature, her grey hair was starched into position and her face meticulously painted.

'I'm surviving, honey. I was thinking about your mom. Is she all right?'

'Oh yeah, Mrs O, she's fine.'

'It's just I haven't seen her in a few days. And you know me, I have to be tormenting myself. I said it to Mossy, I hope Regina isn't unwell again.'

'Don't you worry. It's the weather. She doesn't care for these temperatures, you know? Prefers to stay indoors.' It was a fantastic evening, the sky a seamless blue. A cloud or two would have made it more interesting, but you couldn't have everything.

Bridie sighed. 'I'm the same myself. I said as much to Mossy. This heat will kill us all. Just you look at the damage it's doing.' She gestured towards the rhododendron bush at the edge of her neat, wooden porch, its blooms now brown and shrivelled.

Danny nodded. A conversation with Bridie was rarely a two-way process. When Mossy passed on, he was definitely heaven-bound.

'You off out, love?'

'Uh-huh. Grabbing a beer with the boys from work.'

'Perhaps I'll call in on your mom in a little bit.'

'Ah.' He paused. 'There's no need to go troubling yourself. She'll tell you if she wants anything.'

Bridie pursed her already narrow lips. 'Well, you know best. I suppose.'

The exodus from 19 Emerald Street had begun with Danny's father. Seven years before, Dino had met a woman called Bellissa and, after years of part-time philandering, he'd decided that this was the real deal. In Danny's view, his mom's replacement was poorly named; the second Mrs Esposito appeared quiet and drab. There must, though, be more to her than met the eye because the old man was a changed character. When Danny was a kid, his dad's temper could rip the skin off your back. These days he was the very definition of calm.

The rest of the family had taken the departure and remarriage badly. Danny liked to think he took a more balanced approach. If it wasn't working, he reasoned, why continue to make each other unhappy? He had to admit the divorce had not brought any particular joy to his mother. His two sisters had left within a year of each other. Now his brother too was gone. Vincent and his girlfriend were renting the bottom apartment of a sagging triple-decker. The couple had moved just ten minutes away, but without Vincent the house no longer felt like home.

For a moment, Danny considered bringing the car, a twelve-year-old Ford Maverick with an unreliable temperament and a hacking cough. Lately, as often as not, he had ended up walking. Vincent, who acted like the car was a slur on the family's honour, claimed it was a miracle that such a pile of garbage ever got on the road. Danny avoided the obvious retort; he drove what he could afford to drive.

Bridie O'Connor was becoming a nuisance. He was sure she meant well. Actually, on second thoughts, he wasn't, but that was a worry for another day. His immediate concern was keeping her away from Ma. If there was one thing he knew about Regina, it was that she hated fuss. And Bridie was a mountain of fuss.

Besides, what was it she wanted him to say? 'To tell the truth, Mrs O, my mother is depressed as hell. She hasn't been out of bed in three days. I could hold an orgy in the front room and she wouldn't notice. Do come on in, though. And, while you're at it, why don't you invite the rest of the street?' He could picture her face.

This was one of those days, and there were many, when Danny imagined he was treading water, waiting for his real life to come into view. A couple of nights back he'd said as much to his brother. They had been having a beer in a local bar, a squat brown-brick place with rusty grilles on the windows, when he'd tried to broach the subject. With Vincent you had to be careful how you phrased stuff because it didn't take a lot to get his brother worked up. 'Do you ever think,' Danny had asked, 'that there's more to be had?'

Vincent had thought for about half a second. 'More money? Every day of my life.'

'You know that's not what I mean.'

His brother had grunted and given him a look that suggested he wasn't up for this conversation. 'Sometimes, Dan,' he'd said, 'I don't know where you get your ideas from. Or what's going to become of you. Really I don't.'

Chapter 2

'Now remember,' said Donal, as they approached the doorway of O'Mahoney's bar, 'say nothing. Stand back, smile at the nice man and follow me.'

Elizabeth was doing her best not to notice the carpet of broken glass and cigarette butts beneath their feet. 'Is there any chance you'll tell me what you're doing?'

'Not a hope,' he said.

Donal was a man for stories and schemes. The more ludicrous the tale, the more outlandish the game, the more he liked it. At college, he had progressed well beyond the normal student pranks. Where some would take a traffic cone or two, Donal had stolen an entire set of traffic lights. Where most student houses possessed a bit of 'borrowed' crockery, Donal had acquired a diverse collection of bar stools and souvenirs. 'I only take one item at a time,' he'd say. 'I wouldn't want to be greedy.' Occasionally, Peter would get worked up about one of his wilder wheezes – even Donal would concede that trying to raise a fox cub in the kitchen hadn't been that smart – only everything was done in such high good humour, it was impossible to stay annoyed. Attempting to control Donal was like trying to herd cats.

His latest initiative was to try and get Elizabeth into a bar. The youngest of the five, she was still two weeks shy of her twenty-first birthday. Around their way, in Brighton and Allston, the door staff were wise to the full range of student tricks, making it impossible to get past the entrance, let alone have a drink. Over here in Dorchester, she was assured, people were less uptight about the licensing laws. Still, she was nervous about her chances, so Donal had decided to help.

With a flourish of his liquor licence, he loped towards the bouncer. After a minute or so of murmuring and head-shaking, he beckoned Elizabeth forward, put an arm loosely around her back and shepherded her inside. She turned back briefly and saw that the doorman was smiling.

'You can tell me now,' she said. 'What was that all about?'

'Oh, just having a laugh.'

'Go on, what did you say to him?'

Donal ran a hand through his red hair which had been moulded into wiry tufts by the humidity. 'I told him we got married a month ago, and that you were new to America. And I was worried you were a touch flighty, so I needed to keep an eye on you.'

'You're an awful chancer,' she said, her head shaking in mock annoyance. 'How do you come up with this rubbish?'

He gurgled with laughter. 'It worked, didn't it?'

One look at his silly face, and Elizabeth joined in. She went through phases of trying not to laugh too hard. Friends said her round blue eyes were her best feature. The problem, in her view, was with the rest of her face. It was so small that when she laughed or frowned it crinkled up. Even the slightest movement could change her face completely.

Over at the bar, Peter was talking to two men who she guessed were in their mid-twenties. One was definitely Irish. He had the build of a construction worker, a thatch of brown hair and a shiny red face, like he'd already got several beers on board. The second man was unmistakably American. It wasn't so much his tan or dark hair that gave him away as how he held himself. He had an eager air, as though the world was full of possibility. Irish people never looked like that.

'Folks,' said Peter, as they reached where he was standing, 'this is Brian Byrne from Bray. He's over here for the last three years.'

'Practically an American, so,' said Donal, as the red-faced guy nodded in acknowledgement.

Peter tapped the second man on the shoulder. 'And this is Danny Esposito. A real American.'

Danny smiled. 'Sorry about the bar. It's a bit of a dive, only Peter said someplace with a relaxed door policy would be best.' His voice was pure Boston: deep and laid-back with hardly an 'r' to be heard.

'No, man, you're fine,' said Donal. 'I've seen far worse at home. It's good to meet ye. We weren't sure that Peter here,' he gave his friend a playful clip around the ear, 'was telling the truth when he claimed there were lads on the site who were willing to talk to him. Or worse, listen to him. Strangely, it seems to be true.'

O'Mahoney's, Elizabeth reckoned, was the type of Irish bar you never saw in Ireland. On the far wall, there was a washed-out copy of the 1916 proclamation. Another poster urged support for a jailed IRA man. Like everything else, they were coloured by a thousand nights of grime and nicotine. The customers were a curious combination. For every group of elderly men with bulbous noses and Brylcreemed hair, there was a knot of tattooed youngsters in stonewashed denim. Most of them were transfixed by a baseball game on the television. The occasional yelp of 'yeah' indicated that the Red Sox were winning.

Beside her, the boys were dissecting events at Euro '88. Peter, who could talk for a nation when it came to the significance of sports results, claimed that Ireland's win was 'about much more than football, you know'. Brian proposed toasts to Jack Charlton, Ray Houghton, Mick McCarthy, the little fellow who looked after the kit and anyone else who came to mind. Donal promised he would never again get worked up about the team, half of whom were the sons or grandsons of emigrants, not knowing the words of the national anthem. 'They're as Irish as we are,' he said. 'And that's a fact.'

'Boring, huh?'

It took Elizabeth a couple of seconds to realise that Danny was talking to her. She was consumed by her own thoughts and didn't know what it was that might be boring.

'I'm not so good with this soccer either,' he said. 'I mean, around here we have baseball and football and basketball and hockey. I'm not sure as we have room for much else.'

Slightly confused, Elizabeth shrugged. 'Don't mind me. I was … thinking.'

Danny put on a comic expression, like he was trying to figure out what was on her mind. He had interesting eyes: not fully blue, not quite grey. 'You're not having a good time in Boston, then?'

'I didn't say that.'

'You didn't have to. Why else would you look all miserable?'

She looped her wavy hair behind her ears. 'I'm not miserable. It's …' She could hardly start telling this strange American man about Liam getting into a huff. 'It's one of my flatmates.'

'What's she been up to?'

Elizabeth wondered whether he was a bit weird. He certainly asked a lot of questions. 'How do you know it's a girl?'

'Oh, just a little intuition.' He tapped his forehead. 'What did she do?'

'Nothing really … but …'

'It's so bad you're not going to tell me, huh?'

Feeling more rattled by the second, she decided she didn't have much choice. 'I know this probably sounds stupid, but I'm the target for all her jokes, and if I don't laugh along I'm scared that people – even my real friends – will think I don't have a sense of humour. Honestly, I'm beginning to think the girl lies awake at night thinking of new ways to make fun of me. It wasn't so bad in Dublin, but out here she's impossible to avoid.' Elizabeth was about to continue when it struck her that this Danny guy must consider her an awful eejit. She raked a hand through her fringe. 'I'm sorry. I'm acting like a fourteen-year-old. For all I know, you might have *really* bad stuff happening in your life and here am I—'

Thankfully, Danny intervened before her wittering got out of control. 'That sounds like a big enough problem to me. How can I help?'

'Short of banishing her from America, I'm not sure that you can.'

He smiled again, and she noticed how on one side his teeth were slightly crooked, like right at the back there might be a tooth too many. 'Hmmm,' he said. 'I better have a word with the immigration guys. See if they can get working on her deportation. A girl like you can't come to America and be unhappy.'

Crazy as it might sound, she got the sense that Danny knew exactly how corny his lines were, but was content to toss them out there anyway. She couldn't help but smile. If the dreaded Orla was with her, there would be flirting galore. Or worse, Orla would make out that Elizabeth was interested in him. She was searching for a non-flirtatious way of asking what sort of girl she might be when Peter interrupted their conversation.

'Elizabeth, you agree with Brian, don't you? About London?'

'I was telling the boys here,' Brian from Bray explained, 'how I went there after I left school. Worked on the buildings for more than a year. Couldn't settle. You'd go up to Kilburn on a Saturday night, and it'd be all plastic pint glasses and pointless fights.'

'I know just what you mean,' she said. 'My sister is nursing up that way. I went over to see her once, and it was unbelievable. We met these fellas from Thurles, and in Ireland they were regular young lads. Suddenly they're in London and they have this overwhelming desire to watch show bands and act like it's the 1950s.'

'You get the other ones, mind,' added Brian, 'who don't want to admit they're Irish at all. They're barely off the boat when they start going on about what a great woman Mrs Thatcher is.'

'I know the men,' said Donal. 'There's a fella at home. I'd say he was working in the Vauxhall plant in Luton for eighteen months, maximum. Then, didn't his father die and he had to come back. Not only did he already have the English accent, he insisted on calling the parish priest "vicar" and the guard "constable". Named his children Charles and Diana.' He took a slug of his drink. 'Which category will we fall into, do you think?'

'Neither,' said Peter, giving him a withering look, 'because we're going home.'

Brian said that after London he had returned to Wicklow where he'd spent six months on the dole, watching quiz shows and pretending to sleep. 'I decided I'd go insane if I didn't get on the move again. Luckily enough, I knew a fella over this way. Been here ever since.'

'Three years,' said Elizabeth. 'When were you last in Ireland?'

Brian bristled, swallowed the last of his beer and signalled for another round. 'Are you joking me? How could I go back? I'd never get into America again.'

Elizabeth silently cursed her stupidity. She had read often enough about the thousands of Irish people who lived in fear of the knock on the door, and one of her own cousins was working illegally in Queens. 'I'm sorry, Brian. I was being really thick.'

'You're all right.' He smiled, only when he spoke again there was a wistful undertow to his voice. 'It's odd, being cut off like this. It doesn't matter if you hated the sight of Ireland on the day you left, it's still home. I can't say as I'd like to live there again. I'd just like the freedom to visit, you know?'

She fiddled with the hem of her red T-shirt, smoothing it between her thumb and index finger. For a few moments there was silence, and she tried to imagine what it must be like to be in Brian's position. She wouldn't be able to handle it, that's for sure. She turned around to see what the American, Danny, made of their conversation, but he had drifted off. He was at the far end of the bar, chatting to a woman with DIY-blond hair and a tattooed ankle.

Peter sighed. 'Makes you think.'

'It does that,' said Brian. 'How long are you here now?'

'Only three weeks,' Elizabeth replied. 'The visas last six months but I doubt any of us will stay that long.' Actually, this wasn't true. She didn't plan on staying, and she knew that Peter was of like mind. But the others? Like Liam had said, there wasn't much for them in Ireland.

Brian started on a fresh beer. 'That's what everyone comes out with, though, isn't it? All the time I hear people saying, "Oh, I'm only here for a few months." And then they get sucked in. I'm not saying this city is perfect, but you know what the great thing is? Nobody cares what you did before you got here. Or who you know, or where you went to school. They just want you to work.'

'Sounds good to me,' said Donal. 'It's like you can be whoever you want to be.'

'Yeah, only what if you're happy enough with life at home?' asked Peter.

'Happy enough with what?' said Brian. 'What are you going to do?'

Peter raised his shoulders as far as his ears. 'Can't say as I have any definite plans at the moment.'

Brian sucked hard on his cigarette. 'You return to Dublin and you'll end up like everybody else – sitting around arguing about which of you is the poorest. Listen, it doesn't matter what you say now. When your visas are up, I can guarantee you won't want to go back.'

Danny and Peter were taking a break from work, their backs to the wall, the sun dancing on their faces. In the near distance, a drill throbbed through concrete; a cement mixer clattered and whirred. Someone called Danny's name, but he decided not to hear.

He blew a curl of smoke into the sky. 'It was good to meet your room-mates the other night. You all seem pretty tight.'

'Mmmm,' Peter replied. 'They're not a bad bunch. Donal's shocking clever. As mad as a ditch, though. I don't know what'll become of him.'

'And the girl … Elizabeth, right?'

'Yeah.'

Danny smiled. 'What do I have to ask to get some proper information?'

'You're interested in Elizabeth?'

'Jesus, man, you make it sound like I'm trying to score Mother Teresa. She's a fine-looking girl.'

'It'd probably be easier to get a result with Mother Teresa. Anyway, do I not remember you mentioning a girlfriend?'

'I've kicked that into touch for a while. Cindy and her mom were starting to hear wedding bells.'

'Ah, the dreaded mammy.'

'Yeah. Time for a change, I think.' Looking at Peter, Danny didn't reckon the guy would understand his predicament. His mousy hair was cropped short on top and hung in spindly tails at the back. The heat had glued those tails to his neck. It was hard to imagine any mother seeing Peter as the answer to her prayers.

Peter squinted at him. 'How old did you say you were?'

'Twenty-three.'

'Sure, that's only two years older than me, and I'm just a child. You've years of freedom ahead of you yet.'

'That's the way I see it. Cindy's on a different wavelength.' She wasn't alone. Everyone in his life, especially Vincent, was looking for him to settle down. He would have to be staring down the barrel of a gun before he'd admit as much, but Danny knew he was good-looking and he exploited his good fortune to the full. When life offered so much opportunity, only a fool would walk away too soon. Anyway, he had already fallen into line by getting this job, and by staying here. They were working on a regeneration scheme, giving a new lease of life to one of the city's decrepit housing projects.

Danny wasn't entirely sure why he was interested in this Elizabeth girl. Usually, he went for beauties, and she didn't fall into that category. Adequately pretty was probably the best description. He could say he was attracted to her foreignness, except being from Ireland was hardly exotic. Not when you lived in Dorchester, and just about every face you saw was Irish. There was something different about her, though. Something that made him think, why not? Plus, unlike local girls, she didn't come with strings attached.

Next to him, Peter was muttering something about the

existence of a boyfriend. 'Seriously,' he was saying, 'Elizabeth is well spoken for. Going out with a lad from home. Steady. The sort who could be steady for Ireland.'

'As exciting as that, huh?'

'Well, you never know what women will go for. Liam's considered good-looking, I'm told. And he has a job. Engineer with the council. Played minor hurling for Tipperary too. Never made the senior panel, mind.'

'You've lost me.'

'It's a big game at home – with sticks. I guess it's kind of like being the top baseball player at school, but never getting the call from the Red Sox.'

That was more Danny's language. He looked at his watch. Time to get back down to work. There were, he figured, another six or seven months in this job. Eight, tops. And after that? What he hadn't told anyone was that he was thinking of travelling. Not for too long. A year or so, maybe. It was a shame no one in the family had been to Italy, to see where they came from. Never had the money, he supposed. As far as he knew, his mom's family were from down south: Calabria. His dad's folks he wasn't so sure about. He had asked Vincent, except the reply – 'wherever the low life hang out' – wasn't of much help. There were other places too, like Berlin. Now that was a city he would like to visit; it was hard to get your head around a place with a wall down the middle.

Of course, all the Irish people urged him to go to their country. He would *love* Ireland, they claimed. No disrespect to them, he didn't see it being first on his list. It may look pretty but, man, did it sound dreary.

'Irish, come on in here, wouldya?'

Elizabeth was resigned to a summer of being renamed. The culprit was her boss, Mike Anderson, the co-owner, co-manager and all-purpose dictator of Anderson's Electrical in downtown Boston. Mike ran the store from a yellow-walled basement office. Elizabeth and her colleague Jackie worked in an adjoining room.

They answered the phone, dealt with confused customers, placed orders and tolerated Mike's temper.

'For freak's sake, Irish, what's keeping you?'

'Coming, Mike.'

Her feet rooted under the desk for her pink court shoes. Shoes located, shoulder pads rearranged and skirt smoothed down to a respectable level, she girded herself for the morning's moan. Back home, Mike might have been nicknamed 'O'Connell Bridge', for he was as wide as he was long. He did, however, have surprisingly attractive brown eyes. There was a hint of joviality about them, like he'd once had fun but didn't want to overdo it. His laugh reminded her of Ernie from *Sesame Street*.

As usual his desk was laden with paperwork. This morning, though, his attention was taken by some small print on the sports pages of the *Boston Globe*.

'Shame your crowd couldn't lick the Reds,' he said.

The soccer. The night before Ireland had drawn one-all with the Soviet Union. If they won their next match, they would go through to the European semi-finals. Donal had called his brother in Leitrim to get the result. The brother said Ireland was driven demented with anticipation. The excitement had travelled as far as Lantern Street. Peter had stuck a makeshift Irish flag out the window, and Elizabeth was revelling in the team's unlikely success. The two lads were trawling Boston's Irish bars, trying to find somewhere to watch the next match live. If this didn't work out, Orla and Michelle were clamouring to go to O'Mahoney's. Elizabeth had surprised them with her positive description of Peter's friends. Orla claimed that if she had noticed what they looked like, they must be movie-star quality.

'It was a pity all right, Mike,' she said. 'Apparently, the USSR equalised with a few minutes to go. No shame in the result, though. Sure, there are hundreds of millions of them and hardly any of us.'

Her boss scowled. 'And on a bad day it feels like every last freaking one of you is in Boston.'

Elizabeth waited to be dismissed.

'Irish, as you're here, what's the story with the air conditioners? How are we doing?'

'Sold out, as far as I know. The suppliers say nobody can cope with the demand. I gather it's not normally this hot in June.'

'That's no freaking good. I have a whole floor of salesmen out there with no AC to sell. What's the point in that? People don't want new ovens or VCRs. They want colder air.'

Elizabeth had drawn up a list of the day's jobs. At the top were two phone calls, neither of which she wanted to make. Both calls were to women who had expected air conditioners to be delivered today, and neither was going to be in luck. The others in the apartment knocked all sorts of fun out of Elizabeth's job. As she said herself, she couldn't recall having seen an air conditioner until three weeks before; now she was an expert. Despite Mike's tricky temper, she was enjoying the work. Every day yielded new insights into America, and she got to speak to all sorts. Sometimes, when a customer rang to complain, they were thrown off-course by her accent. Where was she from, they'd want to know, and how was she finding Boston, and wasn't the heat just unbelievable?

Mike would be appalled if he knew that Lantern Street was reliant on a half-hearted electric fan. It was also dingy and sticky, and fear persisted that a rat was lurking; intermittent scratching sounds could be heard from one of the kitchen cupboards. Donal, who claimed to know about wildlife, said there was no way a mouse would make all that noise. Their apartment had two poky bedrooms – one for the lads, one for the women – and at night they all collapsed in various states of exhaustion. That was something else Elizabeth had learnt: you can have a surprisingly sound night's sleep on a wooden floor.

Jackie had taken the morning off. When she turned up, Elizabeth would escape from the bunker, take her book up to Boston Common and eat her lunch in the sun. In the meantime, she decided to take a walk around the sales floor. The men and women who did their business there were keen-eyed creatures, adept at spotting a target and mesmerising them with sales patter. Affable as they all were, she knew they'd walk barefoot to New York for a big sale. In the land of commission, she was discovering, the shameless man is king.

Mike had emerged from his cave and was summoning her towards the televisions where he was watching CNN. Most days, the news people were consumed by the contest to replace Ronald Reagan in the White House, but her boss was signalling with such vigour, she wondered whether a report was coming up about the big soccer match. As she got closer to the screens, she saw the images were of a darker kind. A woman reporter was talking about 'high explosive Semtex'. An eyewitness spoke of 'bodies lying all over the street, bones scattered'.

Mike made a sound that was halfway between a sigh and a whistle. 'That's some part of the world you come from, Irish. Six guys dead. One of 'em only twenty years old. Now you tell *me*, is that gonna make any difference to anything?'

She was surprised at how many Americans enquired about 'the troubles', as they were called. At home, unless something particularly heinous occurred, most people – Elizabeth included – were skilled at turning a blind eye. 'I don't know, Mike. I don't think it will achieve anything. But what can you do?'

'Well, you should have a word with some of the boys around here who have one beer too many and want to die for freaking Ireland,' he said.

Back in her windowless office, she turned on the radio. The dial was set to the rock station Jackie liked. The one that played 'Sweet Child o' Mine' by Guns N' Roses at least ten times a day. Now that she was on her own, she would drop a few lines to Liam. It was his turn, but he'd been in such rank humour the other day he would appreciate a letter.

'How did you meet?' the girls at college had liked to ask. After all, it was a rare teenage romance that survived the distractions of university. The truth was so spectacularly unglamorous that Elizabeth had been tempted to invent a story. Her dad had dragged her along to one of those club hurling games where the weather is always foul, and the players are either knock-kneed kids or beer-bellied old lads. That day there had been one exception: a midfielder with boot-polish black hair and an appealing curve to his legs. Afterwards they got talking, and when Liam asked if she'd like to go to the pictures, Elizabeth was so flattered she almost keeled over. At nineteen, he was three years older than her, and she knew he was a real catch. Halfway through *Footloose* an arm slipped around her shoulder, and that was that. Her parents were delighted with the match. Her mam said Liam was such a good worker, he put other young men to shame. Her dad thought he was very sharp. 'He'd mind mice at a crossroads, that fella,' Syl had once declared.

Among her housemates, the relationship was an endless source of sport. Peter and Donal were especially inventive. If there was a jibe to be made about small-town boys or life outside the capital, she had heard it. It was hard to take offence. The two lads were townies like her: occupants of the halfway house in Irish life where Dubliners dismissed you as rural, and genuine country people looked down on you for having no land. What did get to her were Orla's antics. Her latest stunt was to ask what Liam was like in bed. Keep on asking, thought Elizabeth, but I'll never talk about that.

Still, and she could barely admit this to herself, there were times when she wondered if she *was* too young to be so settled. A tiny voice at the back of her head would say, 'If you're this cautious now, what will you be like in twenty years' time?' Worse, it would ask if she was really, truly sure about Liam.

There was no denying that he was a good boyfriend. He was smart and considerate, and she always looked forward to seeing him. Well, almost always. Sometimes, at college, she had made up an overdue essay or a Saturday lecture so she could stay in Dublin and go on the tear with Michelle and the two boys. The four of them would go on a pub crawl of Baggot Street, drinking Guinness in the Henry Grattan and Toner's and Nesbitt's. Occasionally, if a grant cheque had arrived, they would move on to a

Leeson Street nightclub and spend extortionate sums of money on toxic white wine. There, they would dance and laugh until it was bright. Afterwards, Elizabeth would be dogged by guilt. But the guilt wouldn't stop her from doing it again.

Weekends with Liam were a more sedate affair. Usually he had a match to play, so he didn't like to hit the town too hard. From time to time, they would go for a quiet drink with her parents. Liam would have a pint of Harp, and she might have a glass of shandy or a Malibu and pineapple.

What worried Elizabeth was that she never felt any of the exhilaration that other girls spoke about. They never spent the day in bed together, or went anywhere without a tribe of others tagging along. There was nothing daring or unexpected or particularly joyful about their relationship. The tiny voice suggested that this was the real reason she had come to Boston; that she was looking for an escape.

Then she copped herself on. Oh listen to yourself, she thought. You should remember how lucky you are. Anyway, maybe Liam wasn't the problem. Maybe it was her.

Chapter 3

The football fairy-tale ended on Saturday night. The final score was Netherlands 1, Ireland 0. The winning goal came eight minutes from the end. Elizabeth was determined to look on the bright side, but Peter told her that he didn't want to hear any guff about moral victories or the best fans in the tournament. The Netherlands and the Soviet Union went through to the semi-finals. Ireland went home. They weren't able to watch the match live. The closest they'd found was a man in Allston who said he might have the video by Monday, so Michelle called her parents to get the result.

A deflated Donal maintained it was as bad as the Montreal Olympics. Although he'd only been a kid back in 1976, he remembered the family getting a colour television especially for the 1500 metres final. Eamonn Coghlan had finished fourth. His father still claimed the useless bastard owed him two hundred pounds.

Elizabeth had no trouble getting in to O'Mahoney's. The same doorman was on duty and he recognised the Irishman and his wayward wife. The bar was like she remembered: dark and hot. Like a cross between a Bruce Springsteen video and the Ballinasloe Horse Fair, according to Michelle. Within minutes, Donal descended on the horse fair element, a group of 1950s-style immigrants with hardly a sound tooth between them. As they swapped stories, Elizabeth noticed a sign behind them. *God made liquor to stop the Irish from ruling the world*, it read. Donal's new friends looked as though they'd have difficulty ruling a straight line.

Peter had delivered a full contingent of men from work. 'No

compulsion now, women,' he said to Michelle and Orla, a laugh in his voice, 'but I'll be upset if I don't get at least one result.' Elizabeth watched the frenzy of swaggering and flirting and scheming, and felt like a child fobbed off with endless soft drinks while her parents got tanked at the bar. Everyone was on the prowl, and she was out of place. She gulped down her beer and contemplated going back to Lantern Street.

She was scoping out her escape when Danny appeared. The next she knew, he was handing her another beer, pulling up a stool and asking questions. Since the previous Sunday, she'd been trying to pinpoint who it was that he brought to mind. Now he was sitting in front of her, the riddle was solved. Back in Tipperary, her father was friendly with a local politician, a minor league figure who had that knack of appearing to be interested in every word you came out with. Danny had the same capacity. You would swear there was no one else on the planet he'd rather be talking to.

'Which one is it?' he asked. 'Curly or blond?'

'I'm not with you.'

'The bitch of a room-mate? I'm guessing it's blondie. She looks kind of mean.'

'Most men can't get enough of her.'

Danny peered at Orla and gave her an elaborate once-over. 'Nah. Doesn't do much for me.'

'Jesus, Danny, what are you trying to do to me? If she sees you, I'll be in even more trouble.' Elizabeth made an effort to look annoyed. She was, of course, pathetically pleased.

And that was how it began. Their conversation whizzed along, enjoyment crept up on her, and in no time at all he was laughing at her Mike Anderson tales and threatening to come in and sort him out. He asked a stream of questions. Why Boston? How long had she known Peter? Apart from Blondie, what were her flatmates like?

'They're cool, actually,' she said. 'Well, now that I look at the state of them,' she glanced towards Donal and the old lads, 'they're obviously not cool at all, if you know what I mean. But

36

they're great crack.' Danny laughed so she continued. 'Michelle's my best friend. Donal keeps us entertained. And Peter – sure, you know Peter, he's forever finding fault with something but he's got a heart as big as a house. I'd be lost without him.'

'You're looking more cheerful tonight,' he said. 'Will I call the immigration guys, and tell them Orla can stay?'

'Hmmm. I'm not sure. Let's not do anything too hasty. She does want to stay in America, by the way. Permanently. Says she'll do whatever it takes to get a green card. Including getting married, if needs be.' Elizabeth shocked herself by what she did next: she winked at Danny and said, 'So, consider yourself warned. Unless you're already taken, that is.'

'Nope. I'm open to offers.' He rubbed his neck. 'My standards are probably too high for her, though. What about your other friend? Is she looking to hook an American guy too?'

'I think Michelle has already found her man. She has a crush on a fella in the supermarket where she works, a supervisor named Ray. He's a recovering alcoholic which she says is grand because, being Irish, she's attracted to suffering.'

Danny unleashed his laugh again, a low throaty chuckle. 'And do you have a crush on anyone, Elizabeth?' he asked.

This was going too far. Elizabeth felt herself turn as red as a rash. But she didn't mention Liam. In fact, she said nothing; just knocked back the last of her beer and waited to hear what he'd come out with next.

'So assuming you don't plan on staying in Anderson's for the rest of your days,' he said, 'what do you want to do with your life?'

'Teach English, I think.'

Danny played with his bottle of beer, digging his nails, such as they were, under the damp label. The nails were bitten; the skin looked jagged and sore. 'Why teaching?'

'You ask a lot of questions.'

'So I'm told.' He touched her hand. 'You hold that thought, and I'll get us another beer.'

She watched him go for the drinks, then risked a few furtive glances around the bar. She didn't want to make it look like she was seeking out additional company. The last thing she needed was one of the others lumbering in and diluting or disturbing their discussion. Elizabeth tried to herd her thoughts. She feared she was out of practice at gauging these situations. When he returned, their hands touched again. A tremor went skittering down her spine. She uncrossed and recrossed her legs. Their easy chat picked up pretty much where it had left off.

'Why do I want to teach?' she said. 'I suppose I've always had this belief in the importance of education, and how it can change your life. At home, you get all these people saying that school doesn't matter, and that exams deaden the mind. But, if you ask me, the types who come out with that stuff are usually well connected; they know that Daddy will be able to fix them up with a job anyway.' She took a deep breath. 'Sorry, Danny, I'm sounding way too earnest here. Orla says I'm like a headmistress when I get going.'

He smiled. 'I thought we'd agreed not to pay too much mind to what Orla says.'

May God forgive me, thought Elizabeth, but that smile could do a lot of damage. 'What about you?' she managed to ask.

'Well, my mom had high hopes. Wanted me to go to university. Except all I managed was six months at community college. Right this minute, I'll bet the poor woman is studying my high school grades, trying to work out why the boys in Harvard wouldn't make room for me.'

'You're a carpenter, though. That's a good job.'

'I suppose. It wasn't something I'd planned on. The problem was I hadn't planned on anything else either. My dad's a carpenter. All the family were on my case, so I figured I'd just do what he did. Mind you, the old man says that if I work till I'm ninety I'll never be as good as him.'

Although Elizabeth found his self-deprecation entertaining, she did wonder if it was *too* entertaining, too practised. She

38

made a fist and lightly rubbed his upper arm. 'Do you know what, Danny? I'd say there's fear of you.'

He returned the gesture, gently brushing her forearm. 'Ha. You see, I've learnt over the years that most Irish phrases mean the precise opposite of what you think they mean. So I'm assuming that's a compliment.'

She had to laugh. 'Do you like Boston?'

'The place must have something going for it. Enough of you come over here and don't want to leave. Seriously, though, it's home. I mean, what hope have you if you don't like where you're from?'

Elizabeth smiled in acknowledgement. She felt just the same.

'Place has plenty of faults too, of course.' Danny took a swig of beer. 'But we can leave those for another time. What about you, Elizabeth? Could you live here?'

'I'm only in America a month. You'll have to ask me in October.'

'Perhaps I'll do that.'

'What are you going to ask her?'

Elizabeth hadn't spotted Peter sidling over to them. 'Ah, nothing,' she said. 'Just chatting. You want another beer?'

They both nodded.

Peter was the catalyst for a general movement in their direction. When she returned with the beers, Michelle was nearby, talking to Brian from Bray. And there was Orla, top to toe in white Lycra, tossing her hair away from her upturned face while a circle of potential conquests looked on. Danny was on the fringes of the group with a man she didn't recognise. She caught mentions of Wade Boggs and Roger Clemens. Red Sox. Their moment had passed. Someone bought her another drink and engaged her in mundane chatter. Something drew her attention to the door, and she thought she saw Danny leaving. Shortly afterwards, she scanned the bar. No sign.

People always said alcohol clouded the brain. 'Oh, it's all a blur,' they'd claim. In Elizabeth's experience, it did the opposite. Several drinks in, you got to a point where the distractions receded and you were able to focus on exactly what you wanted. Anyway, she wasn't blind, incoherent drunk. She was more spirited drunk, daredevil drunk.

'I'm heading out for a minute. Going to get a little air,' she said, although she wasn't sure that anyone was listening.

As she left, she grinned at the doorman who was giving hell to a group of lanky teenagers. Plainly, even O'Mahoney's had to draw a line somewhere. The girls all looked like junior Joan Jetts, and the boys were going through a savagely spotty phase.

Outside was only slightly cooler. Elizabeth felt the night air circulate around her legs. She filled her lungs with carbon monoxide and the stale smell of bar. She heard him before she saw him.

'Hot in there, isn't it?' he said.

Elizabeth had a little time to talk to herself, about ten yards' worth of time. She reassured herself that she was only there to talk. After all, talking does no harm. Then she instructed herself to look casual. The thing was she didn't feel casual. She was exam hall tense, her muscles tight, and her mind racing. Beside her the walls were releasing the heat of the day. Waves of muffled sound leached from the bar.

'It got too hot for me,' she said, as she reached where Danny was standing. 'I thought I'd come out here to cool down.'

'I was hoping you'd follow me.'

She was on the verge of launching into some offended spluttering, when her instincts told her that Danny would see through an over-dramatic display. In a heartbeat he had managed to switch from self-effacement to self-confidence. He knew his worth, all right. She gave what she hoped was an indifferent shrug. 'What gives you the idea I'm following you? I might be trying to escape from someone. Or I might be following someone else.'

There was a hint of a smile on his face. 'True, true. Only, I don't think so.'

'As they say at home, you've got a great welcome for yourself.'

'Another phrase for me to remember.'

'Well,' she said, relenting a little, 'I was enjoying our conversation.'

'Me too,' he said, as he took a half-step towards her. 'Until the others came and broke it up.'

She produced another slight shrug. 'We could always talk out here.'

'We could.' Another half-step.

They looked at each other. For a short time, neither spoke. By now, Elizabeth knew they were too close. Her mind see-sawing, she fumbled for some appropriate words. She had talked a mile a minute for most of the night. If anything, she was worried she had talked too much. Now she wasn't able to summon one sensible sentence. 'I—'

'Sshhh.' Danny took one hand, tickling the palm with his fingers.

Elizabeth knew what was meant to happen next. Or she knew what would happen at home. They needed to draw out the flirting, gradually ramping it up while getting closer and closer. Inching towards the inevitable while pretending it wasn't so. That was the accepted way to play the game, and it was a complicated business. But home felt very far away. Orla's barbs remained in her head. How satisfying would it be to confound her expectations? Elizabeth scrutinised Danny: the blue-grey eyes that dipped ever so slightly at the corners, the tanned skin and the vague air of trouble. If she was ever going to kiss anyone other than Liam, this, she believed, was the man. A few kisses would hurt no one. So why play games? Why not plunge on in?

Danny held her gaze. Message received, he let go of her hand and brushed back her hair. 'I've been wanting to do this all night.'

Her mouth twitched at the corniness of the line. 'Mmmm.'

He cupped her chin, stroked her cheek and they began to kiss. To start with, Danny's kisses were gentle. Gradually they became more insistent. Then he slowed again. One moment he kissed hard, the next he paused to nuzzle her face and her neck. He smelled of cigarette smoke, beer, faintly of soap. Buzzing with alcohol and enjoyment, Elizabeth tried to catch her breath. Her mind blurred. This is not the slow set at the teenage disco, she thought. She was in the grown-up's league here.

Sometime later, they moved to the back of the building. It was dark and cramped there, but private. She was against the wall. Fleetingly, the bricks felt rough against her back but mostly she was aware only of the man who enclosed her. From time to time, he murmured small endearments, or said 'Oh' or 'Mmmm'. She didn't say anything, except perhaps his name. Her head hummed.

After that there was a jumble of sensations: of Danny moving one hand slowly over her body, of him somehow removing her bra, of more kissing and grazing and of the assorted lurches and whooshes of pleasure that accompanied all of this. Who knew that kissing alone could provoke that much whooshing?

At some point, she began to wonder if he was hoping to go all the way. Right there at the back wall of O'Mahoney's. Did they say 'all the way' in America, or did they have another phrase for it? Whatever it was called, that's where they looked to be heading. Between whooshes her head started to clear a little. Elizabeth was in the car park of the seediest place she had ever seen with a man she barely knew, and he was making resolute efforts to remove her clothes.

'Danny?'

'Huh?' He was biting an ear while easing a hand inside her denim skirt.

'Do you think we ought to, ah, slow it down?'

'Uh, no. This is great. Just go with me.' He kissed her again, a barrage of kisses, and his hand crept further.

She turned her face to one side. 'No, Danny. Please.'

He didn't stop quite as quickly as she would have liked, although he did stop. They disentangled. She told herself to move away, except her feet wouldn't obey.

'Are you OK, baby?'

Elizabeth didn't think anyone had ever called her baby before.

How could such a silly word sound so appealing? It undoubtedly was not a word Liam would use. Lord, she thought, Liam. Stupid as it was, an image of her real boyfriend – all heavy brows and wounded eyes – flashed into her head. She attempted to rehook her bra. Danny appeared to have more skill with the damn thing than she did.

'I …' she said, realising she was out of breath. 'I think maybe we were going too far.'

Danny drew a finger along her chin. 'I can slow down. I can do whatever you want. I'm just crazy turned on, you know?' He exhaled. 'Or, if you like, we can go someplace else? My brother's apartment isn't far from here. He's got a spare room.'

'No, it's …' She hesitated. 'I shouldn't be doing this. Not at all. I'm going out with a fella at home.'

Clearly, Danny wasn't going down without a fight, especially when his competition was three thousand miles away. He stroked her hair and then the side of her neck. 'Hey, it's cool. I'm not going to make you do anything you don't want to do.' He gave a full-wattage smile. 'I had the impression you were enjoying your-self too.'

'I was. But—'

'This is not the most romantic spot in Boston, I'll give you that. I do know better places.' He chuckled. 'I even know better parking lots.'

She thought, I'll bet you do. She said, 'I didn't mean here. I meant anywhere. I shouldn't have kissed you.'

Finally, Elizabeth did manage to take a step away from him. Danny was wearing a look that seemed to say, 'This isn't quite how it's supposed to go, so give me a moment and I'll fix it.' He ran one hand through his hair. 'Can I see you again?'

'Oh gosh, Danny, I'm not sure. I mean, I'd like to see you again with Peter and the lads and that, but … like this … it's probably not a good idea, you know.' She was appalled by how inarticulate she had become.

'That's a real shame, baby. Are you sure?'

43

'I'm sorry I gave you the wrong idea. I sort of lost the run of myself there. I hope I didn't mess you around too much.'

'No, you're fine. I'm fine. I guess I'll see you around.' He kissed her cheek. 'You should go back in the bar. Your friends will be worrying.'

'You're right. Good night. Take care.' By then she was so addled with drink and desire and guilt that she almost added, 'God bless.'

As Elizabeth watched Danny walk away, she tried to regain her poise. In the darkness she kicked an empty bottle against the wall.

Sunday morning saw Elizabeth sitting in the basement laundry room of their apartment building, waiting for the dryer to finish. Her feet were on a chair as she read her book, *The Grapes of Wrath*. She loved the basement and its linty residue of years of washing and drying. It felt completely American, like she was playing a bit part on the *Mary Tyler Moore Show* or *Rhoda*.

Donal peered around the door. 'Morning, wife. Hope Tom and Rosasharn and all the gang are doing well.'

'They're suitably miserable, all right.' She beckoned him in. 'How's the man? I thought you'd be at work.' Donal had a job doing room service in one of Boston's most upmarket hotels.

'Nah, they've given me a day off at last.' He found another chair and sat down. 'Good night?'

'It had its moments.' Truth to tell, her conscience was giving her an almighty battering over those moments. 'Have you seen Orla and Michelle?'

'Not a sign. The last I saw of them, they were with a crowd heading back to Brian's apartment. Orla was swinging out of one of them.'

Elizabeth inspected the dryer. Another few minutes were needed. She got the sense that Donal had more to say. 'So?'

'So, I'm on to you,' he said.

Her stomach gave a quick lunge. 'Sorry?'

44

'You weren't quite yourself last night. Disappearing on us. Then showing up with the hair bedraggled and the skirt skew-whiff.'

'I don't know what you're on about.'

'My friend, Albert – the door man at O'Mahoney's? He marked my card. Said you were up to your old tricks.' He paused. 'Kissing a man in the car park.'

The lunge progressed into a series of somersaults. She gazed at the ground. 'Will you get away, Donal.'

When she looked up again, his face was pure mischief. 'You're right,' he said. 'That's not *quite* what he told me. He was more specific. Said he saw you kissing Danny Esposito in the car park. Quite an exhibition, apparently. Believed he could have sold tickets.'

Chapter 4

Elizabeth was not having a good midsummer. She was at work, Jackie was away, and Mike was like a briar. In the end, he moaned himself out and left for the day. Now she was knee-deep in one of the most tedious tasks imaginable: invoice filing. Somehow, the combination of stationery and electrical equipment gave the place a peculiarly dead air. Lethargy descended, and she wanted to curl up and sleep. Either that or escape, although she guessed the air outside was similarly listless.

She'd also had to contend with a slew of callers asking moronic questions about their appliances. She gave them short shrift. Instead of coming on the phone to torment her, could they not read the instruction manual? Elizabeth was not given to reciting poetry – she left that type of thing to Donal who had a real feel for words. But a line from Thomas Hardy, etched on to her brain at fifteen, kept coming to mind: *And every spirit upon earth Seemed fervourless as I.* She quoted the line to Mike, just to watch his bewildered reaction.

In her spare moments, she continued to reflect on Saturday night, running events around and around her head. It wasn't just the cheating on Liam she berated herself for. Danny must have thought her a shocking fool. One minute she was draping herself around him, the next she was dashing away like a little girl. As for Liam, she was thankful at least that what he didn't know couldn't hurt him. Funnily enough, even though she had kissed Danny to convince Orla and Michelle she was no different to them, she hadn't yet got around to passing on the news. Perhaps tonight.

Elizabeth had been in America for a month now, but some

thoughts from home kept coming back to her. One episode in particular played on her mind: what had happened on the Friday evening before she left. She had been out with Liam. Nothing wild; they had gone for a walk before the gathering drizzle forced them back indoors. There, they had found her mam and dad, Syl and Stacia, sitting in the kitchen, a pot of tea in front of them, the tension like a slap in the face.

'You'll have a cup,' Syl had said as he got up to fetch two more mugs.

Elizabeth had known that asking questions was futile. With her parents, you had to wait for the story to emerge. Her immediate instinct had been to connect the gloom to the fate of the sugar factory. For months now, her father's workplace had been facing closure, yet he continued to insist it would get a reprieve.

The Kelly family lived in the middle house of a cream-walled terrace. It was damp at the best of times, and as they sat there, the fustiness was overpowering. Too nervous to look either of her parents in the eye, Elizabeth focused on a stain on the wallpaper, created years before when her little brothers – Colm and Eoin – had gone through a phase of flicking cornflakes at each other.

It was Stacia who broke the silence. 'Your sister called. Herself and Keith are after getting engaged.'

Relief coursed through Elizabeth. 'But that's brilliant, isn't it?' she replied, her mother's despondent face more of a mystery than ever. Alice had been going out with Keith for two years. He was a mechanic from Enfield; his father owned three garages there. The year before, when she had spent a week in London, Elizabeth had been in the family house, and it was obvious the Barkers were on the wealthy side of comfortable. They had a beautiful conservatory out back and a small bar in the corner of the front room.

Syl picked a tea leaf from his mug. 'I don't think you understand, pet. Your mam is upset because this means Alice won't be coming home.'

'Of course she will,' Elizabeth said. 'Weren't they over this

47

way just a couple of months ago?' Keith and Alice had visited in March. They'd rented a fancy car at Shannon Airport, and had toured all around Munster. At the time, Elizabeth had got the impression her dad wasn't overly impressed by Keith. 'Lucky his father was born before him,' had been his verdict. Then again, Syl was notoriously hard to please.

'We don't mean for a visit,' Stacia said. 'We ... we didn't think Alice would stay in London. We always assumed she'd come back to Ireland. That she'd get a job in the hospital in Nenagh or in the Regional in Limerick. Or even in Dublin. But, sure, now ...' Her voice tapered off.

Elizabeth recalled Liam sending her a look, like he was urging her to say something, anything, to console her parents. She tried, but her efforts were little more than gibberish. 'London is so close nowadays,' she said, 'and the price of airfares is coming down all the time,' and, 'Who knows what the future holds.'

Stacia gave her a flat-eyed stare while Syl rubbed his knuckles across his forehead. Eventually, Liam intervened. 'At least this girl won't stray too far,' he said, as he patted Elizabeth's arm. 'Once she gets this America lark out of her system, that is.'

Elizabeth knew she couldn't do anything about Alice's decision. She wouldn't want to. During her week in London she had been taken by her sister's lightness of spirit. Contradictory as it might sound, Alice was at home in England. And yet now, four weeks on, Elizabeth couldn't forget Stacia's face. Her mother was a young woman – only forty-seven – but that night she had looked defeated.

Eventually, her daydreaming was disturbed by a rap on the office door. She looked up to see her favourite salesman, the soft-spoken Artie. 'There's a guy over there who wants to talk to you,' he said. 'Reckons you might be expecting him.'

It must be the man from Needham with whom she'd had a fractious phone conversation an hour or two before. A man badly in need of conditioned air, he had threatened to come in to check for himself that the unit he ordered was not in stock. He sounded large. Elizabeth braced herself for pointless confrontation. The longest day could not get any worse.

On the other side of Boston Common, Donal was gliding towards the end of his day's work. At the Five Oceans Hotel, he was keeping the Irish storytelling tradition alive. That very day, a charming couple from Wisconsin had thrilled to the tale of how he and his two brothers had shared one pair of shoes at school, taking it in turns to keep their feet dry. This was total nonsense, although it was far from his most extravagant story. In his back pocket, he kept a photograph of a particularly shabby thatched cottage which he declared to be the family home.

Guests were not alone in being fed a diet of hungry donkeys, barefoot children and on-the-run IRA men. Occasionally, colleagues got the full-scale story of hardship and misfortune. Donal wasn't sure why he did this, except there was only so much you could say about eggs Benedict, and it did add to the gaiety of his day. Neither did he know whether anyone truly believed his stories. They humoured him all the same. 'They're lapping it up, man,' he said to Peter. 'Lapping it up.'

Obviously, Donal had to be careful not to spin his yarns in front of the other Irish workers. There were a handful of these, the most significant being the man who had secured him the job: his cousin Cathal, or Charlie as he called himself these days – he said it was 'best to meet the Yanks halfway'. Donal claimed Charlie had left school in Leitrim without being able to read or write, and that he'd got his own start in the USA from another relative. He was a bone fide 'man who'd made it big in America'.

When he got back to Lantern Street, he was met by a pair of unfamiliar faces. The two boys – he guessed they were eighteen or nineteen – were camped in the middle of the front room floor eating luncheon meat sandwiches. 'Pleased to meet ye, lads,' he said. 'Donal Mulvihill's the name. Are ye just off the plane?'

'Aye,' said the taller of the two, a plain fellow with mottled skin and a moustache of sweat. He stood and extended a hand.

'Tim Lawlor and Tom Burke. From Roscommon. Mrs Rooney, Michelle's mam, gave us the address. We were hoping we could crash here for a couple of days. Until we get sorted, like.'

The other lad also scrambled to his feet. He was blockier, with slanting grey eyes and what Donal called a 50p haircut. It was so misshapen, he couldn't possibly have been charged any more. He smiled, revealing teeth to match his hair. Jesus, thought Donal, we're a terrible ugly people.

'Not a bother,' he assured them. 'We've plenty of floor space. Do you think you'll be staying in Boston?'

'That's the plan. We've nothing lined up, though.'

Donal assumed they were illegal. This limited their opportunities. They also looked hopelessly out of their depth. A pound to a penny this was the first time they'd been further than Dublin. Now they would have to adjust to life on a different continent. Still, chances were they would find work and be swallowed up by the city like all the others. It was amazing how even young fellows as hapless as these found confidence and purpose when they went abroad.

'Are the women upstairs?' he asked.

'Aye,' replied Tom. Or Tim. They wouldn't be driving anyone mad with their incessant chatter anyway.

He found Orla and Michelle flat out on the roof, slathered in the sort of suntan oil that made them shine like they were dressed in butter.

'Afternoon to ye, ladies.'

'Afternoon, Donal.'

He set about laying out his accoutrements: a towel, a can of beer, a greasy paper bag of leftover hotel pastries and a copy of the previous day's *New York Times*, also salvaged from the hotel.

'Sit down there, and give us all your news,' said Michelle. 'How's life in the world of upscale breakfasts?'

He winked at her. 'No mocking there, please. I haven't had the chance to bring ye up to date. I have developments which may be of interest.'

Back in Anderson's, Elizabeth was bending down to file the last of the invoices when another knock shook the door. 'OK, OK,' she said. 'But if it's the man from Needham, I hope he understands there's nothing I can do for him.'

'Ahm … you must have got the wrong message. I'm obviously not the person you were expecting. Is it OK if I come in?'

Feeling like most of her internal organs had rearranged themselves, she jumped.

'Oh hell, Elizabeth, I didn't mean to scare you.'

She stood up, turned around, pulled down her skirt. There he was, wearing khaki shorts and a navy T-shirt, looking like he was fresh out of the shower.

'Um … Danny, hi. I thought you were … oh, never mind.' She was totally blindsided. Thankfully, he looked equally unsure of his footing.

'Hi,' he said.

For what felt like half an hour, but was probably ten seconds, neither said anything.

'Yeah … hi,' Danny continued. 'Your boss …?'

'Isn't here,' said Elizabeth. 'You're fine. I—'

'That's good. What it was … I happened to finish work early today and I was in town. So I thought, why not say hello.' He ran a hand over his hair and looked down for a moment. 'Would you like to go for a coffee? If you can. I mean, you may have other plans.'

Somehow, under the fluorescent glare of the office lights, he appeared less full of himself. Besides, she couldn't refuse; he was standing in front of her. 'Um, I'll have to sort this out first.' She gestured at the filing. 'It shouldn't take too long, though. I'm nearly through the alphabet.'

'Cool. I'll wait out there.' Danny smiled. 'Let them see if they can sell me something.'

As he ambled out to the sales floor, Elizabeth noticed for the first time how flat-footed his walk was. She leaned against the filing cabinet and took a deep breath. Mr Angry of Needham might have been easier to handle.

All the regulars were on the Common. A man with a huge brown coat and a polystyrene cup shambled up and down, asking for a quarter for the veteran; pale-faced kids extolled the glories of scientology; a pair of tame squirrels circled a tree. Early evening commuters, filing into Park Street station, ignored them all. For some reason, Elizabeth noticed detail here in a way she didn't at home. Everything was sharper, more vibrant. She unfurled her legs, shed the pink shoes and pointed her feet towards Tremont Street. Danny sat beside her. They ate ice cream. Neither spoke.

Since leaving Anderson's, they had exchanged a few faltering words, mainly about the fineness of the weather or the beauty of the city. Elizabeth tried to guess what he was going to say. Or was she expected to say something? She ate her ice cream slowly, taking small licks as she turned the strawberry cone around. Danny bolted his. Then, rubbing one knuckle back and forth across his chin, he watched her. The air hummed with the babble of sunbathers and the click-clack of high heels. An age passed before he spoke.

'So, Elizabeth, first off, I wanted to say I'm sorry for coming on too strong the other night. Sometimes I get carried away. I can be kind of dumb like that.'

She crunched the last of her cone. 'You know, Danny, there were two of us there. I didn't do anything I didn't want to do.'

'Yeah, only I wanted to tell you that I enjoyed talking to you. I didn't want you to think that was just an excuse to make a move on you. Not that any guy wouldn't want to kiss you because you're … lovely.'

A lock of hair fell over his forehead. He swept it back again. From the way he was speaking, Elizabeth suspected that Danny had rehearsed what he was saying. That must have been what gave her such an unexpected sense of self-possession.

'And I remember what you said, but I was wondering if I could see you again. So I can show you there's more to me than that. Like a proper date. No parking lots, you have my word. What do you think?'

What she thought was that he was either an accomplished operator or something much better than that, and she didn't know him well enough to determine which. She remembered what Donal had said on their first night in O'Mahoney's: out here you could be whoever you wanted to be. What was to stop her discovering a little more about Danny? There was no reason why anybody at home should find out. And what harm would another few kisses do? She glanced at him, gave a small grin and a slight nod. Danny moved a large brown hand along the grass and placed it over hers, which by comparison looked absurdly pale and narrow. The alien troop of butterflies that had invaded her stomach fluttered up a storm.

For a while they were happy to talk, and gradually the ease returned. Their conversation was unpredictable, rambling and ranging across so many subjects that Elizabeth lost track. One moment they were discussing her contention that people in Boston spent too much time talking about money. (She accepted that people in Ireland might be exactly the same if they had any money.) The next, they were talking about Danny's tentative plans to go into business with his builder brother. 'At some point in the future, mind. I've other stuff I want to do first.' Elizabeth asked about Vincent, and Danny started to laugh. 'I can't name one subject we completely agree on, but we get along really well.'

As they sat there, it struck her that he could recite his twelve times tables and she would listen. Almost everyone you met in Boston enthused about the Irish accent, but to her the cadence of his voice was far more attractive. Realising she couldn't say this without sounding certifiable, she contented herself with a gentle imitation of his pronunciation. 'Pahking lot,' she repeated.

He ruffled her hair. 'Now, you should know you can't come to my city and make fun of the way we talk. There are lots of us – and only one of you.'

'I'm not making fun. I like the way you speak.'

Danny made exaggerated play of narrowing his eyes. 'Hmmm, I'm a touch suspicious here. What do you say?'

'I would say "car park".'

'OK. Cah pahk.'

'Nope, there should be two "r"s in there somewhere. Car park.'

He purred back 'carr parrrk'.

'That's closer. I can tell you're a good student.'

'Ha. You were saying on Saturday night how you want to teach? I think you have it sorted already. Anyhow, maybe the Irish stole all the "r"s. You love emphasising them.'

'I'll have to make that my summer mission. People of Boston,' she laughed, 'the letter "r"? There's nothing to be afraid of.'

'I can see how that might work. When you go home to Ireland and do that teaching course, you can tell them you already have plenty of experience, introducing the letter "ah", sorry, letter "rrr" to Massachusetts.'

'I'll have to use you as a reference, of course.'

'Of course.' Danny inserted a battery of 'r's into the word, then leaned in and tickled her. She squealed, which only encouraged him further. Dissolving into giggles, she collapsed onto the grass.

It was dark when she got home. Orla was in the front room, painting her toenails a lurid pink. Elizabeth waved.

'Come here to me,' said Orla, her eyes like laser-guided missiles. 'Don't go slinking into that bedroom until we've had a word. I hear you've gone over to the dark side.'

'Where is everybody?'

'Gone to the cinema.' She tipped her head towards a stash of sleeping bags and assorted male belongings in the far corner. 'We have a couple of new arrivals. Harmless lads. They've gone too.'

Elizabeth went into the kitchen and fetched a mug of water. She eased herself onto the scratchy beige carpet beside Orla. 'Donal, I presume?'

'Who else? Why didn't you tell us?'

Elizabeth took a long drink of water. She wished Michelle was there. She'd still have to face an inquisition, but it wouldn't be quite so intimidating. 'I haven't really seen you … we've all been working different hours. And … I wasn't sure there was a lot *to* tell.'

Orla wriggled her freshly lacquered toes in front of the electric fan. 'Is there something to tell now?'

Looking at Orla, she couldn't suppress her smile. It was like she had lost control of the muscles at the corners of her mouth.

'Elizabeth Kelly! I am shocked. Have you been with Danny this evening?'

'Mmmm.'

Orla clapped her hands. She was taking a strange delight in the story. Mind you, it was preferable to her usual disdain. 'Come on,' she said, her voice laden with syrup. 'You can tell me. Where were you?'

'Sitting on the Common, talking and that. And then we went for coffee.'

Orla plucked a strand of grass from Elizabeth's shoulder. 'Messy business, the old talking. When are you meeting him again?'

'Listen,' she said, twirling a wisp of hair around one finger. 'Will you do me a favour and not make a fuss? Like you always say, it's an adventure. No big deal. I want to keep it that way. But I invited him along on Saturday.'

As he drove home, Danny sang along with WBCN, his favourite radio station. Tapped the beat on the steering wheel too. Even though it was dark, the sky was glowing, the way it did at this time of year.

Hopefully everything was OK at home. Vincent had promised to look in on Ma. He maintained he'd be all casual, so she wouldn't feel like he was there to keep watch. Danny didn't believe he was capable of this. Subtlety was not his brother's strong point.

He was four or five blocks from the house when he spotted a familiar figure in familiar white jeans, sauntering along the side-walk, hips swaying to and fro. It was an unmistakable walk. It said,

'Yeah, I know you're looking. That's cool. I understand.' He pulled over.

'Hey you,' Cindy said, manoeuvring herself into the passenger seat. 'Long time, no see.'

'Must be all of ten days. What are you up to?'

'Oh nothing. On my way back from a friend's house.'

'Do I know him?'

She stared at him, her brown eyes slightly hooded. 'Don't get smart on me, Danny. It's none of your business who I'm seeing. You're the one who wanted to cool it for a while.'

Cindy had a high-pitched voice, and there were times when she didn't so much speak as quack. This was one of those times. 'How have you been doing?' he asked.

'Still getting over the shock of being dumped, I suppose. Never happened to me before.'

Damn, this was awkward. 'Aw, baby, don't be like that.'

She put a hand on his leg and dug her talons into his thigh. 'Don't worry. I'm not going to give you a hard time. Am I getting a ride home, or are we just going to sit here?'

'Sure.' He restarted the car and gave her what he hoped was a friendly look. 'You know, women who look like you shouldn't be walking the streets on their own at this time of night.'

'Spare me the bullshit, Danny, would you?'

He sighed.

Cindy stretched out her legs and leaned back into the seat so that her top rode up to reveal an inch of tanned stomach. Her scent, a combination of Virginia Slims and drugstore perfume, was beginning to fill the car. Danny had learnt early on that there was a strict hierarchy to physical appeal, and he'd always believed that he and Cindy were pretty evenly matched. There was even a chance she was a notch or two above him. He was sure she understood that too.

When he arrived at her house, they sat in silence. Like him, she lived with her mother. Unlike him, her mother was rarely there. Mrs Martinez ('call me Nina') liked Danny. It wasn't just that she saw him as son-in-law material. He suspected that if the well ever ran dry elsewhere, Nina would be more than accommodating.

Call him old-fashioned, but Danny wasn't that comfortable with Mrs M's behaviour. There was something wrong about a woman trying to usurp her daughter. Besides, for all Cindy's wiggling and preening, she was a good-hearted sort. And even if she wasn't too talented at conversation, couldn't the same be said about lots of girls?

Then there was the other business. The previous December Cindy had told him she was pregnant. They had only been together for a couple of months, and he had been stunned. He prided himself on being a safety-first type of guy. You had to be nowadays. To begin with, she had been adamant she was keeping the baby. 'I'm nineteen,' she had said. 'Plenty old enough.' He had wheedled away at her. 'Think of all you'll be giving up. Your hopes of being a model. Nights out. Freedom.' Worse, he had made it clear that she couldn't count on his support. Six months on, he had almost managed to convince himself that she had wanted the abortion too.

Danny and Cindy had never had an exclusive relationship. He'd never been in love with her. That was just as well. All the signs were that Regina still loved Dino, and look what that had done for her. But taking everything into account, he couldn't simply shuck the girl aside.

She smiled, revealing all of her small white teeth. 'You can come in if you want.'

'We-ell ...'

A look of suspicion passed across her face. 'You're not ... seeing someone, are you?'

He kept his mouth closed and did his best to appear nonchalant.

'Christ, it didn't take you long.'

Danny was wrestling with his best and worst instincts. 'Am I allowed to say it's complicated?'

'That's you, Danny,' she said. 'It's always frigging complicated.'

This was hard. Really hard. 'You know, Cindy,' he said. 'I better head on home. Ma will be expecting me.'

Chapter 5

On the morning of her twenty-first birthday, Elizabeth woke early. The soft click of the apartment door announced Donal's departure for work. She stretched out on the bedroom floor, a gentle anticipation washing over her. For the first time that day, she told herself not to think too much about seeing Danny. In the movie in her head, he already featured too prominently.

One of her presents hung from the rail over the bedroom's slender window, like a temporary blackout curtain. The rest, including a clutch of books from Peter and Donal, formed a neat pile beside her. A silver necklace from her parents and two brothers, a scarf from her sister Alice and earrings from Liam had all arrived the previous day. She'd unwrapped them straight away and put the whole lot on at once. The necklace and scarf were lovely, but the earrings … well, they weren't quite right. They were gold with a little pearl, when she was more of a silver person really. Plus they were kind of middle-aged, like something Liam's sister would wear. There was every chance Lourda had chosen them. Obviously she would never say this to him. It was the thought that mattered, and even if your birthday present turned out to be a spare part for the washing machine (like her father had once given her mother), you had to smile and say how delighted you were. And that's what she did.

A letter had accompanied the earrings. Liam was brimming with apologies for his bad humour on the day of the match. *I was a complete tool*, he wrote. *I've been feeling rotten ever since*. Then he spent pages and pages giving her the news from home. He told her how he'd met her parents down the town during the week.

They had been in better form. Syl had slagged him about being abandoned by his girlfriend and Stacia had joined in the laughing and joking. There were two pages about a local wedding, and three on the Munster hurling championship. He signed off with several rows of kisses.

Elizabeth had been struck by a twist of guilt. 'What *am* I doing?' she'd said to Michelle.

'You're having a laugh,' her friend had replied, 'and the instant it stops being a laugh, you can give Danny-boy his marching orders. Don't go agonising when there's nothing to agonise about.'

At the time she had been trying on her present from Michelle and Orla: a dark blue dress, so dark it was practically black. It was splashed with minute white stars, had cap sleeves and a scoop neck, and finished a good five inches short of her knees.

Michelle grinned while Elizabeth twirled around the bedroom. 'Cindy Crawford will be in the ha'penny place next to you, missus. In fact, I'm having second thoughts about going out with you. I don't like being out-glammed.'

At this point, a snide interjection from Orla might have been expected. Unusually, there hadn't been a peep out of her for ten minutes or more. She was transfixed by a letter from her parents. When finally she stopped reading, her face suggested that her prize bonds had come up.

'You know the way I'm always having to hear about the wonders of my sister, Caitriona?' she said. 'The one who's over in London, living somewhere upwardly mobile and working in a solicitor's office?'

Elizabeth and Michelle nodded.

'Seems the girl has a touch more spark than I gave her credit for. Some busybody has informed my mam that she's actually living in a squat in Peckham. Worse, she's shaved off all her hair. The full Sinead O'Connor, as the mother put it.'

'That's shocking,' said Elizabeth.

'That's fucking brilliant, more like,' replied Orla. 'I'll be left in peace for a while. My parents are convinced even worse news is in store. Wait until you hear this.' She scanned the letter before beginning to read. '"You only have to open a paper to read about those feral English youngsters taking drugs and dancing all night in fields. I'm sure Caitriona is at this rave malarkey too, and your father is considering getting the bus over to London to bring her home.'"

Michelle made a face. 'Ouch, the poor girl.'

'I'll bet the parents never thought they'd see the day where I was the well-behaved daughter,' said Orla with a smirk.

Now, as she lay in the semi-dark, Elizabeth thought of her own parents. She reached out for her watch. Seven thirty. The grocery store on the corner would be open soon. She could get some change there. Then she would ring home and thank them for her present. She would give Liam a call too. That's what he would expect, and it was the right thing to do.

Danny was late. Stunningly late.

'You did give him the name of the bar and the address and everything, didn't you?' Elizabeth said to Peter.

'I did. It's not my fault if he doesn't turn up.'

She couldn't understand it. The other night he had been so keen. Before she got out of the car, they had kissed for an age, and he had said, 'Twenty-one, huh?' as though this was the most important day of her life.

'He'll be here,' said Michelle, stroking the slinky shoulder of the new dress. 'What class of fool wouldn't show?'

Elizabeth sipped her martini, a drink chosen by Orla as being sufficiently sophisticated for the occasion. At least she was confident about how she looked. She had spent for ever in front of the fan drying her hair. It was as big as it was ever going to be.

As bars went, The Zenith was several steps up from O'Mahoney's. Peter had found it while he was over in Cambridge looking for the shop that sold Irish newspapers. It had a calm clean feeling, like nothing messy could happen. And the customers? They were blessed with the type of glossy good looks that only generations of affluence can bring. In Dublin, university had teemed with their Irish equivalents. They all knew each other because they'd all been to the same schools. Their clothes were artfully distressed, their hair perfectly behaved. Oh, and somewhere along the line, they had been instilled with unyielding confidence. As Donal put it, 'You couldn't insult them.'

Michelle hadn't quite penetrated their inner sanctum, but she'd got close enough for the occasional cashmere-scarf-wearing girl to sit beside them in the canteen. Elizabeth would remain on the margins, her insecurities preventing her from voicing an opinion. Despite three years of acclimatisation, she couldn't relax in their company. Her words tumbled out in the wrong order, and any wit she possessed just evaporated.

Peter edged in beside her. 'What's the crack?'

'Oh, you know me, not a bother. And thanks again for organising everything.'

He gave her a look that suggested he saw through her bravado.

'Well, it's just … I thought he'd be here,' she said.

'Now, Elizabeth, you've more sense than to let a man you hardly know ruin your big night. And aren't we better off with just the five of us?'

She knew he was right. He usually was. She remembered her presents. It was safe to assume that while Donal had decided which books to give her, Peter was the man who had trawled the city to find them. At college, if an essay was causing her trouble, Peter had ironed out the problems. If she was hung-over, up he had popped with two Solpadeine and a rasher sandwich. If she was mopey, he'd had time to go for a pint or see a film. Elizabeth hoped that she was a good friend too, although she worried that she often fell short. She squeezed his hand. 'What would I do without you?' He smiled at her. Thankfully, he hadn't noticed that she still had one eye on the door.

Michelle and Orla were attempting to speak quietly. Unfortunately for Orla, even her softest voice was probably heard three streets away. 'She must have played it all wrong the other day,' she was saying. 'I *told* her she should have invited him in.'

Donal tapped the table. 'Now, women, this evening is becoming way too serious.' He looked around the bar. 'Orla, I'm particularly disappointed with you. I expected you'd be well in there by now. Trying to score an Ivy League type. With a rich daddy and a flashy car.'

'And furniture,' added Michelle.

'What about yourselves, lads?' tittered Orla. 'There must be eligible women here too. You might find a nice girl with superior teeth. And a horse.'

After a month in Boston, it felt as if their lives were shooting off in different directions. Orla was wallowing in the freedom while Peter was clinging on to his Irishness like a favourite T-shirt. Michelle, on the other hand, was determined to avoid Irish people, especially Irish students. 'This is our chance to understand America,' she'd say, as though she was talking about some unusually complex science. Donal was exploiting every opportunity to tell his tall tales. Just then, he was explaining how he'd sold Leitrim to a hotel guest from Texas.

'I told the fellow, "Listen there's not a lot of coastline. But there's enough. And the countryside is as pretty as you'll find, if a bit damp."'

Peter's face concertinaed with scepticism. 'Will you pull the other one? I'm sure the guy didn't swallow a word of it. How can you sell a county?'

'Petie, you're fierce short of imagination. Negative thinking won't get Ireland out of the recession. Why not sell some land? It's all we've got.'

'How are you proposing to close the sale?' asked Michelle.

'I'll leave that to the old man.' Donal's father worked for Leitrim County Council. 'I told the Texan lad to write to Donal Mulvihill senior, care of the Planning Department, Carrick-on-Shannon. He seemed up for it, so I gave him the phone number as well.'

'Your dad will go mental,' Peter said.

'That's the general idea.'

Elizabeth tried to check her watch without anyone noticing. An uncomfortable feeling was settling into her stomach. 'He's not coming,' she said, her voice so light she thought no one would hear.

Michelle linked arms with her. 'Listen, pet, if he's a bit of a gobdaw, aren't you as well off finding out now?'

'True. I suppose.'

'I mean, when you were talking about him last night, he sounded too good to be true. No man is that perfect. Scratch the surface, and he's bound to have something to hide.'

Elizabeth drained her glass and squeezed out a watery smile. 'It seems I'm never going to find out.'

Peter offered to get another round.

'Thanks,' she said. 'I'll go for a beer this time.'

Orla gave her a pitying look and adopted her most hectoring tone. 'Sweet Jesus, Elizabeth, you're hard work. There am I trying to give you a little finesse, and you insist on behaving like you're back in Thurles. Next we know you'll be up at the bar asking if they wouldn't mind playing some Christy Moore, or a few nice ballads. Oh, and by the way, if you do come across that Danny lad again, you have got to play it cool.'

'Cool,' echoed Elizabeth, who was determined to hide the scale of her disappointment. The clinking and braying that surrounded them were hurting her head. She was trying to think of subjects that had no connection to Danny when, out of nowhere, Donal gave Orla a poke in the ribs. She, in turn, nudged Michelle who slapped Elizabeth on the thigh.

'Well now,' said Donal, 'the dead arose and appeared to many.'

Elizabeth stepped outside with Orla's words ricocheting around her head. 'Remember,' she had cautioned. 'A large amount of grovelling is required. As they like to say around these parts, a *wicked* large amount.'

63

'Don't worry,' Elizabeth had replied. 'I'll be back before you know it. Handling this won't take long.'

Out on the street, she was wrestling with how to behave. She had come around to the idea that Danny wasn't going to show. And now here he was, looking sort of frayed around the edges.

He took her hand. 'I really am sorry. Will you let me explain?'

'You're fine. It's no big deal.'

'I think it is. I told you I'd be here, and then I turn up two hours late.'

'Closer to three.'

He smiled, but it was a limper effort than usual. 'God, Elizabeth, am I forgiven? I promise you, I can explain.'

'There's no need for that. We barely know each other. You didn't have to come.' She removed her hand. 'I better go back in to my friends.' She stressed the final word then castigated herself for acting like a kid.

'Come on, babe. Can't we go for a short walk? I got caught up in stuff at home. I wasn't able to leave and I had no way of contacting you. You should get a phone.'

'What would we do that for? We're only going to be here for three or four months. By the time the phone came, we'd be gone.'

'No, you wouldn't. You apply for a phone on Monday, and you'll get connected later in the week.'

Elizabeth was baffled. 'That can't be true.'

'Why not?'

'At home it takes months. And that's way better than it used to be. In the seventies it took years. Unless you got a TD onto the job.'

'What's a TD?'

'Like a congressman or a senator.'

Danny tilted his head to one side. 'You needed a congressman or a senator to help you get a phone?'

'If you asked him to help, eventually he would call around with a telephone which meant you had to vote for him. And then at some point the phone company would connect you.'

64

'Eh, right. Well, in Boston you don't need to ask Ted Kennedy to get you a phone. You can buy one on Monday.' Danny spoke slowly like he was trying to make sense of her story.

'I can?'

'Elizabeth,' he appeared to be swallowing a laugh, 'you work in a store where they sell phones.'

She did laugh. 'Oh you're right, I do.' She tapped herself on the side of the head. 'Only twenty-one and losing it already.'

Danny's smile was almost restored. 'I wouldn't say that. Can we go for a walk now?'

'OK then. For a small while.'

'The river is down there. That might be good. Do you want to tell Peter and the others what we're doing?'

She thought about it, decided she didn't. He put an arm around her shoulder, which Elizabeth had to admit felt good. All the same, she believed it would be a mistake to ask too many questions about where he'd been. It was too soon for that. She might give the impression she cared, which would be against the rules.

'You know, you have incredible legs,' Danny said.

'So I'm told.'

'I'm not forgiven, huh?'

'For the last time, Danny, there's no call for any forgiveness. You clearly had better things to do.'

They strolled down JFK Street, past earnest drink-fuelled conversations and uninhibited carousing. It was like everyone was luxuriating in the joy of being young and bright and desirable. Gradually, even equable Elizabeth became infected. Danny chatted all the while, pointing out landmarks and chipping in the occasional caustic comment about the area and its residents. Every so often, he kissed her on the cheek or said something else about how well she looked. Staying annoyed with him was not going to be easy.

Despite being moments from the noise-filled streets of Cambridge, it was quiet beside the Charles. Only the buzz of traffic, and the occasional whoop or holler, challenged the silence.

Elizabeth was taken by the view across the river of the elegant buildings that Danny told her belonged to Harvard Business School. They found a bench, and he took a small black box from his denim jacket.

'Happy birthday,' he said. 'And sorry again for screwing things up.'

'Danny, you didn't have to do that. Like I said, it's not as if we know each other that well. I didn't expect a gift from you.'

He burrowed into her hair, kissed the side of her face. 'I wanted to.'

In the box was a silver bracelet with tiny silver stars attached like charms. He put it on her wrist, stroking her hand and fingers as he did. The bracelet was beautiful. This was, she suspected, not his first time buying jewellery. 'It's … it's perfect. Thank you.'

They kissed. And then again. She felt pleasingly strange, as though her insides might be dizzy. As on Boston Common, she was also unexpectedly confident. Orla's rules were retreating.

'Do you do this a lot?' she said.

'Sit on benches kissing good-looking women? Not nearly as often as I'd like.'

'So you do try to make a habit of it?'

Danny laughed, and they resumed kissing. He placed a hand on her thigh, which was largely exposed anyway. She shivered.

'I'm sorry.' He had a different voice now: half ordinary speech, half whisper. 'Are you cold? There's not a lot of material on that dress. I hope they didn't charge you too much money for it.'

Elizabeth whispered too. 'No, I'm not cold.'

She ran the back of her hand down his chest, hesitated when she got to the belt of his jeans then continued tentatively. It was Danny's turn to shiver.

'Cold?' she asked.

'Nah, I'm doing great. I like birthdays.'

They continued to kiss.

'But it might get cold,' he said. 'We can't stay here all night. Perhaps we should go back to the bar?'

'If that's what you want.' It was not what she wanted at all.

'Well ...'

'Well?'

'Would you like to come home with me?'

Elizabeth thought for a moment. A short moment. She real-ised it was high time she came up with some rules of her own. 'Yes,' she said. 'I would.'

Chapter 6

The flimsy curtains blocked little of the late morning light. Danny was facing towards Elizabeth, his sleeping breath steady. For a man he had long eyelashes; their delicate curve appeared at odds with the rest of him. Anxious that he sleep on, she did her best to stay motionless. Somehow he sensed her gaze and his eyes twitched open. Please let him speak first, she thought.

He trailed one finger along the side of her face before kissing the bridge of her nose. 'Morning. You OK?'

His morning breath was surprisingly pleasing which made her worry about her own. She decided to let him do the talking. To be honest, she had never been in this situation before. Liam was the only other man she'd gone to bed with, and it had taken them two years to get that far. Needless to say, even Michelle wasn't aware of this. '*Two years*,' Elizabeth could hear her exclaiming. There would be less amazement if she admitted to kidnapping Shergar or having a secret career as a stripper.

Danny gave a drowsy smile. 'I'm …' he paused, 'more than OK.'

Still she didn't say anything. It wasn't like the confidence of the previous night had completely vanished. It was just that there was more to fret about now. The sex had been surprising. Good surprising. Enthusiastic. Affectionate. Loud. Several times, Danny had said, 'Now you have to tell me what *you* like.' And the terrible truth was she didn't really know. American sex appeared to be like American menus: there were an awful lot of options. But how to broach the subject? She could hardly say, 'Sorry there, as I have your attention, that was brilliant for me. Was it up to your usual standards? If not, maybe you should offer some guidance.'

'Hey, you've gone all shy on me. I didn't see any of that last night. The opposite, more like.' He kissed her. 'I like a woman who shows her appreciation.'

The heat rising in her cheeks, Elizabeth searched for something to say. 'Ah, this is kind of unusual for me.'

Danny brushed his lips along her shoulder. 'You seem to believe I do this every night of the week.'

'I never said that.'

'Well, I don't.'

'That's good. I think.'

'And to prove it, we'll just have to spend some more time together. Do you reckon that's something we could do?' He put on a funny face, like he was scared of rejection. She guessed it wasn't a sensation with which he was overly familiar. He was a real messer.

Elizabeth realised she was smiling. 'Yeah,' she was saying. 'Yeah, that's what I'd like too.'

Danny drew her in even closer, so that he was talking right into her ear. His breath tickled. 'And, by the way, there's no one else in the house. So don't you get worked up about having to meet anyone or explain anything. We're on our own and we can do whatever we like.'

The butterflies were back in force.

Regina Esposito woke slowly. For some seconds she was uncertain of her surroundings. Then it came to her. She was in the spare bedroom of her daughter Teresa's house. A beam of light poked through the blinds, highlighting the pastel prints on the magnolia walls. Downstairs a radio played middle-of-the-road rock music. The sheets and blankets were tucked strait-jacket tight. That feeling clicked in where she knew she was unhappy but couldn't quite say why. Every part of her was heavy, her brain filled with treacle. Gradually her memory's full sweep returned, and she remembered why she was there.

Unsure as she was about the previous night's sequence of

events, she assumed Danny must have called Teresa. Her second daughter was the coping child. Even as a girl, she had organised the others: rebellious Linda, cantankerous Vincent, head-in-the-clouds Danny. Teresa remembered birthdays and anniversaries, and bought the cards the others signed. When she'd arrived at the house on Emerald Street, Regina had been curled up on the bed. Not crying, not sleeping, not doing anything much. She couldn't recall when she'd last been up and dressed. To begin with, she had insisted on staying put. 'Why can't you all leave me be?' she'd asked. Inch by inch, the girl had cajoled her into the car, telling her how she wasn't up to managing on her own, and how Danny couldn't be there all the time. 'For a few days, Ma,' she kept on saying, 'only a few days. It will all become clearer then.'

Those who had never experienced it thought of depression as sadness. For Regina it was much more, although sometimes she imagined she was carrying all the unhappiness of the world. She might see a story on the news about a foreign war or a dead child or even a failed business and feel so bad it was hard to breathe. Not that it was always the same. Sometimes she might go numb, almost paralysed. Other times the pain bordered on physical; she feared she would snap in two. Or she could lose control, crying at the most inappropriate times. At its worst she was beyond caring who saw this emotion. She would walk through a crowd with tears rippling down her face.

For weeks now, she had tried not to leave the house. She would lie there, feeling encased by heat, like the walls were inching towards her. If she did go out, she conspired to avoid those she knew. The thought of their questions terrified her. The sound of Bridie O'Connor on the porch made her hide under the sheets. Some days she even dreaded the turn of Danny's key in the lock. It was easier to cope in bad weather. When all was grey, your own mood was less out of place. There was no pressure to get on out there and be happy. How she loathed the happiness brigade.

In the car, Teresa had assured her that Sam, her husband, was out. That was why her two pyjama-clad daughters, Megan and

Jenny, were there, their faces rumpled and sleepy. By the time they reached the house, Sam was back home. He'd been for a few beers and was intent on making a fuss of everybody. The girls responded by becoming late-night hyper. There were things – colourings and such – they *had* to show their grandma. Right there and then. Unable to look any of them in the eye, Regina stared at the floor. If anything, their loveliness made the sadness more intense.

She would not have chosen to go to Teresa's house, only the alternatives were worse. What if Danny truly couldn't handle the situation, or didn't want to, and she ended up in hospital? Of course the day would come when he was no longer there, when he decided he wanted his own life, in his own place. She wouldn't think about that now.

Others, especially her daughters, tended to blame the depression on the break-up of her marriage. For sure, Dino's cheating had made life worse, but her problems stretched way back. She reckoned the damn disease had always been there. When Regina was young she was so preoccupied with the demands of life she could try to shut it out. Now even Danny, her baby, was an adult, and life felt all the more barren. The older she got, the more insidious the illness became, sneaking up on her so that by the time she was aware of its presence, she was already surrounded.

Regina felt bad about Danny. Evidently, he'd been planning a night out. There had been showering and shaving. A shirt had been ironed. A new girl must be on the scene. With Danny, there was always a girl. Far too many of them, if you asked her. She didn't care for how he treated most of them, but what could she do?

From the yard, the sound of her granddaughters floated in. She fingered the blue nylon bed cover, turned the pillow over to the cool side. At least Teresa had a solid life. Linda and Vincent were getting there. But Danny? He drifted. It wasn't like he was dumb. Exactly the opposite. As Bridie would put it, the boy had brains to burn. At school, he had claimed the tail-off in his grades had no connection to Dino's departure. 'All fuck-ups entirely my own,

71

Ma,' he would say. As she left the previous night, he had been sitting on the porch, smoking one cigarette after another. Maybe he didn't go out after all.

She considered getting out of bed. By now, the girls would be wondering why their grandma was hiding away. She could always say she was ill. At four and five, they were too young to ask what was wrong. The day would come, though, when they would have questions. What would she say?

At one time, Regina had hoped that diagnosis would help. If you put a name on something, surely it must provide comfort? Now she wasn't so sure. The pills helped, she supposed. She would take all the side effects – the dry mouth, the never-ending lethargy – if she thought the medication would banish her depression. Experience had taught her that it didn't work like that. Everything was so imprecise.

There were days when she worried that she was on the fringes of insanity, when she wished it was possible to wipe her head clean. And then, almost imperceptibly at first, the light would edge in again. But even on her best days she was playing the waiting game, knowing it would return. Regina knew it was wrong, yet there were times when she wished for a physical illness instead. She was convinced it would be easier to bear.

Elizabeth was preparing to ask Danny about his epic lateness. She'd side-stepped the issue for hours now, a state of affairs that owed more to apprehension than acceptance. Several times the pair of them had toyed with getting up. They remained entwined, Elizabeth examining her surroundings. The room was strikingly plain: white walls, white sheets on the bed, lightly varnished floorboards broken by two red rugs. There was, Danny maintained, too much junk in the world. From what she could tell, apart from a considerable record collection, he didn't have many possessions.

'Elizabeth?'

'Mmmm?'

'I still owe you an explanation. For being late. I thought you'd ask.'

Here it was. Her mind galloped. She stroked his arm. 'We haven't had a lot of time for talking. I assumed you'd get to it eventually.'

'It's a bit … unusual. No, not unusual … complicated. It was my mom. I didn't want to leave her alone.'

And that was how he told her. It wasn't, he said, that his mother had ever threatened to hurt herself. But you had to be careful. So, when she was bad, he didn't like leaving her alone. Now that Vincent had moved out, this was more difficult. A while back he decided it might help if he educated himself. A book in the public library claimed that, each year, twenty million Americans suffered from depression. Strange then, that he should know only one.

'Danny, I wish you'd told me last night.'

'It didn't feel like the right time. I'd already done enough damage to your birthday without saying, "Hey, let's talk about my mom's depression."'

While Danny spoke, he smoothed a hand up and down Elizabeth's side. She kissed his forehead. 'But that way I wouldn't have acted like an idiot. Saying you had better things to do. I'm impressed you made it at all.'

'I figured I'd get a drink poured over my head. If not by you, by one of the others. The curly-haired girl?'

'Michelle.'

'She was pretty pissed with me.'

'Don't mind Michelle. She assumed you weren't going to turn up. If she had any notion what the real story was, she'd be mortified.'

'I suppose.'

'Depression.' She rolled the word around her mouth. 'Here in America, is it like at home? People say there's no reason to be ashamed. Except they won't use the word. They say, "The nerves are at him" or, "She needs a rest."'

'Sounds about the same. Some people get all uncomfortable.

That's what I've found.' He hesitated. 'Don't worry. I won't go on and on.'

'You're fine. I'm pleased you've told me. Really I am. What about your mother? What does she say?'

'She's not so good at talking about it. It's like when she's ill, she can't. And when she's better, she doesn't want to be reminded.'

'And your sisters and your brother?'

'Linda's in New York. We don't see too much of her. Vincent's not bad. Teresa is great. Just great. It was difficult for her to get away last night, but when I told her I had a date, she put the two kids in the car and came on over here.'

Elizabeth smiled. 'I hope the date was worth it.'

Danny pinched her cheek. 'The report will be positive.'

'I'm not sure there's much I can do. If there is …'

'This is good, you know. It's not a guy's conversation. I can't go into work tomorrow morning and launch into a story about my mother's head.'

'Are you going to see her today?'

'I can go over to Teresa's later.' He played with her hair. 'Before that, though, we should eat. Or else I'll be in real trouble. I don't want the scary friends thinking that first I almost stood you up, then I had my way with you, and afterwards I decided to let you starve.'

'That's OK,' she said, kissing his forehead again. 'I'll tell them I had my way with you too.'

They went to a local diner for breakfast. That is, if you can have breakfast at two in the afternoon. Elizabeth found her appetite had vanished. What was that about? She didn't want him to think she was one of those women who didn't eat. So, toast, scrambled eggs, bacon: she did her best. A lazy silence settled over them. She was wearing Danny's jacket over the birthday dress, the outfit giving her an unmistakable look of 'the woman who had not been home'. Worse, she wore the look with pride. Two women at a nearby table gave her a forensic examination. She had to resist the temptation to say, 'Him? Yeah, I did. I *know*. Lucky me.'

'What's the smile for?' he said.

'Sorry?'

'You're smiling to yourself there while you play with your breakfast.'

'Oh nothing.'

Danny reached over and touched one hand. 'Will you stay again tonight?'

She frowned. 'I better go back to the apartment. I can't go to work like this in the morning. Well, I could, except the display of flesh would give Mike Anderson a heart attack.'

'Hmmm.' He thought for a moment. 'What I could do is give you a ride over to Brighton before going to see my mom. You could get a change of clothes. Or a couple of changes, to be on the safe side. And I could collect you again on the way home. What do you reckon?'

Elizabeth's conscience was nudging her in one direction. To spend two nights in a row with Danny would be to cross a line. As she studied the persuasive face across the table, however, her resolve started to crumble. 'Feck it,' she said. 'May as well be hung for a sheep as for a lamb.'

'You know, baby, I haven't a clue what that means so I'm going to assume you said yes.'

Chapter 7

Vincent Esposito was curious. According to Bridie O'Connor, a woman was living in the house. 'Comes out of here in the morning. All high heels and tight skirt. Irish, I think.' Without even a trace of irony, she managed to make 'Irish' sound grubby.

He had encountered his former neighbour when he'd called around to Emerald Street on Friday night. No one had been home. His mother was still holed up with Teresa. Regina was edging towards recovery but didn't want to take any risks. A quick examination of Danny's room had confirmed that unless the guy had taken to wearing lace-trimmed underwear someone was staying there.

Although just two years older than his brother, Vincent often felt like they were separated by at least a decade. When he was twenty-one he'd met Valerie Farina. Blessed with more than his fair share of common sense (he reckoned he'd got Danny's allowance too), he had realised he would do no better. To his great good fortune, Valerie had also seen something in him. He was honest and hardworking, she said, qualities that were surprisingly hard to find. Also, while he could be a touch grouchy with others (people did insist on provoking him), he was sweetness itself with her. She brought out the best in him. Everybody said it. They hoped to marry the following year.

On Saturday afternoon, he was trying to convince Valerie to accompany him on a return visit to the family home. She was focused on scrubbing their poky kitchen. His fiancée was partial to cleaning. Not a fashionable attribute, but you wouldn't hear any complaints from him.

Vincent was all in favour of experience. That's what your teens were for. And your early twenties. Getting on out there, making the most of what was available. A point came, though, when a sufficient quantity of wild oats had been sown. His brother didn't seem to understand this. As far as he could see, Danny was intent on scattering not just oats, but barley, rye and pretty much any other cereal you could mention. The time had come to put him straight.

'You see, Val,' he said, 'I don't understand what was wrong with Cindy. A local girl. A real looker too. But is the guy happy? Of course he's not. Has to go and pull a stunt like this.'

'He was bored.'

'Huh?'

'Danny. I asked him. Sweet girl, he said. Only talking to her could be hard work.' Valerie tapped the top of her head. 'A little lacking in the brains department.'

'My brother, the Harvard professor. What was it he wanted to talk about?'

'That I didn't ask. Oh, and he reckoned they were getting too settled.'

'Too settled? The problem with Dan is he doesn't know what he wants. His life is too easy. *Way* too easy.'

'All right, I'll come with you.' Valerie put down her cloth and surveyed her work. 'But only because I want to see what he's up to now.'

If he was straight with himself, Vincent would admit that he had never been given quite the same womanising opportunities as his brother. Once, the two had got rotten drunk, and Danny had told a story that for some reason he considered funny. Apparently, one of his girlfriends had likened him to the tale of Goldilocks and the three bears. When it came to the rest of the Esposito family, she said, the features didn't quite fit. Danny, however, was like the third bowl of porridge. Everything was just right. Danny had smiled his big irritating smile and said, 'I like that. The third bowl of porridge.' Vincent loved his brother, would do *anything*

77

for his brother, but at that moment he'd come close to driving a fist through his pretty-boy features.

Not, he would stress, that jealousy played any part in his attitude towards Danny. He was trying to do the guy a favour. What did feature was a small element of self-interest. If the brothers went into business together, they would have to get serious. A restless, girl-chasing Danny would be a nightmare.

In the narrow backyard, Elizabeth was installed in a faded deck-chair. She was reading one of her presents from Donal and Peter, *The Poor Mouth*, and had reached the part where people are dropping dead from an excess of Irish dancing. To Danny's apparent amusement, she occasionally laughed out loud. He was cutting the grass, his shirtless back the object of admiring glances from his new girlfriend.

From the start, she had decided that she wasn't going to change herself for Danny. Given how their romance was destined to be a short-term thing, making all that effort to become a more interesting and lovable person would not make sense. Anyway, her behaviour was already out of character. It was complete lunacy to move in with a man when you didn't even know his middle name. And when you had a boyfriend back in Thurles. Every so often, she had to catch her breath and ask, *Am I really doing this?* But for the most part she tried not to think about Liam or her parents or anything connected to home. It wasn't as if this could last. Soon enough Danny's mother would return, and a halt would have to be called.

Since the previous weekend they had engaged in an unspoken conspiracy. A couple of times Danny had ventured out to see Regina. Otherwise they had been alone. Once, a knock on the front door had sent them scurrying behind the sofa, hiding like kids until the threat had passed.

'So, we meet at last,' said a gravel-filled voice.

Elizabeth almost jumped out of her chair in fright. Looming over her were a tall, spare-framed man and a tiny slip of a woman.

A photograph in the living room had given her some idea of what the rest of the family looked like, but it was old; Danny was not much past confirmation age and Dino posed at the back in his seventies sports jacket and sideburns. Despite this, she knew immediately who the couple must be. Vincent had a touch – only a touch – of Danny about him. His eyes had the same shape, but not the same clarity. If Danny was drawn with a sharp pencil, his brother was more a smudge of charcoal. Valerie had large brown eyes, a snub of a nose and a friendly smile. Her boyfriend was poker-faced.

The introductions were stiff. Right from the off, it was clear that Vincent was disgruntled to find a strange woman in his mother's house. He wasn't openly hostile or anything, more watchful. She saw a flicker of surprise on his face when Danny sat beside her and took her hand. When he started to run that hand along her forearm, the surprise became more marked. In the time she had spent with him, Elizabeth had assumed Danny was a full-time hand-holder. Maybe she had assumed wrong.

Valerie was warmer, inviting the pair for dinner. If anything, she seemed to find them funny.

'So then,' she said, 'how long have you two known each other?'

Elizabeth decided to exaggerate. She didn't want the big brother thinking she'd moved in with Danny after one date. He didn't look like a man who would understand. 'Um, a few weeks. My friend Peter works with Danny.'

'And when did you move to Boston?'

'A few weeks ago as well. It's not like we've really moved here, though. I only have a student visa, a J-1. I'll be going home again in the autumn.'

Danny beamed. 'I'm keeping an eye on her in the meantime. Making sure she doesn't fall in with a bad crowd.'

'Going home?' said Vincent, raising one caterpillar-shaped eyebrow. 'That would be a first. In my experience, once an Irish person gets a sniff of America they never leave again.'

'I have … plans back in Ireland, so I'll be heading back.

Definitely.' She smiled at Vincent. 'Danny says you're part Irish. On your mother's side, isn't it?'

'Yeah, Ma had a grandmother from Ireland, all right. But I wouldn't go wrapping the green flag around us, if I were you.'

Elizabeth, who had the Irish affliction of having to know everyone's creed, breed and generation, was undeterred. 'Danny said her name was Lily Ryan. She must have been from Tipperary. We've tons of Ryans in Tipp.'

Vincent produced what may have been a smile, although if you had to guess, you would say he'd been hit by a sudden attack of stomach cramps. 'When did you last see your mother?' he asked Danny.

'A couple of nights back.'

'You make sure you call over there tonight. You don't want her thinking she's been abandoned.'

After that Vincent spoke only occasionally. Elizabeth got the feeling that he didn't so much engage in discussion as hand down commandments. When he did give an opinion, Danny tended to defer to it, like he was anxious to avoid confrontation. Once or twice, she got the impression the elder brother was about to lob a hand grenade into the conversation. Then Valerie would intervene and ask another question.

On the walk home, Vincent found his voice. 'Now answer me this, Val. Where is he getting his ideas from? He's acting like a complete cretin. I mean, can you *believe* the stupidity of the guy?'

'What's stupid?' Valerie was familiar with his concerns, but he was getting the sense that on this occasion she didn't quite grasp where he was coming from.

'He's shacked up with some Irish student he hardly knows. Great fun for her, no doubt. A real blue-collar adventure to share with her university friends. What's in it for him? Two or three months and she'll be gone. Besides, what would Ma think? Her unwell. And Danny moving a girl in.'

The afternoon was hot as hell, ninety degrees and counting,

and Vincent stepped up his pace. The sun glinted off car windows, and yellow grass snaked up through cracks in the scalded sidewalk. Just ahead a collection of stringy kids squealed with delight as another kid turned a hosepipe on them.

Valerie tugged at his arm, a signal to slow down. 'I thought they looked kind of cute together,' she said. 'Maybe it won't last. Or maybe she won't leave. She did say she was finished school. Anyhow, your mom has more important stuff going on. You shouldn't go upsetting her.'

Vincent grimaced. She wasn't getting this at all. And she had stymied his attempts to tackle Danny. She needn't think he hadn't noticed. 'For God's sake, Valerie. *Cute?* He's not sixteen. And tell me this: what have the two of them got in common? Oh, and what sort of girl moves in with a man she's just met?'

'Come on, Vincent, you sound about ninety years old. It seemed to me like they had plenty to say to each other. And even if she does go back to Ireland in the fall, can you not let them have a little fun in the meantime?'

He'd heard enough. 'Danny's whole fucking existence is about fun. That's no way to carry on. How many students are there in Boston? If that's what he's into these days, I'm sure he could find a local girl to do the necessary. I'm looking out for him, that's all.'

Valerie made a silly noise, like she was having difficulty swallowing. If there was one thing Vincent could not bear, it was folks making light of him, especially his girlfriend. And he was getting the notion she was about to start tittering. It truly was an annoying habit.

She reached up and ruffled the back of his head. 'You know, love, I don't think we have to worry about him. Or her. You saw them. They're in that place where nobody else is needed. There was a charge coming off them that could light up from here to Maine.'

Vincent held his tongue. If Val was going to get slushy on him, there was no point in engaging any further. He would have to address matters in his own way.

Chapter 8

The sky was filling in for rain, great purple clouds hurtling together. You could almost feel the electricity crackle in the air. Michelle watched Donal press his nose against the front room window. 'A good evening for the ducks,' he said, as he turned around to his flatmates.

Michelle was crouching on the floor, ironing a T-shirt and her tightest jeans. Why she was bothering with them she didn't know. Only Elizabeth ironed jeans. 'As long as it holds off for another half an hour or so,' she said, 'or my hair will get wrecked.' Progress had at last been made with Ray who she'd been pursuing since her arrival in Boston. They were going to the cinema to see the baseball movie, *Bull Durham*. She hoped he wouldn't be too distracted by the big screen.

Donal resumed his inspection of the weather. 'If you were into omens, you wouldn't be too keen on this. With the exam results tomorrow, and that.'

'Ah, Donal, you've no concerns. We'll all be grand,' said Orla who was perching on one of the two chairs they now possessed – footpath salvage, taken from outside a nearby building. One of the women in the supermarket had told Michelle about the moving ritual: at the end of every month large numbers of people moved apartment, and if they weren't sure about a piece of furniture, they simply left it on the street. A telephone had also been added to the apartment, the process being as smooth as Danny had promised.

Peter was on the other chair, the stuffing poking out of its dirty yellow cushion. It wasn't hard to see why it had been abandoned.

He argued that the next time they searched for discarded furniture, they should head down towards Brookline. That was where the presidential candidate Michael Dukakis lived so there was bound to be a better quality of rubbish. Michelle gave a glance in his direction. Peter never bothered to mask his emotions or irritations. His face gave the whole lot away, and right then it had the look of a well-squeezed lemon.

He heaved a noisy sigh. 'Good to see the iron in use. I think its owner has deserted it. In fact, I'm beginning to wonder why she's paying rent. When was the last time anybody saw her?'

For a day or two, Michelle had sensed that he was working himself up to a good vent about his semi-detached flatmate. And, like the rain, here it was at last. 'Elizabeth was here last week,' she said. 'To pick up some clothes. And we're bound to see her tomorrow.'

He made a harrumphing sound.

'In fairness,' she continued, 'the girl's having a rare old time. And isn't that why we came to Boston in the first place?'

Peter's eyebrows scooted upwards until they were in danger of meeting his hairline, and he muttered something that may have been, 'Give me strength.'

Michelle was unruffled. 'You introduced them. If you're not happy, you've only yourself to blame.'

'I've introduced her to plenty of men. She didn't feel the need to run away with any of the others.'

'You have to hand it to Elizabeth,' said Donal. 'When she cuts loose, she cuts loose in style.'

Giant raindrops were gathering on the windows. Ominous bangs and clatters could be heard in the distance.

'Now, Donal,' said Orla, the mirth dripping from her voice, 'you shouldn't be making any assumptions about what the two of them are up to. For all we know they might be sitting up half the night discussing who Dukakis should choose as his running mate.'

'Or,' offered Michelle, 'they might be debating Ronald Reagan's legacy. Or the war on drugs – can it ever be won?'

Plainly, Peter had heard enough. 'Jee-sus, there's more of it. The two of you are determined to encourage her. I think you take a bizarre pleasure in her behaviour. What was it you called her once – Ireland's most faithful woman?'

'And she'll get back to Ireland, and that's what she'll be again.'

'Except she'll have a few new tricks,' said Orla.

'For God's sake, Orla. If myself or Donal came out with a line like that you'd get all sniffy. I'm sorry, but I can't see how this is as funny as you seem to think. If she's not careful, she'll regret her antics.'

'Would you not lighten up? Where's the harm?'

'Liam's the harm. I don't know how she does it.'

'Who's to say he's not carrying on too? He might have the nightspots of Thurles set ablaze.'

A plume of steam hit Michelle's face. She wasn't able to stop herself from joining in. 'A legendary rampage, I'd say. Hayess Hotel has probably never seen the likes of it. The *Tipperary Star* will have to print a special supplement.'

Orla snorted with laughter. 'In colour, with a parental advisory sticker on the cover.'

'Lookit,' Peter said, 'if the same trick was played on either of you, I'd have to listen to "Oh woe is me – all men are bastards" for at least six months. Yet we're all supposed to laugh along with Elizabeth. I don't get it.'

Orla tugged at the hem of her grey cotton shorts which she'd teamed with a white halter-neck top and flimsy red runners. No matter that she was no longer fifteen, and that the TV show had long since been cancelled, Orla had a habit of looking like a refugee from the set of *Fame*. 'OK, OK,' she said. 'But, as they say at home, we'll be a long time dead. What Liam doesn't see can't upset him.'

'Yeah well, Orla, I'm aware that your world vision doesn't stretch much further than that. Michelle, I thought you'd have more cop on.'

Michelle made a face at him. 'Don't act the bollox, Peter. It doesn't suit you.'

'I'll fight my own battles, Michelle, thank you.' Orla's voice had taken on an edgy tone. 'What do you mean by that, Peter? What is my "world vision", as you call it?'

'From what I can tell, it seems to involve pleasing yourself at all times and not giving two fucks about how anyone else feels. Oh, and getting some sad kick from trying to turn Elizabeth into something she's not.'

'Aha! Now we have it. You're not worried about Liam. This is all about you and Elizabeth. You reckoned that at long last you'd get your leg over. And now she's gone and ruined your plans.'

'Did I tell ye,' said Donal, 'about the guest from Idaho who believed that Ireland had turned Communist? You see, I told him they were going to build a wall around the border. That way there'd be lots of jobs. And—'

'Shut up, Donal,' shouted Orla and Peter in unison.

Peter had gone a pale shade of grey. 'You really are a piece of work, Orla. The problem is, you assume everyone is as superficial as you are.'

Michelle was getting anxious. This was extending way beyond their normal bickering. She was also convinced that Orla was wrong. Michelle knew Peter as well as she knew anyone, and his interest in Elizabeth was not sexual. She was his most reliable friend: the person who shared his values and prejudices, and had the same fondness for home. Peter was not likely to look kindly on anyone who damaged that bond.

'Ah, lads,' Michelle said, 'this is daft. Will you stop it.'

Orla tossed her hair over her shoulder. 'I'll tell you what. Things have come to a sorry pass when you can't have a bit of crack in your own front room without some freaking asshole telling you what to think. Whatever your issues are, Peter, don't lay them on me.' Paying no heed to her unsuitable clothes, she bounced up from the chair and strode towards the door. 'I'm going for a walk. In the rain. It'll be more fun than sitting here listening to you.'

'Fancy that,' said Donal. 'She's already learnt to swear like an American.'

Elizabeth was in a lather over her exam results. 'You do realise, Danny, that if I fail, I'll have to go home and repeat?'

'I can guarantee you that isn't going to happen,' he said.

They were on the sofa, the living room window made opaque by a wall of water. 'How can you be so confident?'

'Because what would I do if you went home? I'd be here, all by myself. Bored. Lonely. Frustrated.'

'Hungry,' added Elizabeth. 'Surrounded by squalor.'

He hiccuped with laughter. 'Yeah, those too. Seriously, babe, you're going to be fine. You must know that. And if you're not, you'll just have to pack me up and take me back to Ireland with you. I could take up that hurling game, and learn to speak in riddles. I'm sure I'd fit right in.'

She pictured Danny, with his toothy smile and inquisitive American face, wandering around Thurles with a hurley, and struggled to suppress a giggle.

'Ah,' he said, 'she smiles at last.'

Outside, the deluge was intensifying, the thunder and lightning moving closer. So overwhelming was the noise that they nearly missed a knock on the front door.

'I'll get it,' said Danny. 'Although it's beyond me what sort of idiot would go out in this.'

A minute later, the idiot was standing in the middle of the room, easing off her plastic raincoat. She had liquid-brown eyes and caramel-streaked hair that glistened in an almost unnatural way. Her heart-shaped mouth was painted a glossy bubble-gum pink. It took Elizabeth all of five seconds to distrust her.

'I go for a walk and look what happens,' the girl said. 'When it got really bad, I was far closer to your house than my own, so I thought … why not.' She smiled, revealing even white teeth. 'I'm *so* sorry, Danny. I had no idea I would be disturbing anything.'

Danny stood there, surveying the scene, looking nonplussed.

'Ahm, Elizabeth, this is Cindy Martinez. Cindy, this is Elizabeth Kelly.' He paused while they eyed each other up. 'Elizabeth's from Ireland. She's a student.'

'Fancy,' replied Cindy, who sank into an armchair before crossing her golden legs at the ankles. 'Regina must love that – a girl with a college education.'

'Danny's mother isn't here at the moment,' said Elizabeth, wishing she wasn't quite so pale and plain and Irish-looking.

'Beer?' Danny disappeared into the kitchen before either of them was able to reply.

Cindy wasn't dressed for the weather. Or for walking, come to that. She was wearing a cream jumper that might have fitted her when she was ten years old, a brown suede miniskirt and red stilettos. A silver chain hung around one slender ankle. In that get-up, Elizabeth would have looked like she belonged in Duffy's circus. Cindy could have walked out of a Prince video.

'Well, now,' she chirruped. 'Isn't it good of you to keep Danny company? He hates being on his own. Always has done.'

An almighty clap of thunder made Elizabeth shiver. The rain continued to pelt down. She knew who Cindy was but decided to feign ignorance. 'Are you old friends, then?'

'Oh, we've known each other *for ever.*'

Danny returned with three cans of beer. He flopped onto the sofa. Elizabeth did her best to edge towards him.

'Elizabeth's exam results are out tomorrow.' He patted her knee in an awkward sexless way, like she was a small child. 'And she's awful nervous.'

'You're so lucky to be with Danny, then. I always found him very supportive.'

'Really,' said Elizabeth, 'what were you studying?'

Cindy gave a patronising smile. 'Me a student? Ha! No, I meant he was always so helpful with my career. My modelling work and such.'

'You're a model?'

'Part-time at the moment. I work in a jewellery store during

87

the day.' She kicked off her shoes. Her toenails were a matching shade of red. 'I've had some success in pageants. But it's a tough business, you know.'

Danny took a mouthful of beer. 'Cindy almost made the finals of Miss Massachusetts.'

'That's nice,' said Elizabeth, instructing herself not to look interested.

'The problem I have is nowadays they're obsessed with college girls. Girls with fancy qualifications. One of the organisers said as much. Told me if it was down to looks alone, I'd be on my way to Miss America. But what can I do?'

'You could get some qualifications? It's not that hard.'

'I'm OK the way I am. I think.' Cindy looked towards Danny, as though seeking reassurance.

Elizabeth made sure he didn't get the opportunity to reply. 'That's fair enough, I suppose, if you want to be one of those women who spends her life depending on men. I can never understand that myself. It's so … demeaning. And it lets down the rest of us.'

As the words came out, she was pleased with herself. The little madam needed putting in her place. Who did she think she was, stalking in here with her self-satisfied walk and her smug pout? For a second or two, she saw something other than smugness in Cindy's face, but exactly what that something was she didn't know. All the while, the room was silent. One of those suffocating silences where your mind empties, and you can't think how to restart the conversation. Cindy lit a long, thin cigarette. Danny picked at his teeth.

Elizabeth peered out the window. 'I've a feeling the rain is easing up.'

To be honest, the downpour was getting worse. For an instant, the room turned white. A growl of thunder was only a second or so behind.

'I better get on my way then,' said Cindy.

'That's a shame,' Elizabeth replied.

Danny gave her an unexpectedly hostile look. 'You can't go out, Cindy. The lightning is far too close. It's not safe.'

Elizabeth wanted to kick him. 'Why don't we give your friend a lift home, darling?' He didn't seem to be getting the message. In fact, he looked as though all brain activity had been suspended. 'Then we can have an early night.'

Finally, Danny got to his feet and pulled the car keys from his pocket. 'Come on, Cindy. I'll drop you home.'

'*We'll* drop you home,' said Elizabeth.

Across town, Regina and Vincent were sitting in Teresa's kitchen, watching the water cascade down the window, listening to its comforting splashes. Every day she felt a tiny bit better. Soon enough she would be able to handle life again.

Vincent told her she looked much improved. The life was returning to her eyes, he maintained. The previous day, Teresa had revealed that she was pregnant. 'May be a boy this time,' Regina had said as she hugged her daughter. 'I'd like a grandson.' She'd quickly added the standard proviso that any child was a blessing. For Regina the pregnancy was a double bonus. It gave her the opportunity to be useful. She insisted she had guessed the good news, but that wasn't true. When she was ill, even the starkly obvious passed her by.

Vincent tapped his fingers against the side of his coffee mug. It was funny, as old as he now was, he remained remarkably easy to read. There was scheming going on in that head. She waited, and sure enough it came.

'What do you make of Danny then?'

Regina was convinced that if you asked Vincent, he would say his brother was his best friend, and if you asked Danny he would say precisely the same. There was always a tinge of rivalry, though, and sometimes Vincent couldn't help himself; it spilled out into the open. How often had she heard her elder son complain that she'd spoiled Danny, that he got away with too much? She wondered what was going on now.

89

'Danny? He was here yesterday. Talked a mile a minute. Looked well. Must be taking care of himself. What's he been up to?'

'You know. The new girlfriend.'

'Didn't mention anyone to me.'

'Oh. Sorry, Ma. I assumed he must have said *something*. Given how she's staying with him, and all.'

'Staying with him? In our house?'

'Yeah. Not sure what the story is. Forget I opened my mouth. There mustn't be much to tell.'

Small wonder then that he'd been so full of it the day before – swinging his nieces in the air and teasing Teresa. Telling her that unless he was made a godfather he would boycott the baby's christening. But moving a woman into the house? Was that how Danny saw the future: her staying with Teresa while he set up home with his new woman? Regina found this unnerving. She reached for a cigarette.

'Who is she, Vincent? Do I know her?'

'I doubt it. She's only in the country five minutes. Irish. Don't let it trouble you, Ma. He'll tell you when he needs to.'

Regina pulled long and hard on her cigarette. How stupid had she been to imagine that, in her absence, life would stand still? She would have to return to Emerald Street to see for herself what was going on.

'How long's it going to last?' Danny opened a fresh can of beer, and positioned himself in the chair vacated by Cindy twenty minutes before.

Elizabeth was on the sofa, wondering why she hadn't been offered a drink. 'I'm sorry?'

'The silent treatment. How long's it likely to go on for?'

'I don't know what you're talking about. I'm thinking. That's all.'

'Could have fooled me. Anyhow, I'm the one with reason to be pissed. Did you have to be such a bitch to Cindy?'

'Did *I* have to be a bitch? You've got that the wrong way round.

I wasn't the one making all those vacuous comments about how hard it is to be beautiful. I wasn't flirting with someone else's boyfriend.'

'Come on, Elizabeth. You're smart enough to see through her bravado. Cindy only comes out with that bullshit when she's nervous. She was taken aback to find the two of us together.'

'Nervous, my eye. She was taunting me. With her tiny skirt. And her pouting and preening.'

Danny gave a half-smile. 'You're jealous!'

'Jealous of what? Her ill-fitting clothes or the fact that she went out with you?' Elizabeth's voice had risen a register. She needed to calm down before she became too shrill.

'Ah, babe, you don't need to worry about Cindy. I heard she's got a new guy on the go, anyhow.'

'She's a fast mover, I'm sure. No wonder the pair of you were so well suited.'

'All right.' Danny's smile had been replaced by a look of irritation. He put his beer on the floor. 'You know the way you're worked up about your grades? The way you don't want to disappoint your parents?'

She nodded.

'And back in Tipperary, what do you expect your parents are doing tonight? Thinking of you, I'll bet. Hoping you're getting on OK in America. Looking forward to you coming home again.'

'So?'

'Do you have any idea how lucky you are? Cindy lives in a house where no one gives a shit what or how she does. Her mom's been around the block with most of the losers in Dorchester. It's a miracle if she sees her dad more than three or four times a year. Oh, and there's a brother who's on every drug known to man. The guy's such a retard, his own sister crosses the street to avoid him. You think she wouldn't like to swap places with you?'

'I hadn't realised you were so attached to her. If you'd prefer to be with her, that's OK by me. And no doubt she'd be delighted to have you back.'

'For Christ's sake, listen to yourself. You've got this all out of proportion.'

Elizabeth was feeling squashed. Was this, she wondered, where they parted company?

Danny trudged across the room and sat down beside her. 'I don't want to be with Cindy. We split up. Remember?'

'But when she was getting out of the car, and she began prattling on about meeting up again soon, you didn't put her off. You encouraged her. "Of course, babe. That sounds great, babe," you said. You didn't have to be so friendly.'

'It's not that simple.'

'It looks fairly straightforward to me. If she's not your girl-friend, why do you need to see her?'

'Like I said, it's not that simple. OK?'

Elizabeth didn't have the energy to go around in circles. 'Listen, I'm going to head over to Brighton. It'll be easier to get my exam results from there. Michelle has it all sorted.' She stood up.

Two creases had appeared at the top of Danny's nose. 'Sit down, would you?' he said.

'Don't worry. The rain really has eased off now. I can see you tomorrow, or whenever.'

He gripped her wrist. 'Please, Elizabeth. Sit down. I want to tell you something.'

Michelle was sitting on the yellow chair, eating cereal from a cup. It was early. Tom, Tim and the latest arrival, Jim, were snoring merrily. Ordinarily, organisation was left up to Elizabeth or Peter. At the moment, though, she was otherwise occupied, and he was going through one of his awkward phases, so someone else had to take charge.

Back in Dublin a friend was primed to collect the five sets of exam results. The friend, Assumpta Gogarty, had promised she would wait by the phone box for Michelle's call. Peter was going to hang around to collect his results which meant he could let Danny know how Elizabeth had fared. He didn't say as much, but if the extent of the tongue-clicking was any indication, this stuck in his craw. Donal claimed he wasn't fussed and asked her to leave a note for him.

Michelle believed it was noble of Peter to be so worried about Elizabeth. Noble and a complete waste of time. She was clearly enthralled by Danny, so why not let her have her fun? Michelle had always maintained that Orla had got the girl wrong. Elizabeth was an altogether more complex creature than first appearances might suggest. For three years they'd shared a house, and Michelle had seen ample evidence of her more dramatic side. Like, halfway through second year when she'd had a bust-up with Liam; Elizabeth had knocked back most of a half-bottle of vodka, lit the fire with the rest and barely got out of bed for the next ten days. She'd even gone to the shop in her pyjamas. Finally, a contrite Liam had arrived with a gaudy bunch of flowers, a box of Milk Tray and a long list of apologies. He was a grand lad really, if a bit serious for his years. Michelle reckoned he was the sort of fella who actually wore the jumper his mammy bought him for Christmas. Danny, on the other hand, was everything your mammy warned you about.

That morning Michelle was in effervescent form. The trip to the cinema had exceeded expectations. Ray said he would have to go to *Bull Durham* again. On his own. That way he might get to view some of the actual movie. He also asked if he could see her again.

Almost as good, the storm had been a temporary aberration. The sun was back and, after the deluge, the morning felt fresh. The pungent smell of the street's greenery wafted into the apartment. It was like the gods had been out with the disinfectant. Now, if only she could rouse the lodgers, she would ring Assumpta and everything would be grand. How did they put it here? She was all set.

Chapter 9

Sitting at her desk in Anderson's, Elizabeth was so tired her eyes hurt. Her limbs hurt. She could swear that even her hair hurt. All night she had tossed and turned, repeatedly saying sorry for her restlessness. Danny had said the apologising was actually more annoying than the writhing and weaving. By the time they'd drifted off to sleep, light was beginning to seep through the curtains. It was Danny who woke with a shout, the universal nightmare where the exam questions don't make sense still fresh in his head.

The exams. All that palaver and now the damn things barely featured in her thoughts. Every millimetre of space was taken up by Danny's story. How Cindy had got pregnant; how she had wanted the baby; how he had given her the money to get rid of it; how after a few drinks she still got all maudlin.

Elizabeth didn't know anyone else who'd had an abortion. Or if she did, they hadn't told her. She wasn't someone other women confided in. Too judgemental, Orla said. Danny had looked confused when she'd explained how Irish women got the boat to England because abortion was illegal at home. 'That's one screwed-up country,' he'd said. She hadn't argued. She couldn't have handled another scene.

She did feel sympathy for Cindy. And shame for the way she had sniped at her. But there was something else too. Oh, she knew it was wrong, but the little voice niggled at her. If the girl was less beautiful, it said, wouldn't he find it easier to walk away?

The phone burred into life. 'Anderson's Electrical.'

'Can you talk?' It was Michelle.

94

Cradling the phone under her chin, Elizabeth blessed herself. 'Break it to me gently.'

Upper second class honours, Michelle said. In both subjects. English and Geography. She had got the same grades. You could hear the delight in her voice.

Elizabeth sighed. 'That's a relief.'

'You don't sound too happy, pet. Are you not pleased?'

'Of course I am. Totally.' She ordered herself to think some cheery thoughts. What she really wanted was to tell Michelle about last night, but Mike was firing filthy looks from the adjoining room. 'What about the others?'

There was an intriguing pause. 'Now here's the thing. Donal "Yerra, I'm not that fussed" Mulvihill got ... wait for it ...'

'I'm waiting.'

'A first.'

'Stop the lights.'

'Swear to God.'

'What *will* he be like?'

'Exactly the same, I'm sure,' said Michelle.

'As bad as that?' replied Elizabeth, and they both laughed. 'What about the other two?'

This time Michelle's pause was longer still. 'Here's the other thing. Peter got a 2.2. Not ecstatic. Not surprised either.' There was yet another delay. 'But Orla's name isn't there. Assumpta says she spent ages looking for it. Went over the sheets of paper again and again. Even asked someone else to help. There's definitely no Orla Finnegan on the list.'

There were tears: sticky, noisy, unrestrained tears. Orla cried so much she resorted to mopping her face with her hair. For once, she said, she didn't care if it was a greasy mess. She was following her own advice. She always maintained that if you wanted to cry, you should be as ridiculous as you liked and then get over it.

Orla had studied economics, and a phone call to the university revealed that statistics was the offending exam. 'Fucking maths.'

She was only a couple of per cent away from a pass. 'But the miserable bastards didn't have it in their miserable hearts to fix it for me.' She was assured she'd get the resit no bother. 'Easy for them to say.' It was in ten days' time. 'My summer is over. My hopes of staying in America are over.'

Elizabeth was the last to hear about all of this. By the time she pitched up, face flushed and hair shower-damp, the others were well ensconced. They were at a window table in one of those pizza and beer places that littered the neighbourhood in Brighton. Everything – staff included – looked as if it came from an easy-assemble pack. Red and white check tablecloths? Pitchers of watery beer? Waitress from the outer reaches of chirpiness? All boxes were ticked.

Donal and Peter were in a huddle. She caught Peter saying something about missing a good opportunity to say nothing, and she thought she heard Donal say, 'Of all the stupid things to fight about.' It was obviously a conspiracy of two, for when she sat down there was an abrupt silence. On the outside, Orla was resigned to her fate. Taking in the waitress, she remarked that at least she was saved from any more of that lark. Not one of life's natural servers, she particularly hated waitressing in Boston. 'What's all of this "have a nice day" business about?' she would moan. 'If you ask me it sounds like a threat.' Even so, the curtailment of her American adventure seemed to upset her more than the damage to her degree. Sitting beside her, Elizabeth was in line for the full force of her disappointment.

'It's not like I was ever going to be an economist. I'm not weird enough. And I'm a woman. Did you ever see any women economists on the telly?'

'Eh, no,' Elizabeth replied, while casting her eyes around for support.

'I rest my case,' Orla announced, almost triumphantly. She took a sip of her drink. 'What I'm dreading now is telling my parents. I haven't been able to muster the courage yet. My dad will go through me for a short cut.'

'You can't say that,' said Michelle. 'Parents get worked up about the oddest stuff. And then, the day you think you're in for the worst tongue-lashing is the day they rally round.'

'I hope you're right. The sister will be off the hook for a while, anyway.'

'What's the latest?'

'As chance would have it, I got a letter from London today. It sounds like she's – whisper it – enjoying herself.'

Michelle laughed. 'A stop will have to be put to that.'

Donal turned to Elizabeth. 'You're quiet tonight, lost sheep. Were you talking to them at home?'

'Not yet. Didn't get the chance today. Work and that. I'll call tomorrow.' What she didn't say was that it wasn't Anderson's that had occupied her day. To her surprise, when Danny had heard about her results he had bunked off work and taken her for lunch in the North End. At the start, it had been dreadful: the two of them dancing warily around each other, their conversation stilted. Finally, he had seized the initiative. 'I don't know about you, baby,' he'd said. 'But I'm crap at arguments.'

'That's two of us.'

'Are we still arguing?'

'What you said about Cindy … I suppose I understand.'

'Is there anything else you want to ask … about anything?'

Nothing that I want to hear the answer to, she thought. She shook her head.

'So, are we … together? For now, I mean. Until you have to go home to Ireland?'

'If that's what you want.'

'Oh Jesus, Elizabeth, of course it is.'

For a minute or two, Danny turned his attention to the demolition of his pasta. 'By the way,' he said eventually, 'you have me to thank.'

'For what?'

'Getting rid of Orla. When Immigration said there was

nothing they could do, I gave the college authorities a call.' He winked. 'You can show your gratitude later.'

Afterwards they had gone back to Emerald Street. Despite Danny's jaunty words, there was an intensity to the sex, like both were hoping that if they tried hard enough they could erase the night before. God help me, thought Elizabeth, as she listened to the others talk about their exams, if I had the choice I'd be with him right now. Unfortunately, there was no choice; she had to help with the toasting of Donal's success and the drowning of Orla's sorrows.

Elizabeth liked Danny too much. She knew that. She liked his kisses and his touch, his questions and his conversation. She found him exhilarating, like freewheeling down a hill, no brakes on her bicycle. The danger was she might end up in a crumpled heap at the bottom of that hill.

There was more on her mind. Her betrayal of Liam was gnawing at her conscience. Now that the worst of the air conditioning mania had subsided, she had time to write to him at work. Once, Mike had caught her mid-letter. The following day Danny had called in. Right in front of everyone he'd given her a long, hard kiss. Her boss had sniggered until she feared he'd have a seizure. 'Irish,' he said, 'for one so quiet you sure lead an interesting life.'

Sitting in the backyard at dusk, Danny had time to draw breath. This was his favourite spot at his favourite time of day. With the weather like this, you never knew what colour the sky would turn next. At that moment the sun was surrounded by wisps of orange, that luminous orange you didn't see anywhere else. In five minutes' time it might be different. Sometimes he liked an hour of calm. He could get his thoughts in order. Although, to be fair, Elizabeth wasn't a woman to go disturbing his peace. He hadn't expected anyone would share this pleasure. You couldn't even tell most people you liked sitting in the yard, staring at the sky. They'd give you grief about getting old or being strange. She was different.

Last night had been awful; just awful. That doleful face when he'd told her about Cindy and the baby. No doubt, the guy at home would never foist an abortion on some poor girl, and then dump her anyway. Being Elizabeth, she had had to do her amateur psychologist act, prodding and picking at sores that were best left alone. 'Do you think you were affected by your parents breaking up?' she'd said. 'No,' he'd replied. 'Couples split up. Life motors on. Happens every day of the week.' It was clear she didn't believe him.

Truth to tell, she wasn't nearly so keen on talking about herself. This was especially true when it came to Liam. The last time his name had been mentioned, she'd got all antsy: like a deer or a raccoon, or whatever it was that got caught in headlights. 'Ah sure, we'll see,' was all she'd said. Danny had no complaints. As in most aspects of life, he considered it unwise to go stirring up unnecessary hassle.

Even though Elizabeth wasn't the most beautiful woman he had dated, there was something pleasing about her face. And she was bright; she'd look at you with those light blue eyes as if to say, 'There's no point in spinning any garbage to me, mister, I can see straight through you.' That was cool. He was getting a grip on her too.

A couple of times, she'd really surprised him. One evening he'd been late back from work – car trouble again – and there she was, long limbs folded into an armchair, immersed in his depression book. He pointed out that she didn't even know his mom. She fixed him with one of her earnest looks. 'I want to understand,' she said.

She hadn't said, and it wouldn't be fair to ask, but he suspected he was a lot more accomplished in bed than the Irish guy. Her enthusiasm for having sex, no for having sex with *him*, was great. He joked that she made so much noise the whole street would want to sleep with him. She said he should listen to himself and, anyway, nobody else would be able for him. They joked a lot. There was something else too. He made a habit of figuring out what people wanted from him, what their angle was. Elizabeth didn't appear to want anything.

Danny lit a cigarette, stretched out his legs and watched the sky change to purple. He knew that spending this much time thinking about one girl did not make sense, especially when theirs was a temporary arrangement. Some days he reckoned this was just as well because there was a danger she would drive Vincent crazy. The last time his brother had called around, he'd said something about being disinterested in a TV show they were watching. Cool as you like, Elizabeth had corrected him. '*Un*interested. Disinterested means you're impartial or unbiased. It's a common mistake.' You should have seen Vincent's face. He glared at her like she'd just told him that Valerie was on crack.

She was a terrible fusser too, overly quick to change the sheets or clean the bath. In return, Danny liked play-acting the slob. If she was watching, he'd sniff yesterday's underpants before putting them on again. A thought occurred to him. Was she genuinely that fastidious, or was she doing what she believed was expected of her? For some reason, he suspected the latter was closer to the truth.

Anyway, there was so much else to think about. Work. Family. Friends. Red Sox. Celtics. Bruins. Patriots. Other girls he had been with. Other girls he would like to be with. Fixing the boards on the porch. World peace. So many things. And yet his mind kept drifting back to her. He wondered where she was right then. Whether she was enjoying herself. What she was saying about him. Danny wasn't sure what was going on. Elizabeth had only been gone for a couple of hours. He couldn't be missing her.

The three of them sat on the roof of the apartment building with a bottle of warm white wine. They were already well refreshed. The night was still, the air clean from the downpour of the day before. Just a faint suggestion of traffic could be heard from the Avenue. Orla was talking about her flight back to Dublin, booked for the following Sunday, only five days away. 'You can return to

Boston once you've the exam done,' Michelle was saying. 'Sure, can't you go to the bank and borrow the money for the airfare?' All three knew this wouldn't happen. Her chance had come and gone.

Elizabeth's head whirred with conflicting thoughts. How she had wished for Orla's early departure. In fact, once or twice – and she felt bad about this – she had actually prayed for something to send the girl scurrying home. She'd gone down on her knees, blessed herself, the whole rigmarole. Now, here she was, feeling sorry for her.

Orla and Michelle had stopped talking, and Elizabeth realised she was being asked a question.

'Will you write to me?' Orla was saying. 'To keep me up to date about Danny and that.'

It was odd – the subtle power shift that had occurred. Orla was no longer in charge. Not because she'd failed an exam, but because of Danny. For as long as Elizabeth bore his warm imprint, she was insulated from Orla's scorn. Everything had gone topsy-turvy.

'I promise,' she said. 'And make sure you write to us. Tell us how you're getting on. And what's going on at home. Parents are useless for that. They just tell you how bad the weather is, and who died.'

'Don't you worry,' said Michelle as she clasped one of Orla's hands. 'I'll keep you informed about our friend here and her romantic entanglement. I'm not sure that we can trust her to tell the truth.'

Elizabeth recognised the glint in Michelle's dark eyes. Trouble was lurking. 'I don't know what you're talking about,' she said. 'I tell ye far too much.'

'Hmmm,' replied Michelle. 'Did yourself and Danny have a nice afternoon, then?'

'I didn't say I spent the afternoon with him.'

'You spent the whole day at work, so?'

'No—'

'Whatever you do next, Elizabeth, don't think of a career in the Secret Service. That is if Ireland has a Secret Service. You're the most transparent person I've ever met. You and your, "Oh, I was too busy at work to call my parents." I'd say you were busy all right – busy doing the bold thing with Danny.'

Elizabeth's cheeks were ablaze. She swallowed some wine, but said nothing.

'Do you know,' started Orla, 'I don't think we heard nearly enough about the fabulous Danny tonight. You were remarkably restrained.'

Lord, thought Elizabeth, if only you knew. She had decided to stay quiet about the Cindy episode. 'I wouldn't want to be boring ye,' she said.

'Are we bored, Michelle?'

'We are not.'

'Right then, Elizabeth,' continued Orla, 'what would you say is Danny's most important attribute?'

'Ah, stop it, girls.'

'No, seriously now. His engaging personality, would you say? The strong arms? The manly chest? Those soulful eyes?'

'The crooked teeth?' added Michelle.

'Ah, girls. This isn't fair.'

Michelle wagged her finger. 'It's too late to be getting demure on us now.'

Elizabeth took another drink of wine.

Orla scrunched her fist into a microphone shape and thrust it under her chin. 'Miss Kelly, of the many gifts bestowed on Mr Danny Esposito, to which would you give top billing?'

'No comment, Miss Finnegan. No comment.'

'Let me ask the question another way, Miss Kelly. In the bedroom, where would you say he rates most highly?'

By now the three were shaking with giggles.

'I'm waiting for an answer, Miss Kelly.'

Elizabeth maintained her silence.

'Miss Kelly, I'll to have to press you,' said Orla.

'OK then, Miss Finnegan, if you insist, I would say …' Elizabeth hesitated, then threw caution to the wind. 'It would have to be his tongue.'

Michelle spat out a mouthful of wine. 'His tongue?'

'He's got a perfect one and he knows what to do with it. It's quite a ... precision instrument.'

Even Orla looked taken aback. 'I'm not sure I want the answer to this,' said Michelle, 'but what does he do with it?'

'Puts it to effective use. *Everywhere.*' Elizabeth gave 'everywhere' at least five syllables, then took a further drink of wine. 'In fact, I was wondering ...'

Orla resumed the questioning. 'Yes, Miss Kelly? You were wondering?'

'I was wondering – do you think is it illegal at home?'

Tears ran down Michelle's face. 'God Bless America,' she squeaked.

Orla was looking at Elizabeth like she'd lost her mind – and maybe she had. 'Miss Rooney, Miss Kelly,' she said. 'May I inform you ...' She paused for dramatic effect, assumed her most authoritative voice. 'You are both going to hell.'

Elizabeth lay back on the roof and listened as their laughter drifted out into the night.

Chapter 10

'You're a hard woman to track down.' Liam sounded relieved. 'I'm only in from mass. I met your dad. He said they hadn't heard from you either. Had an anxious head on him. Is something wrong?'

Elizabeth was sitting on the yellow chair, phone in hand. It was shortly after three in the afternoon in Boston, five hours later at home. Liam always went to Saturday evening mass. He liked a clear run at Sunday. He'd have his dinner at ten in the morning if he could. 'I'm fine, love,' she said. 'Totally fine. Maybe I've been working too hard.'

On her return to Lantern Street, she had found a note from Michelle. Liam had called three times. Apparently her mother had passed on the number. Elizabeth had been hit by a pulse of guilt. No, it was more than that. She'd been hit by raw fear. What if he had found out? Stranger things had happened. One day she'd asked a man for directions, and it turned out he was from Carrick-on-Suir. He'd been to school with her cousins.

'Working too hard?' Liam was saying. 'That's what I told Syl. You know your daughter, I said. She'll be tiring herself out, doing everybody else's job as well as her own.'

She did her best to sound light-hearted. 'Well, I wouldn't go that far but I do want to save some money while I can.' In actual fact, Elizabeth was spending every cent she made. After the Cindy encounter, she had gone to Filene's Basement and bought a bagful of what Michelle called 'slapper gear'. The skirts were even shorter than those she normally wore and the tops significantly tighter. Danny would approve. These were not clothes that would ever see the light of day at home. Her father would have a conniption, and her mother would be lighting candles to obscure saints.

She could tell that Liam was genuinely pleased about her exam results. 'Didn't I always say that everything was set up for you?' he said. 'You could always come home earlier, love. We all miss you. Me most of all, obviously.'

Sweat trickled down Elizabeth's spine, and her eyelid twitched. 'My return flight is already booked, Liam. For October. Remember?'

'I'm just saying, like. Sure, people change these arrangements all the time. You'd be here in time for the All Ireland semi-final. Tipperary are playing Antrim.'

She swallowed. 'You're very good to worry about me. Really you are. But there's no need. We're having a party tonight. Before Orla goes home.'

'Oh, OK. You take care of yourself now. Don't go drinking too much. And make sure the partying isn't too wild. You don't want to lose the deposit on the apartment.'

'I promise. Listen, love, I better go or the phone bill will cost me a week's wages.'

Liam sighed. 'Fine. Remember what I said, though. You can come home anytime you like. And ring again soon. So I know you're all right.'

After they had hung up, Elizabeth lay flat on the floor and tried not to think.

The revelation was that Brian Byrne, Bray Brian as they called him, could sing. Not merely hold a tune, or coarsely belt one out like a lounge bar covers band, but really sing. His voice had range and depth and was free of affectation. It was the sort of voice that, at one moment, urged you to stay quiet to appreciate its beauty. The next moment you wanted to sing along for the sheer joy of it. When Brian had told Peter he might 'bring along the ould guitar', none of them had expected this.

It was late and the party was at full tilt. Swarms of raucous

Irish youngsters, with new tans and new clothes, preened themselves. Americans mingled. Elizabeth wouldn't go so far as to
say the apartment had been transformed, but a couple of cheap
lamps, strategically placed, had knocked off some of the edges.
A keg of beer stood in one corner. A fug of cigarette and dope
smoke hung in the air. Revellers were in the front room, the
kitchen, the hall, even the bathroom. A gang were on the roof.
They were drinking, pursuing, kissing. Some were invited; others
got the word from a friend of a friend; more heard the noise and
wandered on in.

Brian was in the lads' bedroom, back to the wall, entertaining a
swelling crowd. In the half-light, his voice soared. The repertoire
was wide: from 'Follow Me Up To Carlow' to 'Brown Eyed Girl'
to 'Sally MacLennane' and on.

'I'm probably gushing like a groupie here, but you were brilliant.' Elizabeth zeroed in on Brian while he took a breather.
Peter and Danny were beside her. 'Honest to God, I've paid to see
people who aren't in the same league as you.'

From the warmth and width of his smile she could tell he was
pleased. 'Ah, thanks, I've done the odd night in a pub here and
there. Mostly it's only a bit of crack.'

'There must be bars in Boston that'd pay you. Why don't you
give it a go?' asked Danny.

'I've thought about it on and off. Only it's like too much of a
gamble. When you get up and sing, you're putting yourself out
there. People have an opinion. Laying blocks is a lot less hassle.'

Peter slapped Brian on the back. 'We're all fierce impressed,
man. You're looking at the worst singer of all time. And there I
am, working with a star and I didn't know it.'

'The worst singer of all time?' said Danny.

'I'm chronic. Always have been. Even as a kid. No cute little
voice. When we were making our confirmation, the entire class
sang. Except me. The teacher said, "Peter O'Regan, I won't have
you wrecking the day, so just you mouth the words."'

Elizabeth had an idea. 'Why don't you come around some

evening, Brian? When there aren't a million other people here. We could all meet up and have a good old sing. And we could put Peter to the test. See if he really is the world's worst.'

At two in the morning, the hordes were multiplying. Leaning against the wall at one end of the hall, Elizabeth realised she didn't recognise most of them. The giddy, strident voices, everyone desperate to be heard, reminded her of a school playground. In the front room people were flinging themselves around to a cassette of the Pogues. The keg had been drunk dry, so alternative sources of alcohol were being mined. The lads from one of the apartments upstairs were drinking a bottle of something called Wild Turkey. The girls from over the corridor were knocking back a slab of Miller. Try as she might, she couldn't banish Liam's phone call from her head. She wished he hadn't been so solicitous, so *decent*. In the past Elizabeth had told the odd white lie, or engaged in the occasional sin of omission. But never before had she been so out-and-out dishonest. She hadn't appreciated how accomplished a liar she was.

Danny was talking to Orla, who was wearing a teeny-tiny white dress, and Michelle, whose black number was only slightly more substantial. Elizabeth admired the breadth of his back and the shape of his head, and tried to guess at the nonsense the two women were putting into that head. Michelle was alone tonight. Ray, who had recently given up drink, was unlikely to be comfortable at a gathering devoted to its abuse.

Brian aside, the night's main discovery was Rosie. With her round face and bouncy fair hair, she was aptly named. Donal introduced her as his 'colleague', but she was clearly more than that.

'Hello there, dark horse,' Elizabeth said as he ambled towards her.

Realising what she was referring to, his slate-grey eyes twinkled with pleasure.

'What's the story?' she asked.

He shrugged. 'We'll see. A spot of diversion.' He paused. 'You haven't been talking to Peter, have you?'

'We had a chat earlier. Him and me and Danny and Brian.'

'I meant without Danny – just the two of you.'

'Is there something we should be talking about?'

Donal scratched his neck. 'You might go for a jar with him. Or a coffee or that. Next week if you can. He's a bit low. I reckon he's missing you. The two of you used to be together all the time, and now he hardly sees you. He has to hear about you from Danny.'

'He's missing me? What's he missing?'

'Ah, you know Petie. He likes everything in its place. His ducks in a row.'

Elizabeth was perplexed. 'If you're sure. Yeah, I can do that.'

Donal patted her shoulder. 'Good woman.'

'So,' she said, 'how's life with you? Have you sold much lately?'

He gave a conspiratorial wink. 'Oh yes, it's been a good week. There's a man from Florida interested in Bunratty Castle and the Cliffs of Moher. And they're queuing up to buy the Burren.'

The two were still laughing when Michelle joined them, wide-eyed. 'What do you make of the exhibition over there?'

With the crowd and the smoke and the muted light, it was difficult to see anything clearly. Donal was first to locate the spectacle. 'Holy fuck,' he said. 'Go on, you good thing.'

Peter was in a corner of the front room, wrapped around one of Michelle's friends from work. They were petting and smooching and stroking.

'Offending public decency,' said Michelle.

'If they were back in Ireland,' added Donal, 'someone would do the proper thing and throw a coat over them.'

Elizabeth was fascinated. 'What's that her name is again?'

'Marlene.'

'More importantly,' said Donal, 'how old is she?'

Michelle smiled. 'About thirty.'

'And the rest.'

'Perhaps a *little* more.'

Donal chortled to himself. 'Get down off that gas stove, Grandma, you're too old to go riding the range.'

'You've a bad tongue on you, Donal Mulvihill,' said Elizabeth.

'Not the best choice of words in the circumstances,' he replied.

'Speaking of tongues,' said Michelle, 'here's Danny.'

Elizabeth shot her what she hoped was the filthiest look in her arsenal.

'Hey there, I thought I'd lost you,' he said before swooping in for a kiss.

'No fear of that,' she responded with enthusiasm.

'I don't know about you, Donal,' said Michelle. 'I think I preferred it when everyone was all Irish and repressed.'

It was then that Orla sauntered over. Someone had given her a camera. 'Not that I'm sentimental or anything,' she said. 'I want you to understand that. But I'd like a picture of you all.'

Danny draped an arm around Elizabeth's shoulder. 'Us first,' he said to Orla. 'You'll definitely need a shot of the best-looking couple in the room.' Elizabeth rolled her eyes, and the two grinned for all they were worth.

'Our first photo,' he laughed.

Danny said he was happy, and Elizabeth didn't like it. Of course, it wasn't the happiness itself that disturbed her. It was the fact that he came out and said it.

They had been for a drink and were meandering home. The weather was so perfect, the evening so mild, that Elizabeth felt impossibly light. Then, a block or so from the house, Danny, having paused to look at the sky, ran up behind her and buried his head in her hair. She squealed, and he made his declaration.

Her response was sharp. Too sharp, she feared. 'You shouldn't say that.'

'What's wrong with being happy?'

'Nothing. You just shouldn't say it. It's bad luck.'

'Why?' he asked. 'What'll happen?'

'You're tempting fate, inviting trouble.'

Danny shook his head. 'You're a funny girl.'

'I may be. But humour me.'

He swept around, stood in front of Elizabeth and looked her straight in the eye. 'I can't. Because I think you're wrong.'

The street was quiet. Curtains were being drawn and bedroom lights extinguished. Up there somewhere, no doubt, the stars were doing their thing, although their efforts were washed away by the city lights.

Danny vaulted onto a wall. 'Come up here.'

'Are we not going home?'

'In a minute. First, you have to tell me you're happy.'

Elizabeth hauled herself up onto the wall and edged in beside him. She was wearing a flower-strewn wraparound skirt left behind by Orla and had to proceed with caution.

'What if I say I'm not happy?'

Danny arched an eyebrow and told her she couldn't say that because it wasn't the truth. Elizabeth decided to play with him. How, she asked, did he know?

'Because I do. I'm not saying you don't have stuff to worry about. Or that both of us wouldn't be even happier if our lottery numbers came up. At the moment, though, I'm happy and I have the feeling you are too. Why not be up front about it, huh?'

She thought for a bit. One large hand started to forage beneath the flap of her skirt, and she had to slap him away. 'You should remember that where I come from we don't do up front. Feelings and compliments aren't exactly our strong point. Calling someone "nothing but an old bollox" is a term of endearment. Saying you were happy would be seen as a touch, em, American.' She could have added and not very adult and not very cool. Elizabeth couldn't imagine anyone in Ireland talking about happiness.

Danny made another lunge for the opening of her skirt which she artfully knocked back. He laughed. 'Maybe then, in this one thing, you should be more American.'

She smiled. 'Yeah, but ... I always think of happiness more as something you appreciate in hindsight. You can't be aware of it at the time.'

'What though when it creeps up on you? And you find yourself thinking, "Hmmm, I must be happy"? Why can't you acknowledge that?'

'Well—'

'Go on, Elizabeth, live dangerously.'

'OK.' She was quiet for thirty, forty seconds. 'Danny, I am happy. Most days I'm unbelievably happy. Things that would normally have me fretting or fuming float straight on over my head. And the reason I'm happy is because I'm with you.' She paused again, kicked her heels against the wall. 'But at the back of my mind is the feeling that this is not quite right. It's not honest. The pair of us ... we talk and talk but we do our best not to mention the obvious. We pretend no one else exists.'

Danny put an arm around her. 'Listen, I don't know whether you'll be here in a few months' time, but I don't want to dwell on that. Simple guy that I am, I want to make the most of what's here now. And you make me happy.'

Elizabeth was part touched, part exasperated. She didn't swallow the 'simple guy' routine. He knew it wasn't true, and she knew it wasn't true. She wouldn't have any interest in him if he was as simple as he claimed. Some days, she felt like he was one of the most complicated people she had ever met.

Danny admitted that, perhaps, simple was the wrong word but he insisted his point stood. 'What I mean is that sometimes simple, straightforward or whatever you want to call it is good. Why make life more difficult than it has to be? That's what other folks are for.'

'Some things are hard. You can't wander around saying if it's not easy I don't want to know. You have to persevere.' As soon as the words left her mouth, Elizabeth realised it could have been her father speaking. You heard men whinging about women slowly turning into their mothers. She was far more likely to morph into Syl.

'I hear what you're saying,' Danny said, his own heels knocking against the wall. 'Where I'm coming from is … well, I think of all the crap my mother goes through, and it strikes me that you have to grasp whatever comes your way. All the small pleasures.'

Elizabeth leaned in and stroked Danny's chest. 'I've heard worse philosophies.'

He gave a trademark smile. 'I think for once I may be winning here.'

'Oh now, I wouldn't go that far.'

'All I know is, I look down this street, Elizabeth, see all these houses, all these people. How many of them are having as good a time as us?'

She was glad no one else could hear their conversation. What she didn't know was whether this was because it could be dismissed as childish, or because, in its own way, it felt incredibly intimate. All the same, Elizabeth wouldn't be swayed. Happiness was best not discussed.

Right then, both of them were conscious that the days of being on their own were coming to an end. Regina would be back soon.

'What's the story with your mam?' she asked.

'She enjoying being with Teresa, what with the baby news and all. Last I heard, she was talking about coming back at the weekend. Asked if I could give her a ride home.'

'That, as my father might say, will put a stop to our gallop.'

'Let's go home then. Continue the galloping while we can. And, Elizabeth?'

'Mmmm?'

He kissed her. 'I'm pleased I make you happy.'

Even then, she knew she would remember that evening. The tang of newly cut grass hanging in the air, a hint of decay underneath; overhead, an elegant sliver of moon. Sitting on a wall in her borrowed skirt, with her complicated American man, Elizabeth had all the happiness she could possibly need. Even thinking about it was scary.

*

Back in the house, she perched on the kitchen counter while Danny poured a glass of milk. The kitchen in number nineteen was small and dimly lit. It was weighed down with the accumulation of two decades of family life, with saucepans and bowls and unidentified utensils and recipe books. In among the books were bills and letters and pieces of paper that someone had probably intended to file away somewhere. Elizabeth had a surprising attachment to the room and always felt comfortable there, maybe because it could have belonged to any house in Ireland.

He handed her the glass. 'Time for bed?'

'Failing any better offers …'

'Tuh,' he scoffed. 'Like there could possibly be any better offers.'

Elizabeth drank. The milk felt silky cool as it washed down her throat. 'Do you want some?'

'Milk? Or you?'

She swatted him with a tea towel. Taking the glass and the towel from her hands, Danny positioned himself between her dangling legs, drank the rest of the milk and started nuzzling her and purring.

'Just like a cat,' he said.

'If it's possible, you get worse.'

He began undoing her sleeveless blouse.

'Danny?'

More purrs. Another button opened. 'Yeah?'

'Should we not continue this upstairs?'

'I'm good right here. I mean, we've been almost everywhere else. I don't see why the kitchen should be ignored.'

'If you put it in such a romantic way, how can I possibly say no?' Not for the first time with one of Danny's suggestions, she wasn't sure how this would work. You had to give him credit for being inventive.

'Come here, gorgeous thing.' He eased her from the counter into his arms. Before she knew it, her blouse was on the floor. As was his T-shirt. Two buttons and her skirt fell there too. Her bra followed.

Slowly she traced a finger along the line of hair that ran down the centre of his chest, onto his stomach and beyond. The hair was soft, little more than fluff, really. While she undid his belt, Danny's breath grew jagged. As she opened the buttons on his jeans, they exchanged expressions of desire. He moaned. Those warm tingling feelings took over – the feelings that left little room for any rational thought.

His sole focus on one imperative, for a moment he must not have noticed her panic.

'Jesus, Mary and Joseph,' she shrieked. 'No.'

A woman stood at the kitchen door. Afterwards, all Elizabeth remembered was a green dressing gown. And large blue-grey eyes.

Danny turned around, his jeans slipping to his ankles in the process. 'Oh hell. Ma? What are you doing here?'

Chapter 11

The last light was bleeding from the sky as Danny arrived at O'Mahoney's. Already the days were getting shorter, the mornings that touch mistier. He wasn't looking forward to this. An older brother was a useful commodity, and for all his funny ways Vincent was a good brother. He had always looked out for Danny. That was the problem. He did too much looking.

Danny was grateful for the use of Vincent and Valerie's spare room, even if his brother was beginning to hum and haw about temporary arrangements. They'd been using the room since what had become known as 'the incident'. They tried to arrive late and leave early so as not to make a nuisance of themselves. Their only alternative was Lantern Street, and in his book that was a non-starter.

In the early mornings, before the silvery softness was burned away, the couple went for coffee together. Amid the steam and the smoke and the forced cheeriness of the exchanges, they sat at a scarred table, smiling and sporadically letting their fingertips touch. It wasn't a hand-holding kind of place. Despite their restraint, he was aware of a few of the regulars – Elizabeth called them the hard chaws – gazing on. He always left first and before walking away looked around, just to see her sitting on a plastic chair, doing her best to blend in, yet managing only to appear more apart.

'You been allowed out on your own, then?'

Danny figured that if this was Vincent's opening salvo, the evening might be even more testing than anticipated.

'Ha, look who's talking. You're the guy with the wedding to plan.'

Vincent gave Danny a cuff to the shoulder and offered a cigarette. 'Don't worry about me. I never expected to see you under the thumb like this.'

'This from the man who's forever going on about the joys of the steady relationship. I do the same – for a few weeks mind, not fifteen years or whatever it is that you've been with Val – and I get all this grief.'

'*Four* years. And there's no comparison, Dan. *No* comparison. You're dating a woman who's going to be back on a different continent in the fall. For all you know, she might have another guy over there in Ireland.'

'She does.'

'Huh?'

'Have a boyfriend at home.'

'Man, you have a knack of getting into awkward situations.'

Now this was what he meant by too much looking out. Why couldn't Vincent let it go? Gradually, Danny was coming to the conclusion that Elizabeth was going to stick around. Hand on heart, he didn't see too much of a dilemma. He wasn't being arrogant, because he didn't view this as him versus Liam. Rather, it was America versus Ireland. Now sure, as he would be the first to argue, America had its faults. All the politicians, for a start. But taking everything into account: America versus Ireland? It didn't sound like much of a contest. He remembered the previous November, on a mist-soaked day with a sour wind whipping in, talking to an Irish guy he was working with at the time. The Irish guy said it was like a day at home. 'You could get this day in July or January. That's what Ireland's like – a whole year of November.' Why would anyone return to that?

Now that he thought about it, Danny couldn't recall the last time Elizabeth had spoken about Liam, although there were days when he was a ghostly presence, his name hovering on the fringes of their conversation. Danny still reckoned it was best not to force these matters or create unnecessary stress. The two of them had enough of that at the moment, which was why interference from

Vincent, no matter how well intentioned, was not what he wanted tonight. He wanted a beer or two to blur the edges, and he wanted some peace.

'Guess who I met this afternoon?' his brother said.

He shrugged.

'Cindy. She was looking good. Looking *ve-ry* good.' Vincent elongated 'very', so that it seemed to last for about twenty seconds. 'She was asking after you. Of course.'

Danny ordered another beer. He wondered if Vincent was about to trawl through all his former girlfriends. That might take a while. 'That's nice.'

'So, I'm looking at Cindy … and I'm thinking what *is* Danny doing with that Irish girl? I mean, apart from her willingness to get naked in the kitchen,' he guffawed, 'what does he see in her?'

'Ah, leave it, Vincent. Would you? I enjoy being with her. It's … different.'

'Different?'

'Like, say, a few days ago, we had this great conversation about sin. About whether something should be a sin if you're not hurting anyone.'

'Calm down, Dan. I don't need to hear about any more of your kinky stuff.' Obviously pleased with his own wit, Vincent looked towards the door. 'I told Cindy you'd be easy to find tonight, anyhow.'

Danny dug a toe into one of the gaps in the tiled floor and sighed. There was no point in trying to explain, because all he'd get in return would be a torrent of sarcasm. He focused on his beer.

'Well, look who it is,' said the elder brother.

Danny looked up to see a figure teetering towards them. 'Uh, hi there, Cindy,' he said.

Elizabeth was not looking very good. She wasn't in the same universe as very good. She was wearing the least flattering T-shirt in her rucksack, a grey tent of a thing, and a voluminous purple skirt belonging to Michelle. The skirt was probably designed to appear bohemian, but swaddled her like a bolt of leftover curtain material. She oozed dowdiness, which to be fair, was the effect she was aiming for. In fact, when you added in the flat sandals and the scraped-back hair, she feared she may have overdone it on the frumpiness.

On the T, people were wedged in nose to nose, the air a patchwork of competing shower gels and deodorants. At Park Street, she changed to the red line. She let the first train go by, convincing herself it was too crowded. The previous night, while Danny went for a drink with Vincent, she had returned to Lantern Street and written to Liam. His letters continued to overflow with stories of weddings and funerals and sports events and nights out. As she read, one part of her was swamped by guilt, but another part loved absorbing the news from home, all the minutiae that no one else would understand. Writing back was beyond difficult. She had the devil's job filling more than a page.

Neither did she know what to say to her parents. In their last letter, her mother had spoken of the sugar factory being in its final months. Her dad appeared to have abandoned the King Canute act and was looking for another job. *But what is there*, her mam had written, *for a man nearing fifty without a qualification to his name?* Poor Stacia. If she had any notion what was going on in America, she would … actually what would she do? She was already a terror for mass going and the like; the parish church wouldn't hold a first Friday or a last Tuesday without her. Elizabeth unburdened herself to Donal who advised her to invent some news. Half of the stories in his letters home were made up, he said. His sister would be ferociously disappointed when she discovered he hadn't really met Patrick Swayze or Rob Lowe.

On occasion, she wondered what her parents, especially her dad, would make of Danny. Would Syl be put off by the superficial stuff: the black leather jacket, the torn jeans, the divorced parents? Or would he see the true Danny: the unpretentious, intelligent guy who worked hard and would go fifteen rounds with Mike Tyson for his family?

Danny knew she was planning on seeing Regina. What he didn't know was that today was the day. Telling him would only add to the tension. On the night of the incident, they had pulled on their clothes and fled for the comparative safety of Vincent's apartment. It was an odd phrase: the incident. Michelle claimed that as euphemisms went, it was akin to the Irish government calling the Second World War 'the emergency'. The following day the remorseful couple had tried to make amends. They'd met after work and had arrived in Emerald Street laden with apologies. Danny had done most of the talking while Elizabeth stood beside him, scrutinising her feet with mortification. Regina had sat bolt upright, hardly a word passing her lips, one thumb rubbing against the other. When the embarrassment could not reach a higher pitch, they had decided that more time was needed.

So, two weeks later, here she was, counting down the stations. She got out a stop early, telling herself this was solely so she would have more time to prepare. She dawdled past the familiar shops and offices: the ever-busy laundromat, the insurance office with brown-tinted windows, the grocery store with the poster that said *Food Stamps Welcome Here*. She saw a young guy with his shirt off washing a car. Danny did that, and it always made her smile. 'Show off,' she'd say.

The walk could only be strung out for so long, and too soon she arrived at her destination. Bridie was on her porch. 'Well, well,' she squawked. 'I was beginning to think you'd gone and left us.' Elizabeth gave a perfunctory wave and pressed the bell. With a tremble of lace curtains, the door opened.

'He's not here.'

Elizabeth felt Regina's eyes sweep over her. Now she was convinced she had overdone the drabness. She lifted her eyes from the doormat and attempted a smile. 'I was hoping – if it's OK – to talk to you.'

The older woman responded with a tepid smile of her own.

'You better come on in.' She walked down the hall ahead of Elizabeth. 'I presume you know your way around.'

Elizabeth, trusting that Regina didn't mean this to be as hostile as it sounded, followed her into the living room. She sat on the edge of the grey and pink patterned sofa. Compared to the day she had left, the room was pristine. The windows were fully open, yet the synthetic scent of polish permeated the air. Keeping house was not Danny's strong suit, and now she regretted not having made more of an effort herself. Imagine, if on top of everything else, Mrs Esposito thought she was dirty.

Sitting across from her, Regina was doing that routine with her thumbs. One rubbing against the other, to and fro, back and forth. It was remarkable how Danny was simultaneously the image of his mother, and not like her at all. The eyes were indisputably hers, except Regina's were framed by a network of narrow lines, and the lids sagged as though she lacked the strength to open them fully.

The principal difference between mother and son was less tangible, and she struggled for a description. Physically, Danny was the essence of solid. Despite his not being particularly bulky, Elizabeth thought of him as shelter. If Boston was hit by one of those savage storms you saw on the news – the full-scale *Wizard of Oz* – he was the man you'd want. Regina, although not unnaturally thin, appeared hollowed out, like a gust from the lower notches of the Beaufort Scale would lift her up and deposit her down the street.

'I was thinking,' Elizabeth found herself saying, 'that, unfortunately, we didn't get off to the best of starts. And I want to try and make things a wee bit better. To see if we could be … not friends as such, but friendly. The way it is … the current situation … is difficult for Danny.'

'If things are difficult for my son, he only has himself to blame. Believe me, I was far more angry with him than with you. He's an adult and he should start acting like one.' Regina shook her head. 'I've said it to him before, more than once. It's not safe to behave like he does. You read about these things all the time.'

For the second time in as many minutes, Elizabeth wondered whether she had been insulted. Was the woman implying that Danny might catch something from her? 'I hear you. I want you to know, though, that the two of us have been, eh, responsible.' Regina said nothing, so Elizabeth continued. 'And I think your son is ... he's one of the good guys. He's been good to me.' She couldn't prevent a grin from forming. 'Really lovely, in fact.'

The thumbs were gnawing away. 'I don't doubt it. He's not short on charm.' She pursed her lips, like she was deciding how to proceed. 'Do you mind if I ask you, because Danny has clammed up on me, how long did you spend here?'

Elizabeth grappled for an answer, couldn't reach a plausible one, so settled on the truth. It came out more like another question. 'Most of the time you were gone?'

Regina's face crinkled, her mouth split open and she chuckled. Trying to take this in, Elizabeth was stuck in one of those moments, where despite being sure that she was now an adult, the response of another one of the tribe left her flummoxed.

'And while you were here, Elizabeth, where did you eat?'

Squirming with embarrassment, but sensing that the use of her name might be a positive sign, she decided to stick with the truth. 'Sometimes we went out or got pizza, but mostly we ate here.'

'Am I right in assuming you did the cooking?'

'Danny helped.'

'Danny? Helped?'

'He was handy enough. Say, not as good as Peter and Donal my flatmates, but way more useful than ...' The words 'my boyfriend at home' came close to popping out. 'Way more useful than lots of men.'

The questions kept coming about cleaning and washing and ironing, and Elizabeth kept answering until she came to the conclusion that it was all going horribly wrong. Of all the receptions she had expected, this one hadn't featured. 'Eh, Mrs Esposito?'

'Regina, please.'

'I'm getting the impression here that you think I'm some

simpleton who Danny roped in to do the housework while you were away. That's not how it was. I suppose I wanted to reassure you that we were civilised, you know.'

Elizabeth's use of the word 'civilised' prompted another laugh, only it was softer than before.

'I'm sure you're not simple, Elizabeth. It's just … the pair of you had me confused.'

Regina leaned forward, like Danny did when he felt he had an important point to make. She revealed how Vincent had told her about a new girlfriend, so she didn't know what to expect. But when she got home the house remained standing, there was nothing growing in the refrigerator and there were sheets on the clothesline. With one thing and another, she was tired and went to bed. When she heard a noise she came down expecting to find Danny.

'Instead, what do you know, I walked in on the *Last Tango in Paris*. And, I swear, I was stumped. I began to wonder if he had an entire harem of women, some to do the laundry, and others to take their clothes off in the kitchen.'

Elizabeth allowed herself a slight smile. 'No, just me.'

Regina made a tiny sound, gentler than a full sigh. 'I guess I didn't expect a woman I'd never met to have become such a fixture in his life.'

Right enough, it had been an unusual situation. But there never was a plan. Had there been more planning and thinking, she might have taken fright and run back to Brighton. Instead they had rubbed along in a way that suited them, and now those weeks were gone she missed them.

Elizabeth accepted the offer of coffee. The heavy lifting was behind her, she hoped. She was curious too. The woman with the string of questions and the wheezing laugh was in many ways like her son. She was hard to reconcile with the withdrawn, desperate figure about whom Danny worried so much. Elizabeth was in two minds as to whether to enquire after Regina's health. She knew that if a problem with any other body part had laid her low, this would be front and centre of their conversation. But expressing interest in the state of a person's leg or throat or breast was child's play; everybody spoke the language. Asking about the balance of their brain involved stepping into the unknown.

She placed her coffee cup on the low wooden table. 'Regina, I hope you don't mind me asking this. You seem so good. How are you?'

Like an alarm that had stopped pealing, Elizabeth hadn't noticed how the thumb rubbing had ceased. Until it resumed.

'I'm fine.'

'I'm glad you're better. And, obviously, Danny is too.'

Regina, her features tightening in concentration, gazed into her coffee. 'Did he talk about me a lot?'

Elizabeth cursed herself for not leaving well enough alone. She needed a graceful way to exit the conversation. 'Enough to explain the situation to me, to let me understand that life has been tough for you. That's all.'

Regina continued to stare into the cup. An ambulance siren could be heard in the distance, cutting through the torpor of the morning. 'I'm sorry, Elizabeth.'

'No, I'm sorry. I should stay out of matters that don't concern me.'

'No, no,' Regina said, and even though she had raised her voice by the tiniest amount, it filled the room. 'I have to get better at this. It's always the same. I want to put the whole episode behind me. Except I should know by now that I can't.' She rifled through her bag, took out a pack of cigarettes and lit one. 'I usually have a plan. I try not to get into situations where I'm asked about it. If it's unavoidable, like with family, I have my answers, and my brush-offs, prepared.' She rested the cigarette on an ashtray that looked like something a child had brought home from a school tour. It was all gaudy colours and cartoon suns.

'Did you ever think that it might simply go away?'

'Oh God. How I wished. Or I hoped that there would be a new kind of tablet. Or there would be a doctor, who I could afford, and he'd perform a miracle.' She took another pull, then another, then with some force stubbed the cigarette into the cartoon suns. 'Now I understand that's not going to happen. You see, it's not like I'm really bad. I've never had to go to hospital. I've never … hurt myself. I think this is – how do I put this? – my cross to bear. If you believe in that sort of thing.'

For a short while, she stopped. Her thoughts appeared to be coming in bursts, so Elizabeth stayed quiet. Regina took a shuddering breath. 'To me, it feels like I've lost connection. Like I'm destined to spend half my life apart from the rest of you. I'm sorry, Elizabeth, I don't expect that to make sense. But that's how it feels.'

Elizabeth tried to look her in the eye, only Regina's gaze remained rooted to the coffee cup. It struck her that even though they'd been talking for some time, neither of them had used the word depression. 'If I was meeting you today,' she said, 'and I didn't know anything about you, I would never have guessed. You're so – I'm sure this is the wrong word – normal.'

At last, Danny's mother raised her eyes. 'Isn't that the way we all work, Elizabeth, honey? Mostly, people let you see what they want you to see. They give you one version of themselves: the version where life is straightforward and work is great and the family are a blessing. You have no idea how much they may be struggling.'

Tears were forming at the back of Elizabeth's eyes. She willed herself not to get emotional. 'I hope, Regina, that my coming here hasn't been difficult for you,' she said.

'No, it's … it's not unreasonable for you to ask. You've become close to Danny.' Regina smiled. 'And you did make me laugh.'

Elizabeth realised the time had come for her to go. Scooping up her bag, she rose from the sofa. 'I'd better head into work. My boss is a bit of a tyrant.'

As Regina got to her feet, she asked how they were finding life with Vincent and Valerie. Elizabeth was non-committal.

'Should you and Danny not think about … coming back here?'

Regina said. 'I'd say the other two have had their fill of you by now.'

They were a step away from the front door when, to the surprise of both women, Elizabeth hugged Danny's mother, squeezing her like she was one of her own family.

Chapter 12

Elizabeth floated to the T station and fizzed into Anderson's Electrical. She careened down the steps into the basement, finding it hard to contain her good humour. She was bursting to tell Danny that everything was sorted. They could go home.

Artie was slouching by the bottom of the stairs. 'Jackie said to tell you she's gone for lunch,' he said.

She looked at her watch. She knew exactly how late it was, but thought it best to appear surprised.

'She also said to tell you Peter called. Sounded mighty worked up, apparently. He'll call again later.'

'Thanks, Artie. Was that it?'

'Uh-huh. Mike's in there, though. I'll bet he can advise you of any developments.'

Elizabeth shuffled across the sales floor, trying to guess what Peter was at. On the one other occasion he had called work it was to inform her, amid an amount of sighing and tutting, that her rent was overdue. In the hope that Mike would be on the phone, or submerged in sales figures, she slunk towards her desk. He might not even notice her arrival.

'Ah, there you are, Irish,' he boomed. 'I was beginning to worry that you'd left the country.'

'Dentist?'

'Dentist my freaking eye. Good lord, what's with the gear? Have you been to see the mother superior?'

'In a manner of speaking.'

Mike looked lost. 'A man called ten minutes ago. Wanted to talk to you.'

'Sorry, Mike. Was he Irish?'

'No, one of us. I think it was that blue-eyed Lothario I've seen hanging around here. Will you be working for us today?'

Elizabeth mumbled, 'Sorry?'

'Work,' he said, the decibel level rising sharply, the words shot out in staccato style. 'Do you think you will engage in any today?'

'Eh, yeah, Mike. Is there anything in particular you want?' Her head was elsewhere now. First Peter, then Danny; what was going on?

For the next hour, each time the phone rang she hardly allowed it past the *brrr* of the first *brrring* before the receiver was at her ear. Each time it was a customer being gormless about their washing machine or oven or perishing air conditioner. When the phone had been silent for the best part of ten minutes, she wandered out to the televisions. Every channel was showing some variety of political attack ad. Either George Bush was an unprincipled, criminal-loving freeloader, or Michael Dukakis was. She tried to imagine this type of approach in Ireland and decided it wouldn't be subtle or sneaky enough. Why go for a full frontal assault when a knife between the shoulder blades was more effective?

The phone came to life again. Before she could reach it, she heard Mike announcing, 'Elizabeth Kelly's office.' She would have to tease him about remembering her actual name. Expecting another tedious customer, she bounced in the door. Her boss smirked as he handed over the phone.

'Hello, Anderson's Electric—'

'At last,' Danny said. 'Where have you been all day, baby? I was starting to worry.'

'Everything's fine. No, better than fine. I went to see your mother and, wait until I tell you, it's all fixed.'

'Listen, we'll have to talk about it later. There's been an accident. I'm at the hospital.'

It was amazing what a lot of worrying you could do in the space of a few seconds. 'Are—' she started.

'I'm good. Peter's good. Brian's ... ahm ... not so good. He fell off some scaffolding. It's a long story. Do you think you can come down here?'

Mike was practising his repertoire of angry looks, as Elizabeth assured Danny she'd be there as soon as possible.

When she arrived at the hospital, Danny was standing outside with Peter and a couple of the other guys from the site. They were in a huddle of smoke, still piecing together what had gone wrong, still arguing and talking over each other. Peter had been first to the scene. He'd found Brian on the floor, unconscious, his limbs contorted.

Peter started to stalk up and down, his fingers tapping against his thigh as he paced. Elizabeth joined him. 'What's the story?'

'I know this won't speed up the news,' he said. 'But I have to keep moving. I can't stand in a circle listening to platitudes any longer.'

He told her how one of the boys had gone to find Brian's flat-mates. Rory, she remembered, worked in a bar in Southie. Nicky was a plumber, but nobody could recall where he worked.

'Will one of them ring Brian's parents?' she asked.

Peter was unexpectedly agitated. 'I think we should hold off. The lad mightn't be too badly hurt. What if he wakes up and everything's cool? Then we'd have gone worrying his parents unnecessarily.'

'But he fell quite a distance. If it was your parents or mine, they'd want to know.'

'Brian's dad's on the dole. He doesn't have the money to come rushing over to Boston.'

Elizabeth thought of Brian's open, pink face, and his undis-guised delight when they'd complimented his singing. She thought too of his precarious status in America. Not a sniff of home in three years, and no prospect of one in the near future? In the same situation, she would be unbearable.

Peter suspended his pacing. 'The poor fella is forever maintain-ing he's well on the way to getting a green card.'

'Maybe he is.'

'Come off it, Elizabeth. Every illegal you meet comes out with the same line. We have this notion that being Irish gives you some class of special status among immigrants. I bet in their neighbourhoods, the Mexicans or the Haitians or whoever convince themselves that they're the chosen ones.' The pacing started up again. 'The killer thing about Brian is that he's so talented. He was round in the apartment last week. Brought the guitar. All of us ended up singing as though our lives depended on it.' He gave her a heavy-eyed look. Elizabeth hadn't made the session because Danny hadn't been in the mood.

'I hate to ask this.' Danny had joined them. 'Do you think he's insured? What with being illegal and all.'

'Would you not lay off the damn questions for once?' said Peter. 'I reckon insurance is the least of his concerns right now.'

Undeterred, Danny began pacing in sync with the two of them. 'OK, man,' he said. 'I know you're cut up over this. Only hospitals aren't cheap. We're talking a lot of bucks here. And then there's the other thing.'

'What thing?' Peter asked.

'The cops will get involved, and they'll know in a flash that Brian has no papers.'

Peter came to an abrupt halt. With the palms of both hands he rubbed his forehead.

Elizabeth remembered reading that all hospitals smelled the same. Now she knew this wasn't true. The one hospital she'd been in at home had smelled of damp coats. Here, the scent of strong disinfectant didn't quite conceal the base notes of sweat and vomit. Along with Danny, she had been to talk to a doctor. Peter had practically shoved her in the door, arguing that authority figures always saw her as someone they could deal with.

'So,' she said, 'they can't say for definite yet, and he is pretty beat up, but they don't think there'll be any permanent damage.'

'He's badly concussed,' Danny added. 'And there's a lot of

bruising and one leg is broken in several places and there's probably other stuff too. But if it's possible to tumble from a height and be lucky, that's Brian.'

'Thank God,' said Peter.

Elizabeth saw Michelle and Ray in the throng. And there was Donal, with Rosie in tow. At such a time, she shouldn't even be aware of these things, but she couldn't help noticing what a mismatched pair they made. Donal's work shirt was flapping loose, and his trousers were at half-mast. His self-proclaimed status as County Leitrim's thinnest man was in little doubt. Next to him Rosie was all inviting curves and apple cheeks. Even after a day pushing trolleys and carrying trays, she left an aroma of shampoo in her wake.

Michelle pulled Elizabeth to one side. 'What's up, missus?'

'Your guess is as good as mine. We passed on every word the doctor said.'

'I meant between you and Danny's mother.' She paused. 'I saw him with his goofiest smile on, and you looking at him like a cat let loose in a creamery. Do I take it the news is good?'

Elizabeth smiled at the reminder of her surprising morning. 'Regina's lovely. I can't believe I was such a scaredy-cat about going to see her. She practically invited me to come and live with them.'

'Just do me a favour, would you?' said Michelle. 'Play it cool in front of Peter. He's in a bad way.'

As the afternoon blurred into evening, there was still no firm news. Nicky and Rory were tracked down. The rest of them maintained their vigil. The jury was out as to whether Brian's parents should be called. Rory said yes, while Nicky said not yet. Donal pointed out that it was already close on midnight in Ireland. Tomorrow so, everyone agreed.

Neither did any of them know what to do about the insurance issue, or what to tell the police who were bound to ask questions of his colleagues. Elizabeth presumed they'd already been to the construction site.

'I bet the cops have a good idea,' said Michelle. They were sharing a scored plastic chair, the two facing in opposite directions. 'They look at Brian. Young Irish construction worker – what are the chances he's illegal? Fairly high, I would have thought. The hospital will know that too.'

'You're right,' said Danny, who was crouching in front of them. 'No doubt, though, they'll get their money somehow.'

'Bloody vultures,' chipped in Peter.

'Vultures don't do much lifesaving,' pointed out Michelle.

'I know, I know. I just feel like hitting out at somebody. Like, fuck it, how many levels of trouble is Brian in now? Why couldn't someone have sorted a visa for him?'

Donal was sitting on the shiny hospital floor, playing with his shoe. It looked like the top was about to shear away from the sole. 'Do you know what, Petie,' he said, with uncharacteristic force, 'there's no point in blaming any American for this. If you want to blame somebody, you've got to look to home. If Brian's own country had any use for him, he wouldn't be here in the first place.'

A week later, Elizabeth, Peter and Michelle were strolling down Commonwealth Avenue, or 'Comm Ave' as Elizabeth reluctantly called it. Danny insisted that to do otherwise would mark her out as a tourist. They were going for a late Saturday breakfast in the diner where Peter did most of his eating. As they walked, Elizabeth noticed how the clusters of magnolia trees were showing the wear and tear of a hot summer. Their once bright leaves were now singed and frayed.

The Princess Diner specialised in food that was nominally Irish, like corned beef hash. The owner had been tickled when Peter told him that, even in Ireland, food had moved on. 'I swear I never had the like of this at home,' he'd said. Be that as it may, he was more than happy to get his fill of it in America.

Elizabeth was pleased to see that Peter was carrying his newspaper clippings. Once a week, his mother or another member of the O'Regan family sent a letter which included cuttings from the local paper and from the *Irish Press*. They always provided entertainment. He had half a notion about becoming a journalist and claimed it was vital he kept up with developments at home. Donal said how right he was, and why would you want to be following a real live American presidential election when you could be reading about the difficulties posed by ivy on the graveyard wall in Edenderry?

With his bacon, eggs, mushrooms, sausages, hash browns and toast piled up high, Peter spread the week's clippings out on the Formica table. Elizabeth looked at Michelle and detected badness afoot.

'Peter?' Michelle said. 'If you get a job in one of the newspapers, will all of your headlines have to start with the words "local man"?'

He didn't bother to look up. 'Michelle, you know feck all about papers. The sub-editor does the headlines.'

'So there's a whole job where you get to type "local man" all day?'

'I'm not with you.'

'You see for weeks now, I've been examining what your mam sends. And it seems to me that's how most articles are headed.'

Seeing Peter's exasperated expression, Elizabeth gave her a kick under the table.

Michelle ploughed on. 'You see there,' she pointed to the largest article, 'you have *Local Man Wins Top Award in Dublin*. And there,' a finger was jabbed at another piece, '*Local Man Wins Side of Beef in Parish Draw*. Or,' she said, 'there's always *Local Man Found on Moon ...*'

'... *with Elvis Presley*,' added Elizabeth, who had surrendered to the temptation to join in.

Peter set about gathering up his cuttings. 'I hope, girls, ye're always so easily amused.'

Elizabeth rubbed his arm. 'I'm sorry, pet. Put the papers down. We're only goofing around, as Danny would say.'

'We haven't had many laughs lately,' said Michelle.

'I won't argue with you there,' he said.

'Besides,' continued Elizabeth, 'we're jealous really. I wish I got cuttings.'

Peter drained his coffee cup and attempted to catch the eye of the waitress. 'There's a few of us going for a drink tonight. We have to talk about raising money for Brian's medical bills. Will yourself and Danny be there?'

Danny had mentioned the gathering to Elizabeth. Neither of them would be able to make it because Regina had already invited Vincent and Valerie over for dinner.

'Aw, the five of you, isn't that lovely?' said Michelle. 'You've got the feet well under the table there.'

Peter's eyebrows knotted, but he stayed quiet.

Talking about laundry and shopping, Michelle evaporated into the afternoon, leaving Peter and Elizabeth to take the scenic route home. Sometimes, she missed Peter's company. Danny was the best in the world, but if your chatter was too obscure, you had to spend so much time explaining that you were better off saying nothing to begin with. The other day, she had left him bewildered by describing a meal as so small it was practically a collation. Clearly, American Catholicism was less convoluted than the Irish version.

'As we're talking,' Peter said, 'do you think you might have reached the stage where, perhaps, it would be best to … cool it a little.'

Elizabeth lifted up her sunglasses. 'Cool what?'

'You know what I'm talking about. Has the Danny situation not got a bit heavy?'

She frowned. 'It feels OK to me.'

'I'm sure it does. He's a good-looking lad, Danny.'

'True.'

'Like, obviously, I work with him and I see him there with the shirt off and the big eyes and the big smile.'

'Are you about to come out to me or something?'

'Ah, Elizabeth, I'm trying to be serious here. I'm saying I can see what the attraction is. I mean, if I did fancy men I'd fancy him. Fair enough.'

'You've lost me, Peter.'

'I'm glad you're having a good summer. We all are. But it is only a summer fling. We'll be going home in October. Back to Ireland, where Liam lives. I know we pull the piss out of him, but he's a decent guy.'

They had come to a bench on a small patch of grass. Elizabeth sat down. She passed her sunglasses from one hand to the other and back again. 'I hear what you're saying. I do. It's … I don't think you're being fair to Danny, or to me. You're making it all sound sleazy.' Elizabeth dug her front teeth into her bottom lip. Peter remained silent. 'I have had … I am having … a brilliant time. Danny's a terrific guy. A clever guy. Kind. Ambitious. You probably don't see any of that.'

He sat down and his brown eyes locked onto hers. 'That's what I'm worried about. You have a boyfriend at home, but yourself and Danny – it's like you're joined at the hip. If you said, listen, Peter, he's a complete ride, and when we have sex the earth moves and the neighbours complain about the noise, I'd be happy that everything was cool. But it's becoming more than that.'

'You forgot the part about the angels weeping.'

He gave a careful smile. 'Like I said, we'll be home before you know it.'

Elizabeth knew she should defuse the situation. Yet she felt an instinctive need to do the opposite. So she came on out with it. Danny had suggested they go on holiday. To Vermont maybe, or Maine. They joked about whether the car would make it that far. What she might do, she explained, was put off going back to Ireland. Only for a small while, mind.

Peter's face curdled and he got to his feet. 'Ah, here we go. I've heard it all now. What are you going to do? Ring them at home and say, "Mam, Dad, I know you've been looking forward to the graduation. First child with a university degree, and all. So, sorry about this but I'm not coming back for another while because

I'm tooling around New England with my new boyfriend.' Elizabeth opened her mouth, but Peter appeared to be enjoying his eruption. 'And, while I'm on to ye, is there any chance you'd tell Liam? "Liam, old bud, sorry that you're already halfway to the airport with a bunch of flowers and an engagement ring in your arse pocket. I'm too busy swooning over this Danny boy to care. Bye now."'

They were attracting rubberneckers. Peter's anger had reached a rolling boil, however, and he didn't seem too perturbed by the audience. 'All right there, folks,' he shouted, 'you're coming to the game a bit late. You can join in if you want, though. I don't mind.'

Elizabeth felt embarrassment ripple through the small gathering, and they started to disperse. She stood up. She wasn't sure whether she was mortified or angry or upset or all three. What she did know was that a vast space had opened up between her and one of her closest friends. 'I was prepared to hear you out, Peter, but if you're going to act the bollox, you can do it on your own. Or Donal must be finished work by now. Why don't you find him and tell him how to live his life?'

'Of all people,' he roared, 'I thought I knew you. Turns out I haven't a fucking clue.'

Elizabeth began striding away.

'I'm only being your friend,' he shouted after her.

She pretended not to hear.

'I believe ye had words,' said Michelle.

Elizabeth was on her lunch break, and the two were sitting in the Public Garden, their tanned legs stretched out in front of them. Close by, a willow tree genuflected towards the pond. 'I think you'd have to say that Peter had most of the words. I sat there getting redder while half the street looked on.'

Michelle tilted her face towards the sky. 'I feared that might be the case.'

'You're not going to have a go at me too, are you?'

'Nope. Don't be too hard on him, though. He means well.'

'He went too far.'

'I think with Petie, it's like he's having a hard time accepting that normal service isn't going to be resumed. We're not going to go back to Dublin and live in a lovely student bubble where we can play at being poor, knowing Mammy and Daddy will step in if the coffers run dry. Even if it means them going without. When we go home, *if* we all go home' – she looked at Elizabeth – 'life won't be the same.'

'Sure we know that.'

Michelle kicked off one of her sandals and examined her coral-coated toenails. 'I suppose Peter wants to hold on to what he's got for as long as possible.'

Michelle was making sense, but three days on from their public set-to, Elizabeth hadn't forgiven Peter. 'He was over the top. He lit into me for suggesting I might go on holidays. Donal is forever rabbiting on about staying here as an illegal, and it doesn't knock a fidget out of him, despite what happened to Brian.'

The park was thinning out, the lunchtime sun-seekers heading back to their shops and offices. Elizabeth knew she should join them.

'I wasn't planning on telling you this,' said Michelle. 'In fact, I swore to Peter that I wouldn't. But after what happened …'

'What is it?'

'Peter blames himself for Brian's accident.'

'That's plain silly. Brian fell. It was nobody's fault.'

Michelle renewed the examination of her toes. 'Except, five minutes before, the pair of them had a blazing row. And Peter has this theory that if Brian hadn't been so agitated, he wouldn't have come a cropper. Apparently, a couple of the lads on the site think the same, which makes life kind of grim for him.'

'The poor fella,' said Elizabeth. 'Why didn't he tell me? Why didn't Danny tell me?'

'Danny doesn't know.' Michelle paused as they watched three little girls running pell-mell towards the sculptures of the ducklings. 'The argument was about the two of you.'

Elizabeth made a spluttering noise. 'What?'

'A few of them were larking around, having a smoke, and Brian came out with some line about you being the crafty girl, getting your claws into a Yank. That you'd have a green card in jig time. As you can imagine, Peter was livid.'

'I never …' Elizabeth's voice sounded unnaturally high, like her mouth was filled with helium.

'It was a joke that went wrong. That's all. And for what it's worth, Brian doesn't blame Peter in the slightest. Insists the accident was all his own clumsy fault. But if Peter was acting the eejit, well, there's your reason.'

'When you think about it, then, it's like the whole episode is my fault. Why did he bother defending me? It's not as though we've even seen that much of each other lately.' Elizabeth's eyelid was dancing like crazy. She swept up her hair and clasped the back of her neck. It felt clammy.

'Yeah,' said Michelle. 'That's Petie, though. He's a fierce loyal sort. And you're his friend.'

'Oh lord. I have to talk to him.'

'Let it be for now, would you? It'll pass.'

She needed to go away and think. If only she had known. Never in a million light years would she have spoken to Peter like she did. She realised that Michelle was still talking. Her words were fading in and out, like a radio not quite on the station. 'Are you thinking about staying an extra week or two?' she was asking. 'Or might it be longer?'

Elizabeth said nothing because the simple answer was she didn't know. She had boarded the plane in Shannon confident that her life was mapped out: a teaching diploma, a job in Thurles or Dublin, Liam, home. Then, at some point, other ideas had crept in. The tiny voice at the back of her head, the voice that had nagged her about being too cautious, had got louder and louder. Sometimes it was like a wailing banshee.

Michelle broke the silence. 'Can I ask you another question?'

'Go on.'

'Are you in love with him?'

'Danny, you mean?'

'Nah, Pope John Paul.'

Elizabeth gave the short grass a close inspection, fingering each parched blade as if it was the most fascinating substance on the planet. 'As long as we've been friends, I've had this different existence to the rest of you. You've all had these flings. The wildness, as Donal would say. Waking up in a bedsit in Rathmines, rummaging through the post in the hall on your way out, trying to see if you recognised a name.'

Michelle smiled. 'You make us sound so classy.'

'I'd only kissed two or three boys before I met Liam. And all the time I've been going out with him, he's never given me any reason to look at anyone else. I was lucky. Wasn't that what I was always being told? And I felt secure with him. Of course, that's not a word you can use when people like Orla are around. But it mattered to me.'

'Believe it or not I understand. The whole Brian episode makes you appreciate how fragile everything can be. Most people, I reckon, would see you and Liam and think you were lucky.'

Elizabeth turned to Michelle. 'In truth, I didn't come here to meet anybody. I hoped we'd have a bit of fun before the real world hit. Only now I see that … maybe I was skating along without asking any real questions.'

'So?'

'Something has happened. And I can't undo it.'

'Would you want to?'

She scrunched up her face. 'I'm so confused. The other night I was lying there beside him. And, in his sleep, Danny sometimes makes a small snuffling noise. Not a fully fledged snore. It's more gentle than that. It dawned on me how much I love that sound. I mean, how stupid is that?'

Michelle stroked her hand. 'It's not stupid at all.'

'Some days I get so guilty, I feel physically sick. I didn't think

I was capable of this much deception. But … I can't help myself. I suppose I've been knocked back by how big it all feels, if that makes sense.'

'You have it bad.'

Elizabeth looked up to the sky where just the occasional scuff of white scarred the perfect blue. She breathed in, then exhaled as slowly as she could. 'I know. But what am I going to do?'

Chapter 13

Now that September had arrived, Elizabeth felt like time was passing at warp speed. Her life with Danny and Regina had developed a rhythm of sorts, with every day bringing fresh discoveries and understanding. Try as she might, though, she couldn't get a handle on Vincent. He was as slippery as black ice, and twice as dangerous.

For a start, there was his animosity towards Ireland. No matter that he was one-eighth Irish, Vincent disliked anything to do with the place. This confused Elizabeth. After all, hadn't he grown up surrounded by Irish people? That, said Danny, was the problem. At school, he'd been given a rough time by a boy called Eddie Jennings. Eddie was a hulking redhead with ugly cornflake-shaped freckles and a hint of his father's Cork accent. The Jennings family appeared to have an unlimited membership and if they chose to pick on you, it was wise to keep a low profile because nobody was going to come to your aid. As someone who was inherently incapable of turning the other cheek, Vincent had spent a large part of his teens sparring with Eddie Jennings. And losing.

Since their return to Emerald Street, Danny and Elizabeth had seen less of Vincent. Valerie was determined to maintain contact, however, and kept inviting them over. Elizabeth wished she could relax into their company but found she was overly conscious of every word and movement, and not just her own. She couldn't stop herself from analysing the dynamics of Vincent and Valerie's relationship. Despite his boundless irascibility, she maintained the whip hand. When Elizabeth was drawn into the conversation, she felt like Vincent was waiting for an opportunity to pull her up or put her right. Inexplicably Danny would sit there, wearing his blandest face, and appear not to notice. She did her best not to say too much, which was hard. Vincent was a man who insisted the Vietnam War was a draw.

On the Friday evening of Labor Day weekend he lay prone on his sofa, flicking through a newspaper and tossing out acidic comments about every second article. Valerie was cooking dinner. Danny and Elizabeth had moved two chairs together and were engaging in some start-of-the-weekend foreplay. There was a good deal of smiling, a moderate amount of stroking and the occasional kiss.

The presidential race was at stalemate, by turns vacuous and venomous. The polls claimed it was a dead heat. Vincent was devouring the campaign, and gave the impression that he was quietly willing it to get even nastier. He was a fervent George Bush supporter (Danny was a lukewarm Dukakis man) and that week there was a hullabaloo over whether Bush's running mate, Dan Quayle, was a draft dodger. As far as Elizabeth could make out, levelling such an allegation was like claiming an Irish politician had a sneaking regard for the Black and Tans. Yet Quayle was ducking the worst of the damage.

Vincent wanted to know Elizabeth's opinion of it all. Well, on second thoughts, she was fairly sure he didn't. More likely, he wanted to break up the silent yet elaborate flirtation she was enjoying with his brother. And if he had the chance to get stuck into her political views, wouldn't that be a bonus? She attempted to fob him off with some blather about how hard it was to follow another country's election. There was an element of truth to this. Sometimes, she was genuinely bamboozled by the jargon and imagery of American politics, by the donkeys and elephants and acronyms.

Vincent was not easily dissuaded. 'Aw, Elizabeth,' he soothed, 'I'm sure you have an opinion.'

'Oh, I agree with Danny,' she said, while caressing the younger brother's forearm.

'No great surprise there.' He placed his paper on the floor and swung into a seated position. 'The Irish are never good at thinking for themselves.'

'I must say I wasn't aware of that. Are all Italians good at making gross generalisations?'

'Very funny. We're here four generations now, as American as you'll find. Not all of us feel the need to be part of a tribe.'

Danny was tapping an imaginary beat on Elizabeth's thigh which normally would be enough to distract her. 'What do you mean?' she said.

'After twenty-five years marooned among you, I've learnt a thing or two. For a start, there's the way you all band together and mouth garbage at each other about your love for Ireland, even though most of you wouldn't return if your lives depended on it. And the way you wallow in your misery, or your imagined misery. And the way you all sneer at America, yet nothing will stop you from coming over here and taking whatever handouts are on offer.'

'Irish people come here to *work*, Vincent.'

'Yeah, work *illegally*, Elizabeth.'

'I have a visa, as you know,' she said, finding it impossible to keep the indignation from her voice. 'And the people who do end up working illegally? Life is hard for them. Look at what happened to Danny's friend, Brian.'

'Dan told me about him, all right. I feel sorry for the guy, but he belongs on the first plane back to Dublin.'

Danny's tapping grew more insistent. Elizabeth's back stiffened. 'Do you know, Vincent, it's a miracle you stay in Boston at all. What with all of us Irish people polluting the place with our sneering and our misery.'

Vincent lifted one shoulder. 'Just saying. You meet guys around here who are still going on about the potato famine. We learnt about that at school. It was close on a hundred and fifty years ago. I mean, *a hundred and fifty fucking years*, and you get grown men tearing up over the damn thing. You should get over yourselves.' He picked up his paper again, as if to say, 'discussion terminated'.

Elizabeth was seething. To be fair, many older immigrants felt equally alien to her. She couldn't understand their lachrymose yearning for an Ireland that was long gone, but there was no way she was going to tolerate Vincent's snobbery. She was about to pull the paper out of his hand when Danny squeezed her knee really hard and gave her an imploring look. Not that he said anything. He just sat there humming to himself.

Elizabeth stomped the four steps into the kitchen. 'I'm sure Valerie would like a hand,' she said.

'Yerra, I don't know which Kennedy it was. Is there a Joseph?' said Donal.

'It was definitely a Kennedy. Big Kennedy head on him. Fine mouth of teeth too,' chipped in Peter. 'They can't have come cheap.'

The two were back in Lantern Street, telling Elizabeth about their All-Ireland weekend. The day before, they'd gone to a bar in West Roxbury to watch Galway beat Tipperary in the hurling final. They had crawled in at two in the morning, murdering 'The West's Awake'. That morning they'd been for a feed of corned beef and a restorative pint of milk in Peter's favourite diner. On their way home, they had come across a Labor Day Parade.

At Peter's insistence they'd shaken the hand of a tanned man with the cut of a politician about him. Although they were sure he had some connection to Irish America's most famous family, they weren't able to agree on exactly what that connection might be. Peter said that in his next letter home Donal should tell them that he'd met a Kennedy. Donal replied that if he resurrected JFK and his brother and brought the two of them home for dinner, it wouldn't be enough to impress his father.

Elizabeth's reappearance in Lantern Street was motivated by her desire to avoid Vincent. Unfortunately, she was also avoiding Peter. On Michelle's advice, she'd stayed quiet about Brian's accident. Following their row, a very Irish détente was now in place: a case of 'whatever you say, say nothing'. In their brief conversations, neither Danny nor Liam existed.

A letter from Orla had arrived, and Michelle was taking considerable pleasure in reading it aloud. The good news was that she had passed her exam; the bad news, that she was going around the twist with boredom.

'"I get up at the crack of midday",' read Michelle, '"and try to find something to do with myself. I keep drawing a blank. I swear, if one of you doesn't come home soon and rescue me from *Neighbours* and *Going for Gold*, I will go berserk."' Orla said that to counter the boredom she was applying for training courses, and had high hopes for one particular course in radio journalism.

'Maybe she's not so dizzy after all,' said Elizabeth, who was sitting on their newest piece of furniture, a brown vinyl sofa bequeathed by the girls from across the corridor. Around their parts, this was the busiest weekend of the year. Students were moving in, and other tenants were moving on. The streets were jam-packed with vans and pick-ups. Overloaded cars crawled past like a colony of multicoloured ants. There was a formality about the weekend, like it heralded the official end of summer.

'I don't know,' said Donal. 'Being stuck back in Dublin sounds kind of grim to me.'

Peter had his serious face on. 'Do you not miss home at all?'

'There's no point in lying to you, Petie. It was great to see the hurling yesterday. Being in a room with hundreds of other Irish people was mighty sport. And there's the odd person I'd love to meet up with. Other than that, not a bit of it, I'm afraid.'

'Michelle?'

'I'm with Donal. At the moment the only reason I'd head home is to spite the boys in charge. I've been thinking about what would happen if everyone decided they weren't going to be forced out. The politicians would be petrified.'

'I like your thinking,' Donal said. 'You can hear them wailing, "Why aren't ye leaving?" It's not enough to make me want to go back, mind.'

Peter turned to Elizabeth. 'I suppose there's not much point in asking you. You've barely given Ireland a thought since you got here.'

She said nothing to contradict him. He would be stunned to find out how wrong he was. Despite her summer of thrills, and despite her feelings for Danny, there were days when Elizabeth was brought up short by how homesick she could feel. Those were the days she missed everything, no matter how broken or old-fashioned or corrupt.

Had she been brave or foolish enough, this was what she would have said to Vincent. She would have said that there was a village near her home town where for the best part of a decade the main street was dominated by a pile of scrap metal, and nobody had been too bothered. She would have said that if an Irish phone box was vandalised, it was unlikely to be fixed for two months. Sometimes the news was a litany of bombings and murders and maimings. You had to jump through legal hoops to buy condoms, and you had to leave the country to get divorced. There were only two types of bread and two flavours of ice cream. Oh, and nobody turned a hair when an entire family of children emigrated. Elizabeth couldn't understand how anyone could miss such a place, yet some days she did.

Donal put down his tray and jangled the change in his pocket. Officially, his shift was over, but the cousin had sent word that he wanted to see him, and he was floundering as to what the summons was about.

There was the incident with the rock star and the towel, although no reasonable person would blame him for that. In all fairness, if you order room service you should keep your knickers on and not be diving for cover when some young lad arrives with your egg-white omelette. Had Donal owned a camera, he could have got a decent sum from one of those magazines Michelle brought home from the supermarket. And he wouldn't have to worry about meeting the cousin.

Then there was what the staff called the 'war zone premium'.

Within days of Donal's arrival, a colleague with family in Beirut had put him wise to this. 'If anyone asks what part of Ireland you're from,' he'd said, 'be sure to say the north. I guarantee you, the tip will be better.' Maybe Charlie had heard about that.

To tell the truth, he wasn't in any huge hurry back to the apartment. Between Brian's accident and the row with Elizabeth, there were days when Peter walked around under a glower of grievances. He must have a word. There was nothing they could do about Brian's troubles, and all the sulking in the world wouldn't change Elizabeth's mind about Danny. She continued to stump up the rent every week, although he didn't see that continuing for much longer. It was just as well, then, that he had a plan; Rosie could move in. He hadn't worked out the finer details, but he was convinced it was a good idea. She was constantly cribbing about one of her flatmates, and their place was an even worse dump than Lantern Street.

Donal rapped on the office door and barged on in before Charlie had the chance to open his mouth. The cousin had contracted a sort of an American accent so that he sounded like an Irish character in a Hollywood movie. You'd be tempted to ask how things were in Glocca Morra. Mind you, despite assiduous grooming, he looked as Irish as Donal; like he'd just stepped in from a force ten gale.

'So,' said Charlie, who was brandishing a spiral-bound notebook. 'Let's skip the formalities here. How much is it we pay you to work room service in the Five Oceans Hotel?'

Donal sensed there may be a bit of game-playing going on, only he wasn't able to identify the game. 'Five dollars and fifty cents an hour,' he said.

'And how much do we pay you to make up bullshit stories about Ireland?' Charlie's voice rose as he answered his own question. 'Yes, you're right, Donal. That would be zero dollars and zero cents an hour.'

'Well—'

'No, Donal, let me do the talking for a minute now. You've done plenty already. I got you a job here, the finest hotel in Boston, and this is how you repay me.'

'Honestly, Cathal—'

The cousin's face was growing redder. 'How many times do I have to tell you about the goddamn name?'

'Sorry, Charlie, I'm not sure what you've been hearing. Whatever it was, I swear there was no harm intended.'

'No harm intended?' His voice was ratcheted up to maximum volume now. 'You told the general manager of this hotel that I was the inspiration for a film. Let me see if I have this right, a film in which Mickey Rourke plays an IRA man who blows up a bus and goes on the run. And there was,' he paused, 'no fucking harm intended.'

Now that he was hearing it back, Donal could see why Charlie might be put out. 'I think I, eh, may have overstepped the mark there. It was such a nonsensical story, I didn't think he'd take it seriously. Sure, you don't look at all like Mickey Rourke. And the film – *A Prayer for the Dying*? Total rubbish. Rourke's accent is dire. The Hollywood boys should leave Ireland alone.'

'Ah for Pete's sake, I don't give two hoots what the bloody movie is like. You can't go around saying this stuff. What were you at?'

Donal was getting nervous. What if he got the sack? He was not too nervous, however, to notice that the cousin's accent was returning to its origins. If this kept going, he'd be pure Leitrim again.

He explained how he'd realised that many Americans had an idea of Ireland that was rooted somewhere in the 1950s. 'Not that I blame them,' he added. 'Why should they know or care about Ireland? And we're as bad when it comes to America. Sure, Irish people are forever waltzing into Cheers expecting to meet Sam and Woody. So, I decided to tell the odd story. For the sport, I suppose. And I kept on pushing it, to see how much I could get away with.'

Charlie told him that clearly he could get away with a lot.

Following his conversation with the general manager, he'd made some enquiries. He discovered that several hotel employees were of the belief that the Irish government had banned Christmas, or at least its non-religious aspects. 'Too expensive,' Donal had assured them. 'Too much jollity.'

'Here's another one,' continued the cousin as he leafed through his notebook. 'The Irish Army are so hard up that when they're on exercises, rather than using ammunition they shout "bang bang". And on government training courses, you're taught how to answer the telephone with a banana because it's cheaper than buying a phone.' He threw the notebook on to his desk. 'Jesus, Donal, did it not occur to you that you couldn't keep on telling lies? Sooner or later, you were bound to get caught.'

Donal didn't have the heart to tell him that those last two stories were true. 'I'm sorry it got out of hand,' he said, making a mental note to tell the gang in the apartment that the yarn about Charlie not being able to read or write was bunkum too. He had a degree in hotel management from the Regional Tech in Galway.

Charlie's head swayed from side to side. 'How much longer are you planning on staying here?'

'All going well, up until November or so. Then Rosie and myself are going travelling. She's deferring her last year of college, or uni as she calls it.'

'God help her,' said Charlie, before resting his head in his hands. After a minute or so, he spoke again. 'I have to give you a formal warning about your behaviour. Heaven only knows what I'll put on the disciplinary form, though. I don't think there's a category for reinventing national history.'

Donal, wonder-struck that he still had a job, broke into a smile. 'Cathal,' he said, 'you're a true Gael.'

Chapter 14

Cindy's new boyfriend was called Greg Brady.

'Yeah, there's a bunch of us at home,' he said. 'No girls, though. Six boys.' He shook Elizabeth's hand, and she was tempted to check that her arm was still in its socket. Greg was so impressively built, he made Cindy's old boyfriend appear positively puny.

The four of them had gone for a drink. 'Being grown-ups,' Danny called it. In the handful of times Elizabeth had met Cindy, she'd gradually come to change her view of the girl. She was a far more interesting character than some of her witterings might suggest. You could be listening to her beauty pageant chronicles when out of nowhere she'd say something about her family or about Danny that would leave your mouth gaping open.

Elizabeth had expected Greg to be a grunt and swagger sort, but he was actually quite a charmer. His family were originally from County Cavan, so she asked if they ate their dinner out of a drawer. He looked puzzled. 'It's a joke at home,' she explained. 'Cavan people have a reputation for being mean.' He laughed and said he'd have to buy her another drink, just to prove the trait hadn't crossed the Atlantic. She would happily have chatted away to him, only this would have meant abandoning Danny to the lure of his ex. Perhaps it was Greg's doing, but Cindy was gleaming like a newly polished kettle.

Once or twice when they'd been over in Lantern Street, Danny had been forced to endure a conversation about people from college. He would sit on one of their bockety old chairs, trying to look like he cared, while the quirks of various characters were dissected. Right then Elizabeth knew exactly how he must have felt, for Danny and Cindy were midway through a series of reminiscences about people and places that meant nothing to her.

'Of course that was the night Hunter Nolan lost his pants,' Danny said.

'Oh my God, Hunter with the extra-long arms! Whatever happened to him?' giggled Cindy.

'Joined the military like his brother Mikey,' chimed in Greg, who appeared to be acquainted with most of the folks under discussion.

And on it went. As time clicked by, Elizabeth became more anxious. She searched for any opening in the conversation so she could break in and pretend that she wasn't an outsider. The problem was, the lives of the three people beside her overlapped so that every anecdote shot off on a host of tangents. How long, she wondered, before you had a shared history like that? Or would she always be an alien? As she sipped her drink, another thought struck her; Cindy the real person was altogether more daunting than Cindy the cartoon beauty queen.

The next day she was in the kitchen with Regina, folding sheets. The gentle scent of fresh laundry filled the room. Elizabeth remembered as a little girl helping her mother to do the same job. She smiled at Regina who was halfway through a formidable pile of ironing, the iron hissing and gurgling beside her. 'Coffee?'

'I will thanks, honey,' replied Regina. 'Two sugars. Then you can sit down and tell me what's wrong.'

Elizabeth filled the kettle. 'Is it that obvious?'

'What's he done?'

She placed two mugs on the counter and spooned in the coffee. 'It's not Danny.' She was on the edge of saying, 'it's everyone else', but stopped herself. Vincent was a gigantic pain in the arse but he was also Regina's son. She decided to focus on her other irritant. 'It's that Cindy Martinez girl. I understand that she's had a tough life, so I shouldn't give out about her. And I'm not even sure that she does it deliberately. But she sticks to Danny like a big, glossy limpet.'

Regina took a mouthful of coffee. 'And he laps it up, huh?'

'Revels in it.'

'Elizabeth, Danny's not stupid. As vain as a peacock. And far too fond of flattery. But not stupid.' She paused. 'Does all this concern about Miss America mean you're planning on staying with us?'

'Gosh. I—'

'Or will you be going back to your other boyfriend?'

Elizabeth felt the warmth spreading up from her neck. Her cheeks and ears burned. She had no idea Danny's mother knew about Liam. Before a coherent reply came to her, Regina spoke again.

'Danny never said a word, by the way. Vincent thought I should know. "I don't need to hear any tales from you," I said. "I'm sure Elizabeth will tell me herself." You will, won't you?'

'Oh.' Elizabeth realised she was unfolding and refolding a pile of T-shirts. 'It's … well, it's something I have to sort out.' For a minute or two, a strained silence hung over them. The only sound came from the spitting of the iron. She wished she'd never mentioned Cindy's name.

'There is a boyfriend at home, then?'

Elizabeth had no choice but to tell the full story.

'So, correct me, if I've got this wrong,' Regina said. 'This boy Liam thinks you're living with your Irish friends and working every hour that God sends? And you call him and tell him everything is fine, and you'll be home soon?'

'Yes,' said Elizabeth, her voice scarcely louder than a whisper.

'And Danny knows all about this?'

'We never talk about the phone calls. We rarely talk about Liam.'

'And do you intend to go back to Ireland and take up where you left off? Is that what you want to do?'

'No.' Elizabeth held a T-shirt up to her face, like a child pretending to hide. 'Only it's not that simple.'

Steam clouded Regina's face. 'I don't know what to say, Elizabeth. Except it sounds to me like one or all of you are likely to get hurt here.' Her voice wasn't unkind, but it was hard. Harder than Elizabeth was used to. Regina reached for her cigarettes. 'Isn't it about time you started telling the truth?'

If he had set out to design a bad Friday, Danny could not have done a better job. He had about ten thousand reasons to be in a black mood. Had anyone asked, which of course they hadn't because no one gave a damn, he would not have known where to start his list.

At work he was being smothered by the incompetence of others. Why couldn't folks do their job right? Someone, not him, had got a crucial measurement wrong, and no one, including him, had identified the mistake until it was too late. An afternoon of recriminations about waste and time and money had followed.

He was due to visit his dad the next day. It wasn't the visiting itself that was the issue, but the fact that more agreeable alternatives were now darting around his head. The thing was, if he didn't make the effort, none of the others would. He had suggested to Elizabeth that she might come along. 'I'm helping Rosie move into Lantern Street,' she'd said, although what help a grown woman needed to put a backpack in the corner and roll out a sleeping bag was beyond him.

On top of this, he had agreed to go out with Vincent and Valerie the following night. The overture had come from Valerie, so he couldn't say no. Elizabeth would not be pleased.

Tonight the two of them were due to go to the movies, only after the day he'd endured, Danny wanted to go home and stay there. Elizabeth would understand. That was one of the great things about her; you could tell her you were fixing to spend the evening examining the contents of the city dump, and she'd probably say, 'Grand so, is what I'm wearing OK?' Afterwards, she'd most likely give you her little smile and claim it had all been way better than expected. She saw merit in everything. Except Vincent. There was a flip side to this. It was possible to take the stoic, unassuming attitude too far. Occasionally, he wished she assumed a little more. If you asked him, she was better than she'd been brought up to believe.

Danny was flat out on the sofa, blowing smoke rings at the ceiling, when the first thread unravelled. Elizabeth called to say she was going for a drink with a bunch of the women from work. 'I'll meet you at the cinema,' she said. He told her how he was feeling and, unexpectedly, she began to grizzle about being the last person in Boston to see *The Last Temptation of Christ*. He said it wasn't a night for braving a crowd of holy rollers. She replied that they were all protested out by now, so he had no cause to worry. The news that his mother was spending the evening with Teresa turned out to be his trump card. The prospect of having the house to themselves again appealed to her. 'Just a quick one, so,' she promised.

By his reckoning, she must have had at least three quick ones, and possibly four, by the time she breezed in, full of nonsense about Jackie saying she should get her hair permed or frosted or whatnot. Straight up, he wasn't really listening. As much as he loved women, female fripperies bored the ass off of him. Or they did when he'd had a bad day.

'We can go tomorrow night,' she said.

'Go where?'

Half-cut, because in true Elizabeth style she'd neglected to eat, she started to cover his face with kisses. 'To the cinema, of course.'

Normally, he would return those kisses and then some. Tonight, he wasn't up for it. As she might say, he wasn't himself. 'Ah, there's a tiny problem there, darling. I told Valerie we'd meet up with them tomorrow.'

Instantly her mouth curled. 'That's fantastic. Saturday night with Vincent? What a treat.'

'It's two weeks since we've seen them. You have to see him sometimes.'

'You should have given me more notice. That way I could have wiped my mind clean of all thoughts for fear that any would offend him.'

'Ah, baby.'

'No, that wouldn't be enough. Would it?' She gazed at him, her hands all the while engaged in theatrical flourishes. 'Because my very existence seems to offend the man. Why don't you go along on your own and tell him I've dropped off the face of the earth. That way we'll all be happy.'

Danny smoothed a hand over his hair. This was putting the seal on one lousy day. 'Listen to me, darling, you're being too sensitive. Everybody falls out with Vincent all the time. That's what he's there for.'

'He was dismissive of me.'

'He's been dismissive of me since the day I was born.'

'It's not a joke, Danny.'

'I'm not saying it is. You won't change him. You'll just have to learn to ignore his worst excesses. And, let's be honest here, Elizabeth, was there not a *tiny* element of truth in what he said?' Immediately, Danny saw he had made a huge mistake.

Elizabeth's eyes narrowed and she practically hissed her reply. 'Not you as well.' She hesitated. 'But silly me. I forgot. You're the one person who never challenges Vincent, even when he's trashing your girlfriend.'

Danny's head was sore. If there was never a good time for this type of scene, right then was definitely the worst time. He wanted to mollify her, to soothe her and then tomorrow, or sometime soon, they would talk about this rationally. 'I don't agree with most of what Vincent says. He's still my brother, though. And my friend. We're the same, you know.'

'You are not the same.'

He produced his biggest smile. That always worked. 'Well, obviously, I got the looks and the brains. Other than that …'

Far from damping down the argument, he had sent it off in another direction. Elizabeth insisted he was smarter than his brother. He knew she meant well, yet he couldn't prevent himself from disagreeing. 'I'm just inquisitive,' he insisted. Unbelievably, she got even more worked up.

'I'm sorry, Danny,' she said in a strange frosty tone, 'you're not like Vincent.'

'And I'm sorry, Elizabeth, I don't see anything wrong with being like Vincent.'

She made a noise that sounded a small bit like *hmmph*, then there came a *tuh* and a *hah*. He was beginning to think the worst may have passed when she came out with a line that he couldn't let go. It resurrected all the awfulness of the day.

'We wouldn't be having this stupid conversation, if one of the lads at work hadn't annoyed you,' she said. 'And it's not fair that you're taking it out on me.'

Danny stood up and took an envelope from the pocket of his jeans. 'Not fair? That's bullshit, Elizabeth. You're one of the main reasons I'm so worked up. And who'd blame me when I have to put up with crap like this.' He tossed the envelope, a creased, grubby-looking article, onto the table.

The envelope was folded over, so Elizabeth wasn't able to see all the details. She didn't have to. She knew the letter was for her and she knew who had written it.

'Peter gave it to me,' Danny said, in an unfamiliar tone. 'He said, "Will you pass this on. It's from her other boyfriend." He practically sneered at me.'

'He doesn't sneer.'

'I don't give a damn about Peter's facial expressions. It was fucking humiliating. And you talk about stuff not being fair? Are you writing to Liam all this time, telling him you're missing him and all?' Danny kept using his snarling tone. She wished he'd stop. The set of his face was all wrong too.

'I owe him two letters,' she said. 'Three now.'

'I owe him,' he mocked. 'Vincent was right about this much anyway. I do get myself into some dumb situations.'

Elizabeth hated what happened next. She began to cry, and even as a young girl, she had rarely cried. Once, she'd gone over the handlebars of her bicycle and her face had been all grazed, and even then there hadn't been a peep out of her. She remembered her father saying how proud he was of her behaviour. It might not have been so bad now if she had shed a solitary elegant tear. Instead what felt like a dozen of the things ran down her cheeks, and she heaved big ugly sobs.

Danny held her and let her weep onto his shoulder. He smelled of wood and cigarettes and sweat. She knew it was ridiculous to find comfort in the smell of anybody's sweat, yet she did. For all that, her tears continued to hiccup out. He said he was so sorry and he hated tears and please would she stop shaking because he really did hate tears.

In due course, the tears did stop, although it was an age before the tremors fully subsided. She apologised too, saying she wouldn't change a hair on his head. 'Not a hair,' she repeated.

But she didn't mention Liam, and neither did he. The closest they came was when Danny said they would have to talk. She said, 'I know.' He said, 'Not tonight, huh?' She said, 'But soon.'

Their conversation remained disjointed, like each was scared that even one breath out of place would upset the other. When Danny left the room, Elizabeth buried the letter in her bag.

Jaded with emotion, they went to bed and even though they made love, it wasn't right. They were distracted and out of sync. Not the real them.

Chapter 15

The following morning, Elizabeth returned to Lantern Street to find a poster of Mickey Rourke in the front room. Dashing out the door to work, Michelle admitted responsibility but would say no more.

'You'll have to ask Donal,' she laughed.

He was at the hotel and afterwards was going to gather up Rosie's belongings. According to Michelle, Peter was 'taking his bad humour for a walk'. She then thought better of this and said that he'd gone to see Brian. The news there wasn't good. The INS, the immigration officials, had come calling, and he was doing everything possible to stave off deportation. Nicky and Rory were convinced they would get caught up in the debacle and were scared to set foot in their own apartment. Friends in America and Ireland were trying to raise money, but Brian didn't know how he would pay his medical bills. Oh, and he was maundering around the place on crutches and existing on industrial-sized doses of painkillers. 'A great ad for staying at home,' according to Peter.

Elizabeth couldn't remember the last time she'd been on her own in the apartment. It must have been at the start of the summer. Back when they were convinced Ireland would win the European Championships; when the weather had been so hot that walking out into it was like opening the oven door on Christmas Day. In other words, a lifetime ago.

She had come close to caving in when Danny asked again if she would go with him to see Dino and Bellissa. Truly, he was the most persuasive man she'd ever met. He sat at the kitchen table with his hangdog expression and his sorry-looking nails and appeared so glum that you wanted to say, 'OK, whatever it takes.' But they were still circling each other, weighing up each word for fear it should cause offence, and she couldn't spend a day like that. What she needed was a little time to herself. Besides, her eyes remained swollen from the night before, and she didn't want Dino thinking his son had gone downmarket. So, as gently as possible, Elizabeth had declined the invitation. 'Next time, baby,' she'd said. 'I promise.'

The mid-September weather was less sunny and the nights carried a keener edge. But that Saturday afternoon had a mellow warmth, and the roof beckoned. She picked up her sleeping bag and a pile of Michelle's supermarket magazines. Danny was reading one of her birthday presents, *Bonfire of the Vanities*. Only that morning she'd been about to ask how he was getting on, and had then checked herself. She didn't want to make it sound like she was correcting his homework. That's how wary she felt.

Danny suspected that a curse had been placed over his weekend. Driving home, he was furious with his father. Dino had got it into his head that they should sell the house on Emerald Street. 'You'll be moving on soon enough,' he'd said. 'And Regina will hardly want all that space.' The way he told it, you would think they were living in a gilded mansion, rather than a three-bedroom house on a rickety old street. And, anyhow, what business was it of his?

Danny had wanted to say all of this and more. Instead he'd confined himself to a few non-committal nods. He couldn't bear the thought of another row, especially with his father. To be honest, the man was looking old. He was ten years older than Regina which made him, what, sixty-three? These days that was nothing. Yet his dad, who Danny always pictured as big and vital, looked unreasonably tired. Withered, almost.

Bellissa hadn't been there which was a nuisance because he would like to have asked if things were OK. There had been no point in asking the old man. He would have huffed and puffed and still not told the truth.

Dino being off-colour wasn't enough to cool Danny's anger. He hoped his mother didn't get wind of this house-selling nonsense. He noticed one of Elizabeth's hairclips on the dash – a scrap of green velvet. There were pieces of her everywhere. It was a shame she hadn't come along. Without even trying, she would have charmed Dino. And it would have been nice to show her off, to say, 'Hey, look what a classy woman I can attract.'

Last night had been dreadful, but he didn't believe his reaction to the letter was wrong. It was Elizabeth who was out of line here, stringing Liam along. The poor sucker was over there in his small town thinking she was saving herself for him. It was high time the two of them sat down and thrashed it all out. He knew he wasn't blameless; he'd been content to let the situation drift. If anything, she was worse.

First things first, though. Danny was gnarled and raggedy, and there were only two cures for that. The first was to get drunk. Properly drunk. Vincent said he'd invited a bunch of others along, and that was good. His brother and Elizabeth wouldn't have to engage too much. Tomorrow they could talk about the future.

It was funny her saying she never cried because he had seen her cry. A couple of weeks back, they'd been making love when her eyes filled up. In no time at all her face was wet. She apologised and said she didn't know what she was thinking of, that the tears had caught her unawares.

Danny was first to arrive, and he set up camp in a far corner of Whispers. It tended to get crowded and he wanted to have a drink or two in peace, as far away as possible from the mayhem at the bar. Whispers was a place he didn't particularly like. Not alone did it have a God-awful name, there was a shade too much plastic for him. Vincent might mock, but in his book there was nothing wrong with O'Mahoney's. At least the dirt was honest. This place reminded him of Cindy. She'd always liked the music. That was plastic too. Cindy listened to Gloria Estefan and Tiffany and such-like garbage.

Vincent was unlikely to be drinking in O'Mahoney's any time soon. The previous weekend he'd got smashed and roared, 'INS, INS.' The suggestion that there might be immigration officers about had caused the customers to scatter at top speed. When they'd discovered it was a hoax, they'd been mad as hell, and you were better off not annoying those guys.

Danny had already knocked back two beers and a whisky by the time Vincent and Valerie arrived. Vincent must have been warned about his conduct because, as phoney as you please, he was full of enquiries about Elizabeth. 'I know Ma loves having her about the place,' he said, while Val stood beside him smiling encouragingly, as if she was controlling his strings.

As it happened, Ma did like having her around. She didn't have to say it. He knew from the way she fussed, telling her not to lose weight or she'd feel the cold come the winter. He figured this doubled as a hint to him to get a move on and regularise the situation. It was great the way the two of them were so tight. He even enjoyed it when they ganged together to make fun of him.

He got a beer for Vincent and a tonic for Valerie who said she was driving. That he didn't understand; they lived four blocks away. They must be getting lazy in their old age. While he was at the bar, he downed another Jack. It delivered the desired kick – tingling and burning all the way down. He saw two guys from high school. He hadn't met them in an age, and they were all on for catching up. 'Wait up, boys,' he said, 'I'll be right back.' He deposited the drinks with Vincent and Valerie who'd been joined by several others. By the time he returned to the boys from school, they'd lined up another beer. Danny was feeling slightly blurred, and that was exactly how he wanted it.

Elizabeth woke to the sound of high-pitched laughter and the sight of Donal standing over her with a cup of water. She shrieked, and he backed off. The laughter belonged to Rosie who was clutching a bottle of sparkling wine.

'We're celebrating Miss Marsh's arrival,' said Donal as he

attempted to tickle his girlfriend with one hand. 'Would you like to come down and join us?'

Elizabeth rubbed her eyes. 'Why not?'

'Do be careful, Donal,' said Rosie, 'or I'll drop the wine.'

Elizabeth wished she spoke like Rosie. She had the loveliest English accent, not royal family-strangulated, but properly well spoken like a BBC newsreader. One thing she couldn't do was pronounce her boyfriend's name. The best she managed was 'Donnell'. Like the infatuated man he was, he insisted this was an improvement on his real name. Until she'd met Rosie, Elizabeth had never given much thought to her own voice. By comparison, she sounded like a complete bogger. Donal said not to worry; the way she was headed, she'd be dropping her 'r's soon enough, and then she'd have a whole new set of problems.

Up on the roof, she'd thought about the night before and about her conversation with Regina. It was well gone the time to have a proper talk with Danny. Not just about Vincent, but about the future.

Elizabeth and Rosie shared a fondness for Fleetwood Mac so they cranked up the music and, with mugs of wine in hand, they danced around the front room. When 'Seven Wonders' came to an end, Elizabeth rewound the cassette and played it again. That song always made her think of Danny, even though he didn't like Fleetwood Mac and said there were hundreds, *thousands* of better songs she could choose. Bless his heart, he was such a musical snob. There wasn't much crossover in their tastes. Neil Young and Bruce Springsteen were about all they agreed on.

From a battered tin, the sort old lads in Ireland used to store their tobacco, Rosie plucked out a joint. She appeared to have a row of the things, all neatly rolled like a line of cheroots. 'A leaving present from one of the guys in my old gaff,' she explained.

Donal sat under Mickey Rourke and pronounced himself as happy as a trout. Elizabeth was reminded of the conversation she'd had with Danny on the night of the incident. She was about to give Donal a similar warning but, as her dad would say, she saved her breath to cool her porridge. Why give out to Donal for being happy?

At the thought of Syl, she couldn't help herself; she giggled. What would he make of this scene?

'What would the who make of the what?' asked Donal.

She hadn't realised she was talking out loud. 'I was trying to imagine what my mam and dad would say if they could see us.'

Donal passed her the joint and gurgled with laughter. 'Elizabeth's old man is kind of traditional,' he said to Rosie. 'Well, I'd bet, Lizzy, that if poor Syl had any inkling of your antics, he'd be swimming the Atlantic with his hurley strapped to his back. He'd scoop you up and leather you all the way home. And Stacia's knees would be worn out from saying novenas. Every saint in the heavens would be asked to intercede.'

The three of them sat there and laughed at everything and laughed at nothing until Michelle bounded in the door from work, dark curls bouncing in about four different directions at once. She was in a huge hurry because she was meeting Ray. Before disappearing in the direction of the bedroom, she cocked her head at Elizabeth who was all made up and rigged out in her birthday dress. 'Should you not be with Danny, missus? You don't want him getting worried.'

'I hate to say this, Dan. It's looking like you've been stood up.' Vincent was sitting across from his brother, leaning in and finding it hard to put a veil over his smugness.

'I haven't been stood anything, Vincent. She'll be here soon.'

The bar was creaking with people. Everywhere Danny looked there were faces from his past. Mostly, he was happy to see the men. Seeing the women reminded him how quickly a guy got out of touch. It was a shame that some of them appeared so hostile towards him. He noticed two or three shooting evils in his direction before stroking the arm of the guy they were with, as if to say, 'I did very well for myself, thanks.' Although he knew it was no reason to brag, he was amused that he couldn't quite put a name to one of the arm-strokers. Layla? Laura? Lola? If memory served, she'd had wicked long nails and had lacerated his back.

He'd lost count of how much he'd had to drink. Enough, probably. He was absolutely trashed. He wasn't ready to come down just yet, though, and that's what would happen if he stopped drinking now. He'd get a headache and come over all morose. The book they'd given him in the public library said that depression was hereditary and, occasionally, the idea disturbed him. What if he ended up like Ma – sad and fearful and disconnected? Ah, hell, that wasn't any way to be thinking on a Saturday night. What he needed was Elizabeth. Where was she? He was happy to feign indifference because he didn't want anyone thinking he'd turned into a sad sap who got lonesome if his girl wasn't there. All the same, he hoped she turned up soon. Was the no-show connected to last night? Or was she still worked up at the idea of meeting Vincent? Perhaps he should call the apartment. The problem was, he'd have to go out to find a phone, and that would be a pain in the ass. Chances were she was on her way. For all he knew, there might be a delay on the T or something. Yeah, that was probably it.

Danny registered upheaval beside him. Folks were standing up to let other folks in. There was a lot of bunching of knees and nudging and shuffling. Another bottle of beer was placed in front of him.

There was a delay on the T. Only ten minutes, but it was all stacking up. When she got to Park Street, Elizabeth decided she would have to find a bathroom. That diversion took another ten minutes and she began to get hassled. She urged herself to calm down. Hopefully, she wasn't talking out loud any more.

This was her first time going to this Whispers place. Danny said she wouldn't like it, and his judgement was enough for her. She didn't have to stay for too long. One drink, a bit of God bless all here, and they could go home. He would want the same.

When at last she got in the door, she was struck by how bright the place was. Never a good sign. A couple who lived further down

Emerald Street nodded in acknowledgement, and near the bar she spotted two of the men who worked with Danny and Peter. She waved, and they called her on over. Best not be rude, she thought. She would find Danny in a moment, or better yet, he might see her. Elizabeth inched towards the construction lads. They wanted to talk about Brian and the accident. Danny was around somewhere, they said. They'd had a beer or two with him earlier.

After a few minutes, she spotted Valerie at the far end of the room. Valerie signalled as if to say, 'At last.' Elizabeth mouthed 'sorry', and held up a hand to say 'five minutes'. Not far from Val, she recognised Vincent. His back was turned, his head shaking vigorously. No doubt, some misfortunate character was being put straight about something.

And there in the corner, his shoulders slumped, was Danny. He was talking to Cindy. Nothing short of shooting would get rid of that girl. She was falling out of a black lacy top with a deep V-neck. Elizabeth would have to go over and move her on. And while she was at it, she'd advise her to buy a top that wasn't three sizes too small. Greg must be around somewhere. For a moment, she resumed her conversation with the construction lads.

Elizabeth would never be sure why she turned around again so quickly. It was almost as if some previously unknown sense told her what was about to happen.

As she turned, Cindy was touching Danny's cheek. Slowly, he ran a finger down the side of her face. She leaned in like it was second nature to her, like that's what she was there for. They kissed. Their every movement seemed to have slowed. Danny put a hand on one of Cindy's breasts. She broke away, smiled at him. There was a roaring sound in Elizabeth's ears, like she was under water. The kissing resumed.

She looked away and attempted to run towards the door, except the bar was too busy. As she bobbed and weaved she bumped into people and sent a drink spinning into the air. 'Stupid bitch. Why can't you mind what you're doing,' one woman shouted. Elizabeth didn't care. She couldn't watch any more.

Chapter 16

Elizabeth had read countless books where people complained of a bad feeling in the pit of their stomach. Yet it wasn't the pit of your stomach you needed to worry about at all. Feeling funny there was great. That was the sensation she got when Danny walked in and kissed her hard, or when he whispered something outrageous to her in a public place. No, it was the feeling at the bottom of your throat that you needed to be warned about: the terrible catch and the rush of salty liquid into your mouth.

She tore back to the T station at such a clip that she was walking up Lantern Street before she had fully absorbed the scene in the bar. This was a blessing because she couldn't have handled getting emotional on public transport. By the time the real tears hit, and by the time she had to spit out the salty liquid, she was only a few steps from home.

She hoped Donal and Rosie had gone to bed because she didn't want to face them. She wanted to sit in the dark and unpick her thoughts and regain her composure. She was at the top of the stairs, nearly at the apartment door, when she found she had forgotten her key. She knocked, gently at first, followed by a harsher volley, then an-all out hammering. No one came.

She paced the corridor for a minute or two before trying again. No answer. Both Rosie and Donal were working in the morning; they had to be there. She hollered. Another door opened, and a woman began to complain. When she caught sight of Elizabeth, she changed tack and asked if she was OK. Elizabeth gave a small nod, and the woman went back to bed. More than once that summer she had cursed the fact that there was a gaggle of strangers parading around the apartment. The one night an extra pair of ears was called for, the front room was bare.

It hit once more. Finding it hard to breathe, she rolled herself into a ball and made a slight sound. Not a whimper, it was more guttural than that. She rocked backwards and forwards and prayed no one would see her. Slowly, she came to realise that she was being punished. Well, perhaps 'punished' was overdoing it. She was being taught a lesson. That was it.

What registered was that this wasn't about Danny. For really, what had he done? He had got drunk and kissed Cindy. Maybe he'd been kissing her all night, although Elizabeth guessed not. Maybe he was making love to her at that very moment. Again, she guessed not. This was about her own behaviour which was far less forgivable.

She remembered the letter from Liam, the one she'd hidden at the bottom of her bag. She'd read it that afternoon before falling asleep. It was so kind and concerned. He was worried that he hadn't heard from her. Every time he called, she was out. Was there a problem? he wondered. Her parents were worried too. Whatever about me, he said, do write to them, because Syl is fierce stressed about losing his job.

And what had been her response? She'd got stoned with Donal and Rosie and pulled the piss out of her dad. It was hardly surprising that she spent half her time either crying or shouting. As the same man might say, she had lost the run of herself. She'd been living in a bubble, pretending she was someone else. And her treatment of her lovely, dependable Liam was little short of disgusting.

The time had come to put an end to her fantasising. She had taken everything too far. It wasn't so much that she was at odds with everyone else, which she was. She was at odds with herself. And, while she was at it, how pathetic was her arrogance? Thinking that more than one man might want her, and that this was a problem?

Elizabeth lay on the carpet, her brain racing and jumping.

Later – she reckoned about two hours later – she heard a creak from inside the apartment followed by the flush of the toilet. She tapped on the door. It opened a sliver and a confused Rosie stared at her.

'Terribly sorry, forgot my key,' she said, as if she was sailing in from a wonderful night.

Rosie drawled something about it being almost time to get up, and disappeared.

In the dark, Elizabeth ripped off her dress and wriggled into her sleeping bag. Incredibly, she fell asleep.

Danny woke shortly after ten with a mouth like animal hide, a steel band tightening around his skull and a sense that something was missing. He took off his clothes and went back to sleep.

Around midday he was roused by his mother. Vincent was on the phone and wanted to talk. 'I'll call him back,' he groaned. Speaking hurt.

There was a brief lull while she delivered the news.

'He's insisting, Danny. You know what he's like. Anyhow, isn't it about time the two of you got up? Morning, Elizabeth,' she trilled.

Danny sat on the stairs wrapped in the old bathrobe that Elizabeth usually wore. His hands trembling, he gripped the phone and croaked to Vincent about Elizabeth not turning up. He could hear his brother's breath, heavy and slow.

'Valerie,' Vincent yelled. 'You ought to talk to him.'

'God, Vincent. Tone down the voice, would you man? I'm suffering here.'

Valerie came on the line and asked what he remembered.

'Bits,' he said. He recalled talking to lots of folk. Cindy turned up, but by that point he was totally out of it and … 'Oh hell. Oh Jesus.' He hesitated. 'It's coming back to me. You—'

'I pulled the pair of you apart. Vincent brought you home.'

'I remember that too: puking on the street.'

'And on Vincent.'

'At least Elizabeth wasn't there. She didn't see what happened.'

'This won't make you feel any better.' Valerie's voice, soft as it was, drilled through his head. 'She was there. She saw Cindy nuzzling into you, and you not putting up too much of a fight and she left.'

'Why didn't—'

'I tried to find her, only she was gone. Between you and Vincent, I wouldn't blame her if she never wanted to see us again.'

All the little men in his head were hammering and banging and clattering. There were a couple of particularly persistent fellows at the back of his eyes. Ma trudged past, wearing a look that was almost funereal.

'Danny, are you there?'

'Yeah, yeah. What am I going to do, Val?'

'You're going to get your act together, and go on over to Brighton and apologise like you've never apologised before.'

He didn't want to say anything much to his mother, although she'd already twigged that something was up. When he explained, she told him he was a fucking fool, and she never swore. She said she'd fix breakfast.

The thought was enough. He went to the bathroom, kneeled down and threw up. Although his stomach was empty, he continued heaving. He was reminded of this prank that Elizabeth said she and her friends pulled when someone had a bad hangover. They kept naming revolting foods, like runny eggs and gristly meat, until their victim had to puke.

The floor was cold and hard against his legs. Danny knew he should have a shower, but he wasn't sure he'd be capable of standing for long enough. He needed a chair, like an old man. He was a shocking lightweight. Shocking. He'd have a coffee first, take a handful of painkillers. After that, he'd be fit for what had to be done.

Ma had other ideas. 'You can't wait any longer. Call her now.' She handed him the phone. He was still wearing Elizabeth's bathrobe. It smelled of lavender.

The first time there was no answer. Danny wondered where she was. He'd go over there, sit outside until she came back. The second time, he heard a click, and a familiar voice said hello.

'Uh, hi there, Peter. Is Elizabeth around?' He didn't get the opportunity to say a lot more.

'Why don't you do yourself a favour and fuck off.'

'I can explain. I have to—'

'She says she doesn't want to talk to you.' The phone went dead.

Strictly speaking, this wasn't true. Elizabeth knew she would have to speak to Danny at some point, which was not to say that she didn't appreciate Peter's efforts on her behalf. He had the right to be sanctimonious, and he wasn't. He was better than that.

Peter had spent the night with Brian and some of the other lads from the site. When he'd rolled up, Michelle had ushered him into the front room. Their voices had become hushed; you'd think they were in the morgue. Without even asking, Peter had gone out and bought Elizabeth a coffee and a doughnut, one with apple in the middle. There was another one in the kitchen for when she wanted it, he said. He assured her that she didn't have to say anything, and then she really did weep. Small squeaks accompanied her tears, and a skein of snot hung from her nose. She said how sorry she was about Brian; how the accident definitely wasn't his fault, and how he was the best friend anyone could have. God love him, he looked embarrassed. That, she promised herself, was the last of the crying. She wasn't going to get sentimental and foolish, and she wasn't going to let herself down.

She passed most of the morning on the bedroom floor, staring at the ceiling. 'It's what I deserve,' she said to Michelle, who admonished her for being silly. At first she was gentle but after a while it was clear she was getting annoyed. With Michelle you couldn't push your luck too far.

'For pity's sake, Elizabeth, will you shut up with your rubbish about what you did or didn't deserve,' she snapped.

Elizabeth sat up although she continued to maintain that what

169

had happened was for the best. It was a sign, she claimed. Seeing how easily Danny was diverted had brought her to her senses. 'I've been saved from making a bigger mistake. And, perhaps the row with Vincent was an early warning that I didn't heed.'

'I know you don't believe in any of that mumbo-jumbo about signs and omens.'

'Maybe I do. Or maybe I needed reminding of my priorities. Like, if a person can let you down in a small way, the chances are they'll let you down in other ways too. If it wasn't that conniving little bitch, it would be someone else.' All the time, more ideas, just like those ones, were surging into her head. There were now so many thoughts bubbling around that there was no room left for dissension. Each idea bolstered the one before.

Michelle was sitting on the floor beside her, rubbing her shoulder. 'You said it yourself, pet. He was manky drunk. Stotious. And even you do stupid things when you've too much drink on board. Why don't we go for a bite of lunch? We'll put on some music first. Then you can have a shower and face the day. You can't sit here in the dark.'

Elizabeth said thanks for the offer, but that's what she'd like to do for another bit. And she'd be better off without the music too. She didn't want to be like their next-door neighbour in Thurles – Mrs Maher. When Mrs Maher's husband took up with a young one, she had played the Dire Straits song, 'Romeo and Juliet', for three days. Non-stop. Elizabeth's mam had asked if she wouldn't mind taking a break for a while, so the boys could get some sleep. Mrs Maher had played country and western instead.

Danny didn't have to knock. They must have seen him from the front window, for by the time he got to apartment number ten, the door was open. Peter was on the threshold, his face surprisingly passive.

'Did you not get the message?' he said. 'That was a real low-life trick you pulled. Sitting there shifting your ex, while Elizabeth was forced to look on. Ve-ry classy.'

'I have to tell her how sorry I am. Can I see her?' Danny was scared he might throw up again.

'No.'

'I know you're angry, Peter, and that's fine. Except shouldn't it be up to Elizabeth to decide?' He tried to move forwards. 'Elizabeth, baby,' he said, his voice straining. 'Please, can I talk to you? I need to talk to you.'

Peter appeared to grow larger. Normally gangly and insubstantial, he now filled the entire doorway. His tone remained level. 'Move back, will you? You're not talking to her.'

'But—' Before Danny had the opportunity to say any more, he heard a voice from the rear of the apartment, and for the briefest time he thought it was her, but it was only Michelle.

'Oh, for God's sake, Peter, will you just tell him?' she said.

Peter looked towards the heavens. 'You can't talk to her because she's not here.'

Danny was about to ask where she was when the door slammed shut.

The best course of action, he figured, the only course of action, was to wait. He would sit in the car, or better yet on the steps of the building. At some stage she would have to return. He was prepared for yelling or weeping. He was prepared to put up with Peter acting the goon. He had it coming.

In the late afternoon, it was mild. Small clouds were scudding across the sky. Students came and went. They were all in their new term uniform: carefully ripped jeans and work boots that would never see any work. Danny was examining one of the small clouds – a comically shaped guy – when the door creaked open behind him. As he went to move aside, he realised it was Michelle. Best steel yourself for another burst of animosity, he thought. She stood there and examined him with such intensity he was almost frightened.

'The state of you,' she said. 'Come on. Thankfully, Peter is a fiend for sleep. I had to wait until I heard the snores.' With that she set off around the corner at high speed. He was forced to trot in her wake. After a minute or so, she spoke again. 'Sorry about the secrecy but there's no point in antagonising him any further.'

'I guess I'm not the most popular man around here.'

'Let's get that out of the way first. How could you behave like such a bastard? Did you have sex with that girl – Barbie or whatever she's called?'

'Cindy. No. I swear. I'm so sorry. Like really really sorry.'

'Funnily enough, I believe you. And, as much as I love her, Elizabeth drives me crackers at times. I mean, she should have owned up to Liam ages ago. Both of you are in need of a good shake.'

Their pace had slowed. Danny rubbed his chin. 'Where's she gone?'

'For once, I haven't a clue. She's probably having a meander. You know her as well as I do.'

'I suppose I do.' For the first time that day he smiled. He quickly thought better of it. 'How is she?' An elderly man passed by. He was walking gingerly and carrying a bunch of pale pink roses. He must be in the doghouse too.

'In a bad way. Which, if I were you, I'd take as a positive sign. Elizabeth doesn't do excessive emotion, or she didn't until you came on the scene. She was all over the shop. Quivering like a kitten. She must be mad about you. Well, I know she is.' Michelle shook her head. 'You're a right pair.'

'I'm mad about her too. I hope you understand that. I truly am.' He ran a hand over his head. 'This is a big deal for me. She'll forgive me, won't she?'

'I think she has to get herself together, and I'm not sure if now is the best time to talk to her. Besides, if Peter sees you hanging around, there'll be violence.'

'I have to talk to her, though. I have to explain, and let her know I'll never mess her around again. I swear to God. Lesson learnt.' There were at the edge of Comm Ave now, the incessant drone of cars starting to disrupt their conversation. The T clanked past.

'Why don't I talk to her for you? I can pass on what you said. And I can reassure her that you looked as woeful as she did.'

'But … when will I see her?'

Michelle pressed her lips together. 'Hmmm, I have an idea. What if you call around in the morning, before she goes out? Make sure Peter's gone first, mind. I'll tell her to expect you. I'm sure Mike Anderson can manage without her for an hour or two.'

'Thanks. I mean it, Michelle. I owe you. I won't forget this.'

She shooed him away, but her face was reassuring.

Back when he'd first met Elizabeth, Danny had seen her as a summertime distraction – a bright spark with long legs and a funny little face. Not to be taken too seriously. Gradually this had changed; she must know that. As he walked towards his car, the little men in his head were as busy as ever. Banging, rattling, drilling – you would think they were tunnelling to Australia. He was feeling more optimistic, though, and would cope for now.

Chapter 17

Valerie was curled into a small ball on the sofa. No, not small, thought Vincent. That didn't do her justice. Neat. She was so neat you could fit ten of her onto the thing.

She gave him a sleepy smile. 'What did your mom have to say?'

'Perhaps it would be easier to tell you what she didn't have to say.' He sat down, and she stretched out her legs until her feet were resting on his lap. 'I'm surprised the phone didn't melt.'

'Oh.'

'Haven't heard her so worked up since Danny flunked out of college.'

'Would I be right in guessing this was about Elizabeth?'

Vincent stroked Valerie's feet. Such *tiny* feet, he would bet she could wear kids' socks. 'What else? Danny screws up. I get the blame.'

A needle of early evening sun pierced the window. He was dismayed by how scrappy the room looked, how basic. It was like a single person's room. Valerie was cautious about these matters, but he was convinced they should find a more appropriate place.

'She didn't blame you for last night, did she?'

'Nope, it wasn't that. Said she was less than impressed by my attitude towards the girl. I asked her what Danny had been saying, and she went totally loco on me. Claimed not a word had come out of his mouth. Told me she had eyes and ears of her own. Didn't like the way I found fault with Elizabeth all the time.'

'Was that it?'

'And I wish. Then she banged on about how any fool could tell they were in love. And what was my problem with that. Didn't I want to see my brother happy and settled. Especially with a beautiful girl with a …' Vincent paused because he knew Valerie would be able to complete the sentence.

'College education,' she laughed.

'Got it in one, Val.'

'What did you say to her?'

'Obviously, I said she was exaggerating.' Vincent detected a small snort from the other end of the sofa. Normally, that would set his blood pressure surging. At that moment, though, he couldn't get annoyed about anything. He was full up with happiness, *steeped* in happiness. He tickled her big toe. 'Am I sensing you're on Ma's side here?'

'You know I like Elizabeth. If I had her number, I'd give her a call. She must be mighty upset today.'

Vincent extended his tickling. 'Ma said he'd gone over to her apartment. She figured he'd need all his charm.'

Outside some boys were playing with a basketball. He heard the ball thumping and thwacking against the sidewalk, while the kids yelped with energy.

Valerie swung her legs off his lap, edged along the sofa, and cuddled into him. 'You didn't have anything to do with Cindy being there last night, did you?'

'Ah, Val,' Vincent said, his heart beating that touch faster. Truth to tell, he was feeling pretty lousy.

'I had to ask. Are you going to listen to Regina?'

'Best not to go upsetting her, I suppose.'

'True. She's been in such good form lately. It would be a shame to destroy that. And …' She hesitated, and he kissed her hair. 'For a while now, you've wanted Danny to settle down. And, OK, we didn't see it at first, but what if Elizabeth is *the* girl?'

'Hmmm. It's possible. I mean, I know I sometimes come the heavy on the guy. Ma said to me, "You've got to remember, you're not his father." But the thing is, Val, Dino was never much of a father to him. I'm just doing my best here. You understand, don't you?'

She squeezed his hand. 'I do.'

He gave her another kiss. 'And I definitely don't want to upset you. In fact, I almost told Ma not to go annoying me, that we'd more important matters to be thinking about over here.'

'Vincent!'

'Don't worry. I know what I promised. I'll hold out for another couple of weeks.'

'And Elizabeth?'

Vincent smiled. 'She doesn't know it yet, but she's my new best friend.'

It took an age. An absolute age. And a few downright lies. As Elizabeth waited, she watched the comings and goings, the blasé business people and the twitchy first-timers. There were squeals of delight and a couple of arguments. Mostly, though, the conversations were more prosaic: about parking and the weather and who would win the election.

In the end, a man with monumental black eyebrows listened to her request and gave a grave nod. He said the paperwork might take half an hour or so, but he understood her situation. Given how dreadful she must look, all crumpled and streaked, they were never going to doubt her story. She hadn't even bothered to get properly dressed. She was wearing an old pair of baggy-kneed leggings and an ugly grey T-shirt. Her hair was matted, her lips scaly and her eyes like two raspberries.

Elizabeth thanked the man over and over. She wasn't sure how she felt. Numb, she supposed. But when you had your mind made up, everything had to be better. That stood to reason, didn't it? Her task completed, she went to find a phone booth.

'Hello, Mrs O'Hara?' she said.

…

'It's good to hear your voice too and I'm the finest, thanks. Is he there?'

…

'Oh, of course. I always forget. I'm an awful fool. It's nearly midnight with you. No, don't wake him up.'

...

'It would be great if you would pass a message onto Liam for me.'

...

'The noise? That's what I'm ringing about. I'm at the airport. I've managed to change my flight and I'm coming home a wee bit earlier.'

...

'No, I'm grand. I've had a brilliant experience and all the rest of it. It's time to come back, though.'

...

'Tomorrow.'

...

'You're dead right. I don't do things by halves.'

...

'The flight is in the evening and, with the time difference, I'll get into Shannon on Tuesday morning. Eight o'clock. That mightn't suit him, I know.'

...

'Do you think so? That would be brilliant. I'm desperate to see you all.'

...

'Thanks, Mrs O'Hara. See you soon. God bless.'

'I'm sorry, run that by me again. *When* did you say?'

Michelle was patrolling the bedroom while Elizabeth crouched on the floor, folding her T-shirts and placing them into her rucksack. Packing wouldn't take long because more than half of her belongings were in Emerald Street. The pink shoes were there for starters. She'd bought those in Filene's Basement with her first pay packet, and would be sorry to leave them behind. Still, she couldn't imagine they'd be very practical in Ireland.

It was best to be organised because she would have quite a lot

177

to do tomorrow. First off, she'd have to go into Anderson's and let them know she wouldn't be back.

'I do realise I'm leaving you in the lurch, Michelle. I'll give you the rent for next week, so you're not left short. Rosie's here now too.'

Michelle kicked the wall, distracting Elizabeth from her task. 'I don't give a rat's ass about the rent. Have you taken leave of your senses entirely?'

'I know tomorrow's kind of soon. But I told the man from the airline that I needed to go home because my father was seriously ill. I could hardly request a ticket for later in the week. Something is either an emergency or it's not.'

Elizabeth gathered up her bits and pieces of jewellery and hairclips and whatnot. Should she keep the bracelet with the tiny stars? On balance, she thought yes. It was lovely, and if anyone asked she'd say she had lots of money when she was in America, and you had to treat yourself sometimes. Donal, Rosie and Peter were all in the front room, having been banished from the bedroom by Michelle. Elizabeth was relieved to see them scatter. She wasn't able for a mass inquisition, although she had expected Michelle to be more understanding. She was doing her best to explain the situation to her friend. Surely, she knew that Elizabeth wasn't like her and Donal?

'I'm like Peter. I belong at home,' she said. 'That's what you all used to claim, and now you've been proved right. If last night hadn't happened, something else would have come along to make me see sense.'

Michelle did a sudden about turn and kicked Elizabeth's rucksack clean across the floor.

'Please, Michelle. Stop it, would you? I'm trying to get myself together here.'

'And I'm trying to stop you from making a big mistake. Are you not even going to talk to Danny?'

'Of course I am. You said he was calling around in the morning.' On her hands and knees, Elizabeth scrambled to retrieve her belongings, only to find her path was blocked. No matter where she went, Michelle was there first. 'Anyway, this isn't just about Danny; my dad's about to lose his job and my parents are still upset about Alice staying in London.'

'Right, so if you go home the sugar factory will stay open, and Alice will dump Keith for some local yokel?'

'There's no need to be smart. I'm trying to do the right thing.'

Michelle's hands were on her hips and she was practically spitting out her words. 'For the whole summer, Elizabeth, you've spent every minute of the day with Danny. Or talking about him. Or thinking about him. And, God help him, he's as bad as you. And, I don't care what you say, you've never had so much fun. You probably don't realise this, but you're a different person.'

'I wasn't aware that you had any particular issue with me before.'

'Don't get snippy on me. You know what I'm saying. Listen, I'll admit I wasn't completely sure about him to begin with. I thought he was one of those lads who are so into themselves, they don't need a girlfriend.'

'That's not the way he is at all. Not when you get to know him.'

Michelle sighed. 'That's what I'm saying to you. I was wrong. He's ... what's the word? Interesting. Good interesting. Now, I don't want to mention Liam—'

'Please, don't compare Liam with Danny. It's not fair.' Elizabeth didn't like the direction this was taking. Could Michelle not accept that she'd made her decision?

'OK. He screwed up. He deserves a hard time. But, Jesus, Elizabeth, you should have seen the state of the lad today. You get one setback, and you're going to run home to Liam?'

'Three months, Michelle. That's how long I've known Danny. It's nothing. If it takes the same length of time to forget, I'll be over him by Christmas.'

'It doesn't work like that.'

'How would *you* know?' Elizabeth couldn't take any more. She had been with Liam for more than four years, and throughout those years Michelle, and the rest of them, had been messing around. They were in no position to tell her how things did or didn't work. She was the grown-up here.

Michelle crouched on the ground so that they were eye to eye. Small smudges of pink scarred each cheekbone. 'What I know is that for once this isn't all a lark. If last night is the worst thing that ever happens to you, you're going to live a fairly quiet life. Please don't do this. You have to take more time.'

'I'm sorry, I don't agree. If I was really sure about Danny and about America, I would have rung Liam and called it off. But I never did, and that's got to tell you something.'

'And if you really wanted to be with Liam, you wouldn't be in love with another man. Because, even though you seem to have some crazy phobia about using the word, you are in love with Danny. And he's in love with you. What's wrong with you that you can't see that?'

Elizabeth had to shut down this conversation. She closed her eyes as tightly as possible, so tight that the blackness faded to a caramel brown, the way it had done when she was a schoolgirl and the class were told to put their heads on the desk and go to sleep. She pretended she was on her own. Music spilled in from one of the other apartments: Tracy Chapman, 'Fast Car'. She must have heard it a thousand times that summer.

Some time passed before she opened her eyes. Thankfully, they were only a tiny bit moist. Michelle was still there. She was picking up the earrings that were strewn across the floor when the rucksack toppled over.

Elizabeth saw that her friend was crying. 'Please don't,' she said. 'Please.'

'I just wish you were brave enough to live your own life, Elizabeth,' Michelle replied. 'That's all.' She handed her the jewellery and left the room.

Chapter 18

It was not quite bright when Danny slipped on his running gear and left the house. Even Bridie O'Connor was not yet out of bed. There was a chill to the early morning that burned his hands and his face and his knees. He'd warm up soon enough, though, and his head would clear. He hadn't been doing enough running lately. That was something else he needed to put right. He turned a corner, waved at a mailman and some guys on a garbage truck. The morning was beginning to groan into action. His shoulders were unlocking, and he felt good.

Last night, he had expected to have difficulty dropping off. Instead, he'd enjoyed a near-perfect sleep. Of course, there was too much space in the bed, but fingers crossed that would get sorted today. Ma had said she wouldn't get involved, but did anyway. She had made dinner for three because she'd presumed Elizabeth would come straight on back with him. He'd joked about her preferring Elizabeth to her own son, and she'd replied that if she had to lose one of them, she knew who it would be. In truth, he hadn't really wanted to eat. His stomach had been shredded and queasy and his throat raw, but he couldn't have handled the nagging, so he'd done his best. 'Don't be too cocky,' she advised before turning in.

When Danny got back from his run, she was still asleep. He hoped this wasn't a bad sign. He showered and shaved and dressed, and even though he said so himself, he looked good. It was too early, but he figured he'd drive on over to Lantern Street anyway. He would loiter around the corner until he was sure Peter had left for work.

He would give work a miss, and if Elizabeth was up for it, they could go for a drive someplace. Get back on track. He knew that, to use a phrase of hers, he was rushing his fences, yet he was more sure about this than anything he could remember. He wouldn't do too much gushing. That wasn't his style, and thankfully it wasn't hers either. Without being too explicit, he'd let her know his commitment was long term.

Elizabeth had an uneasy night. Then again, she had a lot on her mind. She did her best to concentrate on practical matters, like how she would work out her share of the electricity and phone bills, and where she would get presents for her brothers. Eoin had got brilliant results in his Leaving Cert and, because she was so wrapped up in herself, she hadn't sent him so much as a card. Now she had the chance to make amends. She ought to get a gift for Liam too. He'd always been generous to her.

She watched Rosie leave and then got up. She wanted to make the most of her last morning in America. In the shower, she let the water run and run until her skin began to shrivel. She would definitely miss the plumbing in Boston. There was no shower at home, just one of those rubber attachments for the bath taps. You had to kneel on the lino to wash your hair, and the hot water always ran out before it was fully rinsed.

In the early hours, she had decided on a plan of action. She would keep an eye out for Danny and dash down the stairs as soon as he arrived. Then they could go for a walk. She didn't want him to see her packed bag before she had the chance to tell him about her intentions. Nor did she want an audience. If he had time, they could be civilised and go for a coffee. She wanted to tell him how much he had meant to her.

As quietly as possible, Elizabeth got dressed. She put on the jeans that she'd been saving for their New England holiday. Then she sat beside the front room window and did her make-up. It was important, she believed, to look nice. She told herself this was for reasons of self-respect, but if she was honest, she wanted Danny to remember her at her best.

Peter was up by now, and foostering around the place. He too was grumbling about her imminent departure. 'There's no need to rush off,' he moaned. Lord, she thought, there's no pleasing some people. Not that she said as much. She wasn't going to have any cross words with anyone today. There'd been too much lurching between up and down, and she wasn't cut out for it.

After she'd put her make-up away, she went into the kitchen and took down a sign that Donal had made. It read *Beware of the Vermin*. At the bottom, he had drawn a cartoon picture of a rat. She knew this was a bit daft, but she wanted a memento from Lantern Street and the rat poster was the first thing that came to mind. Not that she'd ever seen the actual beast. To the best of her knowledge, none of the others had either.

Peter was only out the door, and both Michelle and Donal were still asleep, when she saw Danny approaching the building. She would know his flat-footed walk anywhere. Elizabeth had a quick word with herself then hared down the stairs so that he wouldn't get further than the lobby.

'Well now,' he said, the smile so wide that every last tooth was displayed, 'don't you look fine this morning?'

'I thought I looked fine all the time.'

'Ha, you got me there. I was expecting a bucket of water over the head at least.'

'It's what you deserve, right enough. You're lucky I thought better of it. Let's go for a walk.'

She linked his arm, and although her throat was tight and her legs were unsteady, she stayed calm. She guided him towards Brookline. The streets were quieter and prettier there. They might even make it as far as the park.

Immediately Danny's apologies started. He was a useless drunk and he'd never be dumb enough to get in that condition again. He had no interest in Cindy. And he wouldn't blame Elizabeth for running out of the bar, except she shouldn't have done because it wasn't safe to be walking the streets on her own at that time of night.

Elizabeth had to stop him. 'Did you and Cindy, you know ...?'

'No, baby. You have to understand that.'

'I can see why you'd want to. I mean, I look at her and ... well, she's really beautiful.'

'Oh Jesus, Elizabeth, she's nothing on you. Nothing.' Danny stopped walking and moved in to kiss her. She turned her face away.

A row of imposing trees lined the way ahead, their foliage so heavy that the street felt unnaturally dark. Soon, those leaves would crumble, and all would change. The house they were standing beside was shielded by a blazing red maple. A blue child-sized bicycle was propped up near the door.

Elizabeth couldn't put it off any longer. 'I'll be home by this time tomorrow,' she said. Obviously, she said lots more too. She explained how it was for the best. They'd had a brilliant summer, the best anyone had ever had, but when it came down to it, what had they in common? They were too different. She didn't belong in Boston. 'This is your home,' she said, 'but it isn't mine.' When she'd formulated that line at three in the morning, it had seemed clever. Now she wondered if it didn't sound trite.

Danny kept nodding. Even by his standards, he looked great. His eyes were so clear you could see the dark rim around the iris. He was wearing a plaid flannel shirt and black denims, and the smell of his shaving foam hadn't yet faded. She could see his chest move beneath his shirt. When she stopped talking, he remained quiet. After a short interval, he looked up at the canopy of leaves and took a deep breath.

'OK,' he said. 'Did you not understand? There's nothing between me and Cindy, or any other woman for that matter. The only person I want to be with, Elizabeth, is you.'

'No, you don't understand.' She launched into her spiel again. Repeated all the lines about missing home and taking control and doing the right thing.

He took her wrist. 'I think you're the one who doesn't get this. Go for a visit, sure. But come back. Don't make a bad decision just to punish me. Think about what you're doing. Please.'

She wriggled her arm, forcing him to let go. 'I've done all the thinking I need to do, Danny. I'm convinced this is the correct decision. For both of us.'

'I won't grovel. That's not what I do.' He scuffed one toe against the ground. 'But is there anything I can do or say here to make you change your mind?'

She closed her eyes because, as she'd discovered the night before, it worked. Then she shook her head.

'One thing, Elizabeth. Did it occur to you at all, that leaving like this ... without even troubling yourself to say goodbye ... that it would hurt my mother?'

A rogue tear escaped. 'I—'

'I nothing. Perhaps you're not the person I thought you were and, perhaps, this *is* for the best.'

Another flurry of the bastards seeped from behind her closed eyes, and she made a stupid little sound, like *glug*. Before she could do or say anything more, he stepped forward and embraced her. He said he was sorry, which she didn't want. She made another *glug* sound. He kissed her head. 'Sshhh, no more now, my darling. Sshhh.'

When they kissed, he tasted salty. It took some time, but eventually she decided it was safe to open her eyes.

'Why don't you come home with me?' Danny asked. 'For a small while. You can say goodbye to my mom. And you can collect your clothes. I'll give you a ride back later. Or, come to that, I can take you anywhere you need to go. To the airport, if you like.'

Elizabeth watched a pinched-looking woman with a child of three or four make great play of walking out into the road in order to avoid them. Of course she couldn't go home with him. She believed he knew that too. 'Will you tell Regina that I wish her all the best? And say thanks. I mean that. On my life I do, Danny.'

Her voice trailed off. She realised now that Michelle was right; she wouldn't forget about him in three months. But her memories would be happy ones. And wasn't that what she came to America for?

He made a gentle humming sound and pulled her in tight again. 'Would you like me to write?'

'Best not, I think. A clean break, isn't that what they say?'

'OK, but … you know where I am.'

She rubbed her fists along his back. 'They'll be queuing around the block when they hear you're single again.'

'For what it's worth, I think you're making a mistake.' He hesitated. 'I think … we belong together.'

She said no more. To be honest, she didn't trust herself. When they disentangled, Danny asked if she wanted to walk back to Lantern Street. She said she might go to the park, to collect herself before she went to Anderson's and said her goodbyes there.

He took both of her hands and squeezed. 'I reckon I should get along then. Let you do what you have to do.'

'Danny?'

'Hmmm?'

'Thanks.'

He made a face as if to say, 'What for?'

'Thanks for … for everything. And I hope you know … I think you do … I wish only good things for you. And happiness.'

He kissed her forehead. 'Isn't that bad luck?'

'I think it's OK if you're wishing it for someone else.'

Elizabeth watched him walk away. Even when he was no longer in sight, she stayed as still as stone.

He couldn't let it end there. Danny sat in the car, thoughts sluicing around his head. Self-loathing thoughts and self-pitying thoughts and every half-baked thought in between. At first, he was angry with her. He'd fucked up. He'd admitted it. Said he was sorry. What more could he do?

186

It wasn't like they'd known each other for long. Three months. A couple of haircuts. Less than half a baseball season. Not long enough for them to do a quarter of the things he'd been planning. He couldn't even say *why* he was so mad about her. I mean, why was it you made a connection with some people straight away? Why could you know other folks your entire life, yet never reach that same place?

The way it had always seemed to him, there was a long list of subjects you weren't supposed to discuss, and thoughts you weren't supposed to have. You couldn't be a whole bunch of things. Like, you couldn't want to read books *and* play sports *and* ask questions about the world *and* be a regular guy. He'd only known Elizabeth for a week when he'd said this to her. And she'd understood. What she said about them having nothing in common wasn't true. Surely, she knew that?

Short of kidnapping her, Danny couldn't think how to make Elizabeth stay. His headache had returned, worse than ever. What he needed to do was go home and talk to Ma. It was pathetic: a grown man looking for advice from his mom, but where else could he turn?

The moment he entered the house, he realised something was wrong. There was an unnerving quiet. No *Ryan's Hope* or *Days of Our Lives* on the TV, no silly pop music on the radio. Regina was in the front room. He recognised the look in her eyes: the inert stare. 'Night of the living dead,' as Vincent called it. Behind her back, of course. She was darning a sock. The needle was going over and over the same spot, so that the darned piece was about an inch high. A cigarette smouldered in an ashtray that he'd brought home from the Cape years before.

It should have occurred to Danny that Elizabeth would call. 'What did she say?' he asked.

Regina focused on her sock. 'Does it matter?'

'Yeah, it does. Yeah.' He sat down opposite his mother. 'Do you think I can change her mind?'

'Haven't you left it too late for that?'

'What should I do, Ma?' She continued to stare at the sock, the damn needle flying up and down. 'Ma, look at me, would you? Please.'

'She said she missed her family, and that they needed her at home. There was a wobble in her voice, like she was trying not to cry.' Regina put down her darning and lit another cigarette. 'She said she'd miss us too. And then she said thanks. I said what for. I told her I owed her an apology. Given how my sons had caused her nothing but trouble. "That's the truth," I said. "I thought they were better than that. But they're an embarrassment to me. As selfish and spineless as their father."'

'Oh lord, Ma.'

'I asked her to stay. When she said she couldn't, I offered to pack up her clothes and send them on to Ireland. She got upset and hung up.' Regina put the sock in her sewing basket and stubbed out her cigarette. 'If you'll excuse me, Danny, I'm going for a lie down. Bridie was threatening to call in. You can deal with her.'

An hour passed. And another. Danny kept seeing Elizabeth's face. Only it wasn't the face he knew. It was the face he had left some hours back. Unusually for her, she was wearing a heavy mask of make-up. Her freckles were camouflaged and her eyes ringed with black. They looked even bigger than usual, except all their colour seemed to have washed away. That wasn't how he wanted to remember her. Ma had said she was crying. Was it possible she was having second thoughts about leaving? He had to go to the airport. He knocked on the bedroom door to tell his mother. There was no reply.

Afterwards, Danny couldn't recall the first blow, although he guessed it must have hit him on the chin. The second punch connected with his left eye; the third with his right. There was no fourth punch because by then he was slumped against the side of the car. He tried to get up, but a quick kick from a steel-capped boot sent him reeling. Danny attempted to recover his breath. Too late he identified his assailant.

Greg Brady squinted at him. 'You go down pretty easy. Like a big sack of shit.'

He made another attempt to stand up. He had to return at least one of those hits. This time the kick was straight to the groin. The world turned purple. He may have squealed. Speech was beyond him.

Brady released a heavy sigh. 'I think I'll leave it at that.'

Danny whimpered.

'Ah, hell,' said Brady. 'Maybe I won't. The first few were for me.' He took another kick. This one, perhaps not quite so vicious, connected with Danny's side. 'That was for your girlfriend. I gather she had to watch you sucking face with Cindy.'

He gasped for breath. 'It wasn't—'

'Granted she's no stunner. Not compared to Cindy. She's pretty enough, though. Smart too, and funny. Don't know what she's doing with a retard like you.'

At last he managed to squeak a reply. 'She's leaving.'

'Going home, I hope.'

Pain was ripping through Danny's body. Every nerve ending was screaming. Bile was collecting in his mouth. 'I'm going … to the airport.'

Brady leered. 'The fuck you are. What would she want with you? Huh? A small-time carpenter who can't keep it in his pants.'

'I need to … talk … to let her know.'

'And I want you to leave her be.' He directed a further kick into Danny's side. A real sharp one. 'Besides, you're in no fit state to go anywhere.'

The pain was becoming unbearable. His eyes were stinging like hell. 'I have to talk to her.' The bile dribbled from his mouth. 'I love her. She's got to—'

'Aw, "I love her",' Brady chuckled. 'Are you asking for another kick?'

Before he was able to say any more, Danny heard a wail from down the street. 'Sacred heart of Jesus,' a voice rasped. 'Danny, honey, what's happening?' He could just about make out Bridie O'Connor. She dropped her shopping bag, and its contents scattered across the sidewalk. 'I'm getting the cops,' she screeched. 'The cops. Do you hear?'

At that point he must have passed out.

Two

2010–2012

Dublin and Boston

Chapter *19*

Janey hurtled into the room at gale force and let her bag ease from her shoulder until it thumped onto the floor. She shrugged off her coat and threw it into an armchair. 'It's lovely out. Snowing again.'

'Mmmm,' replied Elizabeth, eyes rooted to the television. 'Close the door there, would you, love? There's a terrible draught.'

Janey did as she was told. 'I don't know how you can watch that shower without throwing something at the telly.'

'Shush, would you,' snapped her sister Stevie. 'Some of us are trying to keep ourselves informed here.'

'Do you know, Stevie, you must be the only fifteen-year-old in Ireland, nah, probably the only fifteen-year-old in the *world*, who would sit down on a Sunday evening and take this carry-on seriously.'

Stevie was cross-legged on the floor, two or three feet from the television screen, watching a phalanx of grey men, jowly men, shocked men and a downcast woman read sombre statements. 'Mu-um, will you tell her to shut up?'

Elizabeth was perched on the sofa, back as straight as a board, a purring mass of black fur on her lap. 'Girls, will you both pipe down for a minute. Janey, if you don't want to watch this, you can go and make a cup of tea. And pick up your bag and coat, would you? You're making the place look untidy.'

'What do you want a cup of tea for?' asked Janey. 'Haven't you a glass of wine sitting in front of you?'

Elizabeth ignored her. 'Oh, and will you take off those boots? You're melting on the carpet.'

'For God's sake,' said Stevie, as she repeatedly pressed the volume button on the remote control. 'We're missing the best bits. They're going through the terms of the deal with the IMF.' She gave the button several further taps so that the drone of morose politician boomed around the room.

Janey made a hissing sound. 'Stevie, there are no best bits. These fuckers have the country wrecked.'

'Janey, please,' said Elizabeth. 'That's no way to be talking in front of a guest. And Stevie, that's far too loud.'

'Michelle hardly qualifies as a guest,' said Janey as she scooped up her bag and coat. 'But I'll be a good girl and make the tea.' She stalked out of the sitting room, dark brown ponytail wagging as she walked.

Elizabeth looked at Michelle who was lounging across the other half of the sofa. 'I don't know. There are days when I get more sense out of Grover here.' Recognising his name, Grover kneaded her lap with his tomcat claws and ramped up his purring.

Stevie renewed her shushing. 'They're getting to the good questions. A guy has just asked about the bank bondholders.'

Michelle tickled Grover between the ears. 'You'd have to wonder,' she said, 'what sort of a country we're living in, when a teenager is talking about bondholders.'

Stevie's small earnest head turned around. 'A broke one. And please don't patronise me. I get enough of that already from Mum and Janey.'

As soon as the small head was facing the television again, Elizabeth winked at Michelle who looked like she was finding it hard to swallow her laughter. She noticed her younger daughter was absent-mindedly twisting her long fair hair into slender plaits. It was something she did when she was concentrating, which was most of the time. Elizabeth was often heard to ask how she'd got such a serious child. She wished her friends didn't respond with hoots of amusement. Surely, she hadn't been *that* bad?

Janey returned, her overloaded tray clanking with cups and plates and spoons, the offending boots still on her feet. 'You should turn over to the other side. Orla's on. She's standing outside Government Buildings, freezing her ass off.'

Stevie flicked immediately. Elizabeth knew she got a kick out of seeing an actual friend of her mum's on the telly, talking about important issues and giving a tough time to pompous folk. Orla had been back in Dublin a lot since the country started to fall apart. Not surprisingly, her television station liked having an Irish person covering the country's downfall. And an Irish person with an economics degree? She was made for the job.

Orla never had time to meet up. 'You know the way it is,' she would say. 'Busy. Busy. Busy. What about Christmas? I'll surely be free by then.' In fairness, the girl had done well. To Elizabeth, though, she never seemed like her real self. She wanted to tap the screen, and say, 'Come out, Orla. The real, raucous, slutty you must be hiding in there somewhere.' She certainly didn't sound like the genuine Orla. Twenty years in England and more than a decade as a presenter on one of the big satellite channels had stripped away every last trace of Dub.

She did look the same: smooth blond hair, wide green eyes, crease-free face. Some months before, Elizabeth had read a magazine feature in which Orla claimed she would never inject anything into her face, that a serious journalist couldn't go messing with their expressions like some bimbo entertainment presenter. Actually, she wasn't quite so blunt, but that was obviously what she meant. Amid considerable chuntering and eye rolling, Elizabeth had shown the article to Michelle.

'She's telling the truth, right enough,' said Michelle. 'She cut out the middleman. Had her eyes done and her brow lifted two years ago. Apparently, they all do it. Saves them the bother of getting injected. She claims she'd be pensioned off otherwise.'

'She's only forty-three,' replied Elizabeth.

'That's right. Old.'

Janey lowered the tray onto the table, and they all focused on Orla who was talking about billions of euro and banks and budgets and further billions of euro and … well, with the best will in the world, these were difficult matters to get your head around right now, especially when you felt powerless to change anything. The country was full of Stevies, torturing themselves with the details. Elizabeth would devote some time to it all tomorrow.

'That's a gorgeous coat,' Janey said. 'The pale colour suits her.'

Stevie snorted in response, yet Elizabeth was certain the elder girl was only trying to wind her up. She was no fool, Janey, even if sometimes she did a passable imitation of one. Elizabeth would barely admit it to herself, let alone anyone else, but she was proud of her daughters. She kept waiting for it all to go wrong; for them to lapse into surliness or fall for a total louser of a man. Normal girl issues. Instead, they sauntered along in their own fashion. One could be too dippy and the other too deep, but those didn't count as problems. 'More luck than judgement,' she would say when people complimented her, pride coming before a fall and all of that. Not, God knows, that her life was coming down with reasons to be proud.

'Will you pour the tea there, love?' she said to Janey. 'The cat has me handicapped.'

'Did you see Orla a couple of weeks ago?' asked Stevie. 'When she savaged Peter?'

'I did. She gave him quite a skewering,' replied Michelle as she took a cup and ladled in the sugar. 'What was it she said again? "I put it to you, Mr O'Regan, that your bank is largely responsible for the sorry state in which Ireland finds itself today."'

'I thought she was over the top. After all, he's only the PR man. It wasn't Peter who lost all the money,' Elizabeth said.

Michelle tittered. 'I worried he was going to get personal.' She made an attempt at Peter's voice, his lazy midlands accent now cut with southside Dublin. 'I put it to you, Ms Finnegan, that you weren't always so sure of your economics. Didn't you to have slink home from America after you failed your exams?'

'Wouldn't that be hilarious?'

Stevie was surprised. 'Did she really? Fail her exams?'

'Only the one. Still, it was enough to ruin her summer.'

Janey was blowing the surface of her tea, creating small brown ripples. She was a desperate fidget; wouldn't eat or drink anything unless she played with it first. 'Michelle, did Mum tell you I'm going to America?'

'She did. Lucky you. I'd give my eye teeth to be a student going off to the States for the summer.'

'It's different now, though,' said Elizabeth. 'The J-1 is wasted on them. Sure, they've all been to America already. Half of Janey's friends have been to New York for the weekend. The *weekend*, I ask you.'

'To be fair, I think we've seen the last of that lark.'

'All the same, it's not like our day when nobody had been further than the Isle of Man.'

'Ah, the good old days,' said Janey. 'We always get to them eventually.'

'Funnily enough, I don't remember too much about them that was good,' said Michelle.

'You haven't listened to Mum, so. Isn't that right, Stevie?'

Orla and the International Monetary Fund temporarily forgotten, Stevie turned around and giggled. Elizabeth sighed. Unfortunately, her beautiful daughter had inherited Liam's laugh. It had always been a little too high-pitched for her tastes.

'Now, Stevie,' said her sister, 'when Mum was a youngster, what was she happy with?'

'What she got.'

'And what did she get?'

'Next door to nothing. But she knew better than to ask for anything more.'

'And,' said Janey, voice rising along with her mirth, 'did anybody ever have a holiday?'

'If they were extremely lucky, they got a week in a caravan in Ballybunion. And even though it rained every single day, they went into the sea all the same.'

'And why did they go into the sea, Stevie?'

'Because they were tough, Janey, not like the soft young ones today.'

Elizabeth saw that, beside her, Michelle was shaking with laughter. She was shaking so much her tea was in danger of spilling onto the sofa. If she wasn't careful she would disturb Grover who had fallen asleep. 'I don't know how the pair of you think up this nonsense,' she said.

Michelle gave another titter, and Stevie displayed her small teeth. Janey, who had a mime artist's skill for making faces, looked deadly serious. 'And, Stevie,' she said, 'if they went on a school tour, where were they taken?'

The answer was embedded in a small squeal of laughter. 'The power station in Ardnacrusha. Every year. Except once, as a special treat, they were taken to a fish farm outside Portumna. Everyone was allowed an ice cream on the way home. A handy-sized one, mind. Nothing vulgar.'

'Well, you've got that part right, at least,' said Elizabeth. 'I'm convinced I never said any of that other rubbish. It must have come from your father.'

Michelle's tea sloshed over the side of her cup.

For the second time that year, the country was covered by an accumulation of snow. 'Snow in Ireland in *November*,' everyone kept saying. 'Have you ever seen the like of it?' And not only that; it wasn't their normal rapidly disintegrating slush. It was proper powdery stuff with staying power.

'We've definitely got another country's snow,' said Michelle as she and Elizabeth trudged down the street, arm in arm towards the Luas station.

'Lucky us,' said Elizabeth who had decided to walk to the tram stop with her friend, turning down offers from both Stevie and Janey to accompany them. 'Will there be school in the morning?'

'I doubt it. I'll have to turn up anyway though, to let everyone know what's happening. Thankfully, Andy doesn't mind driving. And, if the worst comes to the worst, we can bring the boys with us.'

Michelle was the deputy principal of a large community school on the south-western fringes of the city. Five years before, Andy Joyce had arrived as a substitute woodwork teacher. Within a year they were married, and eleven months later Shay and Senan arrived. The twins had their mother's brown curls and their father's persuasive hazel eyes.

Andy was a fine-looking man. He was also six years his wife's junior. Elizabeth knew Michelle got tired of people remarking that she'd 'landed on her feet, there'. What if she had? In Elizabeth's view, she had endured more than her share of loneliness.

'What's the story with yourself?' said Michelle.

'Have you forgotten I don't do Mondays any more?' Elizabeth worked on an inner city literacy scheme. Most of those on the course were women who had missed out on learning to read and write first time around. Their enthusiasm for this second chance was in equal measure to their lack of confidence. Like so much else, the course had been hit by cuts, and Elizabeth's teaching hours had been scaled back.

'I don't mean the job. I mean … the Liam situation. I don't like to ask when the girls are there.'

'OK, I suppose. We spoke yesterday. It was thirty-two degrees with him.'

'There's no reason why you can't go over there and get some sun.'

'Ah, it's not a great time. Both Stevie and Janey have exams. And he'll be home for a while at Christmas.' Elizabeth kicked a clump of snow into the air and watched as it made its powdery fall. On the other side of the road, a pair of amber eyes flashed and an urban fox disappeared down an alleyway. 'And I'm enjoying this too, you know.'

'In other words, you'd rather not see him.'

'Yeah.' Elizabeth stopped to admire a snowman, an old-fashioned character with a carrot nose and twigs for arms. He was meticulously togged out in a scarf and peaked cap. Somebody had put real work into his construction. Almost without realising it, she found herself sighing, her breath creating a plume of vapour.

'To be honest, Michelle, I wish I could persuade myself to think differently. But even the idea of spending time with him makes me feel weary.'

According to the official version of events, Liam was working in Abu Dhabi because it was impossible for a civil engineer to get work in recession-ravaged Dublin. (It was a long time since he'd moved on from his good pensionable job with the council.) This wasn't a lie, but it wasn't the full truth either.

There had only been one affair. Liam was an incompetent liar, and it had become increasingly clear that something was wrong. Eventually, Elizabeth had confronted him. No, that wasn't right. You couldn't call it a confrontation; a pitiful wheedling would be more accurate. He had been upfront. She was called Nicola, she was a thirty-two-year-old accountant, and they'd met through a mutual friend. He didn't think there was anything lasting in it. In fact six months in, she was getting kind of tiresome.

There had not been a lot of crying. Elizabeth had never been one for weeping, and she'd already shed enough tears watching her marriage grow more arid and their arguments become more grudging. The relationship had not been good for a long time. To tell the truth, she blamed herself. She had no interest in Liam. Not in his opinions or his conversation, and certainly not in his lacklustre attempts at intimacy.

While her husband spoke, she stared at the carpet, examining flourishes and whorls that had never stood out before. A dart of pain hit her left eye, causing her to shudder. For the most part, she said little.

Three months on, Michelle was the one person who knew the full story. 'A fucking accountant?' her friend had said. 'Could he not have done the decent thing and hooked up with a model, or one of those girls whose full-time occupation is looking good?' Elizabeth said there were some incredibly glamorous accountants out there nowadays, prompting a funny look from Michelle. 'Stop being so bloody reasonable,' she'd yelled. The outburst had given Elizabeth her first genuine laugh in weeks.

The older she got, the more confused she became. She didn't even understand physical attraction any more. She was no great beauty. Never had been. Perhaps that was why she didn't obsess about losing her looks. Liam was paranoid about his. In his twenties and thirties, he had been darkly handsome. Now his skin was tinged with grey and his hair had taken on a scouring pad consistency. And yet a young woman had fancied him.

As the two walked on, the snow resumed its silent descent.

'Do you think that if you give it a bit more time you might feel differently?' Michelle asked.

'Oh God, I wish I could say yes. But I've never had much belief in all that guff about the healing power of time.'

'And Liam? Has he said any more?'

Elizabeth stuck out her tongue and allowed a large flake to melt there. 'He rings to talk to the girls, and we exchange a few words. You wouldn't believe how many ways there are of saying nothing.'

Janey and Stevie chose not to speak about their parents' marriage. They all pretended that one day soon, the clocks would whirr backwards, and all would be well again. There were times when her situation felt less bleak, when Elizabeth felt that reconciliation would be right and proper. More often, she felt the momentum was in the other direction. Occasionally, one of the girls would inadvertently say something that made it clear how much she missed her dad. Elizabeth would be forced to close her eyes and wait for the moment to pass.

She knew she should be more forgiving. Liam wasn't a bad man or an unkind man, even if at times his tongue was unnecessarily sour. For years the four of them had been more than tolerably content. No doubt many people would still consider her lucky. And, after all, it was not as though she didn't have secrets of her own.

Chapter 20

He knew most folks wouldn't agree, but Danny would have preferred snow. On the first day of December, it was cold. The Boston sky was a middling grey with dark ridges. Intermittently those ridges yielded a fine drizzle. The water had merged into a thin slick on the surface of his coat.

'What are you? Ten years old? You'll have plenty of the cold stuff soon enough. *Plenty*,' said Vincent from the passenger seat of Danny's car. 'Even Gina has more sense than to wish for snow.'

Gina was Vincent's seven-year-old daughter, the lone girl in a family of five, and the youngest by eight years. She was his ray of sunshine, the apple of his eye and any other cliché you could mention. Gina had her mother's diminutive frame and the Esposito family's eyes. She was one of the reasons Danny liked to describe Vincent as Boston's grumpiest happy man. He was as taciturn as ever, yet life had given him many reasons to be content.

'I don't know, Dan,' he was saying. 'I don't see why we have to go to Allston today. I've lots of other tasks that need doing.'

'It won't take long. I reckon we should have a look, get a sense of the place, before we put together the bid. We should see what we're up against.'

Vincent scratched his sparsely covered head. 'You know what we're up against: most likely, every construction company within a fifty-mile radius.'

The brothers had gone out on their own shortly before Danny's first marriage. The business had known slumps, booms, famine and feast. On occasion, they'd been a little inventive with regulations and procedures and accounting, although he didn't believe they'd ever done anything out-and-out illegal. They'd been buoyed along by Vincent's determination and Danny's diligence, a quality he had never managed to transfer to the rest of his life.

The school buildings were only a couple of blocks away from where he had parked. This didn't stop Vincent from bleating on about how far they had to walk. 'Won't do you any harm,' said Danny as he marched along the sidewalk, at least two paces ahead of his brother. He could never understand guys their age, guys like Vincent, who didn't look after themselves. OK, Danny had been given the raw material to start with, but how much effort did it really take to keep yourself in good shape? For a man who was going to be forty-six the following month, he was in top condition. Sure, he was a shade heavier than in his twenties, but it suited him. Women, attractive young women, still looked. That very morning, when he'd been getting coffee, a total fox had held his gaze for a fraction too long before giving him a shameless smile. What man wouldn't like that? Vincent, on the other hand, was immeasurably spongier than in his younger years. Perhaps that was what too much happiness did to you.

'Right then,' said his brother, peering at an A4 sheet plastered with official stamps, 'new schoolyard, new parking lot, three new roofs, new doors and windows, boilers, ventilation, cooling tower, wiring. Nothing we haven't done a hundred times before.'

'You said it yourself, though. We've never known such heavy competition for city jobs. For any job. Did you hear the news again this morning? Hundreds being let go at one company, a couple of hundred more at another. And decent guys about to lose their welfare because of some dumb quarrel in Washington. Where's it all going to end, huh?'

'Ever the fucking liberal,' said Vincent. 'Anyhow, it's not like you to be so downbeat.'

At Vincent's insistence, they had left their recce until after school hours. 'Let's face it,' he'd pointed out, 'we'll look like two paedophiles in the playground. Nobody will believe we're there to examine the tiling.' Unfortunately, the late afternoon gloom was now fast descending, making Danny's mood even more melancholic.

As they strolled back to the car, the blanket of drizzle came down again. This time they walked side by side, past a string of Asian restaurants, tattoo parlours and second-hand clothes shops. Danny paused to avoid a group of students who were clogging up the side-walk. Empires might rise and fall, but students always looked the same – like they could do with a day's hard work and a bath in Lysol. Lord, he thought, when did I become such an old grouch?

Vincent was still musing about the economy. 'Besides,' he said, 'there's plenty of places worse off than Boston. I was reading about Ireland. Jeez, what a mess. Do you remember when around here was full of Irish? Place was *infested* with them. Like the rest of the goddamn city.'

'Lots went home when times were good, I suppose,' Danny said. 'They'll probably come back now it's all gone wrong again. Must be grim having the IMF telling you how to run your own country.'

'They sure screwed things up. I reckon they need someone showing them what's what. A couple of years back I was talking to this guy who said real estate in Dublin was more expensive than here. I mean to say, Dan, how could that be right?'

The passage of time had done nothing to cure Vincent of his antipathy towards the Irish. Even the knowledge that he'd had the last laugh on Eddie Jennings – his high school sparring part-ner was doing twenty years for armed robbery – had not softened his attitude. He had moved on from Dorchester with all possible haste. Later, Danny had followed.

Vincent came to a halt in front of a moderately shabby café. 'Buy you a coffee?'

'Sure.' Something must be up. Going for coffee, especially in a spot like this, was not his brother's style.

'Didn't your Irish student live up this way?'

Danny smiled. 'You're going back a ways there. Her place was further up Comm Ave.'

Vincent took a phone call. By the sounds of things, it was from one of his older boys: Vincent junior, most probably. There was mention of a problem with a car, and a girl who had to be given a ride someplace. After three or four minutes, he ended the call with an age-old instruction: 'You'll have to ask your mother.' He fitted the phone, one of those fancy models that does everything except cut your hair and make your dinner, into an inside pocket.

Danny placed both hands around his styrofoam cup. Snow or not, it was cold out.

Vincent was playing with his wedding ring. 'I won't mess around here, Dan. Val said that when you came round to see Mom the other day, you weren't your normal self. In fact, she said you were downright rude.'

Danny blanched. Regina had been living with Vincent and Valerie for the past five years. They had plenty of space, and the arrangement appeared to suit everybody. Danny always visited on Mondays, but that week when he arrived he'd found that she was away on a seniors' trip. He'd been surprised no one had bothered to tell him. Why hadn't she called him herself? 'She's seventy-six years old,' Valerie had replied. 'Maybe it slipped her mind.' He'd been having an awful day. Actually, he'd been having an awful week, and he'd lost his cool, going off on a self-pitying rant about the entire family taking him for granted. Needless to say, he had immediately regretted it and apologised, but he wouldn't blame Val for being put out.

'Not that Val was bitching or anything,' continued Vincent. 'Not *at all*. She was worried. Told me to have a word. What's up?'

'Nothing important. Will you tell her I said sorry again. I made a big deal over nothing.'

'It's Anna, isn't it?'

Danny stroked the side of his cup. 'Ah, Vincent, I don't know as I'm up for talking about this right now.'

His brother raised one of the eyebrows that appeared to grow bushier by the week. 'Have the two of you seen anyone?'

Danny's intuition told him that Valerie was doing the talking here. Vincent was merely following orders. He wasn't a man much given to discussing matters like relationship counselling. At least, Danny assumed that's what he was suggesting. 'Nah, I'm not convinced it would do a lot of good. I don't think either of us is suited to that type of thing, you know.'

He was finding this excruciating and couldn't imagine that Vincent was finding it any easier. He wasn't able to talk about it; the whole business was too humiliating. There hadn't been many occasions when a woman had given up on him before he had grown tired of her. Truth to tell, there had just been the one of any significance. Right then, Danny feared it was happening again.

Elizabeth got the Luas part of the way home and decided to walk the rest. The tram was jam-packed, and she was in the mood for some peace. She was wearing her sensible boots: black leather with thick grooved soles. Liam hated them. If he was there, he'd say she should wear her regular shoes and take the car, or call a cab. But she liked walking in the snow. She enjoyed the methodical pace and the way other walkers showed their solidarity: the smiles and the polite comments about the hazards of the path.

Naturally, you couldn't *admit* to enjoying the snow. If you did, people griped about how much more difficult it was for them. How they had to get the kids to school and clear the path and look in on the elderly neighbours. It was her secret pleasure. As she walked through Ranelagh and on to Milltown, she revelled in the clarity of the air and the uncommon hush. At that time of year, the sun just skirted around the horizon before dipping out of sight again, the snow glittering under its gentle rays.

Elizabeth had gone to work that day, even though she'd been far from sure that anyone else would turn up. In the event, only one woman was missing. They didn't do much actual work. Instead, they spent their time drinking tea and chatting about the weather and the state of the country. Sometimes, that was how things panned out, and that was OK by her. They were adults, most of whom had experienced and survived far more than she would ever know. Who was she to tell them to sit down and practise their spellings?

Her exit from mainstream teaching had been sudden and messy. Up until three years previously, she had taught English at a girls' school, a respected institution where every pupil was expected to go to university before finding a solid husband. There was one problem; Elizabeth disliked her students. Individually they were lovely, or if not lovely, at least tolerable. En masse, they turned into sniggering monsters, and she found it difficult to be civil. She chastised herself for her bad attitude, telling herself their parents were decent, hardworking people who made sacrifices to send them there. Over time her phobia had got worse. When she was a pupil she had never dreaded Monday mornings. As a teacher, the more experienced she became the more miserable she felt. The shadows under her eyes turned from blue to purple to red.

One drowsy Thursday afternoon, Elizabeth snapped. Her sixth-year class – honours students all – were blatantly ignoring her. The room hummed with giggling and yawning. With about five minutes to go, she slapped her book on to the desk. Even then, there was only a ripple of interest. 'All right, girls,' she said, 'it's clear you have no desire to be in this class. So I'm proposing that tomorrow, we talk about shoes. And maybe after that we can discuss the best place to get your highlights done.'

She was beginning to attract a little attention. Orange faces framed by ramrod-straight hair gawped at her, their open mouths revealing pricey orthodontics. Emboldened now, she retrieved her book and waved it about.

'And you know what?' she found herself saying. 'I agree with you about the shower in here. What were they, only a pile of old losers? I can't imagine Sylvia Plath's highlights were all that. W.B. Yeats? He must have been one hell of a weirdo to spend that long stalking Maud Gonne. Patrick Kavanagh? A drunken mucker. And Gerard Manley Hopkins? Sure, who'd listen to a priest?'

For a week, nothing happened. Well, she did notice the swish of gossip each time she walked down a corridor, and the offending class were peculiarly subdued, but that was about it. In the end, one girl spilled the beans to her mother who mentioned it to another mother, and Elizabeth found herself sitting in the principal's office scrutinising her fingernails. The principal was a modern type with ethnic beads and multicoloured bangles galore. 'I have to draw a line somewhere,' she said, 'and those girls' parents pay an obscene amount of money to send them to such a prestigious school.' She went on to stress how, before the year was out, the school would be relying on those very same parents to fund the new computer room and to help with a skiing trip for the transition year class. She asked if Elizabeth would like to take a break for the rest of the term, to get her thoughts together and 'refocus her energies'.

She got a first-class reference and never returned. And, honestly, who would blame the parents for complaining? She would do the same if anyone spoke to her daughters like that. Besides, the pupils were better off without her. With the help of a small bit of late-night cramming and a few expensive grinds, it was As and Bs all the way and a trip to Marbella to celebrate. Elizabeth knew this last part was true because the next time she saw her former charges was in the pages of a Sunday tabloid under a story about holidaying schoolgirls and shocking behaviour. *Posh Totty In Not A Lot-ty*, the headline read. They appeared to have mislaid their T-shirts.

At first, Liam had been supportive of her decision to move on. Like he always said, he was not an unreasonable man. Later, at the height of an argument about another matter entirely, he accused her of being bitter because the girls nowadays had a marginally easier teenage life than she had. 'The way yourself and Michelle go on, you'd swear you grew up surrounded by squalor,' he shouted. 'You had a perfectly normal upbringing in a perfectly normal town.' He was right, and it hurt.

She got more of a kick from her new job. There were days, however, when she fretted that she didn't love it quite as much as she should. She looked at the old gang and felt like she had turned into the dullard of the group. There was Orla on the telly, and Michelle practically running a school, and Donal a big-shot academic in the United States. Fair enough, Peter's job was not one you would choose right now, but he'd made his mark. The last time she'd seen Donal, he had claimed that thirty-six was the key age. If you were going to achieve anything meaningful, you would have done it by then.

Someone she had once known had had a fondness for asking why a person had to be put in a box; why, he'd asked, couldn't they be a whole bunch of things? On her bad days, those words came back to her. At forty-three, she was trapped, the pattern of her life too well entrenched for anything much to change now.

Elizabeth was surprised to discover that she was almost home. As she padded across the road, she noticed Janey in the front garden of their pebble-dashed semi-d. She was wearing an old anorak belonging to Liam and hanging a new bird feeder from the apple tree.

Janey was definitely a whole bunch of things, although sometimes Elizabeth found it hard to know what would become of her. She was in her second year of an archaeology degree, and to put it politely, there weren't many jobs in that. Liam didn't pussyfoot around. According to him, even if it was found that man had actually originated in County Leitrim, there still wouldn't be any bloody jobs in archaeology because the government no longer had the money for such indulgences.

Janey had flashed her big smile, and argued that not even her dad knew what Ireland would be like by the time she left college. 'We might be rich again,' she'd laughed.

Liam had said it was no wonder the country was in such deep trouble.

Chapter 21

'Zip me up, Aidan. Would you?'

'In a minute, Princess.' Two T-shirts and a sock went sailing through the air. 'I could have sworn I had clean underpants somewhere.'

Janey stifled a smile. It was always the same with Aidan. They were packing for their night in a Boston motel. Officially, they were celebrating her birthday, but really they were just looking for an excuse to get a little peace. With seven official residents and numerous hangers-on, their summer apartment was so cramped you couldn't swing a shrew, let alone a cat. Janey had gone to inordinate trouble over her outfit. Aidan, however, had returned at the last minute looking like an unmade bed.

The great thing was, she didn't care. Wasn't it funny how much you could fancy someone, even when they were no one's idea of handsome? Aidan's hair was a mousy colour and, no matter what he did with it, some sections stuck up in little peaks and others were dead flat. His eyes were that nondescript Irish grey, and his nose needed a bigger face. But there were days when Janey would jump through hoops of fire to get to him.

The Princess stuff was their private joke. Aidan was from Shannon and didn't have a lot of tolerance for a certain type of southside Dublin girl. He said that when they'd first met in the college bar, he had presumed she was another of the tribe. Then she had gone and surprised him by being able to name all of the Tipperary hurling team, and by expressing sympathy for the plight of his county, Clare, who were mired in Division Two.

Unusually, there was no one else in the apartment just then.

Their friends, Brendan and Laura, had gone to the cinema, and the other three – Jack, Ronnie and Kevin – were still at work.

'Aha, got you,' said Aidan to the elusive underwear. 'Now, let me zip up that dress.'

'Thanks. I'm going to send a text to my mum, and then I'll be ready.' Janey wiped her forehead with the back of her hand. The day wasn't particularly hot, but she was feeling clammy. 'You know the way she's meeting her college friends tonight?'

'Uh-huh.'

'It got me thinking about the photos – the ones of them over here in Boston.'

'And the mystery man. Don't forget him,' said Aidan. 'Elizabeth – the secret history.'

'Stop it now. Just because she had her picture taken with a big American-looking fellow, it doesn't mean there was anything going on. Remember you're talking about a woman who changed her flight and went home early. My dad used to joke about that. How he knew then that he was stuck with her.'

'Charming.'

'Ah, he meant it in a good way. Sure, in no time at all they were settled down and having babies.' She scrunched up her face. 'I only wish she was happier now.'

'She'll be all right. You can't let your mam's problems ruin your summer.' He rubbed a knuckle along Janey's cheekbone. 'If you don't mind me saying so, you're looking a wee bit tired.'

'Don't worry, I'll be grand. Anyway, I was thinking that we should take more photographs.'

'Aren't you a terror for the photos already? Snapping away there on the phone and lashing it all up on to the Facebook.'

She knew he said 'the Facebook' deliberately, just to annoy people. He also said 'the Twitter'. How could you not love him? 'I don't mean like that. I mean proper photos. On paper. In the old-fashioned way. So one day we can look back on them.'

'Whatever you say, Princess. Are you ready for the road?'

'I am.' Text sent, Janey put her phone in her bag. What she

didn't say was that she had a pain in her stomach or her side or somewhere; she couldn't pinpoint exactly what hurt. She was sure the feeling would pass.

Peter and Donal were on their feet, facing off like eight-year-old boys comparing marbles, or football stickers, or whatever eight-year-olds traded now.

'The last time I saw you,' started Peter, 'we were still the richest people in the world.'

'That's nothing. The last time I saw you, you had hair.'

'Yeah, but while it lasted it was worth having. I see you're still cutting your own with the garden shears. How you've convinced a woman to marry you, I'll never know.'

Just as the pair began to pique the interest of other diners, Donal grinned and threw an arm around his adversary. After all, thought Elizabeth, nobody could insult you like a friend.

'God, it's good to see you, man,' said Peter. 'How long has it been?'

'There's a question.' Donal turned to her. 'You'll remember, Elizabeth. When's the last time we were all together?'

'More than three years ago. Christmas.'

'Back,' said Orla, 'when the politicians were still boasting about the place being awash with cash.'

Donal sighed. 'I'm back in the country ten minutes, and already I've had at least twenty conversations about the bloody money. Does anybody talk about anything else any more?'

'The answer to that would probably be no,' said Michelle. 'Perhaps we should attempt some small talk first. You know, the standard speech about how much we've missed each other.'

'Or better still,' said Elizabeth, 'we can talk about Donal getting married.'

They were in a Dublin city-centre restaurant, one of those places that rattles with brittle bonhomie. In the way that restaurants are always either too quiet or too loud, this was the latter. They were surrounded by an excess of blond highlights, florid faces and mangled vowels: '*Hew er yew? Jest murvellus.*' Elizabeth suspected that before too long Donal would be running the rule over the crowd, deciding who should survive his imaginary revolution.

Nowadays, he was a touch more sinewy and a shade more weathered but otherwise unaltered. 'Still getting away with it,' was his own judgement. Beside him, Orla had the air of a woman desperately trying to prove she was as free-spirited as the day the group first met. Peter, on the other hand, took every opportunity to stress his worldliness. His pronouncements came with a tone that said, 'If you really understood, you wouldn't argue.' Elizabeth reckoned you could listen to him for hours and be baffled that you ever had anything in common. Then one sentence or gesture would remind you of his capacity for kindness, and you would berate yourself for being so shallow. If anyone got emotional, it would be him. Across the table sat Michelle. If anyone got angry, it would be her.

Orla was hitting her stride. 'No seriously, Peter. The longer this goes on the more it gets like the 1980s.'

'Tuh,' he snorted. 'It is no way like the eighties. Back then, Orla, as you well know, the country ran on EEC butter vouchers and tinned meat. Will you look at this place? Full to the rafters.' To support his point, he threw his eyes approvingly over the room. 'There's no recession here tonight.'

It hadn't taken long for him to rile Michelle. It never did. 'You do know I've banned that phrase? And, for fear you need reminding, "We all partied"? Double banned. Even a *suggestion* that Lehman Brothers were to blame for any of our troubles, and you'll be sent home. On the bus.'

'That's you told,' said Orla.

Elizabeth grinned to herself at the notion of Peter on the bus, preferably with a gang of hoodies or a man who'd taken one tonic wine too many and wanted to discuss where it had all gone wrong. She knew it was slightly early in the evening for him to take offence. Later, when more drink was taken, he and Michelle would goad each other about some matter of no consequence. In the end, one of them would be forced to apologise. Once upon a time, they would have ended up in bed. To the best of Elizabeth's knowledge, this hadn't happened since Michelle met Andy, and Peter became middle-aged.

Peter's wife, Claire, was made for words like 'competent' and 'capable'. You could picture her lying awake at night, listing committees she would like to chair. She wasn't much crack.

Donal joined the debate. 'To me, it feels worse than the eighties.'

Peter groaned. Donal, however, was undeterred. 'Hear me out, man, would you? When we were growing up, recession wasn't two quarters of negative growth, or whatever the economics books say. It was a lifelong predicament, and you ploughed on as best you could. But no one gave us any false hope. The kids today were dropped from a height.'

Michelle nodded. 'And don't they know it. The whinging would test your sanity. Not that long ago, one of my fifth years told me that only losers stay in Ireland. That even if she got a job, she wouldn't want to live here.'

'With that attitude,' sniffed Peter, 'she'd be no loss. We coped. As did plenty before us. They'll just have to get on with it.'

By the sounds of it, the conversation was destined to keep winding back to the country's woes. Elizabeth had already had her fill of such discussions. If anybody had anything new to say, she might think differently. But, to her ear, the conversations spun around pointlessly before disintegrating into the recital of familiar prejudices. Her father had a saying: 'There isn't a thought in his head that hasn't been placed there.' It kept coming to mind.

'Still, wouldn't you love to be young again?' said Donal. 'Twenty-one, say? With a bit of sense, but not too much.'

'I would not,' replied Peter. 'Well, only if I knew that all the nonsense I was worried about wouldn't matter in a few years' time.'

'What else would you say to yourself?'

'Get a proper haircut.'

'Orla, what would you say to your twenty-one-year-old self?'

'Be as wild as you like. And then some.'

'Correct me if I'm wrong,' said Peter, 'but was that not exactly what you were? I'm surprised you can even remember being that age, given the state you were in half of the time.'

She beamed, as if proud to be reminded of her giddy youth.

'What about yourself there, Elizabeth?' said Donal. 'Isn't your birthday around this time of the year?'

'Next week.'

'I can remember the night you were twenty-one.' He sighed. 'Those were days.'

Elizabeth smiled, yet said nothing.

'Now, Elizabeth,' said Orla, 'don't be giving us the old enigmatic act. Wasn't that the time you lost the run of yourself?'

She fingered the edge of the tablecloth. The less she said about herself the better. 'It's such a long time ago, it's all kind of vague.'

Donal spluttered his disbelief.

Michelle intervened. 'Don't we all have a big bundle of memories from that summer? The heat and the carry-on and Ray and Rosie and Bray Brian and Donal's madcap stories. Not to mention Ireland beating England. Sure, Peter, didn't you spend years telling us that match was responsible for the Celtic Tiger?'

He had the decency to look shamefaced. 'Now now, I don't think I put it quite like that.'

Donal thumped the table, sending an assortment of cutlery springing into the air. 'Fuck it. It's only just come back to me. A couple of years ago, didn't I bump into him?'

'You've lost me, Donal,' said Peter. 'Who did you bump into?'

'The blue-eyed boy. I was in Boston visiting Meredith's family. Anyway, there was a gang of us in a bar downtown, and who should be in the same place, only handsome Dan.'

'And did he remember you?' asked Orla.

'He did indeed. No surprise there. Wasn't the same fella always as sharp as a tack? He was asking after you all. Especially Elizabeth here, obviously.'

'And ... how was he?' Elizabeth asked, as her stomach performed acrobatic tricks.

'The very same. Well, no – more prosperous-looking. Decent suit on him. A bit more swagger. Classy young piece on his arm. Or classy young wife, I should say. Can't remember her name.'

Michelle quirked an eyebrow at him. 'American universities must have gone downhill in a big way if that's how you refer to women these days.'

'You know what I mean. Put it this way, I doubt you'd run her on a carpenter's wages. She had one of those shiny brown manes you only find on a certain class of American woman. And the teeth were Grade A.'

'Ah, *Donal*,' said Orla. 'You sound like you're describing a horse.'

'Ladies, you came out with a lot worse in your day,' said Peter.

Donal speared a piece of meat. Elizabeth, not quite sure what to say, gazed at him. He winked. 'I'm sorry, Elizabeth,' he said. 'What I meant to add was that Danny always had classy taste in women.'

For the next hour, Elizabeth's head was elsewhere. Oh, she smiled dutifully. Or frowned, if that's what was called for. But she had to get Donal on his own, and, unfortunately, he was the centre of attention. As time wore on, she got more and more antsy. A couple of years ago, he'd said. So why didn't he tell her before now? He must have known how much she'd want to hear about Danny. Or maybe he didn't. Maybe he assumed, like a sensible individual would, that Danny was just a blur in her past. A secret fling about whom she carried vague memories. A faded photograph. A tarnished bracelet.

The others were consumed by talk of Donal's wedding. Like him, Meredith was an Oregon-based university teacher. Unlike him, she was thirty years old.

'That's *fourteen years* younger than you,' pointed out Orla, as though he might not be aware of this.

'Fair play to the man,' said Peter, raising his wine glass in salute.

Michelle produced the scariest fact. 'That means Meredith was born in 1981.'

'We'll have another drink,' said Orla.

Elizabeth had drunk more than was sensible. All the same, she said yes to a brandy. Donal, as rangy-limbed as ever, wriggled in beside her. 'Congratulations to you,' she said, kissing him on a surprisingly soft cheek. 'It took long enough, but that's the last of us settled now.' (Orla had finally succumbed to marriage two years before. She had been engaged five times. Michelle claimed she'd kept all the rings.)

'Please, Elizabeth.' He held up his hands in horror. 'Don't go using that ugly word. Listen, there's been plenty of talk about me tonight. And hardly a word out of you. How are you?'

'Not the worst. Keeping her between the ditches, as they say.'

'I haven't heard that one in a while.'

'That's because you don't come home often enough.' She wound a small loop of hair behind her ear. 'Liam's away, as you know. And Janey's in Boston. So it's just me and Stevie.'

'What does Janey make of Boston?'

'She likes it, but I don't think anywhere holds the same sense of … wonder, if that's not too strong a word.'

Donal laughed his old gurgling laugh. 'It's hard to imagine today's twenty-one-year-old being excited by a supermarket. What a sad bunch we were. The last of the innocents.' He shifted slightly on the seat and leaned in towards her. 'Speaking of Boston, I wanted to say sorry for bringing up the story about Danny and then not giving you the full version. It's just, even after all these years, Peter puts on a face like thunder at the mention of the man's name.'

'Full story?' Here it was. Elizabeth drained her glass. Donal caught the eye of a waiter and signalled for two more brandies.

'I made it sound as though he asked about you in passing, when really all he wanted to talk about was you.'

Her head swam. She thought it wisest to make light of the situation. 'Danny wanted to talk about me? Even in the presence of the "classy piece"?'

'She'd drifted off somewhere. She must have been catatonic from our chat about the greatness of 1988. I'd say she wasn't long out of the pram at the time.' He paused. 'He wanted to know how you were, if you were married, did you have kids, did you become a teacher. The whole lot. Oh, and he said, "Will you tell her I often think about her?"'

Elizabeth searched for the right response. A fresh drink was placed in front of her, and she was glad to have something to do with her hands. 'And … he was good?'

'Has a building company. He's done well for himself.'

'No. I mean, did he look happy?'

'Lord, Elizabeth, you're not tearing up on me, are you?'

'Oh for God's sake, Donal, it's just the drink.'

'He was in good form. I gathered the woman was his second wife.'

'And children?'

'I think he mentioned boys. But, you know me, I'm brutal at the family stuff.'

'Why didn't you tell me before now?'

'I'm going to annoy you and answer a question with a question. If you care what he thinks about you, and if you want to know about him, why didn't you stay in touch?'

'At the time I didn't feel it was a good idea. And you know what happened. Everything moved so fast. Marriage. Children. Moving to Dublin. Returning to college. Work.'

'Why don't you look him up now then? I keep in touch with Rosie. She's a respectable married woman these days. Married to a Conservative MP, no less, with four junior Tories.'

Elizabeth giggled. 'You're kidding me. Lairy Rosie Marsh is married to a Tory MP?'

'Swear to God,' said Donal, and they both shook their heads at the madness of it all. He rubbed her arm. 'I genuinely do think you should give Danny a call. It's not like years ago. A quick search on the net and you'll find him. And what harm could it do? Like he said, he still thinks about you. And it's obvious you still think about him.'

Chapter 22

When her phone rang Elizabeth was standing at the kitchen door, inhaling her all-time favourite smell: rain falling on dry ground. In her view, you could keep your baking bread and your freshly cut grass. Nothing was better than this. It was four o'clock on Sunday afternoon, and although she was making an attempt at the ironing, she remained frazzled from the night before. She picked up the phone to see Janey's name on the screen which was a lovely surprise. It was barely twenty-four hours since they'd last spoken.

Confusingly, it was a man's voice on the other end of the line. Her impulses were so impaired by the night's drinking that it took her several seconds to recognise Aidan. Elizabeth was tempted to call him Hawaii. She reckoned that as nicknames went it was fairly sweet, but according to Janey he found it patronising and got miffed when anyone used it.

The first thing she said was, 'Is everything OK?' The second was, 'Oh, Jesus.'

As Aidan told it, Janey had been feeling unwell all evening, but she had insisted she'd be all right. At four in the morning, she was in a lot of pain and started to get sick. Still she was adamant there was no need for any fuss. 'Typical Janey,' he said.

After an hour or so it was clear she was getting worse. She had a temperature and the pain was so bad she began to cry. When she tried to stand up, she buckled over in agony. Aidan found the guy on duty in the motel, and before either of them truly appreciated what was happening, Janey was in hospital surrounded by people in gowns. 'Ruptured appendix,' he said.

'And …' said Elizabeth, a tremor in her voice.

'She needed an operation. That's where she is at the moment. I'm hanging around here, cooling my heels. I got to speak to a doctor and he says it's not like years ago, that she'll be fine.'

'But—'

'I know you'll be worried, only don't go using the Google or anything, Elizabeth. You'll only scare yourself. You have to trust the doctor. What I'll do now is get the name of a fellow you can talk to when the operation is over, and I'll send you a text with the details. Would that be all right?'

She was taken aback by how good Aidan was. You'd swear he was forty-three and she was twenty-two, not the other way around. 'Bless you, pet. Was she in a very bad way?'

She'd been pretty sick, he said, but quickly added that this was probably for the best because it meant she was seen without delay.

Her brain travelling in about five different directions, Elizabeth insisted he call her as soon as there was any news. 'Don't stress about your phone bill. We'll look after it. And I'll see you tomorrow.'

Aidan maintained there was no need to put herself to all that trouble. Of course there was. She was already making mental lists: Stevie, Liam, Michelle, plane, passport. Didn't she need a security number of some type? Stevie would know. While she ransacked her bag for a pen, a small face appeared at the door. Grover streaked in, his fur spiky from the rain. He snarled a miaow at Elizabeth, like the downpour was her fault. She picked him up. 'You'll have to fend for yourself a bit over the next while, buddy.' He purred, and she sniffed his head. The smell of Grover's head was almost as soothing as rain on dry ground.

Predictably, Liam got hassled. Whatever else she said about him, he did love the two girls. He was talking about getting on a plane himself until she convinced him it made more sense for her to go to Boston. He was due back in Ireland in less than a month. He would see Janey in no time at all.

'I never did get this mania for spending the summer in

America,' he said. 'It might have made some sense in your day, but sure now the US is as screwed as Ireland.'

'Janey has a great job. She's selling jewellery in Faneuil Hall.' The ensuing silence confirmed that this meant nothing to Liam. He had stayed in Ireland during his college summers, playing hurling and helping out on an uncle's farm. He'd never understood that making money wasn't the purpose of the trip at all. After Elizabeth reassured him that Janey had health insurance, they said their goodbyes.

Their other daughter insisted she be allowed to stay on her own. 'I'm *sixteen*,' Stevie said, trying to make this sound like a grand old age.

'Michelle will be here for you in an hour. When your exams are over, you can come back. Not to spend the night, though. The cruelty people would be after me.'

Stevie grunted and gurned, then flicked back her hair and promised, 'no more than fifty or sixty'.

'Fifty or sixty what?'

'People at the party,' she said, giving her mother a cheeky smile.

After several conversations with Aidan, one with a man called Dr Sabatini, a few drowsy words with Janey and a mostly sleep-free night, Elizabeth was on a plane. She was going back to the city she hadn't seen in almost a quarter of a century.

Danny was undergoing a particular type of torture. No matter how much he wanted to leave, he had to sit and listen. For her age, his mother was as sprightly as they came. She paced the floor of the front room, waving one hand like she was conducting an imaginary band.

'If you don't mind me saying so, I've always believed that's your problem. You expect everything to be easy. It will all work out without any effort on your part. Isn't that right?'

'Well—'

'There's no need to answer, Danny. I know it's right. You've always been the same. You let matters drift until the damage is done. Then you come around here expecting sympathy.'

Danny wondered what age you had to be to stop getting a dressing down from your mother. Surely he had passed the threshold? He sat with his hands clasped, trying to guess what she'd come out with next. Would she object if he lit a cigarette? For years, she had puffed her way through thirty a day. Since conquering the habit, she'd become the worst anti-smoking zealot in Boston.

'Have you any plans to talk to her?' asked Regina.

'Ma, I don't want to argue with you, and I know this makes a change, but I haven't done anything wrong here. It's Anna who's been having the affair.'

'Your brother says you've known for months and did nothing about it.'

'He says lots of things.'

'What sort of answer is that? Is he telling the truth?'

This was getting worse. He didn't care what she said; he was having a smoke. He pulled the pack out of his jacket and lit up. Regina picked up an ashtray like it was a bowl of anthrax, and placed it on the nearest table.

'You haven't answered my question, Danny.'

'I didn't *know* she was seeing another guy. I had my suspicions, I suppose. I was planning on asking, only … it was awkward, you know.' He inhaled as deeply as he could. 'Grovelling's not my style. Never has been, and I'm not about to start now.'

'Oh, Danny.' Regina sat down on the deep pink sofa, leaned back and looked up at the ceiling. 'I know this is none of my business. For heaven's sake, your own children are almost adults. I should be worrying about them, not you. But I do worry. How many marriages do you plan on going through?'

For a moment, he stayed quiet. Well, how did you answer that? 'Did you see me and Vincent in the weekend paper?' He attempted a smile. 'I looked good, I thought.'

'Maybe you should spend a little less time being Mr Big-shot-builder, and a little more thinking about your wife. Did she say when she'd be back?'

She hadn't said, and Danny hadn't asked. Anna's behaviour had become so indiscreet that any fool could tell something was up. She disappeared for hours at a time, then came home and went straight to bed. Several times she hadn't returned at all, just called with some bullshit story about staying with a friend. Anna didn't have any friends. She was a man's woman. That was one of the reasons he had fallen for her to begin with. Now she didn't eat with him. She certainly didn't have sex with him. She rarely spoke to him about anything that wasn't utterly mundane. And somehow he ignored it all. He left the house in the morning and tried to forget. Not for the first time, he found that personal unhappiness was good for business.

Looking back, Danny supposed he'd had ideas about himself, and Anna was where those ideas had led. She worked in banking. Not like a teller or anything. High-class banking. She was a cashmere-coat-and-silk-panties type of woman. And he had thought she was what he deserved.

Matters had come to a head because of one of those crazy rows that starts with something trivial and culminates in the two of you pouring venom over each other. They'd ended up like a pair of kids in a schoolyard, calling each other out on their family's failings. She'd called him a low-life, and he'd asked if that's why she was fucking another man. At first she'd made a half-assed attempt to deny it, but it hadn't taken her long to come clean. He was a doctor, like her dad. An endocrinologist. They had lots in common, she said. Almost as quickly as Anna had become enraged, she calmed down again. In a crisp tone, she spoke about being owed leave. She was going to stay with her parents in Connecticut for a while. She needed to collect her thoughts.

Regina was singing to herself while she dusted the dresser. Danny lit another cigarette.

'Plainly, you've forgotten cancer killed your father.'

'Stomach cancer, Ma. Most likely nothing to do with smoking.'

She fixed him with a stare like he was still the rowdy

223

eight-year-old who'd pitched a ball through the kitchen window. 'Whatever you choose to believe, Danny.'

For years, he had been pessimistic about his mother, hadn't expected her to live to a good age. Or if she did, he worried she'd get some other illness of the head. Didn't it stand to reason, after all those years with depression, that dementia or some such would strike? Instead, her older years were turning into the best years of her life. The depression had gradually drifted away, or she had conquered it, or a bit of both. When he asked, she told him how one day she was weeding the garden and it struck her that she couldn't spend the rest of her life being afraid. 'I knew I had to get on with things,' she said.

Danny had the feeling that Regina's twelve grandchildren gave her far more pleasure than her own sons and daughters ever had. Most of them had, or were destined for, college educations. Their graduation photos decorated her bedroom.

There was a story Valerie never tired of telling. About a year back, the two had been shopping together. Val had suggested that Regina might like to try on a particular skirt. 'I don't think so, honey,' she'd replied. 'That's a skirt for an *old* woman.' He couldn't picture Anna trawling the shops with his mother. Still, different was what he'd wanted, and that's what he had got.

Regina was gazing at him. 'You haven't been listening to a word, have you? Will you stay for your dinner?'

'Aw, I don't want to be a nuisance.'

'You have to eat.' She shook her white head. 'Why don't you take a trip down to Greenwich, talk things over? You can't just give up.'

Elizabeth arrived in Boston at almost the same time as she'd left Dublin. She remembered marvelling at this more than twenty years before. This time it really was a blessing for it meant that by late Monday afternoon, she was at Janey's hospital bedside releasing all of her pent-up fussing. She was smoothing pillows and looking for doctors and sending Aidan out for what she knew were totally unnecessary items. She had to be doing something. Eventually, Janey croaked that her mother was doing her head in, and would she quit the messing.

Elizabeth was strangely relieved by her daughter's stroppiness. She'd never seen Janey looking so wan and miserable, or known her to be so quiet. It was like the normal chatty Janey had been replaced by a morose stranger. The skin around her blue eyes was a disturbing yellowish brown, and her lips were so pale they had practically disappeared.

After the first couple of days, the patient began to eat a little, although she remained on large doses of painkillers and antibiotics. She had developed an abscess that needed to be drained, and there was, the doctors said, a danger she would get further infections, so they wanted her to stay in hospital for some days yet. This, they insisted, was all perfectly routine.

Aidan had been an absolute gem. He'd called work to explain the situation, and was taking a few days off. By the time Elizabeth arrived in Boston, he was already on first-name terms with half of the hospital. By Wednesday, he was enquiring after their children and discussing the performance of their favourite sports teams. Apart from going home to sleep, he only left once – to play hurling. He returned four hours later with the makings of a black eye, and the belief that some of those playing in Boston were 'pure savages'.

On Thursday, Elizabeth realised that her constant presence at Janey's side was no longer required. Actually, she got the sense she was becoming an irritant.

'Eh, Elizabeth?' Aidan said. 'Janey was wondering, do you not have any old haunts you want to visit? As you're in Boston, like.'

'Would this be code for, "I've seen as much of my mum as I can handle. Can I be ill in peace for a while?"'

'Ah now, even in her reduced state, I don't think the Princess would go that far.'

On her journey back to the hotel, Elizabeth rang Stevie who was fresh from her final exam and as giddy as a goose. Nothing much was happening at home, she said. Boston was on the news because some criminal called Whitey Bulger had been captured. Otherwise, it was the usual diet of economic misery and deviant priests.

Grover was there each evening when they went to feed him, although he was catching a disturbing amount of wildlife. For some weeks now, Stevie had been attempting to turn the cat into a vegetarian. On night one, she'd given him a bowl of cheese, which he devoured. The snag was that he'd brought Stevie a present in return: a lovely plump sparrow, which when deposited on the doorstep still contained faint stirrings of life. 'You astound me with your ingratitude,' she'd said to the confused feline. Elizabeth had suggested to her daughter that she might be more usefully employed studying for her exams. She should have saved her breath. If the girl got a notion into her head, no matter how ludicrous, it was best to let her get on with it. Janey claimed that one day her sister would support them all.

Today, Stevie was keen to talk, and Elizabeth was happy to let her. The phone bill was a worry for another day. Her dad called all the time, she said, and he promised he'd be home before she knew it. She joked about Janey being a big malingerer, and was desperate to hear how ugly her scar would be. As they said their goodbyes, Stevie chirped, 'I miss you, Mum.' Elizabeth was struck by how small her voice sounded. For all her earnestness, her daughter wasn't much more than a little girl. Mind you, when she was that age, she'd met her husband. There was something unsettling about that.

Liam sounded equally pleased to hear from her. He usually said how he missed 'them all'. This time he said, 'I miss you.' Elizabeth was taken aback. She hoped that whatever she mumbled in reply made sense. He wanted to know when they would be returning to Ireland. In about a week, she figured. He signed off by telling her not to worry. 'Enjoy being back there. You deserve it.'

What did you do with a free afternoon in Boston? You could go for a walk, she supposed. Or sit in the sun or visit a museum.

You could take a bus tour or stroll around Harvard or look at the shops. Or you could stop feeling guilty that your daughter's illness had presented you with an opportunity. You could just make the phone call.

When Donal had suggested she look Danny up on the internet, he couldn't have known that she'd already done just that. The first time she had typed his name, her hands had been slightly shaky. Having made no impression on the World Wide Web herself, she wasn't sure what she would find. Her hands shook a whole lot more when the search engine yielded its results. She recalled how Danny and Vincent used to talk about going into business. She had always seen them as small-time boys, fixing the guttering or building an extension. She pictured them at work; Danny would be lugging around his old box of tools, and Vincent would be wearing a pair of jeans so filthy they stood up by themselves. The Esposito Brothers Construction Company may indeed have built a considerable number of extensions. But that wasn't the half of it. According to their website, EBCC had built houses and shops and offices. They had remodelled and renovated and restored. There was a list of private and public testimonials. There was even a small section on their philanthropic work.

'Merciful hour,' said Elizabeth. So shocked was she that she spilled a cup of tea on top of Grover who was sitting at her feet having a wash. The half-scalded cat promptly sharpened his claws on her right calf. Undeterred by the stinging and the puddle of tea, she searched on. She found other references, including a picture from a local paper showing 'a smiling Mr Daniel Esposito' handing over a cheque to a youth group. Another photograph depicted a beaming pair of brothers being honoured by an association of Boston Italians. She tried not to look at the pictures too often. That wouldn't be healthy or, worse, someone might catch her.

So when she finally convinced herself that there was nothing wrong with seeking out Danny, she knew where to start. A woman with tones of treacle answered the office phone and said he wasn't in the building today. Elizabeth explained that she was an old friend and asked for his cell number.

'I can't give you that, ma'am,' replied the receptionist. 'I can take your message and ask Mr Esposito to contact you.'

Elizabeth gave her details, then another thought struck. She wondered if he was working elsewhere today. He was, she was told, on site in Allston. Elizabeth asked where exactly that might be. There was another pause. Clearly, Ms Treacle feared she had a stalker on her hands. Elizabeth said that she genuinely was a friend from Ireland, and would only be in Boston for a day or two. 'OK then,' sighed the receptionist. 'It's an old elementary school, not far from Harvard Avenue, but he might have left by now.' Elizabeth reckoned she would take her chances.

Within ten minutes, she was standing on the platform at Park Street station. It seemed impossible that after more than twenty years a smell could be instantly familiar. But it was. It was also mercilessly evocative. She was twenty-one years old, waiting for the B line to Brighton, soaking in the heat and the grease and the sweat. The wail and buzz of the T sounded just the same too, and although the diner that had once marked her stop was now a McDonald's, she knew precisely where to get off.

She walked past rows of shops and cafés. Their fronts were new, but the buildings were the same: some squat and ugly, some with curlicues and embellishments. You could still get an all-day breakfast or a second-hand dress or your tarot cards read. She remembered the liquor store with a towering red sign. They had bought a keg there on the day of the party. The sun scalded the pavement like it always had. Even the clothes, the long shorts and shapeless T-shirts, were the same.

At some point, Elizabeth started to feel sick. What if Donal had got it wrong, and Danny didn't remember her? Or what if she had changed so much he didn't recognise her? When she saw the neon vests and yellow hats, one of her knees gave an abrupt wobble. Her eyelid performed a few quick twitches. For heaven's sake, she said to herself, it's like you told the receptionist; he's an old friend. Twenty metres away, a man in jeans and a navy polo shirt – no vest, no hat – was conferring with a small knot of men. She wasn't able to see his face. If it was odd for a smell to be familiar after twenty-three years, how mad was it to remember the shape of a head?

'Excuse me?' she said.

The man without the vest turned around. 'I'm sorry, ma'am, you can't …'

Elizabeth put her head to one side, smiled and thrust out her hand.

He squinted. 'No.' Then he said it again, louder this time. 'No.' He went to shake her hand, but thought better of it. The smile that broke across his face was as broad as she'd ever seen. Two arms enveloped her, the embrace so tight it was difficult to breathe. 'Well, well, well,' Danny laughed. 'You finally came back.'

Chapter 23

Was there a specific word for it? Elizabeth wondered. The moment when something you had visualised actually happened. There undoubtedly was a physical effect. All of her muscles had tightened. In particular, the backs of her legs felt impossibly taut, as if they might go *ping*. They were sitting across from each other, in soft, low chairs, knees almost touching. Elizabeth was flexing and releasing her toes. The two of them were uncoordinated, speaking over each other then lapsing into patches of silence. They were like strangers which, in fairness, was what they were. 'Imagine, twenty-three years,' they kept saying. 'Twenty-three years.'

Danny hardly uttered a sentence without throwing in, 'This is the *best* surprise,' or, 'You haven't changed at all,' or some similar flannel. No more than Park Street station or Harvard Avenue, the fundamentals were intact. Elizabeth noticed how he still leaned forward as he spoke. He was heavier, yet retained a fit, hard look. When the opportunity arose, he said, he still relished getting his hands dirty. Vincent yammered on about this being inappropriate, and his wife reckoned he was mad. His smile was just as endearing.

Other things were new. His voice sounded more mellow, his accent less pronounced. He had that hard-to-pin-down veneer of success. There were ripples of grey in his short back and sides and lines around his eyes.

As she relaxed, Elizabeth decided to see if his sense of humour remained in place. She gazed over the top of her coffee cup and shook her head in mock sorrow. 'I must say, it's a shame about you … letting yourself go like this. I wouldn't have known you.'

Danny twinkled at her, and released his familiar throaty laugh. 'You're a cruel woman. Age has made you bitter, obviously.'

She laughed too. 'Perhaps. But at least I'll always be younger than you.'

Danny reached over and squeezed her knee. He was the same, all right.

On the short walk to the café, she had explained how she found him and why she was in Boston. He had hummed and clicked and grasped her hand. If there was anything he could do, *anything*, she was to let him know. Strangely, she had forgotten how big his hands were.

Danny knew about her marrying Liam, and about the girls. 'Your friend, Donal, told me how well life had turned out for you.' He was all enquiries about her family and her life and her work. She told him how both of her parents were dead: Syl, four years ago, and Stacia a year or so later. He said his own father was dead for more than twenty years. But Regina? The way she was going, she'd see a hundred or more. Elizabeth got a little rush from this. How she would love to see his mother, but she didn't like to ask.

He enquired after Liam, or as he put it, 'the lucky bastard you married'. Things were great, she said, and she was lucky, and the recession wouldn't last for ever. Danny told her how more Irish guys were pitching up looking for work, and that unfortunately there was not much he could do for most of them. Canada and Australia appeared to be all the rage nowadays, she said.

He nodded. 'It's certainly tougher for the illegal guys over here. We try and stay on the right side of the law. And, I suppose, I remember Brian Byrne and what can happen. Have you ever come across him?'

'No. I know Peter kept in touch with him for a while. I have the feeling he went back to London. I hope everything ended up OK.' She sipped her coffee. 'You've got a good memory.'

'Now, how could I forget Brian? He was there the night we met. When you were barely off the plane. With your big eyes. And your big hair. Do you not remember?'

'Oh, I remember you. And your chat-up lines from the ark.'

'I thought I was very smooth.'

'God help me, I thought you were a fine thing.'

'Oh, but I was,' Danny laughed.

'You still have a great welcome for yourself,' Elizabeth said, squeezing his forearm.

He, apparently, was married to Anna. The boys from his first marriage were nineteen and sixteen. The elder lad, Ryan, was at MIT. 'Can you believe that? An Esposito boy studying at MIT. Ma is so pleased she could practically explode.' Elizabeth got the impression she wasn't the only one. Danny said the younger lad, Conor, was, 'more like his dad, a construction guy'.

'Irish names?'

'I met another Irish woman. Not Irish Irish like you. Geraldine was born in Boston. Her parents are from Mayo. O'Connor.'

'The same as the people next door.'

'The very ones. Mossy was Geraldine's uncle. He died last year. Bridie's gone a few years. No doubt she's monitoring activities at the pearly gates.'

'Or somewhere warmer.'

'Now, now.' He grinned. 'Ger and I are good these days. It was … well, you know how it is. My fault all the way, obviously. She got married again too. Has a little girl. A beautiful little thing.'

'How did Vincent cope with you marrying an Irish woman?'

'He said she was far too good for me, actually.'

'And Anna, is she Irish?'

'Lord no,' he said with too much haste. 'Sorry, Elizabeth, that sounded wrong. She's from Connecticut. There right now, in fact. Visiting with her family.'

It was difficult to avoid the sense that Danny was circling around the truth, yet casting something vital aside. Of course, she hadn't been truthful with him, but then she'd become quite adept at misleading people.

They talked some more about Regina, and Elizabeth asked that her best wishes be passed on. 'And to Valerie and Vincent,' she added. 'Vincent, your business partner. You've done well, Danny, so so well.' She threw up her hands, palms to the ceiling, as if to emphasise his success.

His response was not what she had expected. He was reticent. Uncomfortable, even. Business had been a bit up and down, he said. But they'd never overextended themselves. They were keeping their heads above water. Turning a buck.

'It's a good job you're not in Ireland. Every builder in the land seems to have gone wallop.'

'Wallop,' he repeated. 'You were always good with words.'

They both paused. And smiled. The tinkling and clattering of cutlery and crockery and the dull thrum of music receded. Elizabeth didn't believe their smiles were for anything in particular. They were more for the general absurdity of the situation. At least, that's how she felt. It was a long time since that early autumn morning in Brookline. A long time with no contact. Well, that wasn't entirely true; there had been one letter. She couldn't guess how many times she had thought about him during the intervening years.

Danny rubbed his chin. 'This is surreal, isn't it?'

'My thoughts exactly.'

'You're not going to tell me you have a flight this evening, are you?'

'No, not at all. Janey's likely to be in hospital for another day or two and ...' She got the reference. 'Oh.'

'I'm sorry, Elizabeth. I couldn't resist.'

'No, I'm sorry, Danny. It wasn't my finest hour.'

He reached over and lightly touched her wrist. 'There are things I should have done differently too. But, hey ...'

He must have thought better of whatever he was about to say. Elizabeth watched a chattering couple dressed in black and white – two magpies – pick up their belongings and make for the door. This was her signal to go. She didn't want Janey thinking she'd been abandoned. Neither could she leave Danny like this. She swallowed the dregs of her coffee.

His phone rang. After a cursory glance at the screen and a quick frown, he cut off the call. 'What I was trying to ask is, are you around for dinner tomorrow? Or a drink? Or whatever suits you? O'Mahoney's was levelled about fifteen years ago, so you needn't worry that I'll take you there.'

'That's a shame. But I'd love to have dinner. The hospital canteen is kind of limited.'

'And we've an awful lot of life to catch up on,' he said.

When she arrived at the ward, Aidan was loitering at the door, talking to a narrow foxy-haired man. 'Ah, Clare are sunk this year, I'm afraid. The emigration has us in rag order. The captain has gone to Australia. Mind you, we put up a decent performance against Tipperary.'

Elizabeth couldn't believe that he'd found someone to talk hurling with. She'd got to the hospital more quickly than anticipated because, despite her protestations, Danny had insisted on giving her a lift. 'There are benefits to being the boss,' he'd said. She couldn't name the make or model of car he drove now, any more than she would have been able to name the broken-down amalgamation of chrome and rust he had driven more than twenty years before. All she could say was that it was dark and smooth and smelled like vanilla.

Janey looked wretched – white and glassy-eyed. Elizabeth tried to keep the unease from her voice. 'How are they treating you, pet?'

'Oh, Mum, I feel so rubbish. *And* they say I'll have to stay here for the next two or three days to make sure the infection doesn't get any worse.'

Elizabeth was hit by a spasm of guilt. She should have been there. Like so many times before, she began to overcompensate. 'Has anything else gone wrong? Should I talk to the doctor? I'll go and find someone now. This minute, if necessary.'

Janey gripped her arm. 'Mum, come back. It's not that. It's that I'm stuck here being pumped with antibiotics while everyone else is off having a rare old time. I thought I'd have to put up with three or four days of lying among the sick people, and after that I'd be able to go back to work. But, apparently, I won't be able to do very much for a couple of weeks.'

Elizabeth played with the edge of a blanket. 'You do realise you'll have to come home with me?'

'I suppose I do.'

'And old Hawaii out there? What will he do?'

'Mu-um! I've told you he doesn't like that name.'

'He can't hear me. He's with his new friend, putting the world to rights. Or the part of it that plays hurling, at any rate.'

Janey gave the smallest of smiles. 'Go home too, I think.'

'When your dad comes back, maybe we should all go somewhere for a few days? Just in Ireland. I know both you and Stevie are probably a bit old for that now. But Aidan could come, if you'd like.'

The smile became more substantial. 'That would be cool,' she said. 'Anyway, at least one of us had a good afternoon.'

'What do you mean?' said Elizabeth, the words coming out too quickly.

'Look at you. You're all … sparkly. You must have enjoyed seeing the sights again. Have you been able to get in touch with any of the people you knew back in the eighties?'

'I …' Elizabeth decided on a version of the truth. 'Yeah, sort of. I might meet up with a couple of them tomorrow. If you don't need me here, that is.'

'Oh for God's sake, Mum, you go and relive your youth.' Janey laughed. 'I think you can be trusted to behave yourself.'

When Anna next called, Danny was lying on the sofa, drinking a beer and mainlining the coverage of Whitey Bulger's arrest. He was tempted to answer and say, 'Can't talk. I'm watching all my low-life pals on the TV.' Instead he rejected the call. He would get back to her later.

If he came out with a line like that to Elizabeth, she would bubble up with laughter. And, most likely, she'd ask about the crime gangs. Had he ever met any of these guys? When he was a kid were folks scared of them? Why did some folks support them?

Elizabeth. Half their lifetimes had passed without a word from her. Five months after she left, he had poured his guts out in a letter. Embarrassing stuff, as he recalled. She didn't reply, and the time had come for him to give up. Not long after, he'd met Geraldine.

Danny didn't reckon people ever changed that much. The way he saw it, you acquired a layer on top – of polish, or rust, or a shell for protection. OK, you could spring a surprise or two. You might look different or sound different. It didn't mean you weren't the same person deep down. Valuing the same things, and worrying about the same old crap.

It was clear that Elizabeth didn't believe him, but she did look the same. The quick smile, the enquiring blue eyes, the slender limbs; everything he remembered was there. If anything, she was a mite too thin. She must be worried about her daughter. Maybe that explained how guarded she seemed. Nervous, almost. She'd said how Janey was celebrating her birthday when she was taken ill. Imagine that; Elizabeth's daughter was the same age as she had been when they'd spent the summer together. Back then, he'd thought of her as grown up when really she'd only been a kid. And he had been full of it, coasting along, thinking everything would fall into place.

He would have to make sure he didn't overdo the nostalgia. That was one of his failings. A short while back, Vincent had called him out on it. 'You're like an old man,' he said. 'I swear, Ma spends less time living in the past than you.'

To be honest, he wasn't missing Anna. Her testy presence hurt his head and knotted his stomach, but the consequences of another marriage break-up were starting to hit home. His phone jangled to life again, and he zapped the volume on the television.

'Hey you,' Anna said, as if they'd parted on the best of terms.

'Uh, hello there. This is a surprise.'

'I was just wondering how you were doing.'

It sounded as though she was outdoors. Danny heard traffic, a car door slamming. 'Same as ever. You?'

More traffic. There was a substantial pause. 'I've fucked up, Danny, haven't I? I said things I didn't mean. Things that were unkind and wrong, and … I'm sorry. You did nothing to deserve that.'

Man, this was tough. He couldn't handle it tonight. Anna was waiting for him to respond, only for once it wasn't up to him. More silence. 'Ahm,' he said at last, 'I said stuff too. Stuff I didn't mean. I've always been useless at arguments. You know that.'

'We need to—'

'Talk,' he said. If Danny had the power to ban sentences from the English language, that would be first to go. 'Will you be coming back?'

She made a swallowing sound. 'I need a few more days. Until Monday, perhaps.'

'Monday, yeah. Fine.'

'And Danny?'

'Uh-huh.'

'Sorry. Again.'

Danny turned off Whitey Bulger and lit a cigarette.

Chapter 24

'Maybe we should lay down some rules,' Elizabeth said. 'Like each of us to be allowed no more than three moments of pointless nostalgia.'

Danny looked sceptical. 'Hmmm, I'm probably over my limit already.'

They were sitting in his back garden, absorbing the evening calm. 'Like we used to do in Emerald Street,' he said. Elizabeth replied that the vista in front of them was at least three times the size of the old backyard. She could have gone further and pointed out that they were sitting on proper garden furniture, not two dilapidated deckchairs, and that instead of lukewarm beer, they were drinking champagne.

'Do you still like to look at the sky?'

'I never get tired of the clouds.' He smiled. 'That really is one hell of a memory you've got.'

The champagne was connected to Danny's second surprise. The first surprise was that rather than taking her to a restaurant, he had brought her to the house. 'I can cook, I promise,' he said. 'And we'll be more relaxed. Plus, if I'm honest, I want to show the place off.' Elizabeth could see why. He lived in Belmont now. The setting, with its lush gardens and robust trees, was almost pastoral. And the house? Danny said it was built in 1920. 'Quality construction. We could learn a thing or two from those guys.' To her eyes, it was exquisite: all grace and dignity, wooden floors and panoramic windows. She was touched by Danny's obvious pride in the place. She was also more than a little ashamed of how nosy she was. If she could have poked into every cupboard and under every bed, that's what she would have done. She confined herself to oohing and stroking and admiring his taste. 'That's Anna,' he said. 'She's the one with the class around here.'

You could tell that from their wedding photograph. Danny's wife was a true beauty with almond-shaped eyes, symmetrical features and the sort of loose, artfully arranged hair that takes two hours to perfect. 'Breeding,' Elizabeth's father would have said. A picture of Danny with his sons provoked a momentary catch in her throat. It must have been taken by a talented photographer, one with the ability to capture the personality of his subjects. You could have warmed your hands on Danny's smile, and the two boys were narrower, brown-eyed versions of him.

The second surprise was that he remembered. When they had completed the tour of the house, he pursed his lips in thought. 'You were saying it was your daughter's birthday last week?'

'That's right.'

'It got me thinking – about when you were twenty-one? Now I might be wrong, but I reckon it's around this time of year. Your birthday, I mean.'

Pretending to be horrified, Elizabeth hid her face in her hands. 'What a terrible thing to do, reminding me of that.'

'Come on. When is it?'

'It's tomorrow.' She was genuinely knocked back. He truly did have a long memory.

'To the next forty-four,' he said, and kissed her on the cheek before producing the champagne.

While Danny made dinner, she settled on a high stool and kicked off her sandals. Once or twice, she offered assistance. He told her he was fine, that after Geraldine threw him out he'd spent a couple of years living on his own, and that anyway he was only fixing steaks. 'Simple stuff,' he said.

Feeling pleasantly fuzzy, Elizabeth teased him about how he'd always claimed to be a simple guy.

'Brazen as ever, I see. I think you should forfeit all your nostalgia rights just for that. I've a feeling you might remember some things that I'd rather forget.' For a minute he went about his work, then turned round again. 'Isn't it amazing how much we both recall? You know, I can almost see that night. Taste it even. The two of us sitting on the wall.'

'I think that may have been the last time I was in a kitchen with you.' No sooner had she come out with the words than Elizabeth felt the heat edging up her neck and onto her face. That, she feared, was taking the nostalgia kick too far.

Danny didn't seem to think so. He threw back his head and unleashed a full-hearted laugh. 'My poor mother. Scratch what I said yesterday about her living to a hundred. The sight of the two of us poised and ready for action must have taken a few years off of her life.' When finally he wheezed to a halt, he said, 'I'll bet she would love to see you. Would you like to go and visit her? I can take you.'

They agreed on Sunday, which would probably be Janey's final day in hospital. They would go early, before her daughter was released, which by fortunate coincidence was also likely to be before Vincent and Valerie got home. Despite the passage of two decades, Elizabeth wasn't sure she'd be able for Vincent.

They ate at the kitchen table, a frayed antique of a thing. It was just about dark outside, and she felt the right amount of drunk: warm and relaxed, but still sharp. They talked about America and Ireland, and about all that had altered.

'When I was growing up,' she said, 'America was another world into which people escaped. You could be swallowed up by the enormity of the place, invent a whole new life. Now that difference is gone. I mean, it took less than five minutes to find you.'

'Is that so bad?' said Danny, putting on one of his store of silly faces. So, he still did that too. This face said, 'Go on, tell me again how good it is to see me.'

She looked down. 'You know it's good.'

'I guess I do. And even though it's taken far too long … it's wonderful to see you. You'll find that Boston's different too. Your

240

crowd don't rule the roost any more. Even the mayor's no longer Irish.'

Danny fetched another bottle of wine, red this time. She joked about him not being much of a wine drinker in his younger days. He claimed he remained a beer guy at heart. 'I swear,' he said. 'I was forty years old before a drop of this poison passed my lips.'

Their conversation moved on to people they had both known back in 1988.

'What about America's next top model?' Elizabeth asked. 'What became of her?'

'I take it you mean Cindy?'

'I'm sorry. I know I shouldn't be bitchy about her.'

'Nah. I don't think anyone would blame you. She married a fellow from New Hampshire. Dex Tucker. He's in the pest control business.'

Elizabeth threw her eyes to the ceiling. 'What does he really do?'

'I'm deadly serious.'

She took a mouthful of wine. 'Honest to God?'

'That I may be struck down.'

'Danny, you've made my evening.'

'Don't you get all superior now. It's a very lucrative business, I'm told. Hunting down the rats and the roaches.'

She wasn't sure why she was so amused, but Elizabeth gave a contented sigh. 'I can see Cindy at the rat-catcher's ball, engaging in polite conversation about termite infestation.'

'Or discussing the hazards presented by the possum,' Danny said, a chuckle in his voice.

'Or the bed bug,' she giggled.

'Not forgetting the raccoon.'

'Or, indeed, the skunk.' Elizabeth honked with laughter as she said 'skunk', and for a moment they were both overcome.

Danny closed his eyes, tipped back his head, rubbed his throat. 'You know, Elizabeth ...'

'What?'

'Ah, nothing. Let me refill your glass.'

While he poured, she studied him. If anything, it was even harder to get a fix on Danny now than when they had first met. He was part laddish cheer, part urbane businessman, and part something she couldn't quite describe. 'I get the feeling the second Mrs Esposito has you well tamed.'

'Ain't that the truth,' he said. A troubled silence came over them.

'I'm sorry, Danny. If I hit a raw nerve there, it wasn't my intention. I meant that in a positive way.' She hesitated. 'Listen, don't mind me. It's none of my business.'

'Fuck it, Elizabeth. More than twenty years later, and you still have the measure of me.'

She could easily have said no, she didn't actually. But she chose to remain quiet. She stroked the stem of her wine glass until Danny spoke again. He told her the truth about Anna, and she told him the truth about Liam. He said he was minded to try again; he didn't want to leave a trail of marriages behind him. She said she didn't know what she would do.

'It's one strange world where people can cheat on folks as fantastic as us,' he said, as they clinked their glasses together. 'Bloody idiots.'

'It's not our fault they're so stupid.'

'Right, I have a plan. We can't let other people spoil our night. What say we go into the living room, play some music and forget this three strikes and you're out rule? For one night only, we can reminisce as much as we goddamn like.'

'That sounds perfect to me. There's no one else here to complain. And we know we won't bore each other.'

'We never did,' said Danny as he picked up the wine.

They sat on the floor, backs resting against a dark red sofa, the bottle between them. Danny smoked a cigarette. In the semi-dark, she looked at his profile. He caught her gaze, and smiled. Elizabeth was on the side of the crooked teeth. She was glad he hadn't got them fixed. Perhaps it was the alcohol making her braver, but as she saw it, once you had admitted that your husband wasn't faithful, there was little point in holding back on other things. 'Yesterday,' she began, 'when I spoke about your success, the business and that, your reaction was diffident, awkward. Why?'

'I don't know.' He blew a ribbon of smoke towards the ceiling. 'I suppose, I have this notion that if people see you one way, they won't get past that. Once, a long time ago admittedly, you meant an awful lot to me. It struck me that I wanted to talk to you like this, not in some phoney way. I couldn't bear it if, after all these years, we met up and had one of those vapid dinner party conversations.'

'And yet you brought me here. A place that screams of how much has changed for you.'

He shrugged. 'I never claimed to be logical.'

'I think "complicated" was the word I liked to use.'

'So you did. I guess I'm the man who wants it both ways. I want to be the same old Danny, but I also want to be the guy who made it. And, let's face it, Anna wouldn't have looked at me twice if I still came home smelling of wood and sweat. Sometimes, that can be difficult to handle.'

'You don't know that.'

'Oh I do, babe. I do.'

Seconds, minutes passed with no further conversation. The only sound came from the stereo, Neil Young turned down low, and from next door, the whining of a restless dog.

Danny took a last drag and stubbed out his cigarette. 'You don't have to answer this if you don't want, but did you ever have any regrets, any second thoughts, I mean, about leaving America?'

'Do I have the same regard for home as I did in eighty-eight? Not especially. On my bad days, I feel like we managed to catch the worst attributes of the US without the saving graces.' She worried that this sounded bitter. 'Those are my bad days, mind. I'm not always as gloomy as that.' He remained quiet, so she continued. 'I'm not sure if I could have articulated this when I was twenty-one, but looking back I reckon I saw the country as a big blank canvas. Now it seems to have been filled in by other people, and not in a way that I would have chosen. Does that make any sense?'

'Yeah, I hear what you're saying. I think that may be the same wherever you're from. You get older, that's what happens. You feel like you should have more power, except you're sure you actually have less.'

Elizabeth swirled the wine around her glass. 'Obviously, there were good changes too. Like when I was here before, I would never have imagined peace in the north. Never in a million years.'

'I remember that being on the news. Bill Clinton going to Belfast and all. Vincent kept saying, "It won't last. I'm telling you it won't last."'

She drank some more wine. 'I didn't answer the question you really asked, did I?'

'You're OK. It probably wasn't a fair one, anyhow.'

'The real answer, Danny, is yes. There were many times when I thought again about my decision. About the way I handled the situation. About you.'

'Only one more question, I promise. Maybe you'll think I'm lame for bringing this up now, for even remembering it. I wrote to you. Why didn't you reply? Or did you not get my letter?'

Elizabeth's favourite Neil Young song was playing: 'Like a Hurricane'. A lump had grown in her throat. She looked down. 'I got your letter.'

'I guess I expected that even if you wanted to stay in Ireland you'd write back. To let me know how you were. I thought I'd hear from you at some point.'

'I didn't reply, because ... because I didn't want to lie.' It was ironic how this was the truth. Yet she had managed to lie, or at least conceal what she believed to be the truth, ever since. As she often told herself, though, a secret remains so for a reason. You don't tell because to do so would stir up trouble. Trouble you couldn't control.

On the side closest to him, Danny tucked her hair behind her ear then placed one hand gently under her chin so that her face tilted back up. With the back of his hand, he stroked her cheek. 'I don't follow you, Elizabeth. What would you have lied about?'

'When I got your letter, I was pregnant.'

She could tell that Danny was doing calculations in his head. Eventually, he spoke. 'That can't be right. Your daughter is twenty-one.' He hesitated. 'Did you lose a baby?'

An unfamiliar imperative was pushing her on. Elizabeth felt slightly dizzy. She'd always imagined that if this day came, it would be infused with drama. Instead the room was so quiet, she was scared her voice sounded too strident. And Danny exuded a mild puzzlement, as if she was explaining why she favoured one pair of shoes over another.

'You assumed Janey was twenty-one, and I let you. The birthday last week? She was twenty-two.'

His first response verged on playful. 'You didn't hang around when you got back to Ireland. Why didn't you say? Did you think I would be offended? I like to think I would have been happy for you. Jealous as hell, of course.'

'You don't quite get me.' In another second or two he would understand what she was attempting to say. The dizziness intensified.

'What are you telling me, Elizabeth?'

She turned her head, so that she was looking into his blue-grey eyes. They were as clear as the morning she'd left him, when it had been too soon for her to know that she was expecting his baby.

'I was confused, Danny. And scared. More scared than you could imagine. After all, there was only a gap of a few days. I had to assume the baby belonged to Liam. And that was the path I took. No one at home ever asked any questions because, well, no one knew you existed. They had no reason to doubt me. But, as the years passed, I realised I was wrong. It's not just the physical resemblance. It's more than that.'

245

Danny remained on the ground, but almost without Elizabeth registering it, he had moved. He was square in front of her, his expression impossible to read. 'So, what are you saying?'

'I'm saying that I think you are Janey's father.'

Chapter 25

In all the times she had imagined telling Danny the truth, Elizabeth had never pictured what would happen next. After her first words, he said little. Just sat on the ground, picking at his fingers, insisting it wasn't possible. Claiming he knew this because he'd always been careful.

'Plainly, you weren't careful enough,' she said, the words hovering between them before she appreciated how harsh they sounded. 'I'm sorry, Danny, that wasn't what I meant to say. It came out wrong.'

He turned away, and for two or three minutes both were quiet.

'Tell me,' he said eventually.

'Everything?'

'From the beginning. The full story.'

Somehow, Elizabeth had this notion that if she focused on Danny's face, looked right at him, she would make him understand. He seemed equally determined to avoid her gaze. The wine had left a bitter taste in her mouth, but her head was clear. Of that much, she was sure.

'I suppose it begins on the day I left, really,' she said. 'Or at least that's how I think of it. I remember being at the airport, and Michelle telling me it wasn't too late to back down. "No," I said. "Once you've made up your mind you have to go through with it." So, I got on the plane, stared out into the dark and warned myself not to look back. Not to hanker after what I'd left behind. And for the next month or so that's what I did. I threw myself into life at home. Saw Liam every day. Tried to find a job. Tried to forget about you.

'And then … well, it's funny, the day of my graduation was the first day I felt really sick. I thought I'd throw up on the president of the college. Can you imagine? I remember afterwards, everybody heading off partying, and me sloping home to Thurles with my parents. For a while, I convinced myself I was depressed. That explained why I was tired. Why I felt so wretched. Even when I'd missed two periods, I couldn't acknowledge the truth. Eventually … it must have been late November by then … I broke down. Told Liam. I was scared how he'd react. But he was great. Full of plans and chat. Hugging me. Saying that even though we hadn't planned it, everything was going to be good. In fact, the poor fella wanted to go out there and then and tell half the town.'

'You must have known,' Danny said, all of a sudden. 'Right from the off, you must have known there was a strong possibility the baby was mine.'

'Oh lord, Danny, of course I did. I was as miserable as sin. Couldn't think what to do. For a couple of weeks, I did think about an abortion. I could go over to London, I reckoned. Pretend I was visiting my sister, and then claim I'd lost the baby. But you'd have to be an awful eejit to swallow that, and whatever Liam's faults are, being an awful eejit isn't one of them.'

Elizabeth paused to get her thoughts in order. Danny lit a cigarette and poured himself the last of the wine. The music had stopped, and the room was so quiet that even the slightest sound felt amplified tenfold.

'Go on,' he said.

'When I think about that time, the night that stands out most is the night I told my parents. The rain was hopping off the roof. Hollywood rain, we used to call it. My dad was polishing shoes, and I insisted that he stop. God, I was petrified. I thought they'd be beside themselves with anger. And you know what? They were brilliant. So brilliant, I cried. My mother wept too, but not in the way I'd expected. The two of them, they were genuinely happy. And I couldn't understand it. I mean, what was so wonderful about your twenty-one-year-old unmarried daughter being pregnant?

It was years later before my mam told me the truth. They were happy, she said, because they were sure then that I wouldn't leave. They'd already lost Alice and Eoin, and I was wandering around like an apparition of misery. They were terrified I would go back to Boston.

'My parents didn't think there was any question of us getting married straight away, not unless we wanted to. It seems mad now, but in those days plenty of girls were marched up the aisle to avoid shaming the family. That was seen as the respectable thing to do. I made a joke of it. Said I didn't want to get married in one of those ugly 1920s-style dresses and look frumpy and bloated in the wedding photos. The truth was, I wasn't sure I wanted to get married at all.'

'And did you not think that, maybe, I had some entitlements here?' Danny's tone was careful and considered. 'Did you never say to yourself, "There's old Esposito over in Boston. Maybe he might like to know about the baby?" It wasn't as though I was hard to find. We'd been living in the same house.'

'Danny, I thought about you every day. Every hour of every day. But what would I say? And what would I say to Liam and my parents? "There's a chance my other boyfriend might be the baby's real father so I'm going back to Boston?" Not only would there have been a scandal, I would have wrecked their lives. You've got to understand that. And then ... I thought about Cindy and the abortion, and I wasn't sure you would have wanted a baby.'

Immediately she realised her mistake. Danny's mouth curled. He shook his head.

'For God's sake, Elizabeth,' he said. 'Don't go blaming me. It would have been entirely different. You must have known that.'

She shivered. 'I did. I'm sorry Danny. Of course, I did.'

'Did you talk to anyone about your doubts?'

'Who could I tell? Michelle was in Boston, about to get married to Ray. Donal was travelling around America with Rosie. Alice was in London. I didn't trust Orla. And Peter would have been appalled. I was on my own, and, to be honest, I tried not to dwell on who the father might be. I worried that if I had too many corrosive thoughts, I might hurt the baby.

'When I look back on it, I have scores of memories from those months. But sometimes, you remember the craziest things. Like, I remember the day Janey was born was the day after a general election. The sixteenth of June, 1989. A Friday. My dad was preoccupied by the election results, and Mam was ripping. "Your first grandchild," she said, "and all you're interested in is a pile of galoots up in Leinster House." I got a fit of the giggles. I can still see it – the entire ward staring at me like I was a bit simple.

'Anyway, from the very start, Janey was beautiful. Not red-faced or squawking or sickly. And, bless her, did she know how to sleep. She slept so much, we worried that something was wrong. I know what you're thinking – everyone claims they have the best, most interesting baby of all time. But I genuinely did. My mother kept telling me how lucky I was. "Steeped in luck," she used to say. And I'd sit there thinking, if only you knew the truth.'

'Oh come on,' Danny said. 'I know what women are like. They obsess over who the baby takes after. If Liam wasn't the girl's father someone would have realised.'

'From day one, both our families went through the usual rigmarole of deciding who she looked like. Various aunts and cousins were mentioned. Then, as she got older, she had this big head of dark hair. Like Liam. And blue eyes. Like me. Right to this very day, people tell her she's the image of her mother.'

'So what happened, Elizabeth? You just stopped worrying? And then twenty years later your husband cheats on you, and you decide I might be the girl's father after all?' Danny's voice was loud now, steely.

'No, no. You've got to believe me. It's not like that.' Elizabeth knew her own voice had taken on a beseeching, desperate quality. She urged herself to calm down. 'For a while, I did relax. I brainwashed myself into believing that Liam was Janey's father.

'And then … and then Michelle came back. I'd had the sense for a while that she was pining for home, only Ray didn't want to the leave the States. To cut a long story short, she decided to return anyway, and they split up. By that stage ... we're talking the autumn of ninety-one ... Liam and I were married and living in Dublin. I was about to go back to college.'

Elizabeth took a deep breath. 'I remember the two of us, Michelle and myself, sitting in my new kitchen. A pine monstrosity of a thing. Janey was plodding about the place on her sturdy legs. You know the way they are at that age. Never a moment's peace. And I said something about how affectionate she was. Quick as a flash, Michelle replied, "Wasn't her dad the same?" I told her she was wrong. "I don't know how you got that idea," I said. She laughed. Said come off it, she could spot the resemblance a mile off. Needless to say, I got worked up. Warned her never to come out with a claim like that again.

'Liam's birthday was in early December. I must have been going through one of my more domestic phases because I decided to bake a cake. Janey had been like a devil all day, saying no to everything and banging her toys on the floor. Then all of a sudden, it was, "I help Mummy." I propped her up so she could reach the mixing bowl and handed her a spoon. Told her she could stir Daddy's cake. What she actually did was dig into the mixture in such a way that a big dollop of it flew into the air and landed *splat* on her nose. Well, she thought this was the funniest thing in the history of fun. Broke into a smile so wide that all of her little teeth were on view, and she had this look on her face. It was like she was saying, "Aren't I just the best?"'

She hesitated. For the first time, Danny's eyes met hers. 'And?' he said.

'And I remember ... I remember like it was last week ... gripping on to the side of the table. Because that's when I was sure. Oh, I know it sounds ridiculous, but after that day I never doubted who her father was.'

When Elizabeth started talking about her daughter being his daughter, Danny thought she couldn't be serious. But if she was joking, it was a bad joke. For a time, he considered the possibility that she was unhinged. There she sat, on the floor, as clear-eyed as you like, coming out with these lines about being scared and unsure. She spoke for twenty, thirty minutes. Sometimes she rambled, or veered into anecdotes that seemed important to her but were irrelevant to him. Mostly, he let her speak. Frankly, he was too shocked to do anything else. 'By the time I accepted the truth, it was too late,' she said. 'What could I do?'

He shouted at her. 'You could have told the fucking truth, that's what. You could have found me and told me I had a daughter.'

It was at that point that she plucked a phone out of her purse, and showed him a photograph. It had been taken a couple of weeks back in Brighton, she said. Janey had sent it to her. It showed a girl with brown hair and blue eyes sitting on a wooden floor. She went flicking and showed him another photo. It was a close-up of the same girl. This time she was smiling. At first glance, all Danny saw was a darker-haired version of the girl's mother. As he continued looking, it became more apparent. The shape of the eyes, the shape of the smile, the nose; he saw them every day.

He felt cold. Fumbled for another cigarette, lit it, then realised he wasn't able to smoke.

'I'm sorry,' she was saying. 'I'm so so sorry.'

'Does she ... does Janey have any idea?' he heard himself say.

'No.'

'Does anybody?'

'Michelle. That's all.'

Danny didn't reckon he was capable of saying much more. His voice was thick and strange. 'Why now, Elizabeth, huh?'

'You were asking whether I regretted leaving. What could I say? I looked at you. I couldn't lie to you.'

'That's the second time you've claimed you couldn't lie to me. How am I supposed to accept that when you've been able to spend the past twenty-odd years doing a damn fine job of lying to your husband and your daughter? That is, if what you're telling me is true.'

He thought she might cry. Surely any normal woman would cry? Instead, she tried to sweep back her hair, as though it was still long. 'I didn't see it like that. I don't expect you to understand. I couldn't allow myself to see it like that.'

Danny told her she was right; he didn't understand. He said other stuff too, about not knowing how she could live with herself. That made her flinch. He found his own phone and rang for a cab. 'He'll be here in ten minutes. We'll have to talk about this. Not now, though. I'm going to bed.'

That was where he left her, staring at the wall, one hand running up and down the strap of her purse. Some time later, he heard the click of the door as she let herself out.

It was a quarter past seven on Saturday morning when Elizabeth first rang Janey. She knew this was lunatic behaviour, yet she couldn't help herself. She needed to hear her daughter, to know that for now at any rate she was still there.

'Mum?' a sleep-befuddled voice said. 'I think how it works is I'm supposed to ring you. It's your birthday. Is everything OK?'

'I'm sorry, love. I was awake. That's all. I reckoned they might have you up and about already.'

Janey sounded as though she was slowly emerging from her stupor. 'Nope. For once, they left me alone. Happy birthday, by the way.'

'Thanks. How are you feeling?'

She was fine, she said. Lots better. The doctor told her she would be released on Monday morning, after they'd given her a final check. 'Free at last,' she laughed. Elizabeth winced at her daughter's happiness.

'Mum?' Janey was saying.

'Sorry, pet. What did you say?'

She laughed again. 'You're a worse dreamer than me. I asked if you had a good night. With your friends? A guy you knew years ago, and his wife, wasn't it?'

'Good, thanks. Listen, I better go. I'll see you later. Mind yourself.' She swallowed the bile that had seeped into her mouth. 'Love you.'

'Love you,' Janey replied. 'And I'm glad you're getting to meet up with old friends. At least some good is coming from all of this.'

Elizabeth put down the phone and flopped back onto the hotel bed.

Unbelievably, she had managed two or three hours' sleep. She assumed her pills had helped. Now their effect was wearing off, and she would have to think. What had possessed her? Danny deserved to be told. But like that? Like she was telling him there was a stain on the curtains or something? No wonder he had thrown her out.

How did she live with herself? he had asked. She'd had twenty years of practice. The way she'd forced herself to look at it, Janey's parentage was an accident of biology. It was Liam who was *meant* to be her father. Telling the truth would do more harm than good. There were good years with Liam. They had Stevie who, in comparison to her easy-going sister, was a great deal of work. Elizabeth had her job and her family and she threw herself into everything with as much gusto as it was possible to summon. She was careful too. She knew there were books she couldn't read, songs she couldn't play; they reminded her of Danny. 'Shutting yourself down,' Michelle called it. Elizabeth didn't like that.

Of course, she had her rough times. The heart could be such a trickster. You'd think you were getting by, and then something would start you fretting about what you had done; about the fact that your marriage was founded on a lie; about your connection to someone who may well have forgotten about you. But, and she knew people would find this perverse, she tried to think of the values she had been brought up to appreciate. Poor Syl, and his exhortations about fortitude and counting your blessings. If he had only known the purpose to which she put his sermons.

Elizabeth's phone was ringing. It was Stevie. Her younger daughter was her usual mix of seriousness, madcappery and regular teendom. After her birthday wishes and a story or two about

Grover's latest quarry, she informed her mum that she was no longer planning on pursuing a career as a scientist. She was thinking of banking instead, 'because the bad guys had to be cleared out'. Elizabeth suggested she have a word with Peter. Stevie didn't get the joke. She then instructed her mother to check her e-mail. She would find some suggestions as to what her daughter would like from the American shops which were '*way* better than the shops in Dublin'. Elizabeth was about to remind her that the mission to Boston was already costing a great deal; there might not be money for pricey T-shirts that would be better suited to lining the cat's basket. She stopped herself in time.

As if they'd synchronised their calls, and perhaps they had, Liam was next on the line. May God forgive me, she thought. I can't do this. Not today. She pretended to be on a train. 'I'm sorry, Liam,' she roared, 'I can't hear a word. What? Oh, thank you. I better go. There's a tunnel coming up in a—' She turned off the phone. Even after all these years, she was astounded by her ability to lie.

As she lay on top of the bed, the sheets in a knotted heap on the floor, she tried to think of a coherent plan. It was definitely a day for the brave face. She would have to get dressed and be a happy-birthday person. And she would have to visit Janey and talk to Danny. Even his name gave her a visceral thump.

How did she live? In recent years with more difficulty. She had gone through a bleak time: losing her father, then her mother. Somewhere in between she had thrown away her job. She felt splintered, as if she would never be in one whole healthy piece again. She also began to obsess about whether she was bad. A genuinely bad person. How else could she be able to perpetrate such deceit? Mostly now, she clung fast to her memories of Danny, but there were times when she wished it was possible to eradicate all thoughts of him. She was reminded of something his mother had once said: 'People only show you what they want you to see.' That was her, all right. As far as almost everybody was concerned, she was capable, placid Elizabeth, the woman who had it

255

all figured out. None of them could guess how much darkness her life contained.

She glanced at the clock. In ten minutes' time she would get up and write a list of the day's tasks. She didn't think she would be able to eat. She might try a coffee. First, though, she reached over, retrieved her phone and turned it back on. She sent a text to Michelle: *Can you talk?*

Twelve or more hours had passed since he'd told Elizabeth to leave, and Danny continued to lie in bed. He felt like the moorings of his brain had snapped, and he had no control over his thoughts. Every so often he heard his phone ring. By rights, he should be at the gym. That was what he did on Saturdays. He was certain the sun was shining. He could sit out back and do his thinking there. Instead, he stayed where he was, hoping that if he fell back into oblivion he would wake to find he'd got it all wrong.

Finally, he accepted that this wasn't going to happen. He opened the curtains and, although he wasn't hung-over, the light burned his eyes. Normally he railed against clutter, yet for once the room looked too bare. The air was stale, murky almost. He opened the window as wide as it would go. All this did was allow the sounds of normal life to float in.

In the kitchen, while he waited for the coffee to brew, his thoughts turned to Elizabeth. He remembered that it was her birthday. What was it she had said? 'I don't expect you to understand.' She'd said plenty more too. She spoke about how much she'd missed him, how often she'd thought about him. He couldn't help but wonder what would have happened if, back in 1988, she had stayed another month.

He also thought about Janey. What was she like? Elizabeth had said 'lovely' and 'smart'. Those words were meaningless. What was she really *like*? How did she talk and what made her laugh? Was she a worker? Was she in love with her boyfriend? Did she like books or music or sport? Danny supposed that what he needed to know was whether any part of her was like him.

When he found his cigarettes, he noticed a tremor in his hands. He flicked the ash onto a plate and enjoyed the knowledge that Anna would wriggle with irritation if she saw him. Juvenile, he knew. But he would have to grab his kicks anywhere he found them today.

As he poured the coffee, something struck him. The kitchen was looking tidier. Before she left, Elizabeth had cleared away the dinner things. The dishwasher was stacked and the glasses were washed. 'Oh, fuck it, Elizabeth,' he said. He hoped she'd taken the cab, not sent it away so she had time to sort the damn dishes. He would have to call her.

Chapter 26

In Dublin, Michelle was in a quandary.

'Grand day for it,' bellowed her neighbour, as he pushed an old-fashioned mower around his patch of dandelions and grass.

'You're not wrong there, Kevin,' she replied, praying that she'd be able to dodge any further conversation.

He straightened his back and took on the air of a man with a vast store of inanities to share. She practically ran out the gate. 'In a wild hurry,' she explained.

She wasn't lying. Andy was in Galway for a stag night, so Stevie had agreed to mind Shay and Senan. An hour had gone by since her conversation with Elizabeth, and still she couldn't grasp what she'd heard. Given how wistful the woman had been over the past while, she had expected her to try and get in touch with Danny. But to *tell* him? Had she gone completely crackers?

Michelle was left with the feeling that her assistance was required, except she didn't have the foggiest notion what to do. Andy was in the Quays, surrounded by his equally cheery friends. There would be no sense out of him today. She decided to ring the one other person who knew.

Peter was at work in his Dublin city centre office. Important figures were being released on Monday, he said, and he was preparing the press statement. 'I can't talk over the phone. I'll be with you in an hour,' she replied. Before he had the chance to object, she ended the call.

Now she was at the Luas station in Kilmacud, surrounded by screeching girls in the sort of shoes that looked like you'd need scaffolding to climb into them. She peered down the track.

Michelle enjoyed watching the silver tram glide towards the station. It looked too elegant, too other-worldly to be part of the Dublin suburbs. She always described the Luas as the one thing she'd got from the boom. The one positive thing, that is. She'd also got years of negative equity and a school full of befuddled kids. Faster than you could say 'bank bailout', their expectations had gone from Disney World to a weekend in their grandma's house.

After Michelle had raised doubts about the baby's father, Elizabeth had effectively blanked her. For the best part of six months, at the end of 1991 and the start of '92, not a word was exchanged. Michelle remembered it as the bleakest winter of her life. She was renting a bedsit in Rathmines. The place lived on in her nightmares. It was kitted out in shades of landlord brown and orange with a two-bar heater, a Baby Belling and a lumpy single bed. She'd applied to do a teaching diploma, and in the meantime was back behind a supermarket till, working part-time and living on the clippings of tin. Barely a day passed without her regretting the decision to return to Ireland. She would never describe her relationship with Ray as a great romance. Oh, she'd been fond of him; they'd had a laugh. But in the main their marriage had been motivated by her desire to stay in America. Even so, she missed the feel and comfort of him more than she had thought possible. If anything, she became homesick for Boston.

One evening, the doorbell rang. She almost didn't bother answering it. Who would be calling to see her? When she did go down, she found Elizabeth standing in the rain with a bottle of wine in each hand and a pathetic expression on her face. 'I'm sorry,' she said, 'will you help me drink these?'

For a time, Elizabeth sat in silence and drank her mug of wine (Michelle's wages didn't stretch to buying glasses). Once she began to speak, there was no stopping her. She passed a house every day on the bus. Must have passed it a hundred times. Then, one morning, she noticed it had a strange tall chimney. Now the chimney was the first thing she saw, was all she saw. That's what it was like. She looked at her daughter, and Danny stared back. 'If she started dropping her "r"s and telling me about the Red Sox, I wouldn't be any more certain.'

Elizabeth had been trying to get pregnant. Every month her period arrived, regular as rain. She'd got it again that morning. Liam must be baffled as to why it had been so straightforward the last time. She was going to be rumbled. Then she began to sob. Michelle could see her now: her face contorted in misery, the tears carving silver lines through her make-up. 'I have to tell Liam the truth,' she insisted, her speech distorted by drink. 'And I have to see Danny. I admit the way I left was wrong. But he made mistakes too and if he knew we had a daughter, he'd want us all to be together.'

Even though it was a long time since she had seen Danny, Michelle had heard he was married. She found herself unable to tell Elizabeth but did manage to convince her that it was too late to go looking for him. It was hard not to say, 'Listen, if you had stopped to think. If you had done what you actually wanted to do, rather than what you felt some idealised version of yourself should do, you wouldn't be in this mess.' She presumed Elizabeth was well aware of this, and held her tongue.

Two strong coffees and a washed face later, Elizabeth was in a fit enough state to go home to her husband and daughter. After that, the two saw each other all the time. Often they played an elaborate game, where they pretended they were talking about Ray or some other Boston-related topic. The truth was Elizabeth just wanted to hear her former boyfriend's name. As gently as possible, and sometimes it was not easy, Michelle tried to persuade her that the Danny obsessing was unhealthy. There were several occasions when Elizabeth came perilously close to telling Liam, when Michelle had to walk her away from the edge. Once, she completely lost her cool, and warned her friend that she had no intention of visiting her in the psychiatric ward. 'Make no mistake,' she yelled, 'that's where you're heading.'

Bit by bit, Elizabeth learnt to make do. Years passed with

barely a mention of Danny. Michelle, who had once laughed at her transparency, marvelled at how she managed to hold it all together.

'Were you born in a barn?' Peter said when she strode into his office. He'd been able to buzz her up without stirring from his captains-of-industry style desk.

Michelle ignored him. They were the only people in the building; who was going to eavesdrop? The carpet was so thick she wanted to shed her shoes and bury her feet in its pile. The knowledge that it had been bought long before the crash did little to assuage her annoyance at its lavishness.

'You can never be too careful,' he said. 'And I assume you didn't rush in here to talk about the weather or Donal's wedding. Something must be up.' He rose from his leather chair and shut and locked the door.

Michelle quietly added paranoia to Peter's list of neuroses. 'As you mention it, did you get Donal's e-mail? About the wedding?'

'I saw it there all right. Didn't pay a great deal of attention. Other issues on my mind. Not all of us get to spend the summer skiving on full pay.'

'I'm not rising to the bait, Peter. The wedding is in early January. We can talk about it another day.'

'What is it then?'

'You know the way Janey was taken ill, and Elizabeth went over to Boston?'

'I didn't actually.'

Michelle could tell he feared Janey, his god-daughter, was at death's door. 'No, don't worry. Appendix. Big drama. She'll be better in no time. It's Elizabeth.'

He looked at the calendar on his desk. 'Damn. Birthday. I better give her a shout.'

'I'd hold off on that. I don't know what sort of state she's in.'

'What do you mean?'

'She let the cat out of the bag.'

'Ah, Michelle, will you speak English? I've a rake of work to do, and Claire will have me strung up if I don't get home at a reasonable hour. What's up with her?'

'She met Danny and, eh, she told him. And she thinks he believes her.'

'Sweet suffering Jesus,' Peter said, as he ran his hands over where his hair used to be.

Back in 1992, Michelle had sworn to Elizabeth that she would never breathe a word and, for two years, she kept her promise. At some point, she had started sleeping with Peter. They weren't going out as such, but any port in a storm and all of that. Peter was so touchingly grateful that it became a regular occurrence. Besides, he wasn't so bad. And he had a beautiful lump-free double bed. He and Liam had become good pals. They even took up playing golf. 'What are they? Twenty-five or fifty-five?' was Elizabeth's response. The two of them attempted to picture Danny or Ray playing golf and nearly passed out with laughter.

One Sunday, Michelle and Peter lay in bed. She was trying to persuade him to fix her breakfast.

'What do you make of Janey?' he asked.

'What do you mean?'

'I find that when I look at her, I picture myself on a building site in Boston. Guns N' Roses are on the radio, the back is being burned off of me, and a big American lad is flashing his toothy smile.'

At first, Michelle said he must be imagining it and that, anyway, it was none of their business. Peter wheedled and wittered away until she caved in and told him. For months, he had her driven to distraction. He got it into his head that he had a duty to inform Liam. He might have done so, until one Saturday morning he met a buoyant Liam on the first tee. 'Janey's going to get a little brother or sister,' he said. Peter decided he couldn't risk breaking up a happy family, especially when he didn't know for certain where the truth lay. Occasionally, he would take a fit and want to talk about it all. The fits dwindled with the years. He had never told Claire and disapproved of Michelle telling Andy.

'So,' said Michelle as Peter sat there shaking his head, 'what do you think I should do?'

'Sweet FA,' he replied. 'Did she go to bed with him or something?'

'Peter O'Regan! She did not. She saw a photo of him with his sons, and it affected her. In fairness, she always used to say he had one of those faces that made you want to tell him everything. She couldn't help herself.'

'Claire has always said she's a bit funny. She's more to be pitied than blamed, really. Growing up with a father who maintained that central heating was the ruination of the country.'

'Peter, this has nothing to do with her dad. In fact, if the country had more Syl Kellys we might be in a better place.'

'Yeah, right. The government should pass a law: every house to have a Sacred Heart lamp and a collection of Jim Reeves records. That would solve our problems.'

'There's no need for sarcasm. You know full well what I mean. But I'll not get sidetracked.'

'I'm sorry,' Peter said. 'I shouldn't have been flippant. Was she in a very bad way?'

'In a state of shock, I think. Like she said herself, though, now the secret is out, there's no going back.'

When Elizabeth got to the hotel bar, Danny was already sitting there, fingers tapping the side of his glass. His look was nonchalant. It said everything was cool; this was an ordinary meeting on an ordinary Saturday night. But the look was too studied.

He stood and, bizarrely, he shook her hand, like she was asking him to tender for a new block of apartments and a car park. The hand was sweaty, and up close his face was strained, as if he was having difficulty registering what was happening. Elizabeth wasn't feeling overly robust either. When Danny rang, she'd been in the hospital canteen attempting to eat a sandwich. No matter how much she chewed, the food wouldn't clear her throat.

She'd made an effort with her appearance, mainly because she carried this idea that if she looked dishevelled on her birthday, Janey would guess something was amiss. Still, she had a sense that her shoulders had developed a dramatic slope, and she was powerless to do anything about this. Surely someone would notice?

Mercifully the bar was quiet, but not excessively so. They would be able to talk.

'Another drink?' she asked.

'Nah, I'm driving.'

'Of course. I'll just ...'

'Whatever you want.'

She ordered a glass of white wine. She noticed a minute twitch in his mouth before he spoke again.

'Elizabeth, I said some things last night, asking how you lived with yourself. It wasn't my place to say that and I'm sorry. I've thought about nothing else ever since and I guess this can't be easy for you either.'

Elizabeth's drink arrived, so she paused until the waiter went away again. 'I deserved whatever you said. And probably more with it. Thanks, though.'

'You see, there you go. We'll get nowhere here if you carry on with this Irish martyr act. For God's sake, I heard what you said. You think I'll never understand. I promise you, I am trying. I do have some fucking empathy, you know.'

'Danny, I didn't mean ... I don't know what to say.'

He jumped in. 'There's no call to say anything. Anyhow, that wasn't what I wanted to tell you. What I wanted to say was, I need to see Janey. You don't have to tell her anything. I can be an old colleague of Peter's, or whatever. For now.' He took a drink. 'If she is my daughter, and I'm not saying I don't believe you, I have to see her in the flesh. I have to know what she looks like and what she sounds like. I can't not know.'

Elizabeth rubbed the side of the table. 'Would you be able to come to the hospital with me tomorrow? Tomorrow morning. As an old acquaintance, like you said?'

'I can do that.'

She bent down and placed her handbag on her lap. It was a cavernous old thing, the lining stained with make-up and ink. What she was reaching for was right at the very bottom.

'You asked about this yesterday,' she said as she handed him an envelope. It had been opened and closed and folded over on so many occasions that it was torn in three places. It was addressed to, *Elizabeth Kelly, 21 years old, daughter of Syl and Stacia, Thurles, Co. Tipperary, Ireland*, and marked *Very Important, Please Deliver*.

Danny took the envelope and tipped out the letter he had written in February 1989. As he did so, a thin silver chain fell onto the table. A photograph tumbled out too – the two of them at the Lantern Street party. 'Lord, we were young,' he said. Next he picked up the bracelet. 'Have these been in your purse all this time?'

'To be fair, I've gone through a share of handbags. And there have been other hiding places. But by and large that's where they've been. I rip a hole in the lining, and place them inside. Don't worry, by the way. I've never shown the letter to anyone else.'

He placed the chain and the photo back in the envelope. 'Is it all right if I ...?'

'Go ahead.' She sipped her wine as she watched Danny unfold the letter and begin to read. Elizabeth wouldn't claim she could recite it from memory, but she could make a decent stab at it.

My dear Elizabeth,

I know we said we wouldn't write. The thing is I've never been very good at doing what I'm told, so I hope you don't mind me sending this letter. I had this idea too that after a few months back in Ireland you might be glad to hear from Boston and to know how we're all getting on.

I was thinking of you today. Not just today obviously, but you know what I mean. I remember you saying how you don't get much snow in Tipperary, and that you'd like to be in Boston when we got a good big fall. Well, right at the minute, this is the place for you. I'm used to it, I guess. So I've been trying to imagine what it would look like to you. Very pretty, I think. It's funny how even the ugliest of buildings looks better in the snow. I'm off work today – it's kind of difficult to do my job in this weather – so if you were here we could go walking and throwing snowballs and stuff. Like a pair of kids. It's very cold, but there's a big hairy guy here who would be happy to wrap himself around you and keep you warm!

That's the real reason I'm writing. I've tried several times and I can't quite get it right. So please excuse me if this is all over the place. It's five months since you left, and I keep trying to forget about you. The problem is I just can't. I miss you too much.

Of course, I miss making love to you. For me, it was the best ever but I think you understand that. I miss all the other stuff too. I miss being with you and all the things we talked about and how you made fun of me and how you listened to me. I miss listening to you. I miss us sitting there smiling at each other like two fools. I miss the way that sometimes you kissed me for no reason at all. Almost every day I find myself thinking, 'I wonder what Elizabeth would make of this' or, 'I wish Elizabeth could see that.' And I miss your beautiful face and that glorious body. The way I think about it, if I was asked to describe my perfect woman that would be you. Every part of you.

There was something I never quite said, never said properly, when you were here. We talked so much, except when it came down to it, I never said the words that mattered most. I love you, Elizabeth. I am so much in love with you that often I wake up during the night and think about you. I have never felt like this before, and maybe that was my problem. I suppose I thought love was all about sex and drama (we had plenty of those too!). Now I realise it's also about the quiet things. About calm and about feeling at home. Like I felt with you.

On the day you left, I was planning on coming to the airport to ask you again not to go. And to tell you, properly, how I felt.

Unfortunately, Greg Brady got in the way. I ended up in hospital. Nothing serious, but I passed out and Bridie O'Connor panicked. Embarrassing or what? The cops got involved. Needless to say, I kept my mouth shut. Brady has five brothers in his corner – all even bigger than him – and I have Vincent. Not exactly an even match.

Now I keep asking myself – if I'd made it to the airport, if I'd tried harder, would you have stayed? That morning you said we had nothing in common. Did you truly believe that? I know I made you happy, darling. You told me so. Remember? And I wonder, were you in love with me? I like to think you were.

Don't worry that I've gone all weird on you. This is the first time I've ever written anything like this. Not that long ago, I would have laughed at the idea of me being so cut up over a woman. But every line of this is true.

If you miss me in any way, and if you do want to come back, I can sort everything. I don't know whether you've been working, so I can take care of your fare. I know you became friends with my mom, and she would love to have you back under her roof. If you would prefer us to get our own place, that would be cool too. I'm sure you could go to school and become a teacher here. They'd be lucky to have you. And you mustn't get concerned about the visa issue. Whatever needs to be done to fix that would be good with me. One other thing, don't worry about money. I think we both realise I'll never be a millionaire, but I promise I will always look after you.

Ma sends her love, as do Vincent and Valerie. You won't believe this, but even Vincent would be pleased to see you. In fact, he said that if it would stop me moping around, he would personally go over to Ireland and escort you back to Boston. You have been warned.

The big news here is all about V and V. Valerie is expecting a baby. She's due in April. It's hilarious to see such a small woman with such a big bump. Vincent is a complete pain in the ass. You'd think he invented fatherhood. They're still planning on getting

267

married in the summer. So, I'll be a best man and a godfather.
That is if I don't murder Vincent first.

As you can probably guess, he's happy that his guys are still
in the White House. For a while after the election, I considered
leaving the country myself. Would Ireland have me, do you think?

My sister Teresa had a girl (another one) a couple of weeks ago,
and Ma is in baby heaven. We're quite the fertile family! Ma is
in good health at the moment. You never met my dad. The news
about him isn't so good. He has cancer, I'm afraid. He's pretty sick,
but they can do lots more now than they could a few years back, so
fingers crossed.

Anyhow, my darling, I hope I haven't got too far ahead
of myself in what I've said. I'm the same guy who screwed
everything up and who let you go. But I don't think anybody could
love you more than I do. And I would give anything to have you
back in my arms.

Whatever you want to do, please write and let me know how
you are.

All my love,
Danny.

PS. There's a pair of pink shoes in the wardrobe waiting to be
reclaimed.

Danny handed her the letter, and she fitted the envelope into its
hiding place.

'You were, what, five months pregnant when it arrived?' he
said.

'Mmmm. I knew straight away that it was from you. I remember going upstairs, locking the bedroom door and reading it two,
maybe three, times. Then I went to the bathroom and threw up
over and over again. I had consoled myself with the fact that you
didn't come to the airport. He didn't even try, I thought. Then the
letter came, and I knew the truth. I obsessed over it. Wasn't able
to eat. My mother marched me up to the doctor's surgery, only he

268

couldn't find anything wrong. "As healthy as a horse, Mrs Kelly," he said.'

Elizabeth waited for Danny to ask his next question. After all, that was what he did. His brain had always overflowed with hows and whys. When none came, she decided to take the initiative. 'Do you want me to tell you some more about Janey?'

There was a pause, like he was caught up in his own thoughts and hadn't quite heard her. 'Yeah,' he said eventually. 'That would be good. Yeah.'

She took a long breath. 'Janey is a dreamer. She's clever, but some people take a while to appreciate that because she wears it lightly. She's slow to judge and really independent-minded. Like, I've never had to fret about her going with the flock and getting into trouble. Sometimes, because her head is in the clouds, she can be infuriating. She drove us around the twist when she left school because she couldn't decide what she wanted to do. So, she took a year out and worked in a flower shop before going to college. When she did find a course that appealed to her, she worked hard.'

Danny gestured at her to go on.

'Family matters a lot to her. And when I tell her … tell her about this, she'll be devastated. But, given a wee bit of time, I know she'll be friendly towards you. Because, even though I'm biased, I believe her to be a good person. A genuinely good person. One of the kindest I know. She always has time for people. Even cranks and busybodies. The sort of characters that most of us would cross the street to avoid – Janey will natter away to them. She thinks most politicians are a waste of oxygen, yet she manages to be insanely optimistic.' She hesitated. 'And … there is something else, except I can't remember it.' She shook her head. 'It'll come to me. Oh, and if you think I practised that, you're right. And one more thing – despite the fact that I've always claimed to be a supporter of nurture over nature, I hope you recognised someone there.'

His eyebrows shot up. 'One or two bits, maybe. Although I

wouldn't go giving up on the nurture theory just yet, because I recognised her mother too.'

'I'm tempted to say the bad parts are all mine, but you'd only get annoyed with me.'

Danny stared into his drink, and for a time they lapsed back into silence. Elizabeth flailed about for something to say. Something wise or comforting or conciliatory, but she knew that nothing would sound right.

Focusing on his beer all the while, Danny cleared his throat. 'Are you still OK for coming to see my mom?'

'Seriously?'

'Obviously, we're not to bother her with … any of this. We can go and see Janey first and then take a ride over to Vincent's place. It's not too far away. I won't tell her you'll be with me. She'll only get worked up.'

'Thanks.'

He looked up, before reaching over and brushing her hand. 'I know this makes no difference now, but back then, *did* you feel the same? Honestly?'

Elizabeth placed her other hand over his. 'The guy who wrote the letter? How could anyone not love that guy?'

Chapter 27

Danny figured that this was the oddest Sunday morning of his life. He was with the woman who had just turned that life upside-down, and they were walking into a hospital to see a stranger who could well be his daughter. The fact that he had hardly slept didn't help. All night, he would drop off for a few minutes before some force in his brain would wake him again.

Silently, he repeated to himself, 'Stay calm, don't stare, make sense.' He didn't want Janey thinking he was a weirdo. Elizabeth must have been able to sleep because she appeared normal. Maybe she was chanting similar lines to herself. It was a beautiful morning, balmy with just enough cloud up there to make the sky interesting. Good weather suited her, made her look fresh and happy. She was wearing a summer dress, blue and white. That suited her too. A step or so before they got to the ward, she tipped the base of his spine and smiled at him. Neither spoke.

'Morning, pet,' she said, her voice steady and clear. 'Hi, Aidan, how's it going?'

'Not a bother, Elizabeth,' replied an untidy-headed fellow with a black eye. What was with the eye?

Before anybody had the chance to say anything more, Elizabeth launched into her introductions. 'This is Danny Esposito,' she said. 'He worked with Peter. You've met Peter, haven't you, Aidan? Last Christmas, I think.' She was rattling off the words without pausing for breath. She must be nervous after all. 'And don't be misled by the name,' she was saying. 'Danny is one-eighth Tipperary man, so he's one of us really.' Elizabeth gave him another smile, as if urging him to say something, but his mind was as blank as the day he was born. All he could do was gaze at her, sitting up in the bed with her open face, small like her mother's, and her beautiful tangle of hair, dark like his.

'Janey,' he said eventually. 'Like the song, "Janey, Don't You Lose Heart".'

She gave him a bemused look. 'How did you know that?' Her voice was light and her accent different to Elizabeth's, although he couldn't say exactly how. 'When I was small, Mum used to sing it to me, or make an attempt at it anyway. You're the only other person who's mentioned it.'

Danny worried that he'd made a mistake, but Elizabeth was grinning at him, so all must be OK. 'Your mom and me, we're of a certain vintage, you know. It's a Bruce Springsteen song. From the eighties. A B-side.'

'Whatever one of those was,' chipped in Mr Black Eye, with a wink.

Elizabeth was sitting on the edge of the bed, laughing. She boxed the young guy around the ear. 'Don't you find, Danny, that the young people nowadays are too forward?'

'I couldn't agree more,' he said. 'Where's the respect for their elders, huh?'

Janey also started to laugh. *He* had made her laugh. 'Danny, you must have spent too much time in Mum's company if you're coming out with the same old rot as her.'

Elizabeth looked at him. 'Don't you pay her any heed. I always tell her she's lucky she's not called Rosalita or Bobby Jean.'

Danny sensed that he was being scrutinised by Janey. Dumb as this might sound, it hadn't occurred to him that she might recognise something of herself in the man at the end of the bed. While the resemblance wasn't overpowering, it was definitely there.

'Danny?' she said, then hesitated.

Please, he thought, let this not be an awkward question.

'You were in the paper last week, weren't you?'

The relief shot through him. 'I was, yeah. Me and Vincent, my brother. Fancy you seeing that.' He watched Elizabeth stroking Janey's ankle, or at least the shape made by her ankle under the sheet. She had long legs.

'When Danny worked with Peter, he was a carpenter,' Elizabeth said. 'He's done very well.'

It dawned on him that Janey and Aidan must be confused by his presence. 'The reason I'm here is, ahm, I'm taking Elizabeth to see my mom. They got to know each other during that summer.'

'You made a mad amount of friends over here, Elizabeth,' said Aidan.

'I suppose I did,' she said, as she continued her stroking. She looked down, and Danny could tell she was anxious to change the direction of the conversation. Even after all these years, he knew her signals and expressions. At the far end of the ward, a squadron of white-coated men and women were beginning their rounds. He had a dangerous urge to go over to the most senior-looking fellow and have a word. 'You see that girl over there?' he wanted to say. 'The girl who looks a bit like me? You take proper care of her now.'

Elizabeth was asking Aidan about the eye.

'I'm nudging towards the yellow and purple phase, I reckon.'

'Aidan got a belt playing hurling,' she explained.

'They're ferocious rough out here altogether.'

Danny was stunned by how normal, how relaxed everything was. How could they be sitting here discussing sporting injuries? He was mesmerised by Janey, her every movement and gesture. 'It's been too long since I was part of a conversation about hurling,' he said.

Janey smiled. Oh, how he knew that smile. 'Take it from me,' she said, 'you don't want to get Aidan started. We'll all be here for the next week. And I've had enough hospital to last me a long time.'

Danny saw the white coats advancing. He figured this gave him an excuse to go before he said something inappropriate. He tipped his head in their direction. 'You might want to talk medical

273

talk. I'll wait outside. Get a little sun. There's no hurry.' Before any of them could reply, he was saying goodbye, patting Janey's arm as he left. He would be best on his own.

'Well, you were a big hit.' Until she tapped his shoulder, he hadn't realised that Elizabeth was standing behind him. 'Are you all right?'

She must have guessed where she would find him – in the smoking zone. He'd been there since he left the ward, inflicting as much damage on his lungs as fifteen minutes would allow.

'Hi there,' he said.

'Do you believe me?'

'I did anyway. Except ... sorry, I'm ... actually, I don't know what I am.' Danny took a last drag and stamped on the cigarette butt.

'Do you want some more time? We don't have to see Regina right away. It's such a gorgeous day. I can go for a walk.'

'Nah,' he said. 'I've promised her a surprise. She'll get anxious if I don't turn up on time.' Belatedly, he saw that Elizabeth was carrying a bunch of flowers. There were roses and lilies and daisies and other types whose names he could never recall. When it came to flowers, he'd always lived by one maxim: the more expensive the bouquet, the better the result.

She raised them to her nose and then to his. 'For your mother. Wouldn't that scent do you good? Listen, to use that terrible phrase, we need to talk.'

'You don't like that either? You know, when I'm in the White House it's going to be punishable by firing squad.'

She smelled the flowers again. 'That was the line I forgot. In my prepared speech about Janey? She's funny too.'

Regina was in the back garden. Tidying. There was too much garden in her view. And it wouldn't hurt one of Vincent's boys, awkward creatures that they were, to put some work in either. When Danny called and said he was coming over, she hoped he might be of assistance. Then he claimed he had a surprise for her. She wanted to say, 'Danny, the last thing I ever want from you is a surprise. Boring would be fine.' She hoped that Anna would come home soon. Not that Anna was ideal, but she was his wife. And he was getting too old now to be acting the play-boy. Regina could never fathom how such an intelligent man could be so monumentally dumb when it came to women. It struck her that she'd been fretting about Danny's life for nearly thirty years. Much good it had done.

She often said to her sons and daughters that you didn't get to her age without knowing a thing or two about people and about life. What they didn't realise was that she always said this with her fingers crossed. The instant she thought her younger son was settled, he would do something to cause fresh consternation. Before he went on vacation, she'd said as much to Vincent. 'There's a phrase for Danny. It won't come to me.'

'I have it,' he replied. 'Fucking idiot. That's the phrase for Dan.'

She tut-tutted. 'No, Vincent, I've got it. His own worst enemy. That's your brother.'

Still, stupidity and all, she did enjoy him. Even though she lived with Vincent, and even though her daughters did all that she asked, she was closest to Danny. She supposed it was because of the years they had spent together. Just the two of them – and assorted womenfolk. A short while ago, they were talking about her depression. She was left with some uncomfortable legacies, she said. Like, if she was walking down a street, she would only notice the damaged folks – the women with empty eyes or the men muttering to themselves. 'I get you,' he said, 'it's like the way I only notice the hot women.' She slapped him on the hand and pretended to be insulted. Except she knew he did understand. He was the one person with whom she could have those conversations.

Regina heard the crunch of tyres on gravel. Danny and his surprise, no doubt. She walked out to the front of the house. He was carrying a bunch of flowers. There was a woman with him – tall, but not his wife. What was he up to now? Regina took her glasses from her pocket. She stopped and stared.

'This I do not believe,' she said. 'It can't be.' She walked a little closer. It was. 'Good heavens. Elizabeth, honey, where did he find you?'

'Don't I bring you the best surprises?' Danny said, as the two women merged into a hug.

Regina kept touching Elizabeth, for fear she wasn't real. The three of them were sitting out back, talking and laughing as though they'd woken up and it was the summer of 1988. The weather reminded her of those days too. She sent young Tyler to put the flowers in a vase and to fix them some drinks. He was fifteen now and, as she occasionally had to say to Valerie, those boys would be grateful one day that their grandma had made them useful.

Elizabeth hadn't changed. Obviously, she looked older. Her face had lost the roundness of youth, and she appeared more wary. But there was still something about her. As for Danny, Regina wasn't so sure. One moment he appeared as cheerful as the birds; the next, he was all preoccupied. He was doing a lot of gazing at Elizabeth too. They weren't, were they? No, even Danny was no longer that much of a fool, and she was talking about her husband and her daughters. She wouldn't mess around.

There was a time when Regina would have been torn over what to say to the girl. It was quite a trick she pulled. Becoming part of their lives, then running back to Ireland without so much as a proper goodbye. Leaving Regina to listen to all of Danny's bravado when, plain as night follows day, the boy had been lonely and miserable. Except it was Danny and Vincent who had forced her away. One of them hadn't been able to say what he felt, and the other had said far too much. Who knew what might have happened if her sons had been more mature?

Tyler brought out glasses of juice, shared a few shy words, then disappeared again to kill aliens or whatever it was he did in his room.

'My favourite mini-Vincent,' Danny said.

'I bet that's only because he looks like you,' replied Elizabeth.

'Lucky boy.'

At that point, Regina wanted to pinch *herself* to ensure that it wasn't 1988, because that was just the way they had joked back then.

They got to talking about grandchildren, and Regina voiced her only disappointment; there were too few girls. 'In the early days,' she said, 'when Teresa had all those girls, I was convinced there would be no boys. And the way it turned out, there are eight of them. Four in this house alone. Even my one great-grandchild is a boy.'

'Boys have their merits too, you know,' said Danny, putting on his offended face.

'You know what I mean, Danny. I used to have high hopes of you giving me more grandchildren.'

'Not too late yet, Ma.'

Regina liked the sound of that. Perhaps he and Anna were sorting out their difficulties. She knew they were talking again. Then she saw Elizabeth giving him a peculiar stare.

'Danny told me that you've been well for a long time now, Regina. I don't know if you like to say cured, although that's what it sounds like. I often thought about you, you know.'

'Bless you, honey. The way it is … even after all these years, I tend to fear that it's lurking there somewhere. I try not to take anything for granted.' She patted Danny on the knee. 'And as much grief as I give him, this fellow has been very good to me.'

He made a noise that sounded like 'nyaaah', as if to say, 'think nothing of it'.

'I wouldn't doubt it,' Elizabeth said, with a smile in her voice. 'He's not the worst of them. How long have you been this well?'

'It's hard to be precise, but I reckon I was in my mid-sixties by the time I felt truly strong. I remember starting to look forward again. Viewing life as something other than an ordeal.' Regina sighed. 'Of course, by then Dino was long since gone. And I regretted that I'd never met anyone else.' She stopped. 'Heavens, dear, please forgive me. I don't know why I'm telling you this. You don't need to hear an old woman's ramblings.'

'Don't be silly,' Elizabeth replied. 'They aren't ramblings at all.'

'Now I worry about death, about what type of illness will claim me. But I guess most seventy-six-year-olds are the same. I think it's called normal.'

When she looked back, Regina was perplexed by how little she remembered. A handful of incidents stood out. One was the night that Teresa had bundled her into the car and taken her home. The night that Elizabeth had come to stay.

Now, here she was, swapping puzzling signals with Danny. They were definitely up to something. Oh, let it not be trouble. All the same, it was good to see her. Regina touched her hand once more. 'You know, Elizabeth, I often thought about you as well, wondered how life had treated you. Now that you've made contact, don't leave it so long again. Please don't be a stranger.'

In the car, they barely said a word. Elizabeth imagined you could hear the wheels of their brains, clicking and whirring away. There was a lot of thinking to do. And they really did need to talk.

Danny's house was gloriously cool. There was a lingering smell of coffee and cigarettes, and she tried to picture what it was like when Anna was there. Ms Peyton – Danny said she hadn't taken his name – would be back tomorrow.

She was about to follow him from the hallway into the kitchen when he reached for one of her hands.

'How are you doing now?' he asked.

'In ways, I'm good. Like, seeing your mother was brilliant. And telling the truth at last? That's the oddest sensation. I found I wanted to tell Regina too.'

'I guessed as much. When she launched into her speech about granddaughters, I damn near fell off the chair. A job for another day, I think.'

'And the next part? Telling Janey and Liam? Even thinking

278

about it is tough.' They were facing each other now. 'Don't worry, I'll handle it. So, I'm feeling raw as well, I suppose. Like a couple of layers of me have been planed away. And you?'

He took her other hand. 'Raw is about right. And knocked about a bit. And overwhelmed. And probably half a dozen other emotions I haven't got a handle on yet.'

'I understand.'

'And tender.' Danny swallowed, inspected his feet, then finally looked at her again. 'Impossibly tender towards you.'

Elizabeth rested her head on his collarbone, and he folded his arms around her. 'Like I feel towards you,' she said.

They must have kissed for at least five minutes before she fully registered what they were doing. She paused to savour the joy of it, to delight in the small pleasures: like stroking his hair or noticing how his breathing changed. Still standing in the hall, they resumed kissing. Danny pressed more tightly against her. She was hit by an almost-forgotten feeling; a warm tightness took hold of her throat, travelled down her chest and beyond. When they pulled apart, she moved her eyes in the direction of the stairs.

His lips swept along her forehead. 'Are you sure?'

She nodded. 'You?'

His face said, 'Now, what do *you* think?'

By the time they got to the bedroom, two pairs of sandals, one dress, one pair of shorts and a T-shirt had been discarded. All the while holding Elizabeth's hand, Danny drew the curtains. She suggested he might like to close the window.

'Oh no,' he said. 'It's about time folks up this way heard about my prowess.'

'You're an awful man.'

Danny guided her towards the bed. 'Like I always said in the past, I'm going to assume that's a compliment.'

Chapter 28

The room was filled with a cool light. Not that far away, a bird was singing; *toolool toolool* it went. Elizabeth felt Danny's breath, soft and steady, against her neck. He was spooned into her, his wiry chest hair, so different from the boyish fluff she remembered, tickling her back. A substantial arm was wrapped around her. With one finger, she stroked the back of his hand.

'Hey there,' he said, 'I was worried you might never wake again.'

'Did you not sleep?'

Danny's fingers dawdled over her stomach. 'I'm playing with you. I only woke a couple of minutes back.'

Suddenly conscious of the inadequacies of her body, of how once firm parts sagged and puckered, Elizabeth rolled onto her back. She was reminded of the first time she had slept with him, when she was precisely twenty-one years old. Back then she'd been swamped by a sense of being out of her depth. She felt something similar now. Rather than affecting casualness, there were explanations she wanted to offer. She wanted to explain why she kept calling his name, to let him know what a relief it was to be able to say it at all. For more than twenty years, Danny had been a non-person, a spectre. Now he was real again.

He smiled. 'Feels strange, huh?'

'Mmmm. No regrets?'

'Come on now, what's to regret?'

'I'm sure you say that to them all.'

'Twenty-three years on, and you still can't take a compliment. It's definitely an Irish failing.' She turned towards him, and he kissed her forehead, her cheekbones, her neck. 'I'm getting a touch of déjà vu here,' he said. 'Right back to our first night in Emerald Street. I could swear you've the same look on your face. Like you're thinking, "I'll bet this guy spends every Sunday afternoon having sex."'

'You mean you don't?'

'Very funny.'

'Not even with your wife?'

'Especially not with my wife. Seriously, Elizabeth, there are no others. I screwed things up so badly with Geraldine, I tried not to make the same mistakes twice. Made a whole new set of mistakes, but there you go.'

'And this?' she said, as their legs became entwined again.

'Entirely different. You know that. So what about you? Any other men?'

She caressed his head, enjoying how the velvet of his hair gave way to the warm skin on the back of his neck. 'My experience is as limited as the last time we met.'

Danny tickled her. 'I'm still ranked number one of two, then?'

'The final scores are being totted up as we speak.' The tickling intensified, and Elizabeth squealed.

'I am determined to maintain my ranking,' he said, the two of them laughing and kissing, and then just kissing.

Later, after they'd made love again, Danny claimed she hadn't been entirely honest with him. There must be a third man.

'I'm not with you.'

'Who's the guy you talk about in your sleep? This Grover guy? You asked if he was being looked after.'

She hadn't realised she spoke in her sleep. 'The cat.'

'You've become a cat lady?'

'You're making me sound like a total headcase.'

'We-ell, as you mention it …' he said, moving a hand along her thighs.

Elizabeth wished they could stay right where they were, but they couldn't. The mention of Grover made her think of Stevie.

'Danny, you do know I'll have to go in a minute? To the hospital. And I better call home.'

'Is it not a little late?' He stretched out his other arm and retrieved his watch from beside the bed. 'It's a quarter of eight, Elizabeth. By the time you get to the hospital, they'll be shutting up shop. And – ahm, how should I put this? – you can't go and see Janey looking like you've just fallen out of bed.'

Elizabeth sat up abruptly, pulling the quilt over her breasts as she did. Where was her head at? 'It can't be that late. There's too much light. And if I have a shower—'

'This *is* the month of June. Longest day, and all that.' For some unfathomable reason, he was smiling. 'Listen to me, baby. Everything will be fine. Go downstairs and send a message to Stevie. Let her know you'll call in the morning. Then call Janey and say you're sorry and that you'll be there bright and early to rescue her.'

The bird was there all the while, *toolool*-ing his heart out. 'But—'

Danny put an arm around her shoulder. 'Then we'll get a bite to eat, and whatnot. And we might even do some talking.'

Janey stretched out in her narrow bed. The last night of the damn thing. Earlier, she'd been able to have a proper wash. She was convinced she would reek of hospital for the rest of her days. She was going to spend the next couple of nights in the hotel with her mum, and then her trip to Boston would be over. She hoped the hotel had fancy toiletries, small bottles of shampoo and such, although knowing her mother she was likely to be staying in the most utilitarian spot in the city. You probably had to tidy your own room and hoover the lobby before you were allowed to leave. Aidan was late. She would have to remind him of this the next time he bored on at her about timekeeping. He was back at work and was going to stay in Boston for another two or three weeks. By the time he returned to Ireland, her dad would be home too.

Given the mangled state of his face, Janey had expected that Aiden would be banished out back to wash dishes. Instead, he was the star of the show: 'What happened to your eye, son?' 'Oh nothing, a little hurling injury.' The guy who ran the bar enjoyed that; he thought it was 'authentic'. The customers would appreciate it, he said. Janey doubted that most of the customers would know what hurling was. Mind you, that Danny guy did. She was reading a magazine left behind by one of the other patients. It was full of two-thousand-dollar handbags and the like. ('Statement pieces' they were called. A statement of what? That you had more money than sense?) She thought of her mum who always claimed that selling magazines to women under thirty should be banned. 'You've nothing that needs improving,' she would say. 'Go out and enjoy your perfection.' Eventually, up Aidan rolled.

'How are you going on, Princess? Sorry about the lateness. I had to haggle my way in. Has your mam left?'

Janey placed the magazine on her lap. 'She was a no-show, I'm afraid. Said she stayed too long with Danny's mother. After that she met up with someone else, and the time ran away from her. She'll be here in the morning.'

'Oh right,' said Aidan. He had the hint of a smirk on his face as he collapsed onto the bed. He bent in for a kiss, but she moved her head.

'What's the "oh right" about?'

'Danny's mother is obviously quite an attraction. No doubt Elizabeth was big buddies with her when she was twenty-one. Hitting the town every night of the week, I'd say.'

'What are you getting at?'

'I'm suggesting she might have had a small romantic interest back in the day. How else would she know a fella's mother?'

Janey picked up the magazine. She flicked through the pages, but continued to look at her boyfriend. 'Would you get away, Aidan.'

'I'm not saying there's anything going on now, Princess. I'm saying once upon a time. Back in the good old 1980s when they were listening to Bruce Springsteen records together.'

'Tuh, just because they know the same song. That doesn't mean

anything. Sure thousands, *millions* of people must know that song.'
Even as the words left her mouth, Janey didn't believe them. 'I was
about to tell you something interesting, only I don't know that I
will now.'

'Suit yourself.'

They both knew he'd be able to coax out the truth. There was
no point in play-acting. 'Um,' she said. 'You know the man in the
photo?'

'Aha,' he boomed, 'the mystery man is revealed.'

'I'm not *totally* sure.'

'What a day,' he said, the smirk returning, only this time even
bigger and more stupid. 'The day we learnt that Elizabeth might
not have spent nearly as many nights on the floor as she likes to
pretend.'

Janey rolled up the magazine and clattered him across the head.

Aidan burbled with shock. 'Jeez, mind the good looks, would
you?'

'Just adding to your authenticity.'

Elizabeth and Danny were sitting on the living room floor, a
pizza box and two cans of beer between them. He was wearing a
threadbare dressing gown. She was in one of his shirts.

'You know,' he said, picking up a slice of pizza, 'this is something else I always liked about you. Despite appearances, you're a
slob at heart.'

Elizabeth rolled her eyes.

'Or leastways, you were always willing to come down to my
level.'

From where they were sitting, she could see the wedding
photograph and the picture with Ryan and Conor. There was
another photo too: of Danny and Regina and a doughier-looking
Vincent and two dark-haired women, who must be Linda and
Teresa. Presumably Anna also had a family, but there was no evidence of them. This time tomorrow she would be back, having
made up her mind about what she wanted. Janey would know the

truth. In the meantime, Danny must still be grappling with her own deception. Yet there he sat, hairy legs splayed in front of him, munching contentedly. Periodically, he nuzzled into her, rubbed her leg or made an idle observation. He was the man who didn't have a care in the world.

'We're like we always were,' she said.

'Even better, I'd say. All things considered.'

'No. I mean, we're doing what we always did. Trying to ignore the rest of the world.'

Danny fiddled with the belt of his dressing gown, while Elizabeth looked at the photos of his wife and his sons, his mother and brother and sisters.

'I'll admit that's one of my faults,' he said. 'Part of a long list. I have them all written down someplace.'

Elizabeth was annoyed with herself. 'Don't be silly, Danny. I didn't intend to get at you. I was just making an observation.'

'No, you're telling the truth. I go through life assuming that everything will be exactly how I want it to be. And I'm always stunned when things play out differently. Except for work, that is, where for some reason I'm a zealot for planning and precision.'

'Please, Danny. I'm the one who shouldn't be relaxed like this. I'm dumbfounded that you can be so … I don't even know the right word … that you can be so kind to me.'

'Oh for Christ's sake, Elizabeth, it's not kindness. When will we get this chance again? When will we be together like this? On our own? Enjoying each other? And being, if you don't mind me saying so, like we fucking should have been?'

'I can't say.' She wished she'd kept her mouth shut.

'It's not just finding out about Janey, although God knows that's enough for any man to cope with. That letter brought it back. All of it. So for a few hours, is this so bad?'

She shunted the box and the cans out of the way, and took his hand. They went back to bed. Elizabeth reckoned that if ever there was a time for observing her famous namesake's motto, this was it. Tomorrow she would take hold of herself, do what had to be done, and face the consequences. But, like Scarlett O'Hara always said, tomorrow was another day.

Danny had promised an early start and he was as good as his word. Just before six thirty on Monday morning he threw off the covers. 'Rise and shine, baby,' he said. 'Vincent awaits.' Elizabeth must have looked petrified, because he quickly added, 'Awaits me, of course. He's back from vacation today.' Elizabeth offered to get a train or a bus back to the hotel, but he insisted on giving her a lift. 'I can't have you on public transport looking like the woman who hasn't been home,' he laughed.

This made her worry that she must be woefully bedraggled. A glance in the mirror showed a normal, if sleepy-eyed, face. While Danny had a shower, she stripped the bed. 'You didn't have to do that,' he said, as he dripped onto the floorboards. 'A woman, Cassandra, she's from Haiti, looks after these things.'

'Where's the washing machine?' Elizabeth replied. 'I'm not letting anyone else change these bedclothes.'

Danny shook his head. 'Let me get dressed here, and I'll show you.'

She watched as he put on a grey suit, a pale blue shirt and a red and navy tie. Not counting the photographs, it was the first time she'd seen him in a suit. She was struck again by how far he had travelled. She whistled. 'You're looking very handsome this morning.'

'Meetings,' he said, almost bashfully.

Sitting in the car, they kissed goodbye. To her it seemed too brief, but a line of cab drivers, anxious for hotel business, were tooting and shouting. It was time to go.

By eight o'clock, she was in her room, pacing around the tiny space and talking to an unanswered phone. 'Stevie, please pick up, would you?' Elizabeth decided to give her daughter another try before leaving a message. She feared there was sulking going on.

Until that morning, she hadn't noticed how small her hotel room was. And how stuffy. Its brocade curtains and matchy-matchiness were in total contrast to the room where she'd spent the night. There, everything was just mismatched enough to be in perfect taste.

'Ah, please, Stevie,' said Elizabeth to the unanswered phone. 'Don't get crabby on me. I only missed one bloody day.'

'I was about to ring you,' said the adult voice on the other end of the line. 'What's the story?' It was Michelle.

'Stevie's not around?'

'She's out in the garden, trying to tame the two lads. Don't worry, I'll change the conversation if I hear any sort of sound. Andy's in bed. Stag weekend. No stamina, these young fellas.'

It began well. Elizabeth said she'd been talking to Danny, that he'd been to see Janey, and that today she would break the news to her daughter. She didn't have an exact formula of words, but she had a reasonable idea of what she would say. 'If I tell her now, she'll have an opportunity to meet Danny properly. If that's what she wants.'

'And how is he now?'

'He's …' She couldn't help herself. 'He's brilliant. In fact, he's as wonderful as ever he was. Definitely hasn't lost his touch.' She was conscious of a quiver in her voice. She would have to lose that before collecting her daughter.

For two or three seconds there was silence. 'You're having me on? Or, I hope you're having me on.'

Elizabeth didn't reply.

'Merciful hour, Elizabeth. What were you thinking of? Janey's leaving hospital. You're about to give her news that will change her life, and you think it's a good idea to go to bed with the man who got you into all of this trouble.'

'It wasn't like that.'

'Are you on a campaign to make yourself as miserable as possible?' said Michelle, her voice loud and brusque.

Elizabeth hadn't expected Michelle to react like this. It was grand for her. Andy was upstairs, she had years of the twins to look forward to and her parents were in good health. All was rosy in her garden. 'I enjoyed myself, actually. You're probably familiar with that sensation. I'd forgotten what it was like.'

'When's wifey back?'

'This evening.'

'Right. This brilliant night with Danny was a one-off, then?'

'Well, yeah. I mean, we didn't talk about that.'

'You know, Elizabeth, it's a good job you're forty-four years old, or no doubt you'd let him knock you up again.'

She had heard enough. 'I'm not sure when you became such a smug bitch, Michelle, but I preferred you before.' The quiver had gone. 'You can contact me when you're ready to apologise. Tell Stevie I'll talk to her later.'

'Do you know what, Dan? You were easier to cope with when you were down in the mouth. What are you so chirpy about?'

Danny *was* too chirpy. He knew that. And there was no explanation he could offer Vincent. He couldn't say, 'Well, not much more than forty-eight hours ago, I discovered that I probably had another kid. And to begin with I was all over the place. But the more I consider it, it's good, isn't it? And me and her mother? We had the sweetest day yesterday. Plenty of good old-fashioned lust. I know that seems strange, but it was what I needed. Don't think it did her any harm either.' Of course, he couldn't say any of this. And he certainly couldn't reveal how the weekend had resurrected so many memories and emotions, so he gave his brother a playful dig. 'You're looking good, man. Reckon you've dropped a pound or two. I'd say you got plenty down on the Cape. Just you and Val, huh?'

'For God's sake. Tell me the moronic humour isn't connected to the reappearance of the long lost Irish student.'

Fortunately, Danny didn't believe he was capable of blushing. 'You've been talking to Ma. You don't have to worry. It was great to see her, though. She's a good woman.' He thought he better get Vincent off his tail. 'Anna's back tonight,' he said, endeavouring to maintain an upbeat tone.

Vincent punched his upper arm. 'I hope it all works out, man. Really I do.'

Danny's hopes were elsewhere. They were with Janey. Elizabeth would be talking to her soon. He had offered to be there. She was horrified. 'No,' she said. 'It has to be up to her. Whether she wants to meet you properly.' He figured that Elizabeth was scared her daughter would go calling Liam. She was trying to act calm, yet it was clear she was flustered. All that fuss with the sheets. The sheets were fine.

As the morning wore on, a sort of paralysis set in. He tried to read, except the words flew away. Even if he managed to retain an entire sentence, he still couldn't focus on what it actually meant. It was one of those days when he wished he was back on a construction site, elbow-deep in a nice methodical task, the sun pouring over his face, heart and mind at rest.

Elizabeth had promised she would be in touch so he couldn't allow anyone else to tie up the phone. Obviously, there were a couple of exceptions. Ryan called, and Danny ached to tell him. It was too soon, though. All the same, he needed to keep on talking to Ryan, or rather to keep on listening. He wanted to hear his son's laid-back voice and his slightly nerdy conversation.

Janey was inspecting the bedroom. 'Not bad at all,' she said to her mother. 'I'll stay here with you for a couple of days. Once you don't snore.'

'I'll have you know I do not snore.'

'Ooh now,' said Janey, as she climbed onto the bed, 'for years, myself and Stevie blamed Dad. The odd thing is, he went away and the snoring continued.' She made a sound like a baby elephant, and Elizabeth pretended to be hurt. She was pouring boiling water into two mugs. Somewhere along the line, she had managed to buy a box of Irish tea bags. The brew they served in the hotel didn't deserve the name tea. It was, to use a word of her father's, cat. 'Cat melodeon,' he used to say. Once she had asked what it meant. 'Haven't the foggiest,' he'd replied. 'But it sounds good. And isn't that half the battle?'

She placed one of the mugs on the locker beside Janey and took a packet of biscuits from the oversize handbag. God love the girl, she looked fragile. It was a good job she was coming back to Ireland.

Elizabeth was feeling a residual pang from her row with Michelle. Her friend was right. She shouldn't have allowed Danny to pierce her armour. She should have stayed here; weighing and measuring and sifting every word she would say. She sat down with her back to the quilted headboard, extended her legs and cradled the mug. Her left eyelid gave an energetic twitch. 'How are you feeling?'

'Not a bother. Can't kill a bad thing, as Aidan says.'

'Is it OK if I talk to you about something?'

Janey threw a glance in her mother's direction. 'Ye-ah,' she said hesitantly.

Elizabeth went to put down the mug. As she did so, it clanged against her bedside lamp. 'I'm not sure how I should put any of this. So, I'm going to tell you as simply as I can.'

Chapter 29

Janey walked around the centre of Boston in dazed loops. Clumps of tourists insisted on getting in her way. She sighed and shook her head as she made an arc around them. Why couldn't they see the sights in an orderly fashion? In neat lines? She didn't know where she was going but she had to stay moving. She imagined what it would be like to walk until she became so worn out she collapsed. She would be too weak to say her own name. The ambulance people wouldn't know who to contact, and her mother would be distraught with worry and guilt. Then it struck her that this wouldn't be a sensible tactic for Aidan would worry too. She needed to call Aidan. Not yet, though.

At first, what her mother was saying had dripped into Janey's consciousness. Next there had come a deluge of words: caught, fear, impossible, judgement, forgive. The story disturbed her on so many different levels she couldn't begin to count them. Her head was a riot of confusion. If what the woman said was true, she had been lying to everyone for all her daughter's life.

And if what she said was true, Janey was a different person. She was not herself. She was half American, or Italian, or something. She was related to people she had never met and not related to people she knew. 'My father can't be some random man you met on your summer holidays,' she'd said. Her mother had insisted that Liam was her father really, but that Danny was her father too. And he wasn't random. She'd been in love with him. 'He is random to me,' Janey replied. 'He's a stranger at the end of my hospital bed. Why was he there? To inspect the goods?'

Janey knew she was born before her parents were married. She was in their wedding photos, a fat-faced child in a blue dress. Never ever would it have occurred to her that a man other than her dad might have been involved in her creation.

By then, both of them had been standing up. Janey had to keep shuffling around because otherwise Elizabeth would have touched her, and she hadn't wanted that. The room was small, and she had repeatedly knocked into the furniture or stood on some belonging or other.

'Please, Janey. Please,' her mother had said. 'Please what?' she'd replied. Her mother hadn't answered. Instead she had reeled off all these words about how she knew the time had come. How Syl and Stacia dying, and Liam leaving, and Janey being an adult had made it possible for her to tell. How meeting Danny again had pushed her on. It was all self-serving crap, though. The room had been too hot, and Janey had needed air. Air her mother hadn't breathed.

When she opened the door, a startled chambermaid was standing on the threshold. Once again her mother tried to touch her, but Janey recoiled and put up her hands like she was being attacked, which in a way she was. The poor chambermaid uttered a few words in halting English, and the door clunked shut.

As Janey left, her mother was standing beside the tiny maid who in turn was cowering against her iron trolley. A container of small shampoo bottles toppled onto the floor. Her mother may have been crying.

Full-scale summer had at last arrived, and as Janey walked, she felt the sun scorching through her hair and burning her head. From the bowels of her handbag, she heard her phone. It would be her mother – again. The calls had been arriving at ten-minute intervals. Looking up, she realised she was beside the statue of the man with the enormous feet. She was at Faneuil Hall where she'd worked until the operation. Aidan had called in to the shop to explain, and one evening the manageress had come to visit. She'd been lovely, saying it was a shame to lose such a good worker. Her mother had sat on the other side of the bed, posing like she was the one being complimented. Was it possible that the job might still be available? Janey contemplated going in, but if she spoke to someone she might cry. She could do it tomorrow.

She was doing her best to picture Danny. Her images were blurry. There was yesterday's appearance, and there were the two photographs, one old and one new. What she remembered was a square-jawed American sort. Not her mother's type, or so she would have thought. It turned out she didn't know the woman at all. And neither did her father. Her real father, that is. She wanted to ring her dad in Abu Dhabi but she would only talk gibberish, or blurt out the whole story. That was another job for tomorrow. Janey wondered what her mother was like in 1988. In the photo, she practically radiated happiness. But if she was so content, why hadn't she stayed behind like Michelle and Donal?

She trudged around another bunch of tourists. She was almost at Boston Common when her phone started up again. She would switch the bloody machine off, only she wanted to see how many times her mother would call before she either gave up or tried a new tactic. The tally of missed calls had reached twelve. The idea of walking until she fell into an exhausted heap was growing less and less attractive. As it was, Janey was feeling dizzy. She was swaying slightly, and she saw a chubby couple in matching T-shirts going out of their way to avoid her eye. Their efforts were so over the top, they must have assumed she was a junkie.

What she wanted was a bottle of water and a seat in the shade. Then she could think about what she'd do next. She reached into her bag for some money. Except there wasn't any money. She had half a memory of giving her remaining dollars to Aidan. Well, her ATM card would be there. Except it wasn't. Now that she thought of it, her cards were in her overnight bag. That was sitting on the floor of the hotel room, and no way was she going back there. Oh, of all the things to forget, and of all the days to go forgetting. She would have stamped her foot with frustration, only stamping required too much energy.

As she sat down, she noticed that her skirt was back to front. It had slipped around because of all the weight she'd lost. Her phone rang; the intervals were growing shorter.

'Had you not heard of the pill?' she'd asked. Her mother said she didn't go to Boston with the intention of meeting anyone. 'Was there a condom shortage in America?' Janey snapped back. Now, though, she realised her questions didn't make sense. If they had used contraception, she wouldn't be here. Or would she be here, but someone else? Her head was swirling. If she asked politely, would one of the tourists buy her some water?

There went the stupid phone again. This time it wasn't her mother; it was an American number. It must be Aidan ringing from work. He'd be able to get her a bottle of water. She said hello, and a man said, 'Thank God you're all right. You know your mom is frantic? Where are you?'

'Beside the brown fountain. With the squirrels,' she answered. 'It's very hot.' She forgot to say, 'Who is calling, please?', the way her mum had taught her when she was a child.

Danny found her on the Common. She considered refusing to go with him, only she was too wiped out to make a scene. He explained how her mother had called Aidan but didn't get an answer. No doubt he was behind the bar, showing off the remnants of his shiner. Danny was the only other person Elizabeth knew. 'I'm sorry,' he said, as they got into his car. 'I don't think either of us would have chosen to meet like this.'

Although Janey's head had stopped spinning, her thoughts remained chaotic. 'We did meet. The other day, wasn't it?'

'Yesterday.'

'Sorry,' she said, her voice sounding kind of wavery. 'Not feeling too well.' She was staring at him, noticing individual parts rather than the whole. His eyes dipped at the corners. She was familiar with that dip; had never liked it. He was suggesting they return to the hotel.

'No.'

'She's worried, Janey. And you're in no condition to be wandering around the city. You'll end up back in hospital. Or worse.'

'No.'

'I'm not leaving you here. Will you come home with me for a while? Until your boyfriend has finished work?'

She closed her eyes. She wished it was possible to close her ears in the same way. With everything that was happening, it was ludicrous that she wanted to sleep, yet tiredness was claiming her. 'All right,' she murmured.

While she rubbed a bottle of water over her cheeks, Danny spoke to her mother who sounded subdued, and to a man called Vincent – his brother presumably – who sounded like he was in a right strop. 'I didn't just walk out,' Danny said. 'You don't have to tell me how much money is involved. I can explain. I will explain. Later, man, OK?'

Janey woke slowly. She spent ages in that twilight place where you tell yourself you're awake but you feel powerless to move. She was on a large sofa. She remembered lying down there, only now there was a big fluffy pillow beneath her head and she was covered by a soft green blanket. The room was silent, so to begin with she assumed she was on her own. As she opened her eyes, she took a squinting look around and saw that he was there too. He was reading a book: James Lee Burke. Aidan read him, she thought.

'Hi there,' he said, the man who might be her father. 'I hope you're feeling better.' He put down the book and stood up. He was looking crumpled now, his shirt tails hanging out. His tie was tossed over the back of the chair. 'Can I fix you something to eat or drink? I talked with your mom. She said plain food might be best, but that you'd probably just play with it anyhow.'

Janey shivered.

'I'll turn down the AC,' he said. 'Or we can go outside. When you're properly awake, that is.'

He sat down again, like he was at a loss as to what to do with himself.

'Is anyone else here?' she asked.

'If you mean your mom, no. Anna, my wife, will be back later.'

She pulled the blanket closer to her face. 'Aidan?'

'Doesn't know anything. Do you want to speak to him?' They were staring at each other, the unbroken gaze at odds with their stilted words. 'I'll leave you alone. Let you talk in peace.' He was back on his feet.

Janey hauled herself up and swung her legs around so that she was sitting properly. She remained swaddled in the blanket. 'Danny?'

'Uh-huh?'

'Are you … do you think?'

He dug his hands deep into his pockets. 'Yeah, I reckon I am. You?'

'I'm finding it hard to think right now. Maybe.'

'There's no hurry. If you want to ask me anything, that's cool. It's up to you, Janey. Everything is up to you.'

She was trying to collect herself. She set some store by being composed, not gnashing and grizzling like a kid. She got that from her mother. 'No whinging now, girls,' Elizabeth would say. Your leg could be hanging off, and she'd be all, 'no need to make a show of yourself there, pet'. If you absolutely had to cry, she maintained you should do it in private. Mind you, right then, Janey was prepared to jettison every single lesson she had ever been taught by the woman. She opened her mouth again, and her bottom lip wobbled. She was sure Danny wouldn't notice.

Within a minute, she was the complete opposite of composed. Tears splashed down her face at an alarming rate. To begin with, she didn't know if she was altogether comfortable weeping all over a strange man. Then those silly tremors took over, and she had no choice. At least he wasn't too touchy-feely. And he barely said a word, except at one point when she made a whimpering sound, he let his fingers glide along the top of her hair and said, 'I promise you it won't always feel this bad. I promise.'

After she had purged all of the tears from her system, they

went out to the garden. Danny made her the most inelegant sandwich she'd ever seen; a man's sandwich with chunks of cheese and lumps of tomato hanging out the side. Despite herself, she ate. When she finished, he offered her a cigarette. She shook her head. 'Good girl,' he said, as he lit up. For the first time in hours, she smiled.

She phoned Aidan and said she was fine. She would tell him later, after he had finished work. He was putting in a long shift, trying to make up the hours he'd lost. There was no point in him getting into a flap as well.

Conversation with Danny came in fits and starts. One moment it felt as if they had limitless amounts to say. The words came in spurts, and they ended up talking over each other like they were communicating via a long-distance phone line. Then the awkwardness would re-emerge, and Janey would have to fight the temptation to run away. Perhaps he felt the same.

'One of the things my mum said, she kept on saying it, was that the two of you cared a lot for each other.'

'Did she now? Truth be told, Janey, I loved your mom very much.'

'You see, that's what I don't get. Why did you split up? Why did she go back to Ireland?'

'Cindy Martinez. I kissed her. Not a good idea. A completely idiotic idea, in fact. But there was more to it than that. My brother, the potato famine, a letter your mother received, a film we didn't see, Dan Quayle …' He smiled a tight, rueful smile. 'I don't blame you for looking puzzled.'

'Seriously,' she said, 'I need to know.'

'The Cindy part is true. Other than that, I reckon I didn't appreciate how strongly your mother felt about home. How much she worried about her parents. To me it seemed like everyone in Ireland was clamouring to get to America. I mean, folks were arriving from Dublin every day of the week, so I didn't understand how anyone could miss the place. I was too young, I suppose.'

Janey noticed how his shirt bore the marks of her tears. Given the state she'd been in, she reckoned they must make a right look-ing pair.

'And I said the wrong things,' Danny continued. 'Or, to be more accurate, I didn't say the right things.' He lit another ciga-rette. 'But I'm not being fair to Liam. To your dad. She obviously loved,' he quickly corrected himself, 'loves him a lot.'

She didn't know whether this was true, but she didn't want to talk about her dad. The tears would only return.

'What about your fellow?' he asked. 'Does he have more sense than that?'

'Aidan's a law student. He's good with words. Even if some-times the ones he chooses are a bit out there.'

'Law, huh? My mom will approve.' He exhaled a thin stream of smoke. 'Sorry, Janey. I'm getting ahead of myself here.'

'You're OK. Even though we don't know for certain, I don't mind you telling your family.'

He patted her hand. 'Thanks. Did your mom ever speak about Boston?'

'Not very much. I asked plenty of questions – especially when I knew we were going to spend the summer here. But she was always so vague.' She sighed. 'Now I know why.'

'Will you go back to her tonight?'

'I can't.'

Danny frowned. 'You're not sleeping on the floor.'

Janey raised both eyebrows.

'I'm not fooling here. You're fresh out of hospital. Look at you – a little wisp of a thing. You're not sleeping on any floor.'

'You're such a parent.'

That pleased him. 'I'd love to have you – the two of you – stay here,' he said, 'only …'

'Your wife?'

'I think a little explaining needs to be done first. Honestly, though, Janey, not the floor. Elizabeth would kill me.'

They agreed on a hotel, but not the one where her mother was staying. Initially, she demurred. Danny misunderstood, assumed she was scared of being disloyal to Liam. She hadn't thought of that which made her feel bad. She was worried about the money.

'I think I can rise to a couple of nights in a hotel,' he said.

'The man on the phone – your brother, was it? He was talking about money.'

They were back in the living room by then. He pointed to a photograph. He was with an elderly woman, a serious-looking guy and two other women. They weren't in the first flush of youth either. She remembered his brother from the picture in the paper.

'That's Vincent,' he said. 'Pay no mind to him. You're in for a real treat there some day.'

She looked at the other photos, including one of him with two teenagers. 'Your sons?'

'Ryan and Conor.'

She stared and stared. They were unexpectedly gawky, these boys who could be her brothers.

They were in the hall, about to leave, when they heard a car in the drive. The front door opened, revealing a tall woman in a narrow red dress. Janey recognised her from the third photo. Anna's hazel eyes looked her up and down.

Danny embraced his wife. 'Welcome back, darling,' he said. 'This is Janey. She's ... well, I *think* she is ... my daughter.'

Chapter 30

Avoiding Liam was turning into a full-time occupation. He had called three times, but Elizabeth managed to duck any meaningful conversation. She did talk to Stevie who, as usual, had buckets to say for herself. She was worried that Janey had stopped replying to her texts. 'Have I done something wrong?' she asked. Elizabeth assured her that this wasn't the case. 'She's out and about at the minute, pet. I'm sure you'll hear from her soon.'

After Janey left, she had cried. Not for hours and hours, not in any loud or showy way, but quietly into one of her daughter's T-shirts. It smelled of hospital. She went to bed, wrapping the covers around her. Her teeth chattered and her arms and legs turned numb. How anyone could be so cold on such a hot, hot day, she couldn't understand. Time and again, she came up with words or lines she wished she had used. She thought of those court reports you saw on the news. The judge would ask if there were any mitigating factors. She had never got to list her mitigating factors.

Several times she spoke to Danny who had taken charge of the situation. She'd never seen this side of him. Presumably, this was what he was like at work. He was unbelievably composed, his calls so businesslike you would swear he was merely a bystander in the whole mess.

She was on the bed, curled into a comma, when he called again. Janey and Aidan were going to stay in a hotel for the next two nights. After that, he didn't know what she would do, although he had a suspicion she might not go home with Elizabeth. 'I'm warning you, so as you don't get upset,' he said. 'And don't worry about her contacting Liam. She says that's your job.' Elizabeth offered to pay for the hotel. 'No,' he insisted, 'and don't go making any big deal of this, either. Think of it as me helping a friend.'

'Where did I find you, Danny?'

'In O'Mahoney's. And as I recall, I was more than happy to be found.'

Despite everything, she thought, his charm was like a reflex action, as automatic as blinking. 'What was Janey like when you left?'

'I'm kind of at a disadvantage, because I don't know where she's at normally. Quiet. Thoughtful. The tears had stopped, mind. Aidan will be with her soon enough. She seems mighty attached to him.'

'She's a lucky woman. My father had a saying about a couple down the street from us. And, I know, he had a thousand sayings. But this was a good one. "As God made them, he matched them," he used to say. That's Aidan and Janey.'

'I like that one too.' He paused. 'Listen, Elizabeth, I've got to go. Anna got back right around the time we were leaving. I better listen to what she's got to say.'

'Of course. Of course you must. Good luck.'

'You take care of yourself,' he said, and he was gone.

Elizabeth knew she should speak to Michelle. She owed her an apology. Michelle's words may have been severe, but she told it as it was. Going all the way back to that night in Lantern Street, when she had kicked the rucksack across the room and pleaded with her to think again, she'd always told the truth. It was a rare gift.

In those days, Elizabeth realised, there had been a symmetry between her and Danny. Each, in their own way, had been as attractive as the other. Each had revelled in the joy that the person they desired, desired them in equal measure. As they do, the years had shattered that symmetry. Only a fool would imagine it could ever be restored.

*

It occurred to Danny that he might be killing his brother. His face was an unusual colour. Not purple, as such. More ... magenta. And he was spluttering in a disturbing way. When he had finished talking to Elizabeth, Danny noticed that he'd missed a call from Vincent. He made the mistake of getting back to him.

Ten minutes later here he was, in the office, like a fourteen-year-old caught smoking weed at the back of the gym hall. Anna had misread the situation, had assumed he was joking about Janey being his daughter. In a distressed state, she'd contacted Vincent.

'According to Anna, she looked around eighteen or nineteen. And pale. Wasted, like she was doing drugs.'

'She left hospital this morning, Vincent. She's twenty-two.'

'Come on, Dan. Give me some credit, will you? I knew you were too perky. Too *goddamn* perky. Even if she is Elizabeth Kelly's daughter, why was she in the house? Have you got a family fetish or something? Sure, Anna is no Snow White but what in the name of God were you doing?'

Danny pressed his fingers against his forehead. Vincent was mid-tirade and wasn't listening to a word he said. Every dubious episode in his life was being resurrected. Especially the one that had led to their worst ever quarrel. In the hiatus between Geraldine and Anna, Danny had brought home a girl, thinking she was twenty or twenty-one. At the time he'd been doing his bit for Colombia's GDP and he'd been pretty out of it. Still, he was positive that's what she'd said. The next morning, he'd discovered that she was seventeen.

He'd told his brother, who for some crazy reason had informed Geraldine. They were separated; she hadn't needed to know. Predictably, she went ballistic, said he'd gone so far off the rails she didn't want him seeing the boys. Vincent hadn't accepted the twenty or twenty-one story. Anyway, he had maintained, that would have been almost as bad. Danny could still hear him roaring, 'You're thirty-six, for God's sake. *Thirty-fucking-six.* Are you ever going to grow up?' Right then, he was shouting about him being forty-six. As if Danny needed reminding. More than once, the thought had occurred to him that his wooing of Anna was, in part, a reaction to that episode. He'd wanted to say to Vincent, 'Look what I've found, all clean and classy.'

Telling Anna had been another mistake. It was the sort of error you made in those early infatuated days, when you felt the person lying beside you was so extraordinary you could confess your every sin. She must have feared he was at it again.

Danny waited for Vincent's fury to subside. At that moment he was in such a lather he wasn't capable of hearing anything apart from his own words. Anyway, the actual truth wouldn't be much more palatable to the guy.

After a while, Vincent ran out of anger and the haranguing came to a halt. Danny took a deep breath and gave him a version of the weekend. A sexless version. Not too much emotion either. There was no point in making the situation worse. To be fair, as soon as Danny started explaining, it was clear that his brother believed him. His colour faded, his sneer softened and he asked the occasional question. To the extent that he was incredulous, it was because he didn't understand how Danny could forgive Elizabeth. Danny surprised himself with what he said, and by the vehemence with which he said it.

'I was crazy about her, Vincent. I can't believe she went home and turned into some sort of avenging bitch. Sure, she made disastrous decisions. Hell, I've made plenty of those myself. She was scared, and somehow she convinced herself that what she was doing was right. And,' he paused, 'don't imagine she hasn't suffered. Or that her life will be any bed of roses when she gets home.'

'What are you – Saint Daniel of Dorchester, or something?'

'Didn't you hear? They're putting up a statue of me in the parish church.'

'Oh, Dan, I'm being serious. What does the girl think?'

'Janey. Her name is Janey O'Hara. She wants to do a DNA test – when we've all had time to calm down.'

Vincent was twirling his wedding ring around his finger. 'And the husband? The guy she's been hoodwinking for twenty-odd years?'

'That's a bit complicated.' He outlined the situation, and in an instant, Vincent came back.

'Is she looking for money?' It stood to reason, he said. She was probably stunned by how well they'd done. 'When she left, you didn't have a cent to your name. She comes back, hears about the business and thinks "bonanza".' That was Vincent. Still doing too much looking out, spotting conspiracies around every corner.

'Nah. You're wrong there, man. That's not her. If you ask me, Elizabeth has the opposite problem. She never wants to bother anyone or show any weakness. Always thinks she can sort everything out in her own head.'

Vincent appeared to accept the assurance. 'What are you going to do?'

Danny was chronically confused, but there was no point in riling his brother any further. 'Go home. Talk to Anna. See what she wants to do.'

'And Mom? And the boys?'

'Soon, but not quite yet. Tell Val, though. Obviously, tell Val.' He stopped himself from going further and telling Vincent how fortunate he was. He didn't want to go overboard on the schmaltz.

'Thanks. By the way, I know you've got other issues on your mind, but the meeting went well. Despite your disappearing trick.'

Danny high-fived his brother. This was Vincent's project: the one that was in the paper. He wanted to build a housing development on an abandoned site in Dorchester: a mixture of affordable homes and market-rate places. Despite the recession and the formidable list of foreclosures, he was persevering with his dream. As he was fond of saying, 'A good development, Dan, a *quality* development, attracting quality people.' Danny had said to him, 'You do know that what you're proposing here is practically communism?' His brother's only response had been to wink and say it must be catching. Who would have thought? Even Vincent had surprises in him.

In Dublin on Tuesday morning, Michelle returned to Peter's office. He had issued the summons. This time, she did kick off her sandals and her feet sank into the carpet. His face a study in irritation, he muttered something under his breath.

Michelle made the most of her chance to annoy him. 'Don't mess around now. I have a garden that needs weeding. What's up?'

'Well …'

'So?'

'Well …'

'Do you know, Peter, we're like two old lads trying to outdo each other in the well and so stakes.'

Even he saw the funny side. 'Didn't we grow up surrounded by fellows who could get an entire day's conversation out of those two words? How could we be any better?'

'What's the story?'

'Liam. He's been on to me. He's in a bad way. First, Elizabeth stopped talking to him. Apparently, she answers the phone but pretends she's on a train. He figures that if she was genuinely on a train, she'd be in California at this stage. Now Janey has stopped answering her phone. Well, she did once, and guess what?'

'Was a train involved?'

'Spot on. So Liam wants to know why no one will speak to him. He's convinced some major disaster has befallen Janey. He's even threatening to get on a plane. Will you tell Elizabeth to talk to her husband? It doesn't matter what old shite she spins, once she talks to him.'

The sound of city centre traffic leached into the room. Michelle dug her toes into the carpet. 'There's a slight snag. I don't know that she's talking to me either.' Peter frowned. 'We had a disagreement. Something and nothing. You must be up to your tonsils in work. Don't let it worry you.'

Peter extended his frown so that all his features seemed to contract. 'I'm up the walls. But that doesn't stop me from wanting to know what's going on.'

He'd always been able to browbeat her until he got the truth. Way back when they were students, and Michelle had been sworn to secrecy about some illicit shift or other minor scandal, he would cajole and harry until he got the information he was seeking.

'Fair enough,' she said, smoothing a curl between her fingers then letting it spring back to its natural state. 'Only don't go mental on me. You know the way you asked on Saturday if she'd slept with Danny? You were a little – what's the word? – prescient there.'

'Ah for the love of God,' he exploded. 'You're codding me? She's a bottomless pit of surprises, that woman. And none of them good.'

'At least, it doesn't sound like it'll happen again.'

'And what class of character is he? Elizabeth tells him about Janey, and he thinks *that's* the most appropriate response? Although, if you remember, I always had my doubts about him.'

Michelle had no desire to relive 1988. 'What would the world be like, Peter, if we were all logical all of the time?'

He made a funny noise, like a bone was caught in his throat.

'Elizabeth was going to tell Janey yesterday. About Danny being her father, that is. That might explain why she was abrupt with Liam.'

'So ...'

'I'll try to talk to her. Tell her to call Liam. She's coming home tomorrow – out of harm's way.'

'I don't envy you the call,' he said. 'She's not fit to be let out on her own. Honestly, in the annals of eejitry, there'll be a special chapter for Elizabeth.'

'I'm accustomed to dealing with hormonal fourteen-year-olds. They're good practice.'

Michelle slipped her sandals on and got up to leave. She was struck by how tired Peter looked, his face the colour of half-set putty. It was no fun being the spokesman for a national pariah, even if you did have a swanky desk, a plush carpet and a six-figure salary. The way she saw it, he was at the heart of a bitter irony. The man who loved home more than anyone else she knew made a living defending the people who had gutted the place. The phone rang, but he ignored it.

'By the way,' he said, 'I got another e-mail from Donal. Strange one this. He wants me to be his best man. Does he not have any friends in America?'

She paused at the door. 'Oh, Peter, sometimes you can be incredibly thick. Did it not occur to you that he wants to make sure you're there?'

Chapter 31

There were things Elizabeth needed to say, but first she went shopping. Predictably enough, guilt blew her purse wide open. She bought three tops for Stevie, and a pair of jeans so unfeasibly narrow that only a sixteen-year-old could wear them. They were like the ones she had worn at the same age, except in those days the local shops hadn't stocked such fashionable items. You had to turn your Dunnes Stores jeans inside out and take them in with big tacking stitches.

Stevie was as a thin as a lath. Elizabeth told her that one day soon this would be a source of delight. In the here and now, Stevie didn't see it like that. She wanted to be like the buxom girls who started wearing a bra in fourth class and monopolised the attention of the cool boys. She complained that only nerds talked to her: lads with blotchy skin and jumpers chosen by their mothers. It was disquieting to watch your daughter prepare for a lifetime of wanting to be something other than herself. Especially when, in every other way, she was so clever.

She considered buying a top for Janey but thought better of it. The purchase would be dismissed as a bribe. Doubtless at Aidan's bidding, she had sent a text to say she was in one piece. She had also confirmed Danny's hunch. She wouldn't be returning to Ireland with her mother. Elizabeth replied straight away; said that was fine, asked if she needed money or any of the belongings she'd abandoned in the hotel. Every time her phone beeped or rang, she assumed it was her daughter. Every time she was disappointed.

Newbury Street was bustling with well-groomed women. Studying them from behind her sunglasses, Elizabeth concluded that staying that put together must be a full-time job. 'What do you do?' 'I groom.' Occasionally, she saw the merit in being one of those women. Like at the hairdressers when they gave her *Good Housekeeping* while reserving *Vogue* for the waxy-faced lady beside her. Increasingly, she had started thinking about the person she could have been. The life she might have had. She found herself wondering, what if?

If she had stayed with Danny, what would she be doing now? Would they still be together? If so, she'd be an American. Like the people who came visiting when she was a kid. Her mother had dusted off the best tea set, and they'd eaten ham sandwiches and shop-bought cake. But behind the guests' backs, everyone had laughed at their accents and their clothes.

While she was paying for one of Stevie's tops, Michelle rang to warn her that Liam had an inkling all was not right. Any composure Elizabeth possessed went skittering away. She'd been hoping to dodge the difficult questions until she got back to Dublin.

'What can I say?' she asked. 'Now … from here?'

Michelle reckoned that with an ocean and a continent between her and Liam, Elizabeth should say very little. 'Keep it bright, keep it innocuous, try not to tell too many out-and-out lies,' she advised.

'Thanks. And sorry, I was way out of line yesterday.'

A long sigh fluttered across the Atlantic. 'I would have done the same.'

'What – called me a smug bitch?'

'No, you idiot. Had sex with Danny. Just … mind yourself, will you? And take my advice about Liam. Talk, but say nothing.'

So that was what Elizabeth did. She accepted his rebuke for the silences of the past few days, sympathised with his complaints about how oppressively hot it was in Abu Dhabi and enthused over his imminent homecoming. She did this by rote, trying not to think too much about what she was saying. Not for the first time, she cursed the invention of the mobile phone and yearned for the days when you could lie low for as long as you wanted.

Afterwards, she rang Danny. When he didn't reply she felt deflated, like a fifteen-year old waiting for the boy she'd kissed at the school disco to acknowledge her existence. The night before she'd considered the situation, and the more generous part of her hoped all had gone well with Anna.

Walking back towards her hotel, she came across a memorial to those who'd died in the famine. That was new. She sat beside the statues and for a fleeting moment had an image of Vincent with a placard, saying *Get Over Yourselves*. But she was being unfair; there was every chance his views had softened with the years. The memorial's inscriptions spoke of the countless numbers who had died in Ireland, and the countless others who'd made the journey to America.

She reached the hotel but continued on, past the hole in the ground that had once been Filene's department store, and down the gloomy streets of the financial district. She smiled as she passed Milk Street and Water Street. Donal used to claim it was a shocking state of affairs when a city with so many patriot dead had to be naming thoroughfares after non-alcoholic drinks. Speaking of Donal, she'd replied to his e-mail about the wedding. She told him how sorry she was that she wouldn't be able to attend, and explained that she was actually in Boston right then. *I took your advice*, she wrote, *and met up with my first love!* Then she realised her mistake. After all, she'd known Liam for years by the time she met Danny. She reached for the delete button, yet didn't press it.

The sky opened out, and Elizabeth was at the water. The light washed over her face. She remembered ambling down this way on her lunch break from Anderson's, sandwich in one hand, book in the other. Her memories were unusually hazy, but she was convinced the waterfront looked different, that the intervening years had seen it developed and prettified. From her bench, she made out an untidy line of tourists waiting to take a boat trip. Others were gathering around a collection of red buses, preparing for an afternoon of sights and photographs and ice cream. The air was heavy with heat.

A reverie settled over her as she contemplated the beauty of the scene. To her right, three huge cranes guarded the harbour. Now there was a sight you didn't get at home any more. Logan Airport was in front of her, its planes ploughing furrows across the sky. Her mind flicked back to the memorial, in particular to another of its inscriptions which detailed some of the Irish immigrants who'd played a part in Boston's history. She thought of all the stories the harbour and the airport had heard, and of all the people, from whatever part of the world, who still arrived in hope.

Mostly, though, she thought of Janey and Stevie. She remembered a school sports day when Janey was seven or eight. She'd won a handful of medals, and when Elizabeth had said, 'Aren't I lucky you're my daughter,' Janey had taken her hand and replied, 'And I'm lucky you're my mum.' She remembered how the hand was small and pliable. She recalled Stevie at a similar age, her face weighed down with anxiety. She'd been worried that there weren't enough books in the world. 'What will I do,' she'd asked, 'when I run out of things to read?' She thought too of their quirks. Of Stevie's attempts to teach tricks to the cat and her ability to watch four different news programmes at once. Of Janey's daft faces and her mania for low-rent reality shows.

She must have been sitting there for half an hour or more, when the phone throbbed in her pocket. In the seconds before it was in her hand, Elizabeth asked herself who she wanted the caller to be: Jancy or Danny. To her relief, the honest answer was Janey.

Danny apologised for not getting back more quickly. 'Work – forever getting in the way of life,' he said.

'No problem. I shouldn't be making a nuisance of myself.'

'Now, Elizabeth. We've had words about this martyr act of yours.'

His tone was humorous, so she answered in kind. 'OK, the sole purpose of my call was to distract you from your work.'

'That's better. Where are you?'

She explained. He said he'd come and find her, and they could go for lunch. Elizabeth would have the opportunity to say what had to be said.

At the first sight of Danny's flat-footed walk, her stomach gave a disconcerting lurch. He brushed his lips over her cheek and sat down beside her. Apparently, Vincent knew all about Janey. This made Elizabeth feel vaguely sick. She could imagine Vincent, a cackling triumphant Vincent, reminding Danny how he'd never approved of her.

'No,' Danny insisted. 'I promise you it wasn't like that.'

With Anna, the situation was more complex. According to Danny, she had difficulty coming to terms with his story. She had trouble comprehending something so messy happening in her orderly world. In fact, she was certain Janey was not his daughter.

'What if she's wrong?' Elizabeth asked. 'And she is wrong. I know she is.'

'I can't say. There was a lot of silence.'

'To be fair to her, it had to be some shock. There she was, expecting to have one conversation, and she gets plunged into another.'

'Most of the questions she did ask were about you.'

Elizabeth tried to grasp what this must be like for his wife. Presumably, hearing such news must be doubly difficult when your marriage is already in a parlous state. Unfortunately, no deeper understanding came. She was too preoccupied by her own concerns. 'And the rest? The two of you, I mean?'

'We didn't get that far.'

'I suppose that's hardly a surprise. With everything else going on.'

Danny, who had been staring out at the water, turned towards Elizabeth. 'I can guess what you're thinking. Same old, same old. He wanted to avoid the difficult stuff.'

'No, Danny. I doubt Anna felt able for any of that either.' They were too close now, and she told herself she would have to move.

'I'm pretty sure she did. I was the one who was reluctant to go there.'

'Oh.'

Each considered the other, then without a word being spoken, she was inside his arms, and they were kissing. Breathing each other in and out, occasionally stopping to say a word or two, before starting again. 'Danny,' she said, eventually, 'we can't do this here.'

'Baby, we can do whatever we like.'

She inhaled him, great big lungfuls of him. Their kisses had a languid, summer-afternoon quality, and she would gladly have stayed in that moment. Danny, as was his way, wanted to move on. When next they stopped to look at each other, a slow smile spread across his face. He sighed and said, 'Well now.' His signals were unaltered. That was his shorthand for the next stage, for leaving the bench and finding somewhere else. Her hotel room, presumably. Elizabeth caught her breath and pulled him in again. She needed another minute.

'I can't,' was how she began. Danny was close enough for her to appreciate every mark on his face, every line she hadn't been able to watch develop. She felt such absurd affection for them. Affection she was sure he could never share for her lines, no matter how much he cared about her. 'I can't because tomorrow I'm going home and—'

'Isn't that why we should be together? For an afternoon, at any rate. Making the most of our last chance.'

'Danny, I have to go home, and I have to try and sort things out with Janey. I have to tell Liam and Stevie and I have to prepare myself for how they'll react. I've started to worry that Stevie will take this worst of all.'

He nodded.

'With Liam, I'm not kidding myself. Our marriage was so damaged it might not have survived anyway. I don't know what he'll do. If someone had deceived me for so long, I can't image how I'd react.'

He traced one finger along her cheekbone. 'Or he might under-stand, my darling. Not right away. I'm not saying that. But if Liam thinks about the options you had, or didn't have, perhaps he will see why things happened the way they did.'

'It's over. I know that. But last night the realisation hit me that maybe Stevie will want to live with him. And who knows, maybe Janey too. Or more likely, she'll want to find a place with Aidan. Either way, our lives won't be the same. The two people who matter most to me ... who make my life worthwhile ... and I'll have driven them away.' Saying this out loud and watching Danny's face made the prospect of losing her daughters feel even more real. 'So I'll have to toughen myself up. And I'll have to do everything I can to make them trust me again.'

He put his arms around her, and for some minutes she per-formed one of her oldest tricks. She rested her chin on his shoul-der and closed her eyes. A light breeze was coming in from the sea, and the shopping bags rustled at her feet.

When they let go, Danny kissed her forehead. 'I've been think-ing about what might have happened. If you hadn't returned to Ireland the way you did. If you'd known you were pregnant. If I had known.'

'I've had such a long time to consider that. More than half my life. I like to think ... oh I'm sure, really ... I would have stayed.'

'Can you imagine the two of us? In Emerald Street? With Ma.'

'And Vincent calling round every ten minutes. Driving me nuts.'

'I reckon we would have been, sorry to use this word, happy.'

'That's what I think too.'

They kissed again, and kept on kissing. A passer-by whistled. Presently, the time came. Elizabeth was ready to finish what she had to say. Before she spoke, she put her hands to his face and caressed it.

'The reason I can't go any further is the closer I get to you, the more likely it is I'll end up in love all over again. I know you're probably thinking, "What is she on about? It's only sex." But it would become more than that to me. I learnt that on Sunday.' She hesitated. 'And I can't do it. Not with all the other upheaval. I can't be in Dublin, trying to deal with everything. And wanting to be with you. And thinking about you with Anna.'

'I'm sorry, Elizabeth,' was all he said.

'No, I'm sorry. I only wish I'd made the right choice. Back when I had a choice. I wish I'd been brave enough to do what I really wanted to do. And I wish it was possible to reach into the past and give myself an almighty shake. But I can't go back.' She switched her gaze to the water which shone under the early afternoon sun. 'I can never understand when people say "no regrets". Can you? I mean, the arrogance of it.' Danny remained quiet, so she continued. 'I'm not saying we shouldn't be in touch. Of course we should. We can send e-mails, or occasionally we can talk about Janey. That would make sense, wouldn't it? And I genuinely hope that you can get to know her. It's what you deserve.'

Elizabeth started to shake. She wasn't equipped for this. She had spent years making sure she was contained and composed. Shutting herself down, as Michelle put it. Now she'd been opened up again. Beside her, Danny was silent. She watched him absorb her words. What she hoped for was reassurance, but his face was impassive.

After his conversation with Elizabeth, Danny told Vincent that he needed to disappear for a couple of days. His brother pledged that unless something catastrophic occurred he would leave him alone. Danny's next move was, perhaps, not the wisest, but it was what he wanted to do. He called in on his mother and told her that she had another granddaughter. Her face tensed with incomprehension, and the first words she said were, 'What a terrible thing to do.'

'You can't think of it like that, Ma. This is good news. It'll just take a while to ... adjust, you know.'

For a long five minutes, she said nothing more. They were in the garden, and she looked into mid-distance, although he couldn't think that she was watching anything in particular.

'Will you get to see her?' she said.

'It's up to Janey, and obviously she lives in Ireland. But, yeah, I think so. That would be good, huh?'

For whatever reason, his mother began to talk about a spat between two of Vincent's boys: Vincent junior and Scott. Danny wasn't concentrating the way he should, but it seemed one of them had broken up with a girl, and the other had slapped him on the back and said not to worry, he'd pass on one of his cast-offs. A punch had been thrown in response. All of this had taken place on the construction site in Southie where the pair were working for the summer. A colleague had been forced to pull them apart. Vincent senior was apoplectic, claiming they'd shamed him on one of his own sites. His humour darkened further when Valerie laughed.

'The whole episode reminded me of you and your brother,' Regina said. 'When you were that age you were a terror.'

'I would never have been so cruel,' he replied, his tongue planted well in his cheek.

'You said far far worse. And he let you get away with it. Oh, he did enough grumbling and moaning for ten men. But most brothers would have given you the thumping you deserved.'

Danny's limbs were heavy. Elizabeth's words were playing on his mind. 'Life didn't turn out so bad for Vincent, did it?'

'When your brother found what he wanted, he always had the good sense to hold on to it.'

He lifted his jacket off the chair, reached into the inside pocket and pulled out his phone. 'Elizabeth sent me these.'

His mother peered at the pictures of Janey, and then touched the screen. 'Will I be able to meet her, do you think?'

'I hope so. If it's what you want.'

'Oh, Danny, of course it is.'

She told him how confused she had been on Sunday morning because she'd suspected that something was afoot with Elizabeth.

'You know what I thought. And it turns out the real story is even bigger.'

That was when he let her in on the next part of the tale. Almost immediately he regretted it. After all, she wanted him to repair his marriage, not go jumping into bed with old flames. 'Needless to say, no one else knows or can know. Especially Anna. Or Vincent. So, a vow of silence please, Ma. The scenes with Vincent would not be pleasant.'

'And is that what Elizabeth wants? That you try and return to your normal lives?'

'She's going back to Ireland to tell her husband.' Danny told his mother what she'd said.

'Do you still have feelings for her?'

'I can't see as it makes any difference now. We had our chance, and we blew it.'

Regina pressed her lips together.

'Sorry,' he said, 'I blew it.'

She leaned in and gave him a look like she used to when they were living on Emerald Street and she'd been trying to convince him of the superiority of her point of view. 'You know it's not my place to get involved.' She was involved. 'But are you sure you were listening to her?'

'Of course I was listening to her. I gave you her exact words.'

'In my experience, Danny, it's hard to say what you don't want but even harder to say what you do want.'

'I don't understand.'

Regina leaned in even further and, with three bony fingers, tapped his head. 'Time for some thinking.'

Chapter 32

'For pity's sake, Aidan. The way you're going on, you'd swear you were my father.' The words were out of Janey's mouth before she appreciated what she had said.

'I think you've got more than enough of those already, Princess. And I didn't mean to nag. I just have this feeling you should see your mam before she goes home. That's all.'

She punched herself on the side of the head and glanced over at her boyfriend. 'I think I'm going mad.'

They were back in the apartment, sitting at opposite sides of the front room. Everybody else was at work, which was just as well because Janey wasn't in the form for an inquisition. The night before, their friends Brendan and Laura had called around to the hotel where they'd been staying. When she'd given them her news, Laura had said that Danny must have a fair few bob if he could put them up in such a quality spot. Brendan had wanted to know if she was entitled to a visa. Janey had been upset by their response. 'Ah, don't mind them,' Aidan had said. 'Laura's missing the cop-on gene and she's making Brendan as bad as herself. It will be awkward for people, though. Knowing what to say.'

Danny had offered to pay for another night or two, but she'd decided to move on. Despite his decency, she was torn over how to behave. Unlike one of her favourite movie characters, Blanche DuBois, she didn't want to depend on the kindness of strangers. And for now at any rate, that's what he remained. Gradually the belief was taking hold that her mother was right. Danny was her father. Or, as she should say, her birth father. There was no denying she had the look of him, but there was more than that. Right from the start, before her mother had said anything, she'd warmed to him. So had Aidan. She'd recognised his sense of humour. And he had an optimism about him that she hoped she shared. Or was she imagining all of this?

In a way, Janey felt bad for giving these thoughts headspace. Liam was her father, would always be her father. He was the person who mattered most. At the same time, it wasn't as though Danny had rejected her. He had never been given the chance. She had to know the truth. If it turned out she was related to Danny, then Stevie wasn't her only sibling. How odd was that? She had resolved to get the DNA test carried out sooner rather than later, although she wasn't going to divulge this to her mother. In fact, even Aidan didn't know that she'd already looked at some websites. The results were available in days.

Aidan believed she should meet up with her mother before Elizabeth flew back to Dublin later in the day. Janey said she wouldn't be able for the awkward conversation and the pleading looks.

'Because have no doubt,' she told her boyfriend, 'that's what there'll be. She has Danny wrapped around her little finger already. "Don't be too hahd on your mom," he says to me. What am I supposed to do? Tell her everything is tickety-boo, and we should all carry on regardless?'

'Your Boston accent is brutal.'

'Ah here, I'm trying to be serious. Can we be serious for once?'

Aidan walked over and sat on the wooden floor beside her. He patted one of her knees. 'Listen, you don't have to be all nicey-nicey. You can let her know how upset you are. She wouldn't expect anything else.'

Janey patted back. Aidan's knees were knobbly things. He claimed this was from hurling on all-weather pitches. 'You don't know how awful she'll be. She'll have spent the past two days nursing her misery.'

'Princess, I think you're being a wee bit unkind. I doubt she has to fake the unhappiness. It's beyond me how she's managed to hold it together all these years.'

Sometimes Aidan was too decent. 'Could you be here? To monitor our behaviour? Or more likely, to monitor hers?'

'No problem. I'm not working until tonight.'

Janey sucked in air through her teeth and gave a theatrical shiver. 'All right then. So long as you ring her. Plus, *she* can come over here. I'm not putting myself out for her.'

Looking at her mother standing at the apartment door, Janey was hit by the sensation of roles being reversed. The woman looked harried, needy; her smile a pathetic, rictus thing.

'I promise I won't keep you long,' she said. 'This looks nice.' She put on a face like she was inspecting Buckingham Palace. Needless to say, the apartment looked the exact opposite of nice. It was a dingy tip of a place, and the late morning glare highlighted the layers of dust.

Janey didn't particularly want to make eye contact with her mother, but she risked another peep in her direction. It was two days since they'd last met – only two days – yet Elizabeth appeared to have lost a week's worth of weight. She was stringy at the best of times; it was a family complaint. Now she bordered on gaunt: her cheeks sunken and her shoulders spindly. Her eyes were pink-rimmed, whether from lack of sleep or an excess of tears it was impossible to know. She must have stopped taking her tablets. Her mother never spoke about the tablets, although Janey knew she took antidepressants and other stuff besides.

'How are you going on, Elizabeth?' beamed Aidan. 'It's good to see you.'

Janey sent him a look. It wouldn't hurt him to tone down the amiability.

'Oh, you know,' her mother said, 'happier to see Janey looking so much better.'

'You'll have a cup of coffee? It isn't great now, but it won't kill

320

you.' Clearly, he was intent on ignoring his girlfriend. They would be having words about this.

'Once it's no hassle.'

Janey wanted to clobber the pair of them and their saccharine behaviour.

Aidan disappeared in the direction of the kitchen – or the glorified cupboard that passed for a kitchen – leaving the two of them alone.

'I have your stuff,' her mother said, tipping her head towards Janey's bag.

'So I see.'

'That was good of Danny. Getting you a place to stay. I'm sure it was nice.'

'Yeah.'

'Did you thank him?'

'For fuck's sake.' Janey knew it was a mistake to have let her come to the apartment. It hurt to look at her, sitting on the floor, her legs folded under her so as to avoid displaying her underwear. She wished she wasn't so cranky. She wished she was a bigger person. The problem was, every time she tried to think big, the facts returned. Her mother *knew*, and yet she'd spent years spinning her tales. Janey's anger came in waves and wasn't always the same. Mostly she was angry with her mother for not telling the truth, but occasionally she was angry with her for doing precisely that. Why did she have to do this to everyone *now*?

Janey longed to be like Danny who was remarkably even-tempered. Aidan had this theory that he still held a torch for her mother. She scoffed. 'You haven't seen his wife. Stunn-ing.' Aidan replied that there was more to attraction than looks. Then again, if you had Aidan's face you would say that. What, though, if he was right? After all, he'd been first to spot that there was something between them in the past. No, that would be too much. Too too much.

Her mother's reply was almost inaudible. 'I didn't mean to offend you, pet. It goes without saying that you thanked him.'

At long last, Aidan returned, carrying their one decent mug. He must have heard the exchange because he sent a harsh look in Janey's direction and smiled at Elizabeth. 'There you go now. I'd say you could do with that.'

'Aidan, you're a star. The eye is healing up nicely.'

'Nearly back to my handsome best. So, you're off home this evening?'

She gave a flicker of a smile. 'That's right. Back to the other daughter. And the cat.' She turned to Janey. 'When are you coming home, love?'

'Can't remember.'

'Today fortnight,' said Aidan.

'What will you do in the meantime, while Aidan's at work?'

'I don't know. Talk to Danny again, possibly. I'll see.'

'I'd say he would like that.'

This was torture. Janey wanted her mother to leave. Yet the way Aidan was carrying on, she'd be here until it was time to go to the airport. And, of course, they were all skirting around what had to be said. She decided to dive on in.

'Have you been speaking to Dad?' she asked. 'The real one that is. The one in Abu Dhabi.'

'I have. But not about, you know ...'

'Are you going to tell him? Or will he have to guess?' Janey knew Aidan was giving her the evil eye. Feck him. He hadn't spent the past twenty-two years being lied to. Her mother's phone could be heard, chiming away in the depths of her handbag. It went unanswered.

'I'm going to wait until he's back in Dublin. I don't think it's a conversation for over the phone.'

'I'm supposed to lie to him in the meantime, then?'

Aidan's voice was curt. 'Come on now, Princess, you can talk to him without lying. Sure, the time difference is so big, ye only have little chats on the Skype anyway.'

'And what about Stevie? Will you tell her?'

Her mother placed the mug on the floor, and made a steeple

shape with her fingers. 'I … I don't know whether I should tell her right away, or leave it until Liam, your dad, gets home.'

'You do know she's going to be totally screwed up over this? I mean, that time you went mental at school was bad enough. Even in her school they heard all about loopy Mrs O'Hara over in St Attracta's. This will have her in a shocking state altogether. Jesus, what a mother.'

Janey knew she had gone too far. Her mum was leaning against the wall, her eyes shut tight and her lips clamped together. She waited for Aidan to intervene. For once he remained quiet. He was gawping out the window, like there was anything to see apart from another nondescript apartment building.

It was her mother who broke the silence. 'I should head on. I'm sure you both have things to be doing.'

Aidan urged her to finish her coffee.

'No, I'm fine. And thanks again. I better see who's been ringing me. I've missed a couple of calls now.' She clambered up from the floor, and Aidan joined her. Janey decided to stay put. Her mother was rooting through her handbag. There was so much rubbish in there it wouldn't be a surprise if she pulled out a kitchen sink and Grover the cat. She was holding an envelope. 'This is for you,' she said. 'You might need it now you aren't working.'

'I can't take that,' Janey said. 'Anyway, I won't be spending much, and Aidan's agreed to pay my rent.'

'Please, pet. It would put my mind at rest. For fear there's a problem … and you have to see a doctor again.'

'I've told you. I don't want it.'

Aidan stepped forward and took the money. 'That's decent of you, Elizabeth. With any luck, we won't even have to open the envelope but we'll be glad to have it just in case.' The Judas kissed her on the cheek and accompanied her out to the hall. Behind her, the door closed with the lightest of clicks.

Janey stood up and, silently, began to count. She wondered how far she would get before the recriminations kicked in. The answer was six. Aidan's annoyance had bloomed into full-blown rage.

'Would it have killed you to be civil? She's fierce upset. You saw that.'

'I don't think you have any concept of what it's like to feel this … betrayed.'

Aidan was waving his arms about. He always did that when he was angry, except never before had the anger been directed at her. 'And behaving like that … has that made you feel better?'

'It hasn't made me feel any worse.'

'Listen, Janey, you're right. I have no notion what this is like for you. But I don't see how tearing strips off of your mam will improve anything. I don't see that it's any way to behave.'

He had crossed the line. 'Behave? She's the woman who wrote the book about how to behave. "Say thank you. Don't let yourself down. Don't ask for too much." I've had years of her bullshit, of listening to her banging on and on.'

She watched as Aidan went into the bedroom. He returned with his jacket over his arm. 'I'm away out. Jobs to do,' he said.

'No you haven't.' They were facing each other. Janey's hands were on her hips. When anyone else did that it seemed comical. In this case it felt appropriate.

'You're right there too. I want to go. You know what the truth is? Today you really did behave like a brainless princess.'

There were tears at the back of her eyes but there was no way she was going to fold. 'Oh, for God's sake, Aidan, why are you on her side?'

'I'm not on her side. It's not a debate.'

She had never seen this facet of him before. She went to object, but he was speaking again. 'Now that she's left here, who has she got to turn to?'

'Plenty of people. Like, if you're right, she can turn to Danny. Stick out her bony chest and flutter her eyelashes at him. Or she can call Michelle and 'fess up to her.'

Aidan walked past. 'No one, Janey. No fucking one. That's who.'

Saying Michelle's name gave her a jolt. They also knew Danny: Michelle and Peter and Orla and Donal. So why didn't they guess?

Or did they guess? How many of them had been lying?

When Aidan shut the door, the apartment shook. Janey sat down and slumped against the wall. Her mind churned. She wondered where her mother had gone. Despite everything, Janey hoped she was OK.

Elizabeth was glad she had left before the atmosphere degenerated any further. She had needed to see Janey, but there was nothing to be gained by staying there being pulverised by the force of her daughter's disdain. Aidan would look after her. Elizabeth had been touched by his display of kindness. She only hoped Janey wouldn't view it as another betrayal.

The way she thought about it, her last leaving had been worse than this. Then there had been a choice. What she had to do now was focus on the future, on trying to heal the hurt she had caused. But first, she wanted to make one more foray into the past.

In less than ten minutes, Elizabeth was sitting on the steps of number 124 Lantern Street. It was more down-at-heel than she remembered. The pavement was strewn with cigarette butts, and some of the blinds looked like they hadn't seen soap and water since she'd last been there. Not that she cared. For just that moment, all that mattered was being back in the place that, along with Emerald Street, had featured in so many of her dreams.

The previous night she'd received another e-mail from Donal who claimed he was beyond offended that she wouldn't be at his wedding. He must have assumed that money was an issue, for his next few lines were all about how miserable things must be in Ireland. *I don't think there will ever be good conditions for the Gaels*, he wrote, which made her smile. It was too long since she'd heard anyone quoting *The Poor Mouth*. He was thrilled she had met Danny, and, being Donal, he picked up on the 'first love' reference. *How romantic!* he wrote. *I trust the pair of you managed to keep your clothes on this time*. She would have to reply and let him know she'd been to Lantern Street to pay homage to their youth.

Her phone rang again. She was about to answer when she

spotted two young lads with pink Irish faces carrying a keg of beer around the corner. By the looks of them, they had carried rather than rolled it up the hill. It must be treasured cargo. As soon as it became apparent that they were making for number 124, Elizabeth stood up to get out of their way.

'Party?' she asked.

'You're on the ball there,' replied the smaller of the two, who was a ringer for the young Peter. She feared he was being sarcastic until the two of them stopped, put down the keg and started to chat. They were both from Mayo, over for the summer and having a party on Friday night.

'Will you not have it drunk by then?'

The taller boy, who was wearing an AC/DC T-shirt, looked pensive. 'You might be onto something. We should get a second one. What with it being a Bank Holiday weekend and all.'

'I think around here they call it Independence Day,' pointed out the first fellow with a wink.

Elizabeth told them how she had a daughter living a couple of blocks away. While she spoke, a generously tattooed young woman came out and nodded in acknowledgement. She unlocked a yellow bicycle and freewheeled down the street.

'What brings you to Lantern Street?' asked AC/DC.

'I lived here. Apartment ten. There were five of us. I won't tell you how long ago it was.'

'We're in number seven. There's a family in ten. From the Philippines, as far as I know,' said young Peter. 'Did they have J-1 visas back in the sixties?'

'Ah, here,' she laughed, 'I'm not staying to be insulted.'

'We're only messing with you. What year was it?'

'Nineteen eighty-eight.'

'The year I was born,' sighed AC/DC. 'A grand year.'

'That it was,' she said.

Danny had lost track of the number of lengths he'd done. Still he continued swimming, his rhythm and breathing steady, his arms

326

cutting cleanly through the water. So focused was he on pushing himself on, he could have been on his own in the pool. He could have been anywhere. He reassured himself that of all the places a man could seek refuge, he had chosen the least self-destructive. If only he could stay there for the rest of the day. The swimming pool was the perfect place to avoid yourself.

For the best part of twenty-four hours, he'd done nothing but think. He kept running over events, past and present. He sat up half the night in the home office that he and Anna shared. Some-time around two, his wife came to collect him. He pretended it was work that had him so distracted. There had been no further mention of the gland doctor (he'd looked up endocrinology), and Danny wasn't sure whether Anna was continuing to see him. All he knew was that she was back in their bed, trying to re-establish connection. And he was trying to avoid it.

'We really do need to talk,' she said.

'And tomorrow we will. I promise.'

He postponed going to bed until he was certain she was asleep. When tomorrow came, he was gone. He rose at five thirty and paced the neighbourhood, which was at its most alluring at that hour of the morning. The sky was a pale shade of lemon, the sun was gentle, and there were no people to worry about.

As he hauled himself out of the swimming pool, he started thinking again. The day before, when he'd left Elizabeth sitting on the bench, his uppermost sense was of powerlessness. She had looked haunted and there was nothing he could do. Well, actually, he should have made a better job of handling the situation. She deserved more than him saying how sorry he was before van-ishing into the afternoon. He'd been taken aback by her sudden candour and had run away.

After a shower, Danny checked to see if he'd missed any calls. There was only one: Anna. Life would be tough when Elizabeth came clean to Liam. He decided to put himself in the other man's shoes. What would he do if Geraldine told him he wasn't the father of one of the boys? Tear down the house? Refuse to believe her? Cry? He tried to imagine how Liam might view him, the unknown American. He realised he didn't even know what Elizabeth's husband looked like.

Muddled as these thoughts were, they were nothing compared to his attempts at untangling how he felt about Elizabeth. The revelation that they were bound by more than rosy memories of the summer of 1988 had sent him reeling. Of one fact he was certain; five days on, he carried none of the animosity that everyone seemed to expect. Instead, he was weighed down by a sense of what he had lost. This was hard to admit, even to himself, because it felt like he was belittling the other people in his life. He added it up. More than a decade with Geraldine, two sons, eight years with Anna, all of the other women who had flitted in and out of the picture. Out of forty-six years of life, he'd known Elizabeth for three months. And she was right. They couldn't go back.

Although he'd been dressed for thirty minutes or more, he continued to sit in the warm chlorine fug of the changing room, barely registering the comings and goings of other swimmers. He planned on sitting for another while. He needed to strip away the nostalgia and the nonsense, to discount the misgivings and expectations of others. What did he want? And what would be the consequences?

From time to time, his mind went astray. He had been reading a book set in Louisiana, a place he'd never been. He recalled how as a young guy, back when he'd first known Elizabeth, he'd had notions about travelling the world. Vincent had dissuaded him, had said that right then was the time to set up a business – when times were good and they were young enough to hustle. He couldn't question his brother's timing. Danny liked having money. What was not to like?

Besides, he had been abroad. He'd been to the Caribbean with Anna. She was easy to caricature, was Anna. He was wrong to fall into that trap. All of his life he had placed too high a premium on beauty, but even he wouldn't fall in love with someone solely because of the way they looked. In many ways, she was a fine person. What she'd done the previous night, walking into the office, sleepy and naked, was a conciliatory gesture. He couldn't continue to ignore those gestures.

He thought of Ryan, with whom he was destined to spend a lifetime talking at cross-purposes, albeit in a good-natured way. They were too different. And he thought of Conor, the best kid on God's earth but with no capacity for hard work. Geraldine was happier now. She'd got over him with the help of Mitch Dwyer. Mitch could be an exhibit in Ripley's Believe It or Not; roll up and see America's most boring man. But the man adored Ger.

The clock ticked on, and he was starting to get concerned looks from the fellows who came and went. 'Just thinking,' he would say. An unfamiliar guy looked at him, a half-smile on his face. 'I hope she's worth it,' he said.

'They all are,' Danny replied.

As he left the pool, he waved to the girl on the desk. Leah, she was called. She was a real looker with wavy blond hair and a smile that would raise the dead. Once or twice, he had contemplated trying his luck.

'You look pleased with yourself,' she said.

'That's because I know what I want.'

'Don't we all.'

From a distance, Danny threw his towel into the basket. Leah clapped. He bowed. 'Yeah,' he said, 'but perhaps I can do some-thing about it.'

Chapter 33

On the day she left Boston for the second time, Elizabeth had lunch with Danny. She needed to thank him, and she hoped he would be able to keep a subtle eye on Janey.

At two o'clock the restaurant was still heaving with people. They were sitting in a booth, one as weary as the other. Danny looked unusually worn. Under his eyes the skin was purple and swollen, and his T-shirt looked like he'd slept in it. The Anna conversation must not have gone well. From several tables away they could hear a woman's laugh. It was an unfortunate, cackling thing.

He rubbed his temples. 'That laugh goes straight through me.'

'I know,' she sighed. 'At least we were forewarned. I saw her broomstick on my way in.'

He reached over and tweaked her nose.

Two of Elizabeth's missed calls had been from Danny. There was also a message from Stevie complaining that Michelle was too strict. That would be the same Michelle who, in her student days, had guzzled knock-off vodka that was better suited to rubbing on greyhounds, and who had once mislaid her dress at a party. She relayed this to Danny, and for a short time the two discussed how preventing yourself from turning into your parents was like trying to turn back the sea. Mind you, Michelle was showing signs of being stricter than her mother and father which was a novel affliction.

On her way to the restaurant, she had instructed herself not to dwell on Janey's outburst. She didn't want Danny feeling he had to take sides. Her determination held out for all of ten minutes. That's how she was: cogging along one hour, a trembling mess the next. Back and forth she swung, like a broken gate on a breezy day. Seeing how shaken she was, he got up and settled into the booth beside her. An arm slipped around her shoulders.

'So we're saying goodbye again,' he said.

Don't, Danny, she thought. 'You know that's not what I said. We'll have to stay in touch about Janey.'

'For a little while, I don't want to talk about Janey or anyone else. I want to talk about you. And me as well, if you like.' She must have looked uneasy because he quickly added, 'And I'm not trying to seduce you, so there's no need to get wary on me. Besides, I don't think either of us would be capable of too much energetic activity right now.'

'I trust you.'

'Elizabeth, I've been thinking about what I want to say ... and—'

She looked down at the starched white tablecloth, and at the subtle pattern of leaves and roses woven through the material. 'You probably feel you need to say something about yesterday, but you don't, you know. I had to tell you how it is for me, to be honest. That's all.'

'Can I tell you how it is for me?'

Before she had the chance to answer, the waiter arrived with their first course. Danny explained how he was going to sit beside 'the lady', and that there was no need to go rearranging anything. In that peerless American way, the waiter said this would be 'perfect, sir'. Elizabeth got the feeling they could put their underwear on their heads, and he would be equally unruffled.

'Now where was I?' said Danny, as he tickled the back of her neck.

'You were going to tell me how it is for you, and I was saying there's no need.'

His unshaven face grazed the side of hers. 'And I reckon there is. For a minute or two, will you listen to what I have to say?'

She got the feeling there might not be much eating at this lunch. 'OK.'

'You spoke yesterday about making a mistake all those years ago. And, like I said in the letter, I made a mistake too. I've always known that. Of course, we all look back and remember the good times. The games we won and the days when nobody fought. But the thing is, even when we were together, I knew that being with you was different to being with other girls. I remember telling you how happy I was because I couldn't think of any better way to describe what I was feeling.' She kissed his cheek. He smelled of swimming pool. 'That summer was one of the sweetest times of my life. But I had to put it behind me, like you did.'

'It's all right, Danny. I know how it is.'

'Hear me out, babe, would you?' He paused. 'A week ago you walked onto the site in Allston. Within a half-hour, I knew. I wanted everyone else to go away, so as I could be with you. Or think about you.' They had moved around now, so that Elizabeth's back was to the wall and Danny was facing her. The waiter had the nous to stay away. Somehow all of the other voices had faded out. Even the cackle was gone. 'It was like getting an unexpected thump. Sure, I'd often thought about you but I'd never imagined that seeing you would affect me so much. That the tug, the connection, would still be there. Then you told me about Janey, and I didn't know what to think or what to do.

'You see, most of my life I've had a talent for doing the wrong thing, especially where women are concerned. I look at guys I knew at school – guys who weren't blessed with too many smarts – and I see them living contented lives. And I think, how do they do that?'

Elizabeth didn't know quite where this was going but she felt the need to intervene. 'Danny, when I said yesterday that I was scared of falling in love with you again ... actually, I wasn't being totally honest. I've been lying for so long that even when I try to tell the truth, I fall short.' Their fingertips touched. 'The damage has already been done. I love you. Even though there are a thousand other things I should be thinking about, everything comes back to you. That's why I said what I said, why I have to protect myself. I know what it's like to crave you, and not to have you. I don't think I could do that again. Do you understand?'

'You're not listening to me, Elizabeth.' Again he paused. 'I can't believe there is anyone else like you. Not for me. Knowing about Janey hasn't changed that. Actually, the more time I have to consider, the more certain I am. I'm not talking about the past. I love you. Not the memory of you. Or the idea of you.' He tipped forward, and kissed the bridge of her nose. 'You.'

She swallowed. 'I suppose I find it difficult to get my head around. Not just because of what I did to you but because, for me, it's like I've seen you every day for the past twenty years. You were always with me. But for you – there were times when I was scared you might have forgotten about me.'

'I always said it. For a smart woman, you can be awful dumb. How could I have forgotten?' He shook his head. 'I guess some folks wouldn't be able to understand what I'm saying, but I swear to you it's true.'

'You know, Danny, I think most people would reckon that you're suffering from some sort of temporary insanity brought on by shock.' Elizabeth attempted a smile and managed only to achieve what she had wished for twenty-three years previously; a solitary tear slid down her left cheek. 'If only ... if only we were free to be together.' She spoke tentatively, fearing that she may be going too far. Danny brushed the tear away, then prevented another from falling, but said nothing. 'This time I have to leave,' she said.

'I wish I could come with you.'

'I know you can't, my love.'

'You have to go now. Sure. But that doesn't mean you can't come back to me. That's what I'm trying to say here. I want to be with you, Elizabeth.'

She rested her head against the wall. Oh, but this was hard. 'It's like I said yesterday, Danny. It's too late. I made my decision.'

'That's what I thought too. I thought there was no point in

even acknowledging how I felt because there was nothing I could do. Except my thinking was wrong.'

'I'm trapped, Danny. Do you not see?'

'You have this amazing memory for stuff I said years ago. For a change, I'm going to quote something to you. That night when I told you I was happy, you said that some things were tough but if they were worthwhile you had to persevere. Do you remember?'

'Of course I do. Isn't that the problem? I remember it all.' Elizabeth became aware that the waiter was hovering. She cast a glance to left and right. The restaurant was only half full now. Danny assured him they were ready for the next course. They hadn't touched the first one.

'What was that silly saying you came out with the other day?' he said. 'About Janey and Aidan?'

'As God made them he matched them?'

'That's the one. Now, does that remind you of any other couple?' He furrowed his brow and scratched his head, like he was pretending to be stumped. In the end she had no choice but to smile. A tear slid into her mouth. 'Elizabeth, do you want to be with me?'

'Yes, I do. Of course, I do. If only it was possible. It's like you say ... I guess to many people this would sound crazy. I mean, I don't fully understand it. I say to myself, "How do you know?" But I do.'

'Well, then, we have to work this out. We have to persevere. Here we are, being given a second chance. What kind of fools would we be if we didn't take it?'

She stroked his fingers. They were less battered and callused now, the nails no longer bitten. 'I just can't see how.'

'We want to be together. Properly together. Every day together. I wish that could happen today. Obviously, it can't.' His voice was soft. 'I haven't all this sorted out either, but what about in a couple of years, my love? When Stevie leaves high school, and life is a little more settled? This is ... well, all I can do is ask. Would you consider moving here?'

People, even those who knew her – no, *especially* those who knew her – might have expected Elizabeth to say again that she didn't understand. But she did. And if in the minutes and hours that followed she was jittery and emotional, it was precisely because her head was so clear. Her mind was made up, and the enormity of the decision would scare anybody. Danny, bless him, looked every second of his forty-six years, but his face had the same eager cast as the night they first met.

'I know it's a lot to ask,' he said. 'To uproot yourself, to leave your home. But, maybe, the girls might come too. Stevie could go to school here, I'm sure. Like I said, I haven't this all figured out. It's just ... from what you've said ... I think there's more tying me to America these days than there is tying you to Ireland.' He was speaking quickly, the words and ideas tumbling out. 'I don't expect an answer straight away. Take whatever time you need. But ... if we would have been happy once, why wouldn't we be happy now?'

A plate was in front of Elizabeth. She barely remembered what she had ordered. Fish, it appeared. She tried to cut it, but the knife slipped out of her hand and skidded across the plate. There was a question that needed to be asked. 'What about Anna? You said you wanted to give your marriage another try.'

Danny put down his cutlery. 'Everyone knows I'm hopeless at making decisions. I'm the man who lets things drift. Ma says the last time I made up my mind, Gerald Ford was in the White House. If you do the math there, by the way, I was eleven years old, so I'm not sure how significant the decision was.'

'Eleven is a very important age.'

Danny clasped her hand. It's funny, she thought, he knows. Even though I haven't said anything, he knows what the answer is.

'This time,' he said, 'I have decided. The marriage was a mistake, for me and for Anna. I'm convinced she knows that too. If she was happy, she wouldn't be fooling around with doctors. So, I'm going to tell her it's over.' He hesitated. 'And then I'll wait for you.'

'You would be on your own? Like, completely on your own?'

'They say there's a first time for everything.' He smiled. 'I'd manage. As long as I knew the time would come when we'd be together. And as long as I got regular visits. Plus, there's nothing says I can't do a little travelling myself. Especially now I've got family to go and see.'

Another tear slithered down Elizabeth's cheek. For once she decided to surrender to the damn things. She was experiencing the strangest sensation, like she was surfacing after too long under water. Like she was pushing herself up, and her shrunken lungs were filling with air. 'You always said you wanted to travel.'

Danny squeezed her hand. 'Is that an invitation?'

She gave the tiniest of nods.

Chapter 34

Elizabeth and Michelle had long suspected that Donal had a type, and Meredith was living proof. The bride had bouncy fair hair, luminous skin and the sort of chest that required an expertly fitted bra. She would have no difficulty getting cast in a BBC costume drama.

'You do realise he's marrying Rosie Marsh,' Elizabeth said.

'I think they come off an assembly line,' her friend replied. 'I met one about ten years ago who was more Rosie than Rosie herself.'

They had met Meredith for the first time two nights previously. Now, on a raw Friday afternoon in early January, they were standing in little clusters outside a Boston church, waiting for the wedding to begin. Elizabeth, Orla and Michelle huddled together, stamping their feet and blowing on cupped hands. Donal and Peter were already inside; the groom being infinitely more laid-back than the best man. Andy and Danny were just down the street. 'Puffing on cigarettes like a pair of corner boys,' according to Michelle.

'Did you ever think we'd be back in Boston?' said Orla. 'The five of us all grown up. And Donal getting hitched at last.'

'And Elizabeth having her second youth,' added Michelle.

'Her first youth, if you ask me. Back when we were actually young, she was busy being an adult.'

'Apart, that is, from her time in Boston,' laughed Michelle. 'This city has a funny effect on her.'

'Do you have to talk about me as though I'm not here?' Elizabeth said. But there was a smile in her voice. She had grown accustomed to being a topic of conversation, to seeing slack jaws and wide eyes, to hearing whispered comments about still waters running deep and it being the quiet ones you had to watch out for. This was her first time back in Boston since the events of the summer, since she took the first unsteady steps into the rest of her life.

'How are you getting on with the family?' asked Michelle. 'Or maybe I should say, how are you getting on with your old pal, Vincent?'

'He's on his best behaviour. His mother must have him well warned. He goes around brandishing what he probably thinks is a smile, but actually looks like toothache. Valerie's great, Regina keeps getting emotional and the rest of them, well, they look scared. Danny says they stare at me like I've just escaped from Franklin Park zoo.'

'So, all in all then ...'

'Oh, way better than expected.'

Telling Liam had been as painful as expected, albeit in different ways. Elizabeth had anticipated the initial incomprehension and the subsequent rage. His revulsion cut deep, but it was his distress that cut deepest of all. For all the mistakes they had made, she had spent the bulk of her life with him. Twenty-seven years. Meagre times and giddy times. Babies and mortgages. Upheaval and calm. Countless weddings and christenings. Even more funerals. She would not forget the look on his face when finally he accepted that what she said was true.

Afterwards, Liam had been dignified. He'd spent some time with Janey and Stevie, and then he'd returned to Abu Dhabi. His relationship with his daughters was strong. She was thankful for that.

Occasionally, Elizabeth and Liam spoke on the phone about practical matters, like the girls' education or what they would do with the house. Elizabeth found herself listening to the tone of his voice rather than the words. 'Are you OK?' she kept wanting to say. 'Please, be OK.' But she had no right to ask; it was too soon to try and cauterise the wounds, or ask for forgiveness. Some nights she woke up drenched with sweat, her fists clenched tight, her brain waterlogged with guilt. Not the stereotypical Irish Catholic guilt of her childhood, but a real, powerful sensation caused by the knowledge that she had done wrong. She knew she couldn't undo that wrong. She just hoped that by finally telling the truth she could make some amends.

And her daughters? Stevie was a conundrum. At first, she'd taken to her bedroom and howled. After two days, she'd re-emerged, stuck out her little chin and got on with life. Danny liked to joke about her being extraordinarily well-adjusted. 'We'll be paying the psychiatrist's bills for years to come,' he'd say. Elizabeth would shudder and point out that these were not joking matters.

Janey had turned out to be as resilient as she had hoped. Aidan was always there for her, and she was managing to walk the tightrope between Liam and Danny without too many stumbles. Despite Elizabeth's fears, both girls remained at home. There were days when they stepped warily around her, like they weren't quite sure who she was. But there were far more days when she believed that they would come through this. At Christmas, she'd been talking to Janey when, out of the blue, her daughter had hugged her and said, 'I do still love you, you know.' Elizabeth had experienced a happiness that was purer and deeper than she had thought possible.

Back in October, Danny had arrived in Ireland with a new suitcase and a thousand questions. It was as though he'd needed to gather two decades of information in the space of a week. Even though everyone was still reeling from the revelations about Janey, Elizabeth had known then that she had to take the next step. To tell people that Danny was more than a historical figure, and that one day, in the not too distant future, they planned on being together – in America. Finding the words had been hard. First, she had fretted about how the girls would react. Then she'd fretted about deceiving them. Finally, she'd fretted that if *she* was getting restless, Danny must be on the verge of spontaneous combustion.

On the fourth day of his visit, Stevie had come to the rescue. There were just the three of them in the sitting room. Four if you counted Grover, who had taken an immediate liking to Danny and was flat out on his lap, kneading his legs and other more sensitive parts. Twice he'd urged the cat to 'go easy on the tackle there, fella'. Stevie laughed so much, she struggled for air. Janey was out with Aidan, and with hindsight it was clear that canny Stevie had been biding her time. Her face an exercise in innocence, she looked over at their guest and said, 'Danny, why are you staying in a hotel?'

Not liking the sound of this, Elizabeth intervened. 'Do you think he should be in the spare room here, pet?'

'Oh no. Not there.'

'I'm not with you, then.'

'Well, the two of you are so obviously having sex, or if you're not you want to, that I thought it would make more sense if he slept in your bed.'

Danny nearly fell into a weakness, and Elizabeth found that all she could do was gasp her daughter's name. Grover kept on purring. After a long moment of watching Stevie wind her hair into a plait, Elizabeth told her she shouldn't be saying such things.

'Isn't it the truth?' she replied.

Danny had gathered his senses and managed to mumble a string of Americanisms about them caring for each other, but not wanting to take things too quickly or cause upset.

'In all fairness,' replied Stevie, 'it's probably a bit late in the day to be worrying about the upset. Anyway, unless Mum gets a late vocation, she's going to have to get a new man at some stage. And she's unlikely to do better than you.'

While Danny twinkled like he'd taken control of the Red Sox, Elizabeth glared at Stevie. 'Does your sister have any idea that Danny and I may, eh, like to see each other from time to time?'

'Nope. Sooner or later, though, even Janey will wise up to you.'

'We better talk to her,' said Danny, shooting a look in Elizabeth's direction that was one part concern to four parts relief.

From time to time, Elizabeth wondered what her parents would have made of it all. Danny said her dad would surely have had a phrase for her predicament. She thought and thought but drew a blank. Then, a couple of nights back they had been lying in bed, hearts still racing, when out of nowhere a line had come to her. To the best of her recollection, Syl had used it only once, after he'd told some convoluted tale about an elderly father, two sons and a farm of land. 'For what cannot be cured,' he had said, 'patience is best.'

Danny narrowed his eyes and chuckled. 'Hmmm. You do know you've just compared me to a serious illness?'

Elizabeth nuzzled into the crook of his neck. 'Sounds like a good description,' she said.

Beside her now, Michelle and Orla were complaining about the cold. Danny and Andy were sauntering up the street engrossed in one of their construction conversations. Or at least that's what they said they talked about.

Elizabeth shivered. 'Come on, we ought to go inside before we all turn into lumps of ice.'

'You're right,' nodded Michelle. 'We don't want Peter accusing us of wrecking the wedding.'

As he arrived, Danny's smile was on full beam. He leaned in to Elizabeth and whispered, 'I think there's snow on the way.'

Even though Elizabeth had already given him one sharp poke in the side, Danny couldn't help but look around. It was a mighty fine church. He was partial to a vaulted ceiling, and those stained-glass windows were things of beauty. Sure, they were nothing compared to what he'd heard you could see in Europe, but they were worthy of admiration all the same.

The wedding was getting under way. He wasn't quite as familiar with these Protestant ceremonies as he was with the Catholic version, although he figured they were pretty similar. He would have plenty of time for inspecting the building. Plenty of time for inspecting Elizabeth too. As the ultimate boss might say, 'and he saw that it was good'. She was the best-looking woman in the place. He'd said as much as they were filing in. She was wearing a dark blue dress, and her hair was swept back so as not to swamp her small face. She insisted the bride was always the most beautiful woman at a wedding. 'There's one exception to that rule,' he replied. 'When I'm there, the most beautiful woman is with me.' She told him he was a terrible chancer, but her smile was a foot wide.

She was a tough woman, Elizabeth. If you saw the graceful exterior, you might reckon she'd crumble under pressure. Yet, as good as her word, she soldiered on. She had rough times. She told him how some days she felt impossibly low and other days she felt like she was soaring. He knew exactly what she meant. There were days when he picked up the phone, and her voice had a disturbing wobble. He knew not to comment, just to listen, and to remind her that soon they'd be together. Mostly, her worries were about Janey and Stevie, and, hand on heart, he had no trouble reassuring her that they would be fine. They were strong characters. Like their mother.

Elizabeth and Liam were talking again now. He'd even said the girls should stay with her on Christmas Day. Danny had yet to meet him. That day too would come.

The end of his own marriage had been a less fraught affair. Anna had wanted to try again. That was the right thing to do, and she'd been brought up to do the right thing. As he told his tale, her lips had turned pale and tight. Then she'd got all melodramatic. But when the shock had subsided, he suspected she was probably relieved. Their outstanding issues were all related to money. Despite eight years as a couple, they had left little emotional imprint on each other.

Up at the altar, they were exchanging vows. Doing the full 'for better, for worse' routine. Call him a hypocrite, but Danny liked the traditional promises. He was glad Donal and Meredith hadn't gone messing with them like many folks did nowadays. Peter was up there too, looking officious. It was a shame about his hair.

Within a few days of Elizabeth returning to Ireland, Danny and Janey had done the DNA test. He would never forget the letter arriving; the two of them meeting up before opening the envelope and scrutinising the strings of figures and letters. The fifteen markers that told their story. The crucial line was in stark bold type: the probability of paternity was 99.995 per cent.

Afterwards, Janey had been curiously impassive. 'I knew anyway,' she'd shrugged. 'Didn't you?'

'Yeah,' he'd replied, trying to be composed. 'And it doesn't change anything. Liam is your dad. I know that. That's what matters.'

She had wanted to be on her own, so Danny got into the car and drove to Dorchester. He found himself back on Emerald Street, sitting on the sidewalk outside number nineteen, just letting it all sink in. No doubt, the ghost of Bridie O'Connor looked on with disapproval. Three hours later, he received a one-line text. *'You matter too,'* it read. Danny knew he was a sentimental idiot, but he couldn't stop crying. Bawled for thirty minutes or more. What a sight he'd been. Then he got up and went about his business. He told no one, not even Elizabeth.

Often he got lonely. He did his best to fill all the hours with work or exercise or reading. He tried not to drink or smoke too much. He called Elizabeth way way too much. Sometimes, he called at night and woke her up. In an instant, she'd be full of chat, wanting to know what was up, never saying, 'It's two a.m. here, and I only spoke to you a couple of hours back.' Vincent made fun of him, especially the enforced celibacy, making enquiries about his eyesight and the like. Danny flipped him the bird, said he was saving himself for his true love. Mostly, he just got a snort in response.

In the beginning, his brother had been more than a touch put out by the whole Elizabeth business. 'I give up,' he'd said. 'One of these days the guys in the white coats will come calling for you. And I hope it's soon.' Danny had told him to go home and chill out with his Sarah Palin DVDs, watch her skinning a moose or whatnot. Vincent then lapsed into a medium-sized sulk. Valerie talked him around. The woman was one miracle short of sainthood.

This time Danny was getting to spend almost two weeks with Elizabeth. He planned on returning to Dublin in March. Like he'd assured her in the summer, he would manage. Occasionally, the things she said brought him up short. He would remember what an extraordinary leap of faith they had taken, and how much they still had to learn about each other. But, you know what? They had plenty of time.

The minister was cantering through proceedings now. The bride and groom were pledging 'constant faith and abiding love'. He took a glimpse at Elizabeth's face. Her eyes were glistening; she must be enjoying herself. For a woman who claimed she rarely cried, she could weep with the best of them. He reached for her hand and gave the palm a tickle. In response, she kissed his cheek. Her breath was warm against his ear.

Danny hoped they wouldn't have to spend too long at the reception.

Acknowledgements

I owe a considerable debt to many people who have helped make writing *Going Back* such a brilliant experience.

Not only did Wanda Whiteley help me to put shape on a beginner's manuscript, her advice to 'aim high' helped me to secure an agent and a publisher. Thanks Wanda.

Ciarán Kissane - unwittingly - gave me the idea of writing about a return trip to Boston, and both he and Séamus Hanrahan may recognise some aspects of their 1988 summer job. Thanks for the inspiration!

I'm extremely grateful to my agent, Robert Kirby of United Agents, for his enthusiasm - and his ability to answer all of my many, many questions. Thanks also to Holly Thompson.

Much gratitude to everyone at Orion for being so welcoming to me and my characters. I owe a special debt to Susan Lamb and to my editor, Eleanor Dryden, who seems to understand those characters better than I do myself. Big thanks too to Laura Gerrard and Angela McMahon, and to Breda Purdue, Jim Binchy and Edel Coffey at Hachette Ireland.

Thanks to my colleagues and friends on *Morning Ireland*, especially Hilary McGouran for her encouragement and generosity, and to Brendan Fitzpatrick for his extensive store of sayings from Tipperary.

Nobody has more sayings than my dad, Tony. Heartfelt thanks to him and to my mum, Ruth, who first gave me a love of reading.

Thanks to Eamon Quinn for everything.